T0354891

IMAGO

IMAGO

IMAGO

JAMES LAMPASONA

Library of Congress Control Number: 2019904042
ISBN: Hardcover   978-1-7960-2578-1
                 Softcover   978-1-7960-2577-4
                 eBook   978-1-7960-2576-7

Print information available on the last page.

Rev. date: 04/03/2019

To order additional copies of this book, contact:
Xlibris
1-888-795-4274
www.Xlibris.com
Orders@Xlibris.com
791612

For Uncle Tony

IMAGO

[iˈmāgō, iˈmägō]

NOUN
1. entomology

The final and fully developed adult stage of an insect, typically winged

2. psychoanalysis

An unconscious, idealized mental image of someone, especially a parent, that influences a person's behavior

What is that noise?

TerraLuna

CHAPTER 1

The sun had been harnessed. Charley Porter was responsible for the breakthrough, but credit for the work seemed to radiate from *MoonCorp*, the company for which he used to work. This was the sickening conclusion he rehashed again and again as he wheeled the Mustang around a white asphalt bend toward *Sneaky Petey's*. A blinking signal activated on his locator screen catching his eye as it usually did when he auto-turned in his instinctive trail to his comfortable stool next to the bar at which he found himself seated so many nights over the past month.

Charley saw a billboard flash a holographic beer being poured into a large sweaty mug as the worlds "Time for a cold one, Charley?" materialized above the foam. His widened eyes turned naturally back toward the road. Gurgling noises coming from his stomach seemed to urge his foot deeper on the accelerator. His hair curled a bit in anticipation, and his ponytail tightened, exposing his receding hairline without any real worry. The fluorescent orange Hawaiian shirt still smelled fresh from the cleaners and helped him not to think about the middle-aged spread he occasionally noticed. The billboard was accompanied by music that waved in from his stereo on AHAS (Automated Holographic Audio Service). "Here comes the King, here comes the BIG NUMBER ONE!" he sang along, slapping the steering wheel in time.

He also knew that it was 32.75 seconds until he arrived at *Sneaky Petey's*. His onboard computer (or OBC) toned in a sultry voice, "It's 30 seconds until destination, automatic speed control activated." Glancing at his speedometer reading 162 mph, he gave a hum of satisfaction. "Doesn't feel like I am doing 150." The digital readout began to drop from 162 rapidly as the car's computer brought him to a safe speed to enter the parking lot of *Sneaky Petey's* Bar and Grille.

All three vehicles coming from the opposite direction were not turning off. They flashed by quickly, controlled by the National Highway Commissions speed control system, bringing them to a governed slower speed as their destination approached. Most people use these roads on long trips like from Vegas to LA or from Tucson to San Francisco, but Charley liked the automated world. It worked for him. He needed time to work out real problems rather than flipping through levers and shifting gears. He was a solar engineer or SE until recently, dubbing himself a "suds engineer," which always brought a knowing smirk to his wide sunburned face.

The late-afternoon sun seemed to be shining directly on his watering trough, as he liked to call the place, while automated features disengaged his car, relinquishing control to him. He spun the hot tires into his favorite parking spot next to the light pole. Closing down the car's systems with a press on a key chain tab, he turned to the sky, his power sunglasses adjusting the round lenses to the sun's intensity. He scanned the sky to see what he could see of the day, the moon against the bright blue expanse. He shook his head with a sudden curse, "Lousy, thieving bastards took my job." Turning away, his auto-sunglasses readjusted his vision. He focused on the friendly red door with a brass knob.

A welcome blast of frosty air collided with his reddened face as a shaft of sunlight slid through the dark bar, causing a gauntlet of regulars to simultaneously turn just enough to see a familiar face and then turn back to their limited activities.

"Chucky-babe," said an old man with limited volume in his old voice, calling from the bar. "Your Angels lost again. That makes three in a row, and I hope you're keeping track because I am. They will have to win seven out of ten games, that being the remainder of the season for you to beat me. Do I need to review the contest with you again, Charles?"

Charley sauntered to his frie, took the seat, shaking his head. "No, Duke, you do not."

Duke raised his old hairy eyebrows to where they could not be seen under his old St. Louis Cardinals cap. "That's great. However, for the record . . . *if* the Los Angeles Angels do not win at least 50 percent of their games this season, *you*, my dear sun gun, must buy me a beer each and every time you show your sorry ass in this establishment." He raised his half-full beer with a sure nod and took a minor swig.

Charley stared at the man for a moment, knowing the reason for Duke's pointed reaffirmation of their bet. Two young girls breaking in their newly issued drinking licenses giggled during Duke's greeting, adding to their ongoing entertainment by Duke.

"Yeah, yeah, Duke. There are plenty of games left in the season. The boys can pull it off. Then you can buy *me* a drink every time I see *your* carcass in this place. The only reason I made this easy bet with you is because I know I'm never going to miss a free beer because you are always here!"

"I carry a tab," said Duke, aristocratically nodding at the bartender.

The girls laughed, and Duke returned to his dwindling drink. Sam, the bartender watching them, had made a hobby of playing audience to their banter. He kept up a smile, hoping to chime in something relevant or interesting, yet usually seemed to think better of it. "Bud, Charley?"

"Yes, Sam," Charley offered back.

Sam ran through the motions of pulling a bottle of beer from the speed cooler, opening it, and placing it atop a bar napkin as gracefully as a professional skater. He finished with an expectant look as if someone was going to score his performance. "Five dollars," he chimed.

Charley peeled out a World Dollar card with a "$50.00" in the tiny green-lit screen and placed it on the bar, glancing up at the television. "News comes on at four thirty," he said, hovering the beer sale into the computer till.

Charley tapped the bar top, bringing the remote-control panel to his place, and touched the glass panel, surfing the channels to find some news now. The holo-television sat in the corner of the bar closest to the door, above the rows of bottles and stacked rocks glasses. They twinkled unnaturally for a moment as another couple entered the bar, spilling light from beyond the air-conditioned sanctuary.

He finally parked the television station. "Say, Sam, do you know those corporate guys who come up with those specialty drinks? The Branigan's restaurants, for instance, you know they'll have a green monster margarita or something that tastes like apple pie à la mode in a glass. Do these guys have patents for these things? I mean, is there some kind of a law that prohibits you from making me a chocolate guru?"

"You work for a big corporation. You should know somebody who knows." Duke made a sound, something like a snort for some reason known only to him.

"As far as I know, I won't have to swipe my world dollar card every time I sell you Yoo-hoo and vodka."

He carefully removed another bottle for cleaning with the surety of a librarian.

"The corporation police cannot keep track of those concoctions. It's an open field. What would you like me to plagiarize for you?"

He drained his glass with a nod. "No, Sam, I'm not going to test the law, but I'll take another beer."

The young girls who had lost interest in Duke's musings scurried to the jukebox, selecting a popular tune that stopped Charley from elaborating on his corporate politics with Sam. He did need to vent to someone, but both Sam and Duke had heard enough. Also, it wouldn't make a difference. Nothing would change what happened at *MoonCorp*. They were losing the race for the moon and already had his best solar technology modified and, well, stolen. He developed micro induction panels for intensifying stored energy with incredible efficiency. He perfected the self-cleaning panel matrix that increased solar absorption an additional 32 percent. The actualized solar satellite radio power radio relay system, the edge of historical technology, was *MoonCorp's* now.

Charley suspected that his hard work might have leaked out to their rival *TerraLuna* and they silently held him responsible. *A suspect?* he internalized. Working with Dr. Nick on this technology was his career. The developments they added to the science of solar energy were unique and revolutionary not only for interstellar energy usage but also for the sake of the future of mankind's energy needs.

Funding played a role as well. Without funding, *MoonCorp* could not provide solar radio power to heat the swimming pool; Earth glow was not going to warm it much. The pool, and the dream of floating in that warm water and looking up through the clear ultra-polymer panels at Earth, was the reward he wanted.

The investors had been inching out of their deals with *MoonCorp* due to delays caused by safety issues. *TerraLuna*, however, seemed to be plugging right along, secretly harvesting investors with perks and ploys. Without governmental input, private consultation on such matters had a gray area the size of a battleship. All for the glory of being the first commercial resort and convention center on the moon. A great step forward for unsafe lunar habitation and a great leap backward for Charley Porter.

Charley cupped the fresh beer, pausing with a prayerful resolution to stop browbeating himself. His severance package was generous and would last until he found something an overqualified research engineer with seventeen years of college and twenty-three patents pending could do. Nightly, his work on his holography experiments continued to keep him sharp. Charley worked better at night. His brain seemed to feel more comfortable in the dark. For him, it is a natural high to think in the lightless cool quiet of the mind. It's a fact. Politics has always outrun research. As research comes close to perfection, some suit decides the party's over due to funding snafu bullshit.

"I'm not appreciated," Charley mumbled aloud, feeling the effects of the suds.

"What was that Charley? Did you say you miss your friends in Mexico at the whorehouse?" said Duke, angling for a laugh from Sam through his fake teeth.

"No, dork," he snorted, turning to the news as it began.

"The world news as it happens around the globe . . . to you. From our headquarters in Washington DC, here's Harriet Strong."

This newswoman was, by all accounts, the most cynical person Charley had ever heard; dry tones bordering on suspicion infected every story from the uplifting to the tragic. Yet something must be up because this is the first time he saw a black woman look pale. She read the news as if she did not believe what she was saying.

"Earlier today, reports arrived in our news center of a technical accident at *TerraLuna* Corporation's construction site, which has been building since early last year. No word if the mishap would affect *TerraLuna*'s vacation weekends scheduled to begin the third quarter of 2169."

The TV flashed some artist's renderings of the opulent hotel. Its classic Italian designs of white iron-wrought flowers, marble statues, and fountains raised eyebrows in Sneaky Petey's dark reaches. Dining under a clear view of Earth was featured, as well as zero-gravity sports.

Rumors were spreading that they had a secret amusement park with a roller coaster and batting cages. *MoonCorp* had similar recreation plans but did not have 100 percent guarantee that all their safety programs were sound enough to begin construction, so they waited, and they were still waiting for the go-ahead. Based on satellite defense tech, *TerraLuna* went ahead finding several risk elements to be less than minimal, generally speaking. *Now look what happens,* thought Charley, finding a shred of ironic justice in the accident.

"Reports indicate that an accident in the environmental generators left several maintenance crew members injured when a coolant gas valve failed to operate correctly."

Duke had begun to share Charley's interest in the news and chimed in, "You worked for the other guys. That's the company you should go and apply for, ding-dong. They are going to need someone to reload the automatic pitcher at those batting cages."

Duke thought this was the crack of the century and began laughing and wheezing uncontrollably. Charley looked over, hoping to see him fall off his stool. Looking back, he thought about what the old buzzard had said. Why not? He was an expert in state-of-the-art solar technology development, he needed some good PR, and he hadn't used his résumé in at least ten years. A passing doubt seriously asked if he could work for the competition.

Harriet Stone's report continued with highlights of the advanced technology of this first-ever endeavor, most of which Charley had heard before. The report seemed to be more of a promotion of *TerraLuna* rather than an accident report. Some of the reasons *MoonCorp* would not continue its plans for its vacation station may seem overcautious, yet Steele pulled it off in style, assuring them that Skylar's defense array would be sufficient. Since governmental standards did not apply as rigidly as they did in the past it was up to the boss. Being the first space hotel is great, but is it worth the loss of life? If he went to *TerraLuna*, his life might be compromised.

The vidscreen on the wall flashed a taped interview with the president of *TerraLuna*, Gerhard Steele. He was not quite a tall man yet seemed tall enough. His mid- to late-fortyish youth remained intact with a surety in his demeanor designed to appeal to that generation of the new 2100s who have fantastic amounts of money to invest in these kinds of undertakings. His crop of dark hair seemed wet and rarely moved. Mostly seen in unmistakably expensive suits, he was all business and charm.

Harriet Stone asked him, *"Gerhard, this is the first habitation on the moon that actual civilians can access much like Disneyland. How is this going to affect the average vacationing family's budget with the projected cost to be more than the combined yearly salaries of several working families?"*

Gerhard began without wavering; his mild Germanic/Texan accent added a touch of continental appeal that he felt characterized uniqueness to his American constituents.

"TerraLuna is the most fantastic endeavor mankind has ever attempted. It is for all people, not only the extremely wealthy and fortunate. Right now, Harriet, we have programs in review that offer sponsored charity vacations, corporate discounts, trade agreements, sort of a goods for vacation time arrangement. Financing is, of course, available for those interested. We can make it happen. We have several celebrity events and a variety of TV specials, including a Christmas show with which I personally will be involved."

"This guy is full of crap," offered Duke, waving at the television like a foul smell. "Christmas special? He ain't no Perry Como!"

"Harriet, we have taken every possible safety precaution to provide not only a vacation of a lifetime but the safest vacation ever," Steele said, restarting the conversation.

Harriet Stone remained fixed on Gerhard's mien as if she really wanted to believe him. *"Mr. Steele, there has been some sort of problem at* TerraLuna. *What kind of accident occurred, and what are your people doing to prevent it from happening in the future?"*

Steele imperceptibly adjusted in the armchair placed in the friendly den-like interview set. *"Ms. Stone, we had a valve that carries high-pressure oxygen mixes from the main clean air production station to a minor distribution junction rupture. We have remedied the problem, replacing the old valves with these newly designed valves which are certain to do a better job."* He produced a valve made from some heavy plastic, smiled, and waited for the next question.

"Mr. Steele, this occurrence raised the problem of other possible dangers, like interstellar materials such as meteors, comets, and miscellaneous space debris that are so commonly bombarding the moon doing more damage. Can such an impact be avoided at TerraLuna?"*

Steele found a way to sound casual in response to her truly biting question. *"You are correct. Space junk is colliding with the moon as well as the Earth itself all the time. Most of these are comets, which are comprised of ice and dirt. Our outer wall materials are designed to resist impacts of up to several hundred kilometers per hour. This accounts for the smaller pieces. The larger pieces are out there. We have satellite watchdog operations that continually patrol the vast regions of space beyond our* TerraLuna *provided by the Skylar Corporation. One satellite is called the NMAT or Near-Moon Asteroid Tracking. This will inform us years in advance of any impeding danger to our guests. We can destroy them well before they become a threat. Still, we are improving our systems as new technology presents itself."*

Steele turned to the camera and continued with renewed zeal. *"We have taken the challenge that world governments have avoided for more than two hundred years, that being the start of an aggressive colonization of the universe. I have said this before on another network. We are pioneers in search of new living spaces, new opportunity for investment, and new science that revitalizes our natural pioneering human spirit. We have reached the moon. Plans are on the table to expand our facility to offer a Mars program in the next twenty years. Plans that have been avoided for decades by federal redirection of your tax dollars. The bottom line is that the people want to go the stars. I am simply providing what people want, an economic, safe, and pleasurable access to them. If anyone within the sound of my voice would like information, you should access our COM number 2711*TerraLuna. *Costs will come down. Safety will increase. This is the new world. I'd like you all to be there. Share in my dream."* He paused, looking into the camera for a soul that would disagree. He continued, *"Access now for a chance to win a free vacation. The next 500 COM accesses will be entered in the drawing. So hurry!"*

Steele held the audience in the bar like a minister on a cold country Sunday. Several people reached for their nodular phone and entered the number displayed on the vidscreen into the cyber system to enter the drawing.

"Thank you, Mr. Steele," Harriet Stone said, seemingly uncharacteristically flushed by Steele's sermon. The vidscreen abruptly changed images to a commercial.

"That's the man you should work for, Charley," said Sam.

"That man is dangerous," Charley replied.

CHAPTER 2

The night it happened was like any other night on the moon, still and silently dead. Time passed for the staff with uncontrollable slowness. The initial excitement had dwindled. They were overachievers bored easily as problems were solved and tasks completed quickly. Steele wanted the best for his *TerraLuna*. Workers are granted shore leaves while ships are reloaded to spend time with their loved ones. The lives of this crew were good generally. Most requested not to leave. They liked being adrift on the cold gray-white rock.

Before initial air lock structures had been established, sleeping in the ship gave the crew the feeling that they were still on a journey, looking out at the moon's surface as the huge prefab walls were interlocked and atmospheric generators installed. Soon the enormous puzzle came together and, if need be, would come apart. Ten-by-twenty-foot sections interlocked and were sealed with a vacuum weld, which pulled the locking mechanism together like a zipper. Support beams telescoped across to maintain the upper level that housed the guests. The lower level required some digging into the lunar crust for the foundation. This area included a gift shop, storage, staff quarters, and emergency bunkers.

After his duty shifts, Ed Zonic noticed a dirty spot on the wall from hands touching the wall of the landing to the staircase leading to the lounge. *That really marked time*, he thought. After the foundation had been environmentalized, the sleeping quarters had been set up while cargo ships ferried tons of material and supplies. It reminded him of some kind of relay race that might have had a silly name in some other part of the country. Trying to remember the name of that southern kid's game left him clueless. He didn't know many things. This bothered him vaguely. He was not one for trivia. Yet if there were something to learn in this crappy techno world, something to make it better, he would find it. It kept him sane and what some people might interpret as being motivated. The lounge was one of the first rooms built in *TerraLuna*. People like to lounge. This spot he had personally touched had built up from some of the residue from the packing sealant or clear grease from the environmental stabilizer, maybe a combination of these and other dirt makers like his own hands. It seemed strange, he thought to himself, because such care had been taken in keeping this project spotless. Construction was a messy job, and he wasn't going to get a rag and clean that spot.

His instinctive need for a cigarette carried him down to the lounge, and spinning again for the lower flight, he began to fish for a smoke from his shirt pocket under his Terra uni-jumper, which made them all look like children or inmates. This was another critical comment he was too busy to make.

Pushing past the hall door quickly left him staring at the vending machine gauntlet he loved to hate. He continued at the machine until completing his obligatory stare. He reached for his WD card, still holding his gaze like an artist making sure that the finishing touch was really enough. Ed knows that something artificial had to be mixed into the formula of a PAYDAY candy bar to give it that certain texture. Its texture made you wonder. Halfway through his candy, Ed Zonic lit his well-earned cigarette.

Finally, his body was experiencing the initial stages of winding down; he looked over to notice he was alone in the break room. Since this was the only place where smoking was sanctioned, there were usually a couple of his coworkers there. It seemed to him suddenly that there were fewer smokers than when he was a kid. It never stopped killing people, he noted, as he dragged from his filter carelessly. Some people smoke with a death wish; others enjoy it. He figured, if you die doing something you enjoy, life was not wasted. He took another pull and thought how stupid some people are to let something this small bring them down. His ash tipped off prematurely and bounced off his name badge onto the floor. Ed was zoning again. This might have something to do with his name, Ed Zonic, yet he still was always able to come up with the right answer following the "zone." He stared away in some personally sanctioned thoughtway while the minor details of life floated by. Some regarded him in a sage-like manner after being amazed with the ideas he would have after this seemingly rude pause of thought. He blinked, realizing his wrist phone was ringing. He unclipped the lower half, and it pivoted up, making a handset fitting into his palm from the underside of the silver band. He raised his hand to his ear. "Hello, Zone."

"Ed, I need you to come up to OPS. We could have a liner. I need your help on this one now." It was Dave, the other person who knew how this place worked.

He took the final draw from his butt and tossed it into the tray. Clipping his phone closed, he ran to the doorway. Making his way to the far end of the complex, he couldn't think about stains on the wall or how they make candy bars. The call about a liner needed his attention. Something fast was approaching. The ballroom was the quickest way over to the OPS center.

As he half ran, Ed was again awed by the majesty of the Earth as it glowed through the roof of the ballroom. He shot an admiring glance up, musing thoughts of several ladies he would like to bring here when this place was finished. *TerraLuna* gave technicians a free week's stay. That was the real deal. The rest of the world would pay the low introductory price of . . . megabucks.

He threw open the Authorized Personnel Only door, taking the stairs two at a time. Details seemed to find their way into his thoughts. In a way, they bothered him. They spoiled his concentration. He forced the idea of the wall stain out of his head. This perma paint was not supposed to stain. Someone would have to clean that stain on the wall.

Finally, he entered the operations center, and the tension he expected was more prevalent than anticipated. Three of his normally relaxed and contained associates were afire with activity around the needlessly large computer console. Simey sat at the keyboard, sweating, ready to access more information, but there wasn't any.

"How big is it?" said Ed, searching the screen.

"There is nothing to worry about. The thing is just shy of a light-year away," said Tom, tall and precise in his late forties, who stood reflecting light from his console.

"Okay, Tom, that brings us to just before dinner on opening day. It's still too big and too close. Skylar should have spotted this months ago. Dave, are you sure?"

Dave's careful eye remained fixed on his screen. "The figures here scare me, Ed." He pointed with his pen to a flashing section of the screen. "These speeds are inconsistent with any I've ever seen. Its size we may be able to crack down from max range like any other one, but that's not the problem. It's coming in too fast for optimum targeting." Dave twirled his graying beard and adjusted his wire-framed glasses.

Simey tapped the keyboard, clearly proud of his prematurely bald head. "Here is where we first spotted it ten minutes ago . . ." He continued to work the keyboard and then waited for it to give him information.

"It seems to be coming from sector 45.7213. According to the stats, this area never rendered anything. It's clean space. We have over seventy-five thousand objects in our tractable database, and this is not one of them," Simey said, sure of his data.

Dave and Tom remained glued to the screen, and Ed began to zone without noticing the moan that Simey released as new information flashed onto his screen. Tom stooped even lower to reread the information.

"And here is where it is now," Simey added.

"*My god*, Simey, that can't be right. ETA 27.3 minutes. It's faster than anything we have seen."

Dave pulled himself from the screen.

"Maybe it's a burner. Anything moving that fast could easily burn up. Check the mass, Simey. That must be it, Eddie, right?"

Ed looked flatly at the numbers and tried to realize an end to this unwanted feeling that threatened his gut instinct for order. Time was unavailable. Ed was sure there would not be enough time or distance to deploy the attachable direction modifier to push the object away from the area. He needed an answer.

"Yeah, Dave, it could burn. Simey, the LDS targeters, bring them up now. Let me see how they line up to this trajectory. How many shots can we get off starting as soon as possible?" Simey continued his flight over the keys.

"Lunar Defense Satellites One through Seven aligned and bound for intercept." He entered the coordinates, and the system responded faithfully. "LDS substrate targeters number 8 through 10 in place. Shall I automate?"

The four men consulted their fears and, for a moment, knew that a choice had to be made, and it concerned informing Gerhard.

"We have to try this, Dave. If we don't, that is going to be in our area." He ran his finger to the lunar safety perimeter on the screen. Tom swallowed. "Do we tell Steele now?"

Ed reeled to look through the clear polymer space panels as if expecting to see the thing crash right then.

"Simey, automate. I'll call Steele."

Ed stepped into his office for some separation, opened the satellite phone, and called Steele.

Simey began the satellite procedure. "LDS full. Auto target coordinates compensating speed fluctuations. System formatting . . ." Simey's well-receded hairline felt like it tugged back another inch. "System formatted. They've got it *now*."

Dave looked at Ed through the window on the phone with Steele. Steele, hearing the news from Zonic, took some stress off Dave on whom Steele often brought the brunt of anger.

"Take it out before it gets any closer," Steele said.

The wide orbit laser satellites continued their volley of constantly updating information to the laser stations as they delved farther from the safe area toward open space.

"Station is online. All navigational sensors responding to target lock. Deployment sequence activated. Four minutes, twenty-two seconds to automated fire on target Alpha."

Tom planted himself next to Simey to help him monitor the assault. "As if we didn't have enough trouble, satellite radar is picking up another target. It's not going as fast, but it's about as big. This one is about ten light-years away at its current speed. Tracking Alpha Two, assigning logging host Medina. Keep an eye on that one, Dina darling.

Simey looked to find Ed still on the sat phone with Steele. Pushing his chair over to Dave's console now behind him, he said quietly, "Steele would have asked you too many questions. Zone doesn't take any of his shit."

Dave pushed Simey's chair forward then said quickly, "I am activating EVAC protocol."

Automatic routines fed throughout the facility, alerting all sections. Lights flashed, and sirens pulsed warnings to the scattered crew. He thought back to the dramatic advertising video they made to sell rooms on the moon, with happy people milling about the atrium. The scene in the atrium now was utter pandemonium. He hoped there would be a hotel standing on opening day.

Dave rose and went to the office window and pounded on it a couple of times. Once he got Ed's attention, he tapped his watches and pointed to the skylight. Ed nodded, raising his index finger.

Simey chimed, "Dave, they're ready to go, half a minute!"

Zonic hurried off the Sat phone and went to his computer console at his desk. He opened the standard bank of monitoring systems displaying the *TerraLuna* Hotel from a variety of angles. Clicking on the record icon on his computer, he began to record the incoming meteor drama and its hopeful destruction vis-à-vis the dual laser array. Working quickly, Zonic opened a file of access mail addresses and scrolled down to NICHOLAS, N. He established a live uplink and sent his transmission.

Ed entered the OPS center to find his three colleagues huddled around one console, beaming together what seemed to be a collective prayer in the glow of screen light.

"Ten seconds until first fire," Simey reported.

Dave stood behind Simey. "Simey, can you give us any more resolution from the closest laser banks? Can we get a picture of this thing?" Simey complied, squinting at the computer.

"This is the best I can do for now. We are getting upgrades on the second. Here we go. Lasers firing. LDS one, three, and five confirming target's validity."

The flashing cursor continued with no report of a definite hit. "Tom, get me a re-upped mass reading every thirty seconds. I want to see how fast we can chisel this bastard."

Double zeros followed by a percent sign stared at them blankly. Ed looked at the screen for a hard moment and then deliberately said to Simey, "Lower the target probability trigger to 75 percent for fire effect. We have to hit this thing."

Simey adjusted the settings. Flashing numbers appeared on each hit, 1, 6, 13 percent destroyed.

"We have a picture. Direct from maximum telephoto, there it is," announced Simey, controlling a smile.

Rapid shafts of laser light streamed into the blackness at the tumbling rock that measured nearly three-quarters of a mile wide. The first seven LDS laser banks spun about the meteor maintaining a comparable speed, firing powerful bursts at a rate of one hundred per minute each, now perhaps with less accuracy. LDS 8, 9, and 10 laid in waiting in a concave formation programmed to target the smaller sections, pummeling them to dust. The computers regulating these LDS were three times as powerful to allow for higher accuracy.

Normally, these meteor pickoff sessions, as they were unofficially called, were simple, concise, and most importantly, taking place millions of miles away. Progress reports were unable to be read clearly as they changed as rapidly as they were displayed. Terror lived in the quiet control room as each person privately calculated the possibility of precipitate entering the lighted ring on their screens known as the "safe area."

Skylar's LDS arrays had been very successful on distant planetoids, with plenty of space for safe dispersal. They could not imagine encountering something with this kind of speed finding its way to ground zero. Ed silently advocated additional local defenses for the complex like those developed by his friend Nick Nicholas. Costs were already through the roof on the LDS defense.

Ed Zonic was roused from his most recent zone by a hand grasping his arm. It was Dave pulling him over to another console. "Ed, it slowed down."

"Hasn't it gotten any smaller? We've been smacking it. How long? Ten minutes? Tom, get me a mass reading." Tom scanned his monitor fervently.

"These readings are different. The mass seems to fluctuate. It is down as much as 27 percent. Either there is a malfunction, or those little rocks are reattaching, maybe with a magnetic field." His voice trailed off in thought.

Ed stopped and stared at open space for some recollection of meteors with densities way off the charts. It should break up. Iron, stone, frozen oxygen, and nitrogen, it's likely to be the remainder of a broken planet, perhaps one out of our galaxy composed of unknown materials. An explosion sending a chunk this fast must have been of an incomprehensible magnitude. Mostly, super dense metals like osmium, iridium, or platinum are found in planet killers. He paused in thought to fathom the math of the magnetic force able to pull back the broken pieces of itself. Worst-case scenario was that this was merely a pebble in comparison to the rest of it. Moreover, where was the rest of it?

"The lasers are having a 43 percent hit ratio. Yet the mass has been reduced by only 36 percent," Simey reported earnestly.

"We're going to see this thing in our backyard. It's nearing local gravity," Ed droned as he stared through the space light.

"We're going to red alert. Everybody in the shelter! We have less than ten minutes."

Dave tapped the screen's RED ALERT prompts, and a low, loud, and repetitive alarm sounded, followed by a loop tape recording that directed, "All guests and personnel, please move to the designated shelters in the lower level immediately. Attention, attention please. All guests and personnel . . ."

The mass was hurdling toward Earth and her moon with rigor. It seemed to be drawn not only by gravity but also by some kind of hunger. It now spanned over seven hundred thousand feet across. No doubt it was a planet killer. The lasers ferociously kicked off compact car-sized chunks, spinning them in all directions. They spun unmistakably toward Earth. Fortunately for Earth, the moon happened to be in the way. Some of the precipitate reattached itself magnetically.

The engineers, techs, and execs of *TerraLuna* were nearly all in reinforced bunkers designed to protect them from any one of several disasters. Each of them has seen a photo of the moon and the many impact craters visible even from Earth. Now they imagined what it would be like to be present for a new one.

Sirens blared as Dave watched the last remaining people finding their way into the bunkers. People craned their necks to the space light to catch a glimpse of the doom coming to suck them out into space. He activated the sat phone and placed it carefully to his ear. He had to tell Gerhard Steele the status of *TerraLuna* himself. Tom, Simey, and Ed were at the stations, tensely waiting.

"Mr. Steele, we have chiseled only 30 percent from the original mass we encountered. We have less than ten minutes until it enters the safe zone. I think deployment of LINDYMAX would be our best course of action . . . as soon as possible."

CHAPTER 3

Steele hated giving long interviews. They always seemed to lead to sensitive questions he had no intentions of answering. Why did this have to happen during a television interview? He sat in a makeup chair backstage on the set of the television news magazine during a break in filming. His pin-striped suit suddenly didn't seem as new as it needed to be to make him feel comfortable. He paused, looking around the set to make sure no one noticed a change in his appearance.

He gravely gave the order, "Do it."

Steele held the wrist phone silent for a moment for effect and then indicated carefully, "Or we're all finished." He clipped the band back around his wrist and smiled instinctively at the makeup artist who smiled back and began to touch up a glowing spot on his distinguished, yet not graying forehead.

*****

Conducting the crew to action with a thumbs-up, Dave moved to a quieter part of the operations center and tapped on the lunar nuclear defense system. "We have a green light, boys! Steele just turned it on. Activating LINDYMAX. Confirm sequence, Ed."

Ed was at the next console over, keying his sequence as fast as he could. "Sequence confirmed. LINDYMAX is unlocked. Patching to you, Simey. Opening guidance circuits, please enter sequence for control." Ed glanced at Simey not missing a beat.

"Navigational sequence accepted. Transferring current trajectory into LINDY One." He cascaded his fingers across the keys until he hadn't any more to tap.

"Patching to launch site control . . . Tom, initiate stage 3 upon entering launch sequence."

Tom flicked a knob open at his console and then entered his sequence. "Sequence entered . . . confirmed. Automated launch site is active, navigation is ready, stage 3 complete. Download, Simey!"

Simey carefully confirmed the information sent to the missile navigation computer. He looked to Ed. "Transfer complete. Ready for firing sequence. On your mark, Dave."

Dave studied Ed for a moment. He turned to Tom and again to Simey. Once getting their simultaneous attention, he exercised a bit of the authority he actually had. "We meet in bunker number 1. There isn't any time to go back to your rooms. If this thing doesn't work and the shuttle tubes are blown, we're dead. I thought I'd make that clear. Simey, active bunkers 1, 2, 3, and 4 Omega status."

Simey responded with steady skill. He knew a direct hit would leave a crater deeper than they had dug for the escape tubes, no way home. "Bunkers are active." He looked back to Dave.

"Okay, Tom, activate LINDYMAX in 5, 4, 3, 2, 1 . . . Launch!" Tom sent the missiles through the moon silo deep in the rock, straight up into the heavens. LINDY micro targeters spun, zapping the fragments with varying degrees of intensity based on the size of the targets. They hovered back in waiting for the onslaught of precipitate, sensors locked and poised to finish the war on aggregate the nukes were about to start. The nukes would explode far enough away to keep *TerraLuna* safe from the blast, or at least that was the theory. There was no precedent until now. He hoped the new array for targeting these things was as good as they said. The truth would be known shortly.

The composite nuclear missiles and the meteor did not take long to collide. The targeting system was state-of-the-art and really put the old digital system to shame using micro ballast reflection sensors, synthesizing the shifts in the weights of the atomic makeup of the target. The hope was that it would not destroy the meteor but rather that it knock it off its course. The newest nuclear missiles equipping the station were designed with a centrifugal force initiator that spins multiple nuclear blasts about an axis, scattering the precipitate in all directions away from the hotel. The missile was a simple twenty-five feet long, with a forty-foot boost. Since the gravitational pull of the Earth is many times greater than that of the moon, a large rocket is really unnecessary for these lunar shots. Thirty separate nuclear bombs emerged from the nose of the missile and spun into action like a buzzing swarm of bees. Computer guidance calculated the weakest spots for maximum effect, scanning thousands of times per minute.

Climbing with the precision of an eagle, LINDYMAX made her way to her target. Tom and Dave went to Bunker One's command center, while Simey stayed back to review the transfer of the entire complex's command authority to the safety of the bunker.

Nearly ten minutes passed until Ed began to collect his sat phone and cigarettes from his desk. He stared into the drawers and had a hard time finding anything important enough to take or insignificant enough to leave. After filling his pockets with stuff in general, he walked to the door.

Ed yelled over the droning alarm near the access stairway to the bunker. "Come on, Simey, hurry it up!"

The OPS engineer looked to check the various systems to ensure he would be able to access all possible functions. Then it exploded. Through the space light, a burst of orange light popped open and cascaded around itself. A slight tremor eventually shook the insulated quiet of the room. Ed ran down the stairs for cover. Simey remained gazing at the light and then turned away as the light faded. Uncounted flinchless moments passed. He clutched the underside of his console, peering to see the screen, hoping not to feel a hard, fierce death. He opened his wrist phone and tapped the code for Zonic's phone. "Ed, it's done."

Ed was on his way up to get Simey. He entered the room to find Simey clutching the side of the console and staring into it for some hint of what may be left. Ed joined Simey, staring into the console. "Lower the resolution. If that thing isn't out there, let's see what the hell is." He deftly keyed his request, and the screen displayed a horrible sight.

"My god. It's in a billion pieces. Will LINDY hit all those?"

Simey attempted to isolate the trajectory without running a simulation. "I can't say for sure. They are so spread out. One thing is for sure: LINDY has her hands full. Some of that stuff is going to come our way. We should get downstairs."

They finalized the command center's transfer and headed for safety below. Ed closed the door behind them and checked his keycard from his jumper and snapped it into the slot, enabling the electric dead bolt. Soon after they passed the security door and descended the stairs, they detected a musty smell of less circulated air. They took the stairs briskly. It dropped nearly four hundred feet to a titanium-reinforced bunker the designers theorized would withstand major catastrophes. Ed thought, *this would be the test.* They turned another landing, and Ed produced his keycard before he needed it. He looked up as if to see tons of meteor rock crash upon him. It wasn't there. He inserted his card and entered Bunker One.

At first, he couldn't tell what he was hearing in the distance below *TerraLuna.* The trip down the corridor was filled mostly with the sounds of Simey's heavy breathing and Dave's heavy footfalls coming toward them and the sounds of tiny pelts against the outer structure like hailstones. Hail itself was unreal in space. Small pellets of gravitating debris "falling" on the surface like supersonic grains of sand sounded strange given the silence of space. The miniscule rocks from the meteor pelted the outer walls of the hotel. The intensity grew in waves of cascading rocks slamming against the hotel's unnatural presence. It subsided and then resumed with an increasing flurry, so fierce it was as if hate was behind the space rocks. The three men pulled themselves away from the door.

LINDY 8, 9, and 10 fiercely targeted the largest pieces and blasted them after determining a level of energy strong enough with which to obliterate the projectile. They spun and dodged while shooting hundreds of red laser blasts per minute.

The bunkers were equipped with their own generators and communications, each with accommodations for fifty. One bunker was located in each of the four corners of the complex. Intercom systems were installed to keep communication open until evacuation plans were scheduled. Bunker One's accommodations were intended for the operations team who would be able to control the functions of the complex from the auxiliary command station. The low-intensity lights made the glow from monitor screens seem brighter than in the OPS center. Tom had already booted up most of the systems, including the generator, temp control air filtering governors, food, and water.

Simey accessed the cameras from the four tower structures to give him a look at what was happening to them. "Ed, come look at this view from light tower 3."

A barrage of space dust loaded with larger fragments could be seen approaching the complex. "Its trajectory has changed from the blast, 16.4573 degrees.

"Simey, give me fix from the long- range tapes of the point before the impact. I want to know where that second bogey is heading," said Zonic intently.

"I'm accessing the file point where we first sighted target 2. There it is," Simey complied.

"Dave, I'd like to bring the LDS team back to one on this. I want to get a head start on the other bogey. What do you think?" said Ed, verbalizing his thought.

Dave, operating the intercom panel to the other bunkers, turned to Simey. "It would be a great idea. Get on it."

They were both turned away from the screens when a shock blasted the structures above. The men scanned the various views of the bunker furiously for any signs of a cave-in. Ed seated himself next to Simey and tapped into the light tower system to get a look at the range of damage.

"Accessing light tower 4," Ed said as he pecked in the sequence.

Tom sat at the control station screened wall with several views from inside the complex and the light towers. Several large portions of the hotel were unable to be seen in the face of all the dust. Some of the indoor cameras were damaged. The constant pelting continued when suddenly, another crash shook the edifice above.

Simey began checking updated reports from the hotel's various systems. Tom also checked the usual systems when Dave called to him. "Tom, I think this sat phone signal is being blocked by the dust. Try to bring Houston up again. I'm sure Steele is going to want to hear from us."

"Eddie, we are getting the shit kicked out of us here. Look at this!" Ed rolled his chair to see Simey's screen.

"We have lost environmental integrity in six sections. Half of the power grids are not operational. It looks like that last hit got us in the eastern wall, mostly guest rooms. I'm shutting down environmental filters, artificial gravity, and sealing the damaged sections."

Ed briefly scanned the LINDY screen with Simey and glanced over at Dave.

"Let's take a long look at this debris from the right field." Simey complied, offering a wide-angle view from a distant satellite camera. It revealed a phosphorescent wave of debris swirling its way toward Earth. *It would be nice to notify Gerhard and the global community. This kind of encounter could be devastating. I blew it up, and now it is going to tear up the Earth like some kind of sandblasting disaster,* he thought. LINDY's screen logged in over seventy thousand hits so far. Who knows how many of those would have been devastating?

Ed was zoning. Not able to get a clear reading of the reality of the situation, he let his mind slow down to take some of the infinitesimal possibilities into consideration. He began the cycle again. He rationalized away much of the damage, and deep at the core of his session, he found the second meteor. Where was it heading? Ed's zone was interrupted by a voice coming from the intercom. "Bunker One, this is Bunker Two reporting. Do you copy?"

Tom caught Ed's glance, replying, "Bunker One here, we copy. It is good to hear you made it in. What is your head count?"

"We total thirty-nine. No injuries. Bunker checklist is all good. What time does the next bus come through?" the female voice added jovially, considering the circumstances.

Tom paused, trying to keep the entire situation in a professional and calm tone; his fear was calmed by the humor of the crew in Bunker Two. "We are establishing rescue arrangements. Stand by. Please enter the names of the technicians currently occupying Bunker Two. Follow the instructions on the emergency procedure screen. Hang loose," Tom added, trying not to sound dictatorial.

A short pause brought another technician's voice into the room. The young man queried, "What happened out there?"

Dave hesitated, and then in his best assuring tone, which earned him chief of personnel, he answered, "It was some debris from a meteor. We attempted to scatter it out of our area. Some parts of the hotel are damaged. Reports are still coming in."

Dave paused with an audience. "Bunker Three?"

The rapt listener made his presence known.

"Yes, sir?"

"What is your personnel status?"

The young technician tried to maintain composure.

"We have twenty-nine accounted for with some minor injuries. Nothing we can't handle," he replied.

"Stay together down there. We are assessing our situation. Stand by for updates. I want you to check in every thirty minutes on the status of the wounded. Watch your procedure screens as well. We'll get out of here soon. Bunker One out."

Tom broke the temporary silence. "I hate it in here."

The men all looked at Tom for a moment. Leaving levity behind, they went on about their work. The ominous pelting has become less frequent, thanks to the lunar defense system. A larger set of rocks would have sent the entire structure into space in pieces and left a hole a mile deep. The dust and debris were enough to offer a substantial setback to what was going to be man's greatest achievement.

Ed continued to monitor the remains of the meteor from the view. Some of it appears to be lingering between the moon and Earth, tossing around in an orbital belt between their gravitational forces. It seems probable that some amount would enter Earth's atmosphere.

Ed dropped out of his studying of the trajectory and said calmly to Tom, "Tom, when you establish contact, tell them that most of it will drift into space in rotational eddies. Threat to Earth is negligible. LINDY is working overtime."

Dave tugged his beard a bit and nodded, still concerned about how the bombardment of billions of dollars of Gerhard's investment group, a system that was supposed to detect and destroy planetoids like this far away from the moon, could have happened in the first place. Dave couldn't quite admit he liked Gerhard in any way. Yet this misfortune seemed to give some silent ease to his rivals at *MoonCorp* that could be felt even this far away from San Bernardino, California. His coworkers agreed silently that Steele needed to come down a peg. It angered him that it had to be at the expense of their safety.

All staff continued to collect reports from the other bunkers. All totaled, there were 149 survivors. Two bunkers had serious injuries from the falling hotel. Nineteen were missing and presumed dead. He dreaded the negative press, but moreover, informing the families of the dead made him literally ill. He tried to think to whom he could delegate the job, but it was no use. It had to be him. Dave caught Ed's gaze fixed on the phone.

Ed looked across the room. They needed answers before calling Steele. He had too much to say and not enough energy.

"Ed, want some chips? We've been here two hours already."

Zonic took a chip and crunched it automatically, in all the excitement realizing he was hungry. He fathomed they might be there a while.

CHAPTER 4

$\mathbf{D}$r. Nick Nicholas sat in his orange/peach-painted office as he usually did for about an hour before taking his trip home. He glanced casually at his paperweight, a stack of silver balls of descending size, to clear his thoughts. He would stay late tonight. After a vended dinner from the commissary, he would continue to work, retesting his latest arduously funded theoretical experiment. Usually, he reflected on the day's activities comprising pages of mental notes on how imperfect theories would work when applied correctly. He remembered how his teacher used to pronounce the word *correctly* in sort of a singsong inflection. Perfection's high cost was realization. So many impossibilities, so little time. If he could make it work on paper, he had to make it work in practice; the litany of the underfunded. Testing costs money and time, two commodities usually in scarce supply. Not being able to test theories challenged his skill. People confused genius with skill. Genius was something he made a point of avoiding. People in his field had too much to say about geniuses, especially ones in their mid-forties sporting a youthful demeanor.

He was tall by most standards, thirty or so with a crop of blond hair and a characteristic Californian tan. He enjoyed his work more than complaining about it. *MoonCorp* provides for research, but not before committee scrutinized it. Not having funding for some of the company projects forced him to work harder to refine existing schematics. They want a step-by-step explanation before they fund a project or new technology. This was Nick's specialty. His job was to present a schematic that was a sure thing. The extra hour in the office was the difference between success and failure. It was his clincher. His earlier work as chief of scientific development for *MoonCorp* allowed him to assign projects to the sea of hungry interns the company employed in the research department. The best of these thinkers are gone. Budget cuts left them no funding for formative research staffing. Even mid-level theoreticians were let go, case in point, his friend Charley Porter.

TerraLuna, however, received the funding for their hotel complex, thanks to the political savvy of Gerhard Steele. *TerraLuna*'s popularity set the entire *MoonCorp* project into hibernation. The investors who were going to invest wanted to do it now. They wanted to be involved with the first public facility on the moon. Nick was amazed at how trendy these profiteers could be. They backed the project without comprehensive local defense testing, and it looks like they are succeeding.

Nick glanced past his new silver-rimmed glasses at a note on his desk. His mind had zeroed in on that note, and it forced him to fix his gaze. *Amazing!* Nick thought. It was a picture he had doodled earlier of a light ray moving through an equation. The ray moved out under the equation at a different angle.

He took his pencil, added a number 4, and redrew the ray's entry and exit from the equation with careful precision, staring at it attacking the possibility of error. Holding his gaze on the doodle, he reached for the intercom button.

"Eleanor, is there anything up there for me?"

A couple of moments passed, he still held the doodle contemptuously in his glance as if defying it to be incorrect. "No, Doctor," said the pretty voice.

"Thank you," he said robotically as he clicked off the intercom.

"This might work," he said aloud, alone in his rather small office without a window.

The white and orange/peach-colored paint reminded him of a *dreamsicle*. He tried to like the *dreamsicle* as a way to have some fascinating connection with the room. He could not like them; he tried. Experts argued that a window helped people be more productive in the workplace. He noted a context problem again. What kind of work were they doing? Functionaries could use a nice view to hypnotize themselves into performing the routines known as work. An artist could be inspired by some new shadow cast upon the grass. An executive might be motivated by some scent, like the newly mown lawn or the smell of fertilizer. The clerks found hope in the sunshine; their meaningless tasks were done as happily as the sunshine lights the world or drearily as the clouds darken the picture of the corporate lawn below. Reptiles were like that, cold-blooded, changing with the ambient temperature. Now many are extinct.

He needed no window. Distraction is a dangerous game for a scientist. The closed room kept his thoughts controlled. Other minds were meant to be frivolous and whimsical. Nick reminded himself that he was no poet. But he was getting older.

"Quality thinking leads to quality results." To mark time in his great old life, he would muse in efficiency sayings. "Time is not ours to waste," for example, he considered a very efficient principle. This scared him; it was a sign of aging. If they made sense, it was a representation of impending wisdom. He could deal with that. Nevertheless, he was a professional at keeping youthful. It was a skill, having a good attitude; at least, it allowed him a license to invent.

Glancing back at his doodle, he realized he had broken the barrier that had kept him from the next step in his work. He sat back in the reclining mode of his chair and noted the sealed manila envelope with the completed schematics of the defense proposal he had finished months ago. It was on the shelf, and it was flawless.

Tinkering with side projects would occupy his time now in its advanced form. Notes on napkins and sleeves or on walls, scraps of paper filled his pockets some days, all bits of ideas to add on to the great endeavor. He had many projects in manila envelopes. *MoonCorp* wants him to perfect the systemic blueprints for use at a later date when funding provides the green light. *Well. I've already done that,* he thought to himself. As time passed, without utilization of his work, Nick thought they might try to sell his ideas to *TerraLuna*. In the event that that happened, he would go to them for a job. They must know *MoonCorp* has talent they can use. A minor wave of paranoia came over him. Certainly, his work was being protected. Think tanking was not an option for him. Gerry Steele was big on think tanks. He knew too many colleagues who had fallen into that pit of despair. They turned into beady-eyed, squinting mole-like creatures spouting arcane idea, most of which were filed and very few actualized. Had he become such a creature? Adding the years of theorizing and what-iffing, it was possible. Brilliant concepts were mulled over by cautious overachievers whose superiors tried to use them in a way dissimilar from the way they were incepted, that is, for profit.

He shook his head in disbelief when Eleanor's sweet voice entered the equation of the room. "Dr. Nick? I think you are going to want to take a look at this access mail that just came for you."

Nick swiveled to the direction of the voice. "Who is it from, Ele?" Nick wondered which one of his graduate school swells wanted to find him for some theory-stealing reunion or geek club paper party for a science magazine that routinely flunked unperfected theories. Nick would fix it; someone else would claim it.

"Well, it's from your friend Ed Zonic. The message was sent along with video and other charts. I'm downloading them now to your monitor. Dr. Nick, it's from the moon! The originating address is from *TerraLuna* Hotel and Convention Center." Her voice left the room abruptly, leaving him with the science of a new puzzle.

Any communication with a sensitive member of *MoonCorp* would be highly suspicious and certainly monitored for the leakage of classified material. This was unquestionably true for transmissions from *TerraLuna*'s high-boost communications grid. They spent time together at the National Institute of Physics. Ed was brilliant and could think on his feet when most physicists were stumped on their asses. They found the situation problematic; Ed found working explanations. He worked with Freidby and Seltsky on an advanced format for artificial gravity. It was a breakthrough and earned them honors at convocation.

He started his computer. There was a great deal of empty space in his computer. This was a strategy to avoid hacking. Anyone with knowledge of sensory decoding might tap into highly dangerous and potentially valuable information that he would rather keep sequestered in his home lab, away from criminals and corporate snoops. This was why he coded his projects with names that made them unidentifiable.

Nick set his hand on a clear thin piece of plastic that read his DNA, cuing the screen to blip on. Nick loved the advances in sensor technology yet had not enough zeal to devote himself to work at perfecting it in depth. It was necessary, not extraordinary. He tapped at several points and commanded the computer to display the video Ed sent of the meteor and its flight numbers. The film was not bad, taken from the light towers set up around *TerraLuna* and the satellite system. He enabled the de-coder to reveal the message.

Nick read aloud from the letter, *"The speed of the meteor was greater than I had ever seen. We attempted to veer it off course by breaking it into no threatening pieces at a safe distance. Our laser array chiseled it down only 27 percent. It regained mass, seemingly attracting broken fragments as if some magnetic core was keeping it together. I haven't much time. We are preparing to enter the bunker. We deployed the centrifugal nukes and broke the thing into smithereens. LINDYMAX did what it could to decrease the size of the precipitate. The debris is hailing the complex. It was traveling faster than typical meteoritic bodies of this size and not on our tractable database of monitored entities. Refer to the data for speed rations. What is this thing, Nick? I know you will appreciate the problem. Let me know if anything comes to mind, if you can. I don't know if we are going to make it. I should have taken that job with MoonCorp. I wanted you to have this close-up data. It might help. One more thing, Nick, there was something else out there. A second body, moving more slowly, also previously untracked, was not far behind on the same course. Our scanners recorded it, and its coordinates are included within these documents. If I am alive, I'm in the bunker . . . Zone.*

He fingered his controller to replay the recording of the second object. An illuminated entity about ten light-years away was traveling at the same coordinates. Strange. He adjusted his glasses and pulled his dark-blond hair away from his eyes. He viewed the data for what became an hour and collected and organized the information like he would organize a room in a new house. The room was a mess with boxes of stuff and random furniture strewn about. This metaphor helped him sort the elements of a new problem. What was the relationship between the two bodies? Were they twin comets once a single body and now two? Secondly, the behavior of the broken rocks seemed peculiar. If there was some magnetic core to it, it must have been of incredible power, perhaps not magnetic, to draw back the fragments. Thirdly and perhaps most importantly, where did it come from, and why was it traveling at speeds heretofore unheard of? *I'll have to research this when I have time,* he thought. *Oh, man, now that* TerraLuna *is disabled, possibly dead,* MoonCorp *may give the green light to start production. How selfish,* a small voice reminded him from the recesses of his mind. Nick leaned forward, cupping his face in his hands and pulling them back through his hair. "I'm the first one to know," he said aloud.

Nick brought up a clean screen and began typing a reply. "RECEIVED YOUR DATA. HOPE YOU ARE ALL RIGHT. REVIEWING YOUR SITUATION HAS LED TO SEVERAL THEORIES. WILL FORWARD AT A LATER DATE. PLEASE RESPOND TO CONFIRM YOUR SAFETY. NICK."

He sent the message, wondering if there was anything left to receive it. He tried to remember the type of bunker materials used and some of the stress tolerance configurations. He went into his records to find some stored information on the rival hotel. Of course, the plans were very secret. Anyway, anything Ed sent would probably have been screened first by their people, but that did not stop Ed Zonic, who was masterful at coding. Problem number 1, they knew their rival had sensitive information. Nick's eyes rose slightly. Solution number 1, who cares.

He was interrupted by a phone call. "Hello, Nick Nicholas."

He listened suspiciously for a moment. The familiar sound of his employer and sometime friend, Stan Duncan, allowed him to downshift a mental gear that needed to move.

Stan was the administrator who oversaw every aspect of the projects Nick had been developing for close to six years now. He and Nick were close. Yet most of his personal projects were kept from him for professional reasons.

"Nick, you're still there, good. I have news. *TerraLuna* was nearly destroyed today by a comet or meteor shower. The damage is considerable."

Nick slid away from his desk. "Have you spoken to Gerhard?"

"No, I don't expect to anytime soon. It appears that you were right. Their laser banks and nuclear backup still did not prevent an assault by the precipitating debris." Duncan paused to see how Nick felt about his compliment.

Nick looked at the envelope in the basket on the shelves built into the wall across from his desk and behind the door. It held plans for his prize local lunar defense system.

"Well, Stan, you remember when we were able to review some of *TerraLuna*'s defense plans that happened to find their way to us, I had doubts about its effectiveness. I would have advised them they needed a local answer for a local problem. You remember you wouldn't let me advise them. People are probably dead because of that move, Stan."

"Nick, don't do this to me. *MoonCorp* needs your insights, not Gerhard and *TerraLuna*. *MoonCorp* pays for your work. *MoonCorp* will govern what is done with that work. As for your loyalty, we both know that our team has always wanted to win this game. Now is our chance. This is turning into a lecture. Look, we are calling a board meeting on Friday. Several of Gerhard Steele's borderline investors are suddenly interested in some of the developments were have made since we have gone silent. I want to meet with you tomorrow at eight o'clock. We need a strategy for an interested investor. Do we have anything really impressive, they asked, and of course, I said yes . . . I think we do. This could be it, Nick. I'll see you tomorrow".

Stan closed the line and left Nick's head buzzing with ideas, and ordering them to organize was a task he loved. He clicked off the computer, stretched briefly, and walked to the manila envelopes on the shelf. He took them carefully and brought them to the desk, Local Defense System.

The title C. H. Technology stared at him knowingly. He placed both envelopes on the desk. Noticing the pad with the doodle that solved another unfathomably complicated problem, he drew an even breath and thought of the many doors that would be thrown open because of it. He could not wait to begin to open them. He put the pad in the briefcase as well. *I love science*, he thought to himself. *It really is an adventure.* Instantly, he was filled with rising excitement. This was the answer he needed so desperately; it amused him that he cleared a hurdle of his personal experiment just as *MoonCorp* might finally get off the ground. He now had something to make him work twice as much. It would keep his mind off other things. He scooped the envelopes, shaking them a bit triumphantly, and tossed them into the briefcase. He turned off the lights and left the office.

CHAPTER 5

Far above the moon, streams of rock, varying in size from a grain of sand to the size of a small house, tossed about in the graceful cloud beyond Earth and her satellite. Above the hotel, long clouds of smoke and dust were swirling into a gravitational orbit in a slow space dance. The entire complex as it sits was about the size of two football fields. Perhaps some of the larger debris had hit elsewhere on the moon. *TerraLuna* was not quite destroyed and certainly salvageable.

Large sections of the guest rooms sustained the brunt of the impact. The window that framed the Earth in the ceiling of the lobby had not been damaged. Several monitoring devices were ripped away, along with a section of the roof close to thirty feet across. A sprawling crevasse spanned through at least twenty rooms and left a deadly naked breeze from the moon's powdery surface cascading through the rooms. Smashed beds thrown against the walls splintered and floated strangely into space. Chairs, sinks, and Jacuzzis appeared in fragments about the impact area.

The impact mangled the hotel's shape into the moon's surface. Walls were pulled away to reveal a washroom pushed into the buckled wall of the kitchen. At various points, hallways popped open from the pressure and introduced ice buckets, mini coffee makers, and an assortment of towels into the rolling vacuum of space. A white wall burst in several places, looking like pieces of giant popcorn. Without gravity, flotsam floated eerily about the complex. Rolls of toilet paper bounced playfully against remote controls, rocks, and Gideon Bibles. However, there wasn't anyone alive to look upon these peculiarities, only quiet cameras. Any construction personnel that did not make it into the bunkers were drawn into the void of space, a horrible death.

Fortunately, the shuttle system was operational. The escape shuttles that could remand the crew back to Earth safely were "not available." Gerhard Steele felt the crew needed to remain in the event that the reconstruction phase might require them to work. The crew had undergone simulation exercises living in the bunker for three days; they knew what to expect. They were paid to work at *TerraLuna*, not fly home when there was a problem, a typical Steele move.

It really was not so bad, yet showering in locker-sized stalls and eating the freeze-dried food were the preferred choice over floating into oblivion. The accommodations were comparatively comfortable. Fortunately, none of the bunkers were damaged by the deeper fissures elsewhere on the moon's surface. The crew wasted no time enjoying themselves. They accessed the music database and spent time remembering old songs that they rarely had time to listen to during their busy days. Barely an hour had passed from the moment of impact before crew members were choosing partners for a ping-pong tournament and booting up personal computers to link with their families to play video games. All things considered, being paid while the administration teams fumbled through procedural manuals to reclaim order made the time pass easier.

Other parts of the moon weathered damage from the bits of planetoid much the same as it had for millennia. The pockmarked surface, still unshook from its orbit, bore its scars with a durable pride, not unlike that found in the weather-beaten faces of Indians of the old American West. Many faces of chiefs, warriors, and squaws responsibly reflected the sun's light into the infinity of space. Earth's moon proudly beamed its tribal beacon to the heavens, one of many days in an old and proud collection.

Benjamin Skylar's LDS system annihilated the heavy continent bashers from causing an uninvited meeting of heavens and Earth. The smaller chunks were tracked down and snuffed out before they had a chance to enter the Earth's gravitational pull. The moderately dangerous elephant-sized planetoids would not get within a quarter million miles from Earth.

Yet sifting into the atmosphere were millions of tiny meteorites, most of which burned into soot in the Earth's atmosphere. Seen as shooting stars at night, with brilliant trails of blue and red light, they entertained the people of Earth. Their larger brothers nearly destroyed a billion-dollar hotel; perspective is reality. Wishes were made, and young girls were kissed as usual.

Late-afternoon skies were cleared of summer clouds and would soon reveal an occasional shooting star to a fisherman that would signal him that it was finally time to head back to shore as he tested his craft against the diminishing daylight. If the catch wasn't sufficient that day, he had to stay as late as he could to turn a profit.

The shrimp boats speckled the area with bright halogen lights perched high above the water. Shrimp were attracted to the bright lights, yet tonight, only one of such crafts dotted the wide horizon so late in the day. The hold contained maybe sixty medium mackerel, not a big haul. Such an afternoon dwindled into night for Pepe and Tico as their boat sat silently in the awe-inspiring light of sunset in the Yucatan Peninsula off the shore of a small town called Celestún.

The warm Mexican waters usually offered a fine variety of mackerel, grouper, squid, shrimp, tuna, and even some shark. Tico gnawed at the corner of a worn net just to pass the time. He actually wanted to look busy so his master would take the hint and haul in the nets. He looked up unassumingly to Pepe, who was staring off at the shooting stars taking center stage on the darkening horizon. Pepe stood a solid five feet, ten inches. His thick brown arm held a lever that operated a winch to haul in the last catch of the day. He waited nervously, hoping a large redfish would find its way into his net for a late-night supper with his wife, Paloma. Redfish always put her in the mood, and after this day, Pepe was ready for some tender loving care. Tico continued to play since Pepe was not bringing the net into the boat. Looking again into the sky and then to his burning cigarette, he took a final drag and dropped in the boat and stepped it out with his old black boot, scratched and warped from the seawater and sunlight. His jeans were quite new, still holding their shape and color very well, he thought. His curly black hair blew away from his face as he tried to determine the change on the weather. He looked at his watch, and it showed 8:37 p.m. His stomach growled. He patted his tough belly in its red and white cola shirt, tossing a look at Tico.

"You wanna go home, eh?"

Tico stopped tugging and gave one quick shaggy bark, bouncing from paw to paw, shaking his straggling brown and white hair from his eyes, staring intently, hoping the stubborn man would pull the lever. Tico jumped up several times, hurdling his little body up to the level of Pepe's belt, signaling to him that it was really well past time pulls in the nets.

"I know, Tico, we go home soon. We get something good to eat and go see Mama." He smiled reflexively as he tossed the hair around the top of the little dog's head.

"If we come home with nothing, Mama's going to shake her finger and say no funny business tonight." He scratched the dog's ear the way he liked. Pepe was confronted with a sight in the sky he hadn't seen before. A shower of lights like fireworks fell from the dark expanse above.

No, Pepe thought, *it could not be fireworks*. Meteorites were falling straight down from the sky. Pepe vaguely counted twelve or fourteen until there became too many to keep track of. Each had a trail of dark smoke following it until they eventually plunged into the water some five hundred yards off his bow. Strangely, they seemed to be falling in the same general area. Upon impact, huge splashes shot up, sustaining a fountain of spray. They were in such an orderly fashion, it seemed like they were bombs falling from a mechanical bomb bay of a plane.

Pepe intuitively moved the lever forward. The winch kicked as the cable began to roll over the pulleys, raising the nets draped below the long steel arms extending from either side of the craft into the boat. Before any of the nets reached the boat, swells began to softly rock the fisherman's boat. He knew it would take twenty minutes to get all the nets. Pepe urged the lever ahead another notch to hurry the nets into the boat. From the corner of his eye, another danger materialized. A second group of four or five streaming points fell not a hundred yard from the first group. Widening his eyes to take in this incredible sight forced him to blink as if lubricating his eyeballs again and again would make sense of the things he saw.

Pepe forced his body to the winch. At this rate, the nets would not begin to enter the boat for another five minutes. The boat rocked gently. The motion brought his head upward and around to check for more shooting stars. None could be seen. It amazed him how uniformly they were falling into the sea as if they were on a string. Tico must have been barking the entire time, but Pepe only noticed him because he was jumping again. Then there it was, a third group of falling stars again about a hundred yards from the second group. The net surfaced. It disappeared briefly in the slapping swells and then reappeared, drawing nearer to the spool. Pepe pushed a button that turned the boom across the deck. During the normally uneventful process, several large fish flipped out of the net away from the catch into the turbulent sea. Pepe cast a warning glance to prevent any redfish from leaping back into the sea.

The boat, whose total length was less than sixty feet, continued to rock with the swells that were created by the objects entering the blackening ocean. As the last of the net entered the boat, Pepe started the engines, hoping he could push his ship through eight-foot waves. Night crept nearer as the sun began its journey below the horizon.

*****

As the night plodded onward, time carelessly spent on a singular thought became pointless to Charley. Duke had roused himself to leave hours ago after reminding Charley frequently about their bet on the Angels. It would not be long before he stopped himself from having another beer. Charley came from a family that was not always sober, yet usually realistic. He knew his limitation would creep around within the next half an hour. Sam's earlier zeal had steadily waned as the evening pulsed along. Mostly, he leaned against the spotless bar, sipping seltzers Sam began serving after noting it was time to cut him off from beer and perusing the females engaging the holographic jukebox.

The older crowd had left completely by nine o'clock, and gradually, Sam began watching the clock and the door more closely as the hour neared ten. Charley drank what was left of the flat seltzer he designated to be the second to last of the evening. He looked over to the pair of younger girls who occupied the table to the left of his stool. On several occasions, he had entertained the thought of going over to sit with them. What would he tell them? he thought. *Hey, my name is Charley Porter, and I am an unemployed physicist! No. That wasn't a good opening line.*

He whiled away most of the evening, trying to come up with a quip good enough to move from his vinyl perch. The television was always another opportunity to seem interested in something. It changed pictures again, and the ten-o'clock news began. The anchorman was a tall, careful man with advanced graying of the temples. His light-gray suit seemed to lean his seemingly extra-long upper body toward the camera. It was as if he was coming at him, Charley thought. Charley tried to keep from blinking until the reporter blinked. This guy would not blink. *People must have wondered why he was staring so intently at the television,* Charley wondered subconsciously. He really did not care what too many people thought of him or anything for that matter. This guy was aiming himself at the viewing audience! Charley shook his head to clear the image. This encouraged him to pay attention to the news.

"Our top story tonight concerns a tragedy on the moon. At approximately 5:20 p.m., the Space Watch organization based in Australia documented a confrontation in space. Apparently, a near-Earth asteroid was on a collision course with the moon. NASA's early detection systems are able to track an asteroid up to ten years before they become dangerous to our area. Strangely, this particular object appeared quite rapidly on several planetary monitoring stations. It entered the range of the new TerraLuna Moon Resort currently under construction and was destroyed. The debris from the explosion, however, nearly destroyed the entire station. Thirty people are reported dead and at least twenty injured. TerraLuna crews are currently in secured bunkers, awaiting rescue teams

and salvage operations. The grand opening holiday celebrations have been postponed until further notice. Stay tuned later in this broadcast for a special report, Safety in Space. We'll be right back after these messages."

Charley stared at the screen. His drunkenness was nearly gone. *MoonCorp*'s entire operation could be mobilized if the financial situation existed. Work could be in his future. Charley ignored the fast-food jingles during the commercial break, unclipped his wrist phone, and dialed Dr. Nick. Of course, his line was busy. The computer answering machine directed him to enter his code number. This would alert Nick that he had called. He could not take calls from unfamiliar numbers or if he was doing something; he was too easily distracted. It was simply a fact of nature for him to disregard nonessential information. Charley knew he would call him back. Six years they had spent together working on various projects for *MoonCorp*. Charley knew there were smarter, older, and more gifted people who wanted to work closely with Dr. Nick. Yet for psychological reasons, Nick needed Charley's point-blank candor to counter his overcompensating detailedness. Dr. Nick may need him early tomorrow, Charley mused as he fished for some card to pay his tab. Sam, the bartender, mildly offended that his most devoted customer was preparing to leave at such an early hour, threw his over-dampened cloth in a rag bucket and drew a new one from under the bar.

"Leaving so soon? Those two college cuties have been checking you out all night. I'll send them a round for you, and then you can move in." Sam offered, waiting for Charley to reply.

"You're dreaming for me now, Sam. I've got to go, man. This *TerraLuna* thing might get me my job back." He stood and adjusted his pants, which had wrinkled and ridden high on his back during the five hours aboard the stool.

"Sam, this is important. You know I am a scientist first and a stud second."

Sam looked at him and reconsidered. "Okay, go. This is a record for you. This is the first time you left before midnight. I know, science first. Get the hell out of here! That Steele guy is a bad liar. Don't be too hard on him."

Charley met his gaze without a smile. Sam handed him back his world card, which Charley slipped into his shirt pocket without checking the balance. He did not focus to check the balance. Sam wouldn't cheat him.

"See you tomorrow, Sam." Charley dug for his keys as he made for the door. It opened into the bright shimmer of the high-intensity streetlight that made his silver Mustang look even shinier than it was when it was freshly washed. He wheeled out of Sneaky Petey's and back toward his apartment, barely noticing the brightly lit holographic billboard.

"Hey, Charley Porter. Here comes the King, here comes the BIG NUMBER ONE!"

*****

Before Pepe could move the boat, six more groups of meteors had entered the barely lit sky. They seemed to hit farther away than closer. Pepe brought the boom across the length of the ship, poising the dripping flapping load above the deck.

He had already turned on the floodlights to see the net packed with fish. Apparently, the cascades from the impact of these things scared more than the usual number of fish. This kind of load always had a couple of lobsters. Finally, the crane swung over the hold, emptying the net as it came. An avalanche of fish filled the boat. Pepe was up to his knees in redfish, eels, mackerel, octopus, sea bass, and several small sharks. The sharks' bead-like eyes rolled excitedly in the intense white light from the stadium-like halogens. Pepe hauled himself through the catch and found his way to the steering wheel at the bow of the ship.

Pepe thought for a moment that he should have dumped the catch overboard to make better time against the possible tidal wave from the meteors. This being not only against his nature but an afterthought, he adjusted the throttle, raised the anchor, and eased it up to twenty miles an hour, not wanting to strain the motor. He was carrying at least eight hundred pounds of sea life, and that slowed him down. The boat's engine responded sluggishly to Pepe's need for speed. The swells had become increasingly greater. Yet the added weight kept the boat from capsizing. The trip at this distance was normally under thirty minutes. This load would stretch the time to nearly an hour. Pepe's worst fear could not be thought of yet. Steering the boat to the cluster of the buildings and lights on the shore was his only cause; thinking was not in the plan for the evening. A warm breeze caressed his sweaty neck. It stank of dead fish, yet the explosions of space rock hitting the water overcame his sense of smell and replaced it with fear.

*****

As Charley took the illuminated highway home, he tuned his television screen set into the windshield just to the right of his sight of the road. For night driving, the television automatically dimmed to not take focus from the road. Most cars had them. Not everyone used them. It was great if you wanted the six-o'clock news while you were stuck in traffic, yet traffic had been eliminated anyway, so you watch television whenever the hell you want. Does technology inspire us to a higher level of apathy? He mused as he set the car to auto drive to take in the full effect of the television.

The news show indicated that the defense system came very close to wiping out the threat of a foreign object well beyond the range of the Earth. This planetoid or whatever it was came in at speeds over a hundred times than that of a normally monitored space junk. The nonblinking anchorman said further that it was not quite understood how it could have been destroyed at such a speed. Copious congratulations had been given to the quick thinking of the monitoring crew and advanced technology, et cetera. The screen changed, and Charley checked the road briefly and then returned to see a graphic of how the LDS or lunar defense system used a computer-targeting module to chisel the object down while it was in flight. Well, before it reaches the planet, it is scattered into millions of pieces. The report stated that because of the speed at which this entity was traveling, there remained a large enough piece to cause a threat. Then they deployed a nuclear device to either destroy it or knock it away from gravitational quanta of the Earth.

The newscast ended without giving him anything that would help him walk into *MoonCorp* in the morning and get his job back. The rest of the way home, he wrestled with the idea of calling Nick again. He needed to settle in with his thoughts after this bomb. Charley knew one thing for sure: he was going to be ready if the call came; he had a feeling it would be sooner than he imagined.

*****

The warm, dark waters off the Yucatan Peninsula left behind the trailing sound of Pepe's engine and an occasional bark from Tico. The boat's wake was imperceptible in the choppy waters. The rocks that stuck the water slammed into the seabed, disrupting centuries of sediment. Billows of silt and stone cracked and heaved in places still now for millions of years, sending gigantic pockets of air climbing and reaching for the surface. Huge bubbling towers spewed upward to the newly starlit sky. The sea was boiling from the released gasses as well as the heat from the interstellar travelers. The waves from the overwhelming disturbance incited Pepe's boat to coast along a bit faster than anticipated; the worst was yet to come. The seafloor crumbling apart caused enormous water displacement.

Pepe glanced around to find Tico at his feet, ready to get off the boat as soon as she docked.

"Tico, what do you think? Was that mess far enough away not to wash away the coast towns? Maybe it will go out to sea, eh?"

A swell lurched the boat ahead. Tico barked with fear as a flood of fish rolled across the boat and nearly buried him in a pile of expiring sea creatures. Fins, tentacles, and eyes collaged around paws and wild, wet fur as Tico burrowed out from the carnage and quickly planted himself at the feet of Pepe, looking back to see if anything was coming after him. He licked his lips and looked at Pepe as he shook dry his wet fur.

As the cores of the meteorites sank, trails of boiling water sent steam through the tumult of the sea. The rocks themselves finally, after the burn-off, were the size of a baseball and smaller. An earlier group of rock had caused a deep cavern in the seafloor to open. The ancient layers split apart, exposing materials covered for eons.

Deep in the gulf's ocean, subsequent space rock found its way into the open fissures of the seafloor, controlled by the undertows and pulling currents of displacement. The intermittent quakes spewed rocks and debris upward into a different time. Rocks fell inward, meeting newly mined layered rock, like steps deep into the seafloor. Mostly, this sort of geoturbation occurred as in every other similar situation. Some variant of magnetic force seemed to be at work beneath the waters, unseen by human eyes. The space rock rolled erratically along the seafloor as if it were drawing something up from the layers of rock, something to complement the magnetic force within the burned interstellar spheres.

One by one, rocks from deep in the Earth shot up as if from a geyser and then clapped together with the meteors. Together, they fused and fell back into the abyss. By midnight, the sea was silent, and the floor settled in its new configuration. The fused rocks occupied the old sea with an ominous dominance. They slowly began to emit a peculiar white globigerina that thickened the water around the rocks. Like a phalanx across the seafloor, shrimp began to arrive by the thousands to feed on the ooze. After a few nibbles of the gelatin, they were engulfed by it—poisoned.

After Pepe reached the shore, the dock men quickly unloaded the hoard into the packing building and shoveled ice into the bins, sealing the catch away for sale, apparently unaware of the meteors as they worked. They had an agreement that always resulted in fair payment for the catch of the day. "Amigo, I would like to take something back for the wife," he said coyly.

The clerk nodded assuredly. "*No problema*, senor. What would you like?"

"Well, she likes redfish." The clerk nodded again with a friendly grunt, rummaged through the trough, and retrieved a beautiful redfish, which he quickly wrapped, sealed, and handed back to Pepe. "There you are, senor, fresh today."

"Thank you, amigo. Oh, could you wrap up some *camerones*, uh, shrimp? Give me two or three dozen for some soup," he said, tucking the paper package under his arm.

The clerk walked along the trough, occasionally poking through it with a long paddle. After a few minutes, he returned with his hands in the air. "I am sorry, senor. This catch, it has no camerone . . . no shrimp."

Pepe's eyes widened. He turned to the sea beyond the large open front of the clerk's depot as if to get an answer from her. Pepe turned back and shrugged, thanked the clerk, and began his walk to truck. Tico bobbed along at his feet, eager to go home.

"Can you believe that, Tico. After all our adventures today, no shrimp. Every time we come back, we have shrimp." He stopped and looked down at Tico, who stopped and looked him right back in the eye and had no answer for his master.

CHAPTER 6

The summer evening always held Nick in awe. The best thinking he had ever done was when he was not thinking about science, immersing himself in the sounds of a June evening. The warm summer wind twirled throughout his large yellow car with the air-conditioning on full. The mixing of temperatures left him both exhilarated and comfortable. This setting allowed his mind to shift into overdrive where the great ideas roamed.

Nick tapped on his computer that held almost one thousand hours of music downloaded from his personal collection onto the micro-compact disc. The wordless music provided fertile ground for this cherished creativity. Other people singing distracted him. If he felt like singing, he wanted to ensure a minimal amount of competition. He made words to the music based on whatever occupied his thoughts at that time, mostly theoretical subatomic formulae as they applied to engineering realities. Yet invariably, his mental lyrics echoed of a girl, the only girl ever to set his heart and soul in tandem to the timber of her voice.

Nick and Ada met at the University of California at Berkeley in the winter of the year 2150. Nick was eighteen and a freshman in the physics department, a lonely, skinny kid with cold eyes and an expanse of logic, ready to spring on anyone who would challenge his mounting theoretical passions. All totaled, Nick regarded Ada as his greatest discovery, like a new planet. If they married, she would take his name much like planets and comets were named after the scientists who discovered them. Ada listened as no one else would. He felt her hear him and, moreover, understand and respond critically, yet theoretically. While most people were involved with their financial portfolios, broken families, who was going to be president when it was too close to call, Nick thought about how he would take care of Ada.

Ada was also a bit skinny with a pale expression to match her skin. Her eyes glowed with understanding, and her lips curled up in a natural grin kept away from most people. Nick knew that she smiled for him. It was a grin of understanding and uncompromised authenticity. Her long, not-quite-blonde hair held a glimmering golden hue that Nick reveled in when it was exposed to sunlight.

Nick's fourteen-mile drive to his country home outside of San Bernardino was halfway complete. Wooden fences, barn, and cows replaced the traffic lights, restaurants, and offices as the hot and cold air mixed freely, keeping Nick's mood high.

The jazz music kept the majority of his mind locked on the prospect of the experiment he would perform before tomorrow's meeting with Stan. He hoped he would come to some conclusion early. He needed to be alert to address the endless questions Stan would be asking. This evening's experiment would bring light to a longtime darkened corner of his research.

The colors of June's trees lent facets to Nick's latest breakthrough, the Sun Filter. It came from nowhere while he wasn't trying, an absentminded doodle. It was there, shining on him the entire time. It was there now on his arm as he held the car along the country road to his home. It shone on plants, beasts, water, and everything since the very beginning; it is the beginning, then and now. Today, in 2168, the same sunshine holds the secrets to the next dimension of humanity . . . Maybe.

The large yellow Buick turned a tight curve, and five scavenging crows danced in a circle around a dead squirrel, each taking turns picking bits of flattened sun-dried flesh. The cultic birds eventually noticed Nick and reluctantly flew off in their own directions. Occasional gas stations logged off civilization for the last five miles as he approached the dirt road that twisted nearly a quarter mile to his house.

His mailbox stood faithfully at an angle to accommodate his car window. Opening the metal door, he hoped for a package today. Tossing mostly junk mail onto the passenger seat, he wheeled the aging car up the road to a group of pines, which turned the road into a tunnel for nearly three hundred dark, cool feet.

The red and white aluminum pole barn loomed around the bend nearly sixty paces from the house. An oversized antique telephone pole was planted at the corner of the edifice. A large black electric cable ran up the side of the pole that was visible at a considerable distance. A thick strapping cord was used to lash it to the pole. The end ran inside the building.

He pulled the car in front of the laboratory disguised as a pole barn. He enacted the total screen function, turning his windshield into a widescreen monitor. The rear window dimmed, giving him a complete view of the security systems. He habitually checked the lock on the twenty-foot-high white sliding door as it appeared as one of the forty-seven secured items on his screen.

Nick tapped a few keys on the security system uplink on the console that slid out of his dashboard. Everything checked normally in the house and outer perimeter scans, he keyed the motion detection camera to display any movement around the house in the past ten hours; a small deer appeared on his windshield screen at 9:46 a.m. out in the northern end of the grounds. He switched off the computer, bringing the natural scene of his house and grounds back where they belonged.

Pulling up to the house triggered the automatic garage door opener and identification sensors. Nick glided the big car expertly into the attached garage. The house was an old renovated farmhouse modernized to a degree; the majority of the house faced into the woods and mountains beyond. Nick liked to turn his back on some of humanity when he came home. The car's systems shut down, and the windows rolled up automatically as he gathered his briefcase and mail and slipped his sunglasses into the visor. Fingering the final security code, he entered the house.

He stepped into the hall overlooking the huge sunken living room after removing his shoes, placing his keys in the golden bowl on a marble table in the foyer. His feet sank into the stylish, extra thick white shag carpeting. He announced, "TV on cable news channel," and the seventy-two-inch television snapped on to reveal the oddly large head of the broadcaster in his living room.

The view in the room still amazed Nick after living there for almost six years. The lush summer tree branches rocked their ample leaves back and forth as if to refer to the beauty of the rolling hills.

The news offered nothing concerning the incident at *TerraLuna*. He went to the kitchen on the other side of the hall that separated the great house to get something to eat. Nick was the furthest thing from a chef. The large side-by-side stainless steel refrigerator/freezer/oven offered a black touch screen that displayed a readout of its contents: frozen dinners. The "super fridge" slid his selection into the infrared oven, and within ten seconds, a bell rang. Nick grabbed a towel and then pulled open a small oven door jutting out of the unit onto an adjacent counter. Instantly, he was faced with a full, piping hot meal of Salisbury steak and gravy, mashed potatoes, and a vegetable medley. He touched another button on the super fridge and spoke at a small circular microphone built into the panel. "Iced tea, heavy ice." A generic tumbler fell out of a side slot, filled with ice and his favorite beverage. Pleased to hear something about *TerraLuna* in the next room, he took his meal to his recliner. He set up a TV tray arranging his meal and drink with diplomacy, calling out offhandedly, "Raise volume."

The bulbous-headed reporter dipped his head to expose more of the whites of his eyes to further the impact of his words.

"*Reports confirm that* TerraLuna *Hotel and Convention Center has suffered damage from debris of a planetoid, which was destroyed by Skylar Industries' laser defense system. Cable news has just received these satellite photos of the incident.*"

The old, fuzzy moon pictures have truly become higher in quality, he thought as the camera zoomed in to focus. Nick stopped chewing and looked deeply into the screen to view the effect of the impact. The hotel was still there!

"This would never have happened if they had let me use my protection system. Damn!" Nick said aloud.

"I told them that the entire moon's surface is continually pelted by small projectiles as anyone can see by its pocked surface. Some super paint isn't going to be enough to stop them. My system uses local protection for a localized danger. Jerks."

The news show was not showing anything new. His interest fell from the screen to a picture of him and Ada together on campus next to a tree, with the science hall in the background. They were smiling. This was a rarity. Neither he nor Ada smiled much, he recalled. They were shy, introverted, and plain. Yet this picture captures a normal side that they each had that surfaced only when they were together. They seemed complete, real, and not quite unacceptable. Finishing his now-cold meal, he chased it with a long draught of iced tea, went into the kitchen and then placed the tumbler in the machine. He spoke in a comical Mexican voice. "Reefeel." It responded with another serving of tea the way he liked it.

Nick instinctively moved to the hall leading to the bedroom. He changed into some jeans and denim shirt. He sat again to put on his sneakers. "TV off," he said and walked to the hall and grabbed his keys. He peered into the living room, admiring the old inherited furniture from his grandmother. It comforted him. "Close drapes." He tossed into the room, and the thick green curtains closed mechanically. The heavy drapes kept the room dark and cool. It settled his mind for the night's work ahead of him. He gazed into the peaceful room for a moment and went out to work in the lab.

CHAPTER 7

Charley slept particularly late the next day despite the promise of working again. In the murky indifferent fog of unconsciousness and dreams, with the drapes drawn, he had no concept of time. He forced himself back to sleep to confirm his own reality.

He wanted to talk to Nick but knew not to pester him. Pestering him usually yielded impulse decisions that may lead to nonoptimal actions. He had been given that lecture on several occasions. Nick was his best friend. Charley knew his place. Nick had a better way with people and did not drink. He wondered if it was genetic. Just the old jumble of the genes. He thought about feeling hurt that he was not more impressive or deft of phrase; rather he dug deep into the day, assimilating the remainder of the previous night's beer while he slumbered.

His apartment was basic yet not without all the latest toys a bachelor would want. He actually rented two apartments and, after signing a five-year lease, was able to arrange the partition on the balcony to be removed so that he could use both without having to go into the hall. The second apartment was his workroom. He tinkered with practical holography and of course solar energy. The balcony of the workroom was filled with solar collection cells of various sorts, including a working model of his pride and joy, the satellite radio transfer cell. It was a circular solar cell not quite the diameter of a manhole cover. It had a receive device with a thick rubber ducky antenna. The power it could generate was too great to use. The components for a buffering system lay strewn on a table.

He entertained women on a regular basis, yet he was the kind of bachelor who bored easily and didn't always bother replacing a girlfriend with a new one; an imported set of GPS golf clubs with targeting glasses would do fine. Charley thought they were a great way to get the ball to go where he wanted. After all, satellite systems were one of his specialties; there was no reason to not indulge. Wires and sensors placed along his arm, legs, and neck connected to the GPS fixed itself on the hole fed directions to the glasses that informed him how to position his body to construct the perfect swing using electric impulses. He had to practice for real. Practice he did, every day into a white coffee mug. He had an expensive ball returning device but did not like the noise it made when it spurted the ball back to him. It taunted him. Hating the liberties it took as the ball rolled lazily around in the receptacle before activating the return function, he sat it in the corner under some old *Scientific Revolution* magazines. He liked the quiet of the mug. It helped him find center.

The fading grassy green carpet seemed black in the abysmal bedroom. Several golf balls defined the sides of a path leading out into the living room like lights along the sides of an airplane runway. Charley liked to putt in his spare time, which was most of the time lately.

Since being fired, he chose to turn away from theoretical development. He played with the holographic animals and dancers occasionally. Without the company's sanction, he felt like a loyal, unappreciated crackpot. Having enough money to live comfortably for a long time to him was a sensible lifestyle. Keeping abreast of the latest work of his contemporaries amounted to a major part of his daily regimen. Maybe his best years were behind him. Wrestling with this possibility factored irritably into his equation-oriented mind; someday, a company would endorse his solar satellite research exclusively. His invention was as dangerous as it was brilliant, using solar electricity generated in non-atmosphere and transmitting to Earth wirelessly. Until it was properly marketed, he read science magazines, golfed, and drank.

Daily justifications played in his subconscious like elevator music. No family, so what. He could start one late in life. Many scientists did, and they enjoyed happy lives. Who cared if he was sixty when his kid entered college? He had important technological patents with his cooperative solar cell work with *MoonCorp*. He certainly was not bothered by loneliness. He adjusted his position, realigning his conscience, and went back to sleep.

*****

As Nick opened the door, a rush of hot air attacked his air-conditioned calm. He pulled open his wrist phone and began to check his messages during the short walk to the pole barn. The first call displayed itself—Charley's code. Charley was going to be a part of this new deal. He was one of the few people with whom he could hypothesize. This type of person should never be missing from any great invention's actualization. Being on the inner track of scientific possibility required a certain temperament. Charley qualified well as a colleague; his beer belly and cheesy sense of humor qualified him as a fun person with whom to work. He raised his wrist phone and spoke. "Charley."

The wrist phone's beep, buzz, and musical ring could not penetrate Charley's rest after four rings. Nick entered his number so that Charley would receive the message that he called. Nick approached the pole barn door and spoke into the detection device: "Code."

The sensor was programmed to open on his particular voice command. The familiar odor of electrical activity welcomed him. He flicked on several banks of overhead fluorescent lights and activated exhaust fans to circulate the thick summer air. He adjusted the cooling system that jerked on the air-conditioning unit on the side of the barn. The thick, electrically flavored air began to swirl up and around the vent openings located at various increments around the periphery of the barn, allowing the late-afternoon sun to join his project on the dozen experiment tables. Lights fixed on long wires hung over each table no larger than a shot glass; they could be raised or lowered with an electric winch control box on the underside of each table.

The center area of the seemingly unobtrusive tractor storage edifice housed a raised steel platform with a spiral staircase rising fifteen feet above the floor. A service stairway continued from the platform to a ceiling hatch that opened a twenty-by-twenty section revealing the platform to the open sky. A circular catwalk surrounding the platform allowed access to five large instruments bolted to the ceiling. They appeared to be lenses, four inches thick and three feet across, at first looking like a telescope to the untrained eye. These were the cannon-like solar relay devices.

Nick walked past the platform to a large desk set against a square homemade room between the tables and the platform. He switched on his computer and began fishing through the drawer for a bag of licorice bites against the new light of the screen. It displayed the current radar readings, cloud formations, and weather reports. A regional map clipped into place.

"Holoscreen," Nick said aloud.

A holographic screen appeared behind the desk above him roughly seven by ten feet. He adjusted the angle to the table area where he will be working. The screen was being emitted from several projection sites throughout the lab. Nick picked a finger mouse from the desk charger and placed it on his right index finger. Aiming it at the screen activated a large white arrow, allowing him to click from a distance with a squeeze of his hand. He expanded the Daily Forecast icon, which displayed temperature, barometric pressure, and what he was looking for, sunrise and sunset. Nick tweaked his finger to expand the countdown feature. It read sunset 9:44 p.m. Good, lots of light.

He entered the chair behind the computer, pushing himself backward to acquire a better view. When he clicked numerous links, satellite hookups were fed to his computer as it began a new program. The weather map disappeared and was soon replaced by a very close real-time image of the sun. A band of data along the bottom of the screen displayed readings and icons, offering scads of information about the sun. This sun tracking and measuring device was very much to the credit of Charles Porter. It measured magnetic field strength, corona activity, temperature, sunspots, and solar flares. Most importantly, the solar cycle is recorded. It was, by far, the most comprehensive solar monitoring system to his knowledge.

Nick adjusted the dimmer controls on the spectroheliograph to cast a different hue on the star. This view allowed him to get a highlighted view of specific areas of solar flare activity as they whipped off the sun's surface and cascaded into space. Charley and Nick had been working on dozens of solar-related projects. Yet most of the intriguing ones involved the solar flares, the actual matter of which the sun is comprised and how it reacts within their magnetic fields.

Nick's special study done without Charley involved the activity of chromospheric emissions of the sun. Reactions taking place in these emission zones contain phenomenon and material unable to be recorded by Earth before this technology. The

X-radiation and ejecta of solar flare particles cause several effects when they arrive in Earth's atmosphere. One such effect is the aurora borealis, the northern lights.

In addition to the pretty show in the sky, the sun flare's activity can also cause nuisances. Disruptions in radio and television transmission in some areas have been linked to the effects of solar flares. Nick had always been fascinated by this technology and continued studying it until he realized it had become his life's work.

He went to the first table to the left of the doorway and flicked a small local light switch. The light source hanging from a thin wire in the ceiling fell slowly to about seven feet above the table, entirely illuminating its surface like a medical operating table.

The table was a simple fiberglass-topped four-feet-high plane that came up to Nick's waist. Its aluminum legs were adjustable and unusually strong and allowed for zero wobbling. He fussed in his pocket for his keys as he made his way to the far-left end of the barn where three large fireproof cabinets, almost like safes, stood at attention. He unlocked the nearest one, and its large heavy door opened slowly to reveal shelves stacked with oversized ledgers.

The spines were organized by date, the early volumes encompassing essay from 400 BC by the Greek Melton. Theophrastus was emblazoned across the spine of the next tome. Aratus of Soli, Pliny the Elder, Abu Alfadhi Giaafar, and the Roman poet Virgil joined the gauntlet of ancient astronomers who kept records of their observations, which Nick had fastidiously collected over the past ten years. More modern volumes included the notes of Johannes Kepler, 1607; Galileo Galilei, 1610; Thomas Harriot, a contemporary of Galileo; and Jonathan Fabricus of 1611. The volumes continued with the contributions of Apelles (Christopher Sheiner) and Marius (Simon Mair), both of whom wrote under aliases to avoid conflicting interests with the church. Priests wanted to avoid being accused of heresy by promulgating scientific explanations of God's omnipotence.

Later in the seventeenth century, sunspotting watching became popular throughout Europe—and certainly less dangerous. More books of all sizes, acquired through painstaking means, collectively represented the entire record of solar observation throughout human history, including more volumes by Gassendi, Octuol, and Petitus in France. Rheita, Saxonius, Schickard, and Smogulecz filed their findings from Germany, and Vander Miller and Charles Malapert from Belgium continued along the seven shelves of the first cabinet. Several impressive volumes by Philippe La Hire occupied an entire shelf representing the work of a father and son continuing the family business of observing and recording the sun's activity. The bottom shelf's last volume was a docket by William Derham in 1711.

The other cabinets catalog all attainable research over the next several centuries by foremost scientists as well as lesser-known and even unknown devotees. Nick took a slow breath of respect from the piquant-library-flavored air, an extensive list of his own multilayered system. Nick heaved one of the books from the Derham series and placed it on a cart waiting next to the cabinet. After skimming along the names and numbers, Nick chose another volume, a reddish-brown leather tome by John Flamsteed, and placed it on the cart with the Derham book.

He picked some lint from the felt covering on the cart and wheeled the yard-high books to the table closest to the computer. Countless such trips would finally culminate the experiment. He enjoyed not the completion of the project, but the tediousness involved in doing it. Nick hefted the first book on a homemade holder and then the second on its twin. Adjusting the holders so the books angled in on each other permitted Nick to consult both simultaneously. Keeping his gaze on the books, ascertaining how best to begin, Nick realized he needed a notepad and backed to the desk drawer and produced an oversized prematurely ancient spiral pad with a technical pencil embedded in the spine.

The entries were logged with handwritten print and later would be entered in the computer. It read, "HELIOPAEDIA." He opened the notebook carefully to consult the contents page. The pad listed dates reaching back to the late 1900s, with information kept by someone unknown. Nick scrolled his finger, still bearing the finger mouse, along the long columns of dates and technical notation, much like a medieval monk copying data by hand and archaic method of writing by today's standards. Carefully, he checked the number–decimal point relationships to correlate the new pattern interface.

This activity kept his attention for nearly an hour. Without much ceremony greater than popping another piece of licorice in his mouth, Nick moved to the other volume. With the slightest of sighs, he thanked himself for backing up his records on paper. He respected the motivated hacker. The entire body of his work was not stored in his computer, on discs, and even the data nodes were the most progressive form of storage today. Simple pencil-shaped nodes could hold up to ten times the information of a disc, and they fit right in your pocket. The technology is new, and de-encryption constructs are unreachable without proper sequencing. If they had a node reader, they would not be able to get past the personal DNA security code. This vital data, disguised in ancient logs, was well hidden, unless some really knew what they were looking for. The thief would need to be as well versed in this technology as he. Nick wasn't aware of anyone that studied the history of the sun as much.

Nick seriously considered the remote possibility that someone somewhere may be attempting similar experiments in advanced solar science. Every great scientist had contemporaries, yet he knew of no one having gone further than he did with sunspot activity. After about another hour had nearly past, he was satisfied with the references to the Derham and Flamsteed logs for concordance with previous entries. His gaze still fixed on the figures through his glasses, he moved back to the desk, his thoughts firmly held on the latest synaptic connection. The patterns in the solar activity were irrefutable.

He turned instinctively to the computer and began to upload files. The image of the sun clicked away to eventually reveal lists of decimals and dates listed with several entries missing at varying places in the list. Nick began to scroll into the empty lines and then refer to the information from the readings on the computer. It was half past seven when it all fell into place and was correct. Remembering the doodle from the office as the final piece of the puzzle confirmed the theoretical efficacy he was looking for. Incredible, he thought, what this data should do when initialized, nothing short of viewing a new vista of the known dimensions.

His first instinct was to share with his colleagues to confirm and test. Charley was missing again. He resolved to call him again after he woke from his stupor. He remembered Ed Zonic and the accident at *TerraLuna*. He was concerned for their welfare, and they should send a shuttle there as soon as possible. Yet Steele undoubtedly would be up to his usually cruel double standard bullshit. He should write Zonic.

A sharp ping sound startled him to actually pull away from his screen. A sound like a rock hitting the roof of the shed jolted him for a moment. He rose and stretched hard and listened to get his bearings on the brink of this technological plateau. He heard the humming orchestra of insects in the prairie beyond his gravel road. He looked around the building just in case anyone might be there. Sometimes squirrels would crawl across the trees above the barn and drop chestnuts they would gather from the great tree in the field beyond the transformer. When they dropped them, it could be startling.

Not quite satisfied with that reasoning, he switched open his wrist phone and activated the remote motion detector and requested an immediate scan and report to his unit. In a few moments, the small screen indicated motion well below the suspicious limits of squirrels and birds. The technology of satellite locating had been around for a long time, but it offered problems as it was seen to infringe on personal privacy rights. Nick did not have a chip, something for which he was grateful. Criminals and children had them. *Criminals and children had many similar qualities*, he thought for a moment. While he mused on that topic, the phone rang with an identifying ringtone for Charley Porter, a beer jingle. It chimed for a few seconds when Nick activated the answer button.

"Hello, Nick. We have to talk."

*****

Day 2 in the bunker allowed its denizens to try half of the food selections. The novelty of eating survival food had not seemed to dissipate. Ping-pong and video game tournaments now the usual activity. Passing time, or more specifically, wasting time, was like an Olympic sport for the bright crew. One true thing: egghead workaholics relished leisure.

Wasting time and collecting pay was an instinctively activity for the overworked crew. It was a basic reality that there was not much too do until a plan was sent up to Dave, which had yet to happen. Simey was tempted to put names in a hat for a ping-pong tournament. The group knew that a ship would eventually come and ferry them away like a plane trip home from a vacation. The last thing anyone expected, especially Zonic, was a mission. Zone was listening to his headphones in his tiny cement bedroom; it was a simple room about ten by twelve, with a single bed, table and chairs, and even a tinier washroom with its own slight door.

Emergency jumpsuit clothing was available in a small chest of drawers, along with socks, T-shirts, and underwear. Ed had not torn into his emergency toiletries pack. He overheard the others discuss the funny mouthwash and washcloths. Ed was not the kind to indulge in cleaning rituals more often than he had to, so the thought of cute, probably less effective ones did nothing for him. Though he was getting the idea that he should brush his teeth soon . . . or maybe later, Ed zoned off into the music again but was soon interrupted by a rapping on his little door by a very hard fist.

He pulled off his headphones blaring guitar music and reached over to the doorknob and turned it to allow entry. It was Dave. No one else would bother to visit. Simey might, but Ed knew he was at the center of a fighting video game playoff that would not conclude for some time yet.

"I was on the live link with control and Steele," said Dave, feeling out of character in his blue jumpsuit.

"How soon will they be here?" Ed asked pointedly, looking straight into Dave's eyes.

"Oh, it'll be another four days at least. They cannot find anything for us to do structurally," he said.

"Shit."

"They want us to take the rover outside," Dave said directly.

Ed turned away, sliding his head against the wall in disbelief.

"Apparently, they want some material sample, radiation tests, which means some of the rock that hit us. They say it is vital to the survival of the company. The investors will leave soon if we can't come up with . . ." Dave paused to discern Ed's commitment to the corporate demands. "Answers."

"I know that as well as you. However, I'd rather stay here until my shift is over which should be when the shuttle arrives," Ed said with a half-smile and then continued, seeing Dave was listening, and that he was leading up to something he wanted him to do.

"Dave, I took this job because I needed it. You know I was hoping to work with Stan. It did not get off the ground, so here I am. I remind myself daily that it is just a job. Between you and me, I do not like the way Steele treats people. Usually, I care less, but his guy goes out of his way to screw with people and their self-respect. Self-respect is a big issue with me, Dave, and I have very little patience for people like him who look for ways to make others feel like dog shit. So naturally, when he starts blowing fool, dangerous orders at us through his god-horn, I get a bit agitated."

"Zone, it won't take long. FIDO is okay. You can take anyone you want," Dave said, enticingly ignoring his anger.

"Everyone here is cleared to ride?" asked Ed flatly.

"According to the manuals, they all had to train for lunar land duty," Dave offered. "I know you would do it yourself if you could. The rules also state there must be two persons in FIDO in case something goes wrong. So you can take your pick: the redhead or the brunette with the long hair. I don't care.

"When they get here, we have to have our grocery list complete or . . ."

"Or what?" Ed said.

"Or else, you'll lose your job, or Steele will offer to kick your ass . . ."

Dave entered the room farther and continued, "Ed, if you want to go to work for *MoonCorp* after this, it's fine with me. I got the feeling when that thing hit, it sounded more like a job offer than a death threat to a lot of people. That may be. Until then, *Terra Luna* employs us, and we have a dangerous and vital mission here." Dave was getting ready to raise his voice and then paused.

"Ed, let's get it over with."

Ed finally met Dave's gaze and nodded. "No problem."

CHAPTER 8

" CHARLEY, EITHER WAY this thing goes, we are in business again. Look, if *TerraLuna* does not continue, *MoonCorp* might restart work on the plans that have rested, dormant plans we worked out three years ago, man. We have to be ready for this thing."

Charley listened, shaking his head. "Nick, how can you think for a moment that you would work for that Triple Crown asshole Gerry Steele? If he could make a dollar off you or make a dollar off you and screw you, he'd choose door number 2."

Nick turned back to the barn speaking as he walked, crunching the gravel with his boots purposefully.

"Charles, we developed this stuff together, and not only will we get paid for it, we will finally know if it works in the situation. If Steele wanted my defense strategy, he would have to pull some major cash from somewhere, and we know that is what he does best. He does not know what I have, but he might be interested in finding out how he can save his investors. My trust lies in *MoonCorp*. If they do nothing, then our research does nothing. We could save countless lives and actually make this dream of completely safe lunar habitation live, even if it belongs to Steele. We wait and see what Stan wants to do. I want you to be there in case I need you."

Charley moaned in compliance. "Okay, Dr. Nick, you win. I will go, but let's be careful. Steele is a powerful hombre. He does not like to lose. And if it comes to working for him, I do not know what future Duncan and *MoonCorp* can possibly have if Steele has all the investors. Stan Duncan is your friend, and there is the matter of your contract." Nick stopped crunching pebbles and turned back toward the barn, weighing Charley's blunt depiction of the facts at hand, shifting his head silently from side to side. Changing the subject was his only resolve.

"What are you doing tonight?"

Charley paused silently.

Nick's gaze rose to the sun-collecting apparatus atop his ordinary pole barn and wondered if anybody had a clue as to what was going on inside.

"Charley, come over tonight. I am almost ready to run a simulation."

Charley snapped back quickly, "Already? I mean, now with all this other stuff going on? How did you compensate for the wave stabilizers? What about the filter media?"

"Hold on, stud. Listen to me. It is ready, and there is more I have not told you. I've stabilized the wave connection with a modulation device that is hardwired to the

Hilo's central distributor. Think about that as you get your ass over here! We can leave together for the center in the morning. Bring a decent suit. It has to be tonight. You in?" Nick said fitfully as he ciphered the code to his disguised laboratory.

"Holy crap! Are you sure?" Charley challenged, pacing the green carpet, trying to avoid stepping on a stray golf ball.

"There is the only one way to find out, Dr. Porter. Hurry or I'll start without you. Later."

Nick closed the phone and the door behind him, feeling the nearness of satisfaction. He approached the tall cabinet-like machine at the right side of the barn. Gaining some momentum, he pushed the machine for the first time to the center of the lab next to the circular platform, where it was meant to go for a very long time. The screen saver of the sun had clicked on, casting a near-natural light on the laboratory.

*****

The mess hall in the bunker was always busy. One thing lunar personnel had in common was that they like to eat. FIDO did not scare him. Yet he was petrified of that slim brunette with long hair. Ed noticed her and usually had to suppress a smile when their eyes met. He didn't know her name because she was working on amenities safety and was rarely in the same vicinity. Ed saw her and knew that this might be his only opportunity to get to know her. She was waiting in line for one of the dirty microwave ovens to heat her dinner selections from the display case. She was almost listening to a chubby blonde girl with short curly hair who was making small talk. He quickly took a packet of beef stew, buttered noodles, and dumplings, tossed them with a plate on a tray, and made his way to the line next to her. As he took his place in line, she was setting the silver packets in the machine. Before she could close the door, he grabbed the door, startling her.

"Whoa, whoa," he said, turning on a bit of comic charm. "If you put them in that way, your meatballs will be cold, your sauce scalding, and your spaghetti mushy. Allow me."

Ed reached into the machine and rearranged the packets in the shape of a campfire over the packet, with the meatballs in the center.

"The tops of the packets lean against each other and heat more evenly this way."

She looked at him as if for the first time and appeared to be pleased with what she saw.

"Is this what the manual says to do? It probably is because I never read directions. It's an instinct thing. I have one, and I can usually trust it."

He did not expect such a clever retort. He asked, "You have one?"

"An instinctive power," she noted.

"I use the scientific method regularly. It's a procedure I developed a habit for as a kid. I know it works. Ed Zonic, chief operations engineer," he said, extending his had to hers. They shook as her eyes made a fast decision to find out more about this interesting person she had noticed before.

"Haley Williams, amenities safety," she replied, not used to adding a title to her name. "How do you do, Mr. Zonic?"

"Zone. Call me Zone. My friend's do," he said, not wanting to release her hand.

"Zone? Okay, Zone, does this mean you want to be friends?" she said with a hint of kindness.

"Actually, I was considering you for a mission. Interested?"

The person in front of him in line left, and Ed took his place, arranging his meal in the campfire configuration of which he spoke. "It would take about a day, and that day is tomorrow. It involves you, FIDO, and I."

He started the microwave and turned to her for an answer.

"You want me to go for a walk with you and your dog? How much moon dust have you been snorting, Zone?"

"Actually, we won't be doing much walking, and it isn't a dog. It's a four-wheel intralunar detection operator, FIDO."

"I know what FIDO does." She giggled.

"Do you like shopping?" Zone said as he checked his meal.

"Sure, who doesn't," she replied.

"Well, I do not. I do have a very important shopping list for tomorrow in the new mall." He indicated with his head to the outside.

"I need someone to come along for the ride and help me pick out some moon rock, blasted wall fragments, and a piece of the big, bad asteroid that spoiled a free two weeks' vacation."

A bell went off, and Ed pulled his meal from the oven. "Busy for dinner?"

Haley looked at him for a silent moment. "So why me? Am I along to only pick litter, or do I have qualifications?"

Ed walked toward an empty table. Haley followed. "Well, you did say your job here was amenities safety, right? Well, this qualifies you. Think of FIDO as sort of an oversized maid cart with the little shampoos and all those clean towels, only it is out there on the moon. Without finding out what hit us without being detected, we would not have a hotel in which to have amenities—job security?" He paused for effect and then said, "I want you to come with me."

She combined her meal, impressed at the evenness of the temperature, and then said abruptly, "Sure. It sounds more challenging than beating those nerds at ping-pong. Besides, I scored a 97 on my FIDO simulator. When do we leave?"

"Briefing at 0900 hours, mission begins at 1000. Ride through the campus?"

He began his well-heated meal. "Meet me at the air lock?"

"It's a date," she said.

"It's a mission," he said.

CHAPTER 9

Charley swiveled in the chair for nearly an hour as Nick continued his explanation of what his experiment was trying to accomplish. Charley was prompted to be quiet several times while Nick assured him the thought was not yet complete.

Charley understood most of what Nick was saying, yet at some parts, he denoted understanding and then planned to go think about it again at a later time when he came back to Nick with a question. It always seemed to be an involved, multileveled series-of-possibilities type of question, the kind theoretical scientists loved.

"The interest in the subject of solar energy is the opposite of what it was thirty years ago," Nick continued.

"Early in the twenty-first century, with the technology available, corruption prevented the popular commercialization of public solar-based power facilities because it saved the consumer money that would have been theirs. The public became used to paying, and the power companies became used to spending. Energy costs kept the government-subsidized space programs behind by decades until private companies felt the profits of space were theirs for the taking in the late thirties. Having developed the ability to gather the sun's power from space from a satellite and beam it to a relay station and allow for free power anywhere in the world on a small scale is more than they can handle. It amounts to financial ruin for theses archaic power providers. We are still dealing with nonuse. My contention is that we have only scratched the surface of what this power can do. I want you to take it slowly with this theory. Do not jump to your economic conclusions. Simply apply this with pure science." Nick bowed to the computer quickly for effect.

"It might be a while yet before our PPUs are sold to the general public." He looked back at Charley while his files were being brought up. "This is why so many good theoreticians are drunks. They cannot study and use technology that in theory won't make them any money," Nick concluded, attending to his screen.

Charley shook his head acquiescently and turned away to avoid culpability. The overhead computer screen flashed and tripped as the demo file was loaded. "I have been working on this alone because it was nothing to share. Now I want to bounce this off you to see what you think."

A prompt on the screen about the size of a chocolate bar pulsed "Start demo." Nick squeezed his laser mouse.

"Remember when we tried to find a filter media for the sun power to purify it so it would be safe to use? This filter technology, we thought, was the key to allowing the use the sun's power before you improved the radio energy satellite receptors. The age-old wave theory helped us to solve the problem much like the age-old theory of adaptive genetics has helped me freakin' open a new branch of science!" said Nick.

Charley raised his eyebrows in recognition. "Yes, I recall contributing strongly to this concept. It would make millions."

"Not going to happen, Chuck. Let me refresh your memory about sun cycle activity. Remember the highly radioactive sun plasma seen here leaping from the sun? This stuff we have been trying to keep from the Earth because it is harmful, it is that very dangerous power that may answer our deepest and most profound questions. All you have to do is watch it for a couple of centuries to see that the pattern, Charley!" he said emphatically.

Charley looked at the screen of the sun flares, trying to see what had pushed Nick to this level of excitement. They seemed random, yet he paused before arguing with Nick.

"So my scientific mind says to me, where may we find a reflection of this pattern in the natural world. This is where I was onto something. Northern lights, electrical storms, and such are perhaps candidates for study. Severity of some heavy storms is actually attributed to enormous amounts of solar plasma being ejected into our atmosphere. To cause a hurricane or tornado on Earth, this solar burst, I contend, must actually emit a certain intensity that we can measure. It can be found not only in the force and level of radioactivity but in the past and the future. The sun rules this planet in ways we have never understood." Nick clicked the hand mouse that cascades to Earth. Layers of the sand are in motion in their various strata of plasma as it traveled to a diagram of the solar flare and its sandy plasma wave over time, each noted with a different color.

"What do you see, Charley?" Nick said with a high level of authority.

"Well, the plasma seems to be traveling in a natural emanation from the sun, entering the Earth's atmosphere at various locations that may or may not cause changes in the weather and meteorological phenomenon. That is a great graphic, Nick, but I don't know where you are going with this."

"Okay, Charley, check this out," Nick imparted as he clicked the next slide into place. "Over time, the sun will produce a multiplicity of storms that generate unimaginable levels of energy. This energy is conducted through the sun and out through prominences here and here. The solar winds are so intense they create sort of a shoveling effect, tossing the plasma into space."

A subsequent slide depicted a large wave of plasma advancing toward Earth. "Most of this particle activity has not been available because no one had found any reason to study sun plasma."

"Until you did," Charley interjected.

"Right. I have been pouring over the records of past sun activity, and with this new technology, I have been tracking the sunspot cycles, magnetic activity, radioactivity, and most importantly, this shovel effect upon the Earth over time to find patterns. Since the scope is so large from sun to Earth, I needed to find the correlation on an Earthly basis that was global and appreciable. This is essential for my hypothesis." Nick broke his gaze with Charley for a moment and pointed a rigged finger at the screen with a tremor of mounting enthusiasm. The screen offered a familiar family tree of species of animal. Branches from a central trunk brought the birdlike creatures from the reptilian and the amphibious from the sea creatures and so forth, including man's development from the primates. Charley, trying not to ask a stupid question, remained silent as Nick continued.

"The study of evolution has made great strides in the past thirty years primarily due to technology like the nodal computer system, nuclear electron microscopes, and my time satellite experiments . . ."

"Time satellites!" Charley blurted. "Why haven't you included me on this? You know how much I can contribute. Nick, what are you up to?"

"Charley, listen. This is all new. You are being consulted now for your expertise. Relax and follow the program." Charley swiveled and adjusted himself to an objective perspective. Nick composed his next thought with more care before he began again.

"What we are able to study about evolution has not changed so much in the past fifty years, but the way we study it has changed, thanks to the use of advanced computer and satellite dynamics. This evolutionary basic can now be studied at a highly defined stage and, with the help of holo-technology, go beyond previously recognized limitations."

Nick motioned to Charley to wait with one hand while clicking the next image on the great screen. Charley noticed a slight delay while the image of a moving graphic uploaded from Nick's files. The sun appeared behind the first sun, also brandishing solar activity into space. Each of the images followed the next stamped with a date; 2132, 2133, 2134, and the images continued until eleven suns had ejected their flares after each other. The image faded, and a colored flowchart designated each year with a different shade of plasma as it cascaded to an image of Earth.

New graphics clicked into view with a larger model of the blue planet. A long, layered wave approached the planet. Nick's movie played itself into the effects of weather, climate, and natural geological occurrences like tidal waves, iceberg movement, and earthquakes caused by solar influence. As the waves reached the surface, they interacted with trees and animals in a proportionally diffused state. Sparkling bits of radioactivity danced about the heads of bears and tripped among a school of fish. A group of crickets hungrily chewed plants strewn with glitter-like specks.

Nick's narration followed carefully as the film played. He had not taped a soundtrack probably because he was a little nervous about the sound of his voice and dared not hire someone for a voice-over, so it remained silent for now.

"Here we see the sun plasma soaking into the Earth's crust in cycles. It has been known for hundreds of years that the sun goes through an eleven-year cycle, revolving and pulsating with a rhythm whose effect I have been studying for some time. This cycle has more of an effect upon our little planet than we can imagine. I contend that it is the catalyst of evolution. Furthermore, through analyzing the eleven-year cycles, I have found there are other patterns that repeat themselves over even longer periods. If I am correct, additional repeating cycles remain undiscovered. Since we can study the flow of plasma within the pattern, we can also assume that the patterns continued from a sun flow before our ability to record it. So do we have anything that dates before human record that we can look into for the effects of the plasma on Earth? My answer is yes!"

Nick clicked his finger, moving the film that depicted the flowing plasma about different groups of animals in their natural habitats. Plasma infusing the soil is seen buzzing about insects just below the surface. "Now, Charley, I am sure you would agree that before life appeared on this Earth in any form, the sun was pulsating its young radioactive heart at the Earth's crust."

Charley nodded, purposefully not intending to say anything.

"It also stands to reason that when small insects began crawling around on this primordial dust, it affected the lives of these creatures immensely simply based on the fact that they were living in it."

Charley nodded slowly. Nick continued, "This path which binds each species to its genetic ancestors is the link to the pattern of the hidden cycles of the sun whose power remains so utterly misused and misunderstood that it is the task of fantasy to take over from where science stops cold in her tracks and sits down and cries."

Nick was standing directly in front of his friend, committing with himself to stop here and have him ask one of those great questions he had grown to expect from Charley Porter. Charley looked at Nick like a smart kid with the exact answer.

"You have found more uses for the power of the sun through studying the genetic codes of insects that have been around as far back as the beginning of life due to their lengthy solar exposure. The search for the elusive filter media somehow modified the affect."

Nick refrained from elaborating more because it was nearly one in the morning. He let out a deep sigh, glancing over to the space hotel model under the sheet on one of the worktables and said, "Yes. There is more, but you have the concept. We have to turn in. Duncan wants us at his investors' meeting at eight o'clock tomorrow. We can go into specifics on the way into *MoonCorp*. This is big, Charley. But if I don't get some sleep, I won't be able to give my presentation on lunar defense. Help me load the model into the Buick." Nick began the shutdown of the computer, fan, and security. "Grab that bag next to the model. We'll need it for the demonstration."

Charley rose, took the paper bag, and opened it as he followed Nick out of the darkening room. "Tennis balls?" he asked.

Nick nodded, not willing to give the simple explanation demanded of him, and wheeled the model out of the barn, finalizing the shutdown with a code entry.

The night sky was amply peppered with stars as the motion detector light guided them to the garage to load the model in the yellow Buick. They both stared silently upward, their imaginations digesting the victuals now before them. A lightning bug pulsed on and off again nearby, followed by several others here and there around the yard as they crunched along the fine gravel.

"Nick, you were speaking metaphorically when talking about time satellites, right? Alternatively, is this one of those Nicholas bombs that you will not tell me about and let me think out on my own? Is it actually lightning bugs that hold the key to creation blinking some stellar pattern to life itself or something like that?"

Nick paused and listened peacefully to the orchestration of the crickets in the night bushes and then said, "No, Charley, I was referring to the real key to time: crickets."

CHAPTER 10

The suits seemed as if they had never been used. This was fine with Zonic. An instinctive glance at Haley's bottom as she pulled the suit up around herself appeared to be normal safety procedure as far as Zonic thought until he was caught checking her out. Ed did not smile or apologize; he continued pointedly with his preparations.

FIDO's engines seemed surprisingly quiet for horsepower she provided. It was not long before Haley and Ed were aboard, checking systems with Dave at his console just next to the air lock. Driving FIDO was much like driving a car with an excess of luxury features, although most cars do not come with a miniature nuclear reactor and the ability to shuttle into space in case of emergency. Haley had been in several that were more comfortable and certainly roomier.

"Testing, testing, *TerraLuna* base to FIDO One. Sound check confirm . . . over," said Dave with his finger on the dial that controlled the volume.

Ed adjusted his volume and replied, "Loud and clear, *TerraLuna* base. Sounds fine, woof, woof. Request five minutes until disembark. Systems checking okay."

A list of system checks rolled past his screen, each with a green "GO" after it.

"Five minutes locked in, prepare for air lock sequence." The hatch over the unit closed with a slight hiss. A green light appeared, denoting pressurization security. The air lock began to close, and the lights dimmed as Ed flickered on FIDO's headlights.

Haley looked over to Ed and smiled professionally. "Looks good here. Navigation sensors locked on the crater. Geiger array online. *TerraLuna* base, do you recommend infrared sensors engaged?"

Dave raised his eyebrows with a slight shrug, scratching his beard. "I don't see why not, though I imagine the thing will have cooled off by now. Switch infrared detectors on, copy."

Haley scrolled the row of flat pressure switches that ran vertically on her left and found a red one that indicated "infrared." She pushed it. It lit green. "I have infrared."

Ed's check screen was filled with green light. "Dave, we are all green. Air lock depressurized confirming departure in one minute thirty-three, request to use the garage door opener on board."

"Ten-four, FIDO One," Dave chirped as the door slowly rolled open. Swirling eddies of moon dust whipped around the door, spraying the window of FIDO, welcoming them moonward. The stabilizing brakes came off, jolting the rover slightly.

The huge wheels kept it balanced, protecting it from spinning off course. "Ready when you are, FIDO One. Time in five seconds, four, three, two, one. FIDO, fetch some alien rock and we can go home," Dave intoned, adjusting his headphones with a seasoned tap of his fingers.

Ed pushed the wheel forward. The huge tires moved with a lurch through the open door onto a forty-foot ramp, taking the rover into the bright moon day. An area of thirty yards of smooth pavement surrounded the entire complex. Haley remembered one of the activities for the patrons is a moonwalk. They could gather their own moon rock. This air lock was designed for practical maintenance around the complex, making travel rather smooth along the pavement. Haley kept close contact with her radar maps. Ed noticed her vigil and said, "Beautiful day for a drive." Haley sighed an imperceptible sigh and kept her eyes on the screens. She ventured a glance out of the overhead windows.

"Yes, natural light without an atmosphere is genuinely brilliant. You should stay on this inner drive along the entire length of the complex and then continue straight beyond for about one-fourth of a mile before the edge four target craters," she said professionally.

Ed noticed her tone and tossed FIDO into a higher gear. Ed went about his business, wondering if Haley Williams was ever going to warm up to his edgy charm.

"It looks like this side is structurally sound, Dave. Are you getting this?"

Seven screens offered Dave a complete assortment of angles from FIDO's cameras. "Roger that, FIDO One. The southwest side caught a piece of it continue to the crater. We will use your aft camera for some close-ups. Reduce your speed to twenty-four. This isn't a race." Dave sipped his coffee and kept an eye out for anything that might go wrong. He had enough bad news to report to Steele and did not need any further mishaps.

FIDO approached the end of the complex. Haley was looking to ascertain the extent of the damage, and there it was, a rupture along the west wall three-quarters away to the south wall. She spoke to Dave. "It looks as if the rock cuffed the roof near the edge of the west wall. Thirty feet over and it would have missed. This area is where I worked. Jesus, the guest rooms are ripped apart."

Air locks sealed the area off the artificial gravity and environment generators maintaining the inner areas of the complex. Rolls of toilet paper caught on the debris waved out into the lunar sky. Occasional items floated out from the fissure that spanned about fifty feet across from top to bottom. It ended in a crater of undetermined depth. Ed shot a look over the right, spotting something floating out of the hotel. "What is that?"

Haley had a better vantage point as they pulled beyond the hotel for a better view.

"There is a coffee maker, and that is definitely an ice bucket. It is my job to pick them you know. This is unbelievable."

"Nice bucket," Ed added.

The border lights that surrounded the upper walls fell behind as they rumbled over more rocky terrain. *FIDO's cabin bounced along nicely suspended*, Ed thought as he focused the forward light to a wide beam. "One hundred yards to the crater. This could have been so much worse. What if this happened while a hundred guests were on vacation?" Haley said, finally sitting fully forward.

"They all buy insurance. It is included in the million-dollar package," Ed said coolly, laced with the slightest touch of sarcasm. "You have insurance. Your survivors will be well provided for. You do have survivors, don't you?" Haley kept her hands on the keypad and then entered coordinate updates to Ed's screen and subconsciously knew Ed was lobbying for information she did not care to provide at this time.

"Yeah."

FIDO's circle of light designating the location of the second impact crater stunted the conversation. "The tower cameras had picked up at least two major impacts. Others may have found their mark elsewhere on the surface. This one was the closest to *TerraLuna*," Dave chimed in on time during the natural silence between Ed and Haley. "FIDO One, you should check the stats on this crater. If it is too deep, we will have to engage vertical tactics, over."

"Copy that."

Ed looked over the booster drive controls and reviewed their operation, silently hoping he would get a chance to fly FIDO into the crater. The silvery dust road came to an abrupt end as the expanse of the crater lay before them, with the other side an indeterminable distance using plain sight. Ed eased the rover to a stop. Haley ran several depth and distance scans of the crater twice to confirm dimensions. She looked over to Ed, who simply stared ahead in his personal zone, fathoming the intensity of the meteor. "So this is why they call you Zone." He did not respond. She called ironically into the little microphone in her helmet.

"Zone!"

Ed turned to her without embarrassment.

"It's too steep. We'll flip end over end at this incline. Dave, do you see this?" Dave viewed the screens and the data Haley highlighted.

Barely hesitating, he tipped the microphone. "That's an affirmative. We go over, then hover for a bit, and drop in after twenty-two yards and see how she holds."

"Roger Dodger, reversing for inertia." Ed put the rover into reverse and backed up about twenty yards. Haley continued work on locking in on the target sample.

Ed checked the systems quickly before pushing the throttle forward and then, with a sharp motion, jerked the rover and engaged the booster. Blue and orange flames scattered moon dust in all directions as FIDO barreled forward to the edge of the crater. Lifting seven feet from the precipice before the edge offered some relief as they cascaded out into the expanse.

"Attitude adjustors are really smooth on this puppy," said Ed, beginning to enjoy himself. FIDO sailed into the low-gravity pool above the expanse. Ed stabilized and headed for the center, referring to Haley's radar, adjusting the pitch of FIDO's thrusters to gain a working attitude.

"Are we okay?" asked Haley for lack of something to say.

"Dave, how are we?" Ed spoke into the helmet.

"Looks good from here. Haley, switch on your underside camera and floods. Route the image to your secondary screen please," Dave instructed easily from his swivel chair.

"Take it to the center now or you will overshoot. Boost down, Ed, 45 degrees. Haley, as soon as you align with the nadir, the locator will lock in and then bring her in. Are we good?"

"The crater measures 172 yards in diameter and 9,400 deep," said Haley, adjusting her screen.

"It is fairly dark here, Dave. I am switching outer halogens to maximum. We are catching some shadow. I had expected to see more silicon shrapnel. That is strange. A meteor usually offers enough heat to send tons of moon rock into glassy chunks. I see minimal evidence of typical meteor fire. She must have been an icy one."

"Atmosphere causes friction, which causes the heat. No atmosphere up here, no friction, no heat," Haley said matter-of-factly.

The outer lights exploded with brilliance as the expanse came to life. Moon rock still held cliffs of sand as drifts streamed down into the pit. Occasional boulders the size of two car garages speckled the terrain below. Gusts of moon dust swirled around, giving Ed and Haley a limited view.

"I am pulling boosters down to 25 percent. Let's see if we can find this bugger. Approaching eighty-six yards into diameter. This should be about the center. Engaging descent. I can't see anything."

"You have about forty yards yet. Infrared probably won't do any good here. Haley, scroll the sensor selections and activate hard metals. Let's go for the platinum and iridium group," said Dave, keeping calm authority in his voice.

FIDO fell slowly into the pit as sand eddied less steeply to the bottom. The landscape had evened out somehow, and Ed considered the possibility of landing and rolling it to the center. As Haley's screen switched from infrared to hard metal detector, images lined in various colors pulsed while the scanners determined those most likely to be non-lunar, from red to green to the faintest of blue, which suggested hard metal. Yet the colors did not remain in blue for very long before changing back to red.

"Dave, should we hover or land here. I can see the bottom," said Ed, maintaining a slow descent.

"We can use the deep scan to locate it. Maintain twenty yards from the surface and sweep with a deep scan. It must be there. It broke up. There should be something left," Dave ordered.

Lights flickered, reflecting a hypnotic dance throughout the small cabin. Haley studied them with the intensity of a pre-teen video gamer, countering sections of useless red light in search of the blue pigment of success. Ed guided the vehicle in a grid-like pattern to ensure complete coverage.

The minutes passed, and sweat began to appear on Ed's temple. He really wanted to swab it away, but the helmet forbade it. He adjusted the temperature control and routinely checked the conditions of the cabin. It was slightly hotter than average. Noticing Haley hard at work to locate hard metal samples and also sweating, Ed took it on himself to check Haley's stats. He transferred the stats of Haley's suit to his console. Inner alarms that never rang suddenly blotted out the silence in his mind. Oxygen level twenty-four minutes! It can't be right.

Haley's helmet reflected a blinking blue light. "There it is. I found it bearing fourteen degrees starboard! Lots of blue!" Haley said, turning to Ed, only to see his eyes unfocussed in what was becoming to her an unattractive habit.

Ed broke away to her abruptly. "You have less than half an hour of air. Check your suit." Fathoming what he said took a moment of staring; perhaps she stared at the same bit of nothing he stared to when he was lost in thought. A quick look to the console confirmed his timely discovery.

"So we can make it. Let's get it and go. It isn't deep. Readings show it is covered by about two yards of sand." Ed looked at her in a new way. She was bold.

Ed had subconsciously realized this about her all along. He never put words or thoughts to it. Yet this hidden sense of adventure she was displaying seemed clearly the basis of his attraction to her from the start. Ed involuntarily cleared his throat as his gaze remained fixed on her eyes.

"Dave, can we do this and get back, okay?"

An eternal instant passed as Dave did some quick calculations. "It will take you ten minutes to get back here at full tilt. This leaves you about twelve minutes to get the rock. I suggest you dig."

Following the blue center of the screen, Ed dropped the rover squarely ahead of the target area, disengaged the digger arm, and activated the retrieval box. The arm extended fifteen feet ahead of the box and was equipped with a set of what looked like webbed shovels designed to scoop large pieces in its grasp and then dump them into the box. The arm was controlled by a radio-signaled glove that Haley had on in seconds. It allowed her to dig into the sand and clear it away rather effectively. Hard metal detection sensors in the shovel were ready to flash a yellow light once having the specimen in its grasp. Keeping one eye on the pulsing blue light and another on the pit, she dug away at the sand and gravel covering the rock. Ed, with awakening feelings for Haley regarding her tenacity at work, adjusted the temperature control in her suit and then checked with Dave for the time. "How much time, Dave?"

"You have about nineteen minutes left. How far is it, Haley?"

"My readings show five feet, but the sand keeps sliding back." *Damn it! I checked the suits before we started*, she thought to herself. "I am going to clear a few feet away then dig in and grab it."

Just then, the rover shifted suddenly. Ed toggled to the aft camera to find that a small landslide of scree had piled just behind them. "Can you get that thing sometime soon, Haley? We might have a slight avalanche problem on this side."

"I want you out of there in six minutes!"

Dave instructed flatly, "Five would be better, Ed."

Haley looked like a lunatic pantomime clown digging into the small open area of the cabin for the yet unseen chunk, Ed assessed with vague humor. The arm dug deeper as Haley crunched her hand and then widened it, pushing forward to grab the solid bit of celestial junk that made this mess.

"I almost have it!" blurted Haley. Faint flashes of yellow light glinted on and off again immediately. Her body lunged forward, challenging the confines of the cabin, trying to gain some kind of impossible leverage.

"Three minutes, Haley. I am igniting the primary boosters in two minutes. I will get you back from our first date alive, I promise," Ed said with a finger on the control.

"Date?" she yelled. "You told me this was a mission. I hope this doesn't turn out to be one of those first mission/last mission situations I've read about in Cosmo." Just then, the screen lights changed configuration again. "I am there, okay, just a little bit more and I can grab it."

Gloved fingers groped independently of one another as she grasped the robotic hand into a fist around the softball-sized rock.

"I have it!" she shouted, pulling her arm back slowly and returning to a sitting position, her clenched fist before her. Yellow light beamed triumphantly against their helmets. Slowly, the arm retracted from the sand and hung for a moment as moon sand sifted away. It turned, lowered, and dropped the projectile into the bin, which immediately retracted into the rover, followed by the arm. As soon as the arm was stowed, Ed ignited the boosters, and they shot upward, leaving a cascade of sand trickling slowly away in a silver low-gravity shower that engulfed Dave's screen and drew his gaze back a bit.

"We are behind schedule. We have eight minutes of air for you, and it takes twelve to get back to grandpa's house. Let's go!"

Ed looked sharply to his copilot, attempting to respond. "Do me a favor, Haley. Save your breath. We are flying in, Dave. It should save us a couple of minutes. Amen for boosters and brakes." Ed spun the rover about as they rose out of the silvery pit. The sun seemed too bright. He turned off the halogens mechanically and pulsed forward to *TerraLuna*.

Halfway there, he descended. Momentum could be a killer was what his friend Nick Nicholas had said when they heard about an accident when a maintenance crew accelerated in zero-G. *This would be a great story to be told over a cold beer*, Ed thought. Haley sat motionless as Ed checked her vital signs now displayed on the main screen.

"Heart rate is up, Haley. That could mean you're in love."

He looked over to her with an uncontrollable smile for the first time actually without any pretension. Seeing that she was not amused, he turned and accelerated forward, sending FIDO careening fourteen feet above the lunar surface. This brought an uncontrollable smirk to her worried visage. "Open up, David, we're coming home!"

The garage door opened slowly as a silent response from Dave, who had been joined by Tom in the last few minutes. A medical team scurried in their places to handle any emergency.

Tom took the microphone. "Increase in heart rate is due to fear. Take it easy, Ms. Williams. Calm yourself and take slow breaths." Ed engaged the reverse thrusters as they approached the pavement at the corner of the building to counter the forward momentum. FIDO lurched and, after some tipping and countering, fell onto Zonic's control as he made it descend and slowly equalize.

"Watch your pitch, Zone. That dog you are riding is not a lap dog. Keep it off my lap," said Dave, wondering if he should run off into the hallway for cover.

Ed angled the machine rather steeply to land not fifty feet from the dock. It pounded and jostled its way to a halt. Ed threw in the gear and hit the gas as fast as he dared, considering gravitational conditions. The rover cleared the garage door, and it began to close immediately as Haley's oxygen meter dropped away from the final seconds. She knew it took at least five minutes to depressurize the garage. Panic coursed her face, and Ed offed systems and prepared to open the hatch. It occurred to him that she was without oxygen for close to a minute yet showed no sign of asphyxiation. They could see the crew ready through the window to come to their aid. Ed pressed his glass to hers and made her search his eyes for hope. She looked back blankly yet showing no pain for lack of air.

"Haley, you were out of air two minutes ago. Did you have some extra along that you didn't tell me about?" Ed said without emotion.

"I don't know. I can breathe," she managed.

Zonic fussed around her oxygen pack, checking the connections. "You don't have an air leak, Haley. You have a gauge malfunction. We had a good sixteen hours of fun ahead of us. Here I was looking forward to giving you mouth-to-mouth."

She looked back at him in disbelief. "No, I didn't know. Neither did you." A moment passed, and she said, "Or did you?"

Ed undid hid seatbelt as the depressurization light came on. His answer was a dashing glance, and then he threw open the hatch to greet his friends as they crowded around FIDO.

MOONCORP

CHAPTER 11

Charley liked sleeping in the guest room at Nick's house. It was such a big house, and Charley had what he liked to call "his room" near the back of the house that had a view overlooking the forested ravine that dropped into a little river below. No one else had stayed overnight since Ada; as Nick is a loner.

Charley slept with the window open, and the fresh pine-laden air made his lungs stretch a bit further than usual. The wooden paneling was a great deal more comfortable than the off-white painted walls that were brought in truckloads in five-gallon buckets to paint his apartment complex. It was nice to be here. His excitement about the project Nick was explaining last night was severely heightened by the smell of bacon. Charley knew that an early start would be in his best interest, so he quickly showered and dressed himself. He hiked on a pair of long black socks and his everyday underwear, yet as the crisp white skirt and dark-blue suit came on, he felt like a black sheep going to the reading of a will.

After a very brief session of perfecting his tie, he came out into the kitchen where his prepared preheated breakfast sat at the table. Nick was already dressed in a light-beige suit, finishing his pancakes and bacon. He nodded and adjusted his glasses.

"Come on, man, we've got to cruise."

Charley hurried to the service machine. "Coffee medium cream and sugar. Hey, man, aren't you going to put your hair . . . like back?"

"No, I look fine. You are, aren't you?" said Nick, trying to not insult Charley's slight absence of hair in the front.

"Yeah. I'll do it after I eat."

Charley consumed the meager portioned breakfast, not minding that he was still hungry.

Nick began the shutdown of the house as Charley entertained the thought of taking his coffee for the ride. The sound of the garage door opening prompted Charley to take a daring sip of the hot, brimming coffee. It was too hot and too full.

"Let's go, Chuck," Nick called from the garage.

Charley spilled off a fourth of the coffee into the sink and made his way professionally to the car. Nick secured the garage door and filed his briefcase in the backseat.

The cool leather of the car seat made Charley and Nick a bit calmer; they donned their sunglasses. The garage door opened to reveal the warm summer morning. Nick pulled the car out and closed the garage from his wristband.

Driving to *MoonCorp* with the model in the backseat gave them a feeling of scientific importance. Nick designed and built the scaled-down version of the *MoonCorp* hotel and convention center over a year ago. They drove in silence for most of the way, each collecting his thoughts and preparing to deal with a variety of personalities with whom they usually did not fraternize. Lunar defense strategy had been solved for more than a year ago, giving them a welcomed rare edge. Charley drifted off, compiling the information Nick imparted to him the night before. Soon they were up to speed on the highway, and *MoonCorp* headquarters wasn't thirty minutes away.

Nick really did not want to get into much discussion about questions he knew Charley would have because they would require lengthy detail and he wanted to stay focused for this presentation. He hoped Charley would not provoke him with an intelligent question.

"Charley, I think most of the presentation should come naturally. I do not know how much time I will have. I will open the floor to you on some key explanations, but take my lead, man, okay? I sort of didn't tell Stan about the extent to which you were involved in the system's inception," Nick said, keeping his eyes on the road.

"Of course, Nick. I see the guilt trip you are sparing yourself. However, contrary to what you may think, I do not mind, man. I know Stan thinks I'm a drunk. Falling asleep at the morning briefings was my fault, Herr freakin' Franz narcing on me for having the smell of liquor on my breath—my bad. Whatever happened in the past is past! Let's be sure I get a chance to come across as the intelligent, creative genius who contributed countless hours on this project. They love you, and I am the strange and dangerous scientific bad boy. That will be clear to me, and it'll be clear to the whole damned board of directors while I quietly stand around. Just don't have a spastic episode if I chime in with supportive commentary!" Charley said with finality.

Nick nodded involuntarily. "Damn straight, man. I've worked hard on this mother. It's ours. We own it We are going to tag team this one. Do you know why, because we are the dream team!"

"With the antigravitational beam!"

Charley, feeling a bit up, turned the music stereo to find something resembling classic rock and roll as the big yellow Buick sailed into the glass and steel *MoonCorp* complex now visible on the horizon.

Nick drew a calming breath, opened his wrist phone, and turned the music down.

"I'm calling security. We should get in faster if they know we are coming."

Within a few seconds, Nick asked that a cart be waiting for them to carry the model into the building. He closed the phone and turned up the music. Charley slapped the dashboard to the music and enjoyed the rest of the ride in relative satisfied silence.

Soon the car glided to the front of the building where two sweaty security officers stood leaning on a stainless steel cart near the handicap ramp. They virtually rushed the car, ready to help. Nick gave a quick glance to Charley.

"Dude, this is what we've been working for, the presentation of new technology. Ready?"

"Ready, man. Let's smoke 'em," Charley added, instinctively initiating a high five, which was not reciprocated as the security office came on the phone with Nick.

The young security detail, probably some ranking investor's young nephews, carefully removed the model still under the white cloth and gingerly placed it on the cart. The four briskly made their way up the ramp to the tall glass and steel front doors where the overhead cooling unit kept the front of the building cool and shady.

It was eight thirty-two, and Duncan usually started a fashionable ten minutes late at all these meetings. It had been some time since one of this magnitude took place here. Investors and the entire board of directors were gathered to discuss the new future of the *MoonCorp* lunar convention center that had been put on hold for almost three years.

The lobby was alive with a variety of name-tagged strangers, all touting smiles, handshakes, and belly laughs. They moved along the edge of the crowd, holding the sheet to the edge of the cart, making their way to the meeting room.

"Thank you for investing," Charley said to one of the board members as he passed.

A long mahogany table dominated the richly paneled room. Tall windows invited natural light on the wood and steel swivel chairs. At the far end of the room, a large presentation screen covered most of the wall. Several attendants were setting water pitchers and glasses for the sixty chairs around the table. "Let's bring it to the holopad near the screen," Nick directed as they steered past a nice-looking attendant. She shot a smiling glance to Charley, who was found ogling the end of her black-and-white serving uniform.

"Okay, watch out for the legs," said Charley, offering a wink to the young girl, sounding more than authoritative. The girl looked to the door and back at the passing cart. Sure, that no one was looking. She placed a transparent disc, the size of a quarter, with a silver center on the water pitcher. Still unnoticed, she proceeded to place the discs on all the pitchers and set them on the black-cushioned sweat trays among the glasses.

Nick and Charley lifted the model onto the white-lit stand near the table where Stan Duncan would conduct the meeting. The security guards quickly made their way to their posts, passing the water girl on the other side of the table. Checking her watch quickly, she hurried to adjust the few remaining pitchers.

"I have to go to the john, Nick. I'll be right back," said Charley, moving out the back end of the tunnel-like room.

"Here, take this cart and park it outside," Nick added. Looking about the room, he spotted the microphone station and clipped a microphone on his tie, tapping it for sound. The water girl was finishing her work, and he called to her as she began to make her way out the far end of the room.

"Excuse me . . . do you know where the soundman is?" Nick toned, stopping her briefly.

Slightly startled, she replied, "You know, I thought I saw him in the back room earlier." She pointed to the back entrance and continued with her cart to the main entrance.

"Thanks," Nick called back unknowingly and turned to the back door to find a middle-aged unsmiling woman carrying a receiver. "Oh, excuse me, do you know where I can find the sound guy? I'd like to get a sound check."

"You're looking at her. I am the sound *person*. Are you Dr. Nicholas?" she asked, pointing her nose at him professionally.

Nick turned instinctively at the water girl to find her very much not there. "Um . . . yes, yes, I am," he stuttered, fumbling for his ID and showing her.

She spied the microphone on his tie, nearly snatching it off, surprising Nick.

"This one is a bit fuzzy. Here, let's get you wired with a nice new piece. Is something wrong?" she said as he craned to view the entrance.

"No, it's nothing. I asked the water girl where the soundman was, and she said that he, you were in the back." Nick stumbled for reason, looking fixedly at the sound woman.

"Rosa speaks very little English. Pronouns are always a problem when learning a new language. Okay, there you are. Let's give it a test," she said, finishing his new mic.

Turning the dial on the black receiver, she told him to speak naturally. His voice carried well along the room. He liked the sound of his voice and enjoyed these presentations thoroughly. Some of the board members began to mill into the room, talking among themselves. Nick stopped testing into the system and turned to the woman with a smile.

"I think it sounds great."

Charley appeared from the back door, holding a plastic cup with what looked like cranberry juice and munching on the remains of a lemon Danish.

"Do you ever stop eating?" Nick said flatly as the sound lady approached Charley with a nod and a mic. Charley shook his head silently, relishing the Danish. The room was quickly filled with excited guests finding seats, some carrying coffee and chomping breakfast cakes. Stan Duncan emerged from the front of the room, halfway carrying on a conversation with a trio of Japanese men in blue suits and graying hair. Stan was in his early sixties with a mostly bald head, save for the remains of a onetime dignified crop of blond hair that still existed like an antique around the edges of his regal head. Chairman Duncan was the likeable leader whom people saw as an honest and frank diplomat with a flair for the sensible and an intact sense of humor, except for when it came to certain people with whom he had issues.

"Okay, if we will all be seated, I think we can begin." He nodded to the sound lady, who pinned him professionally as he made his way to Nick, pausing for a brief sound check.

"Everyone, please take your seats." Stan sat graciously, his voice commanding the room completely. Switching off the mic, he approached Nick, pulling him off to the side. "Is everything ready with the model?"

Nick bobbed his head with assurance. "Yeah, we are good to go."

Stan met Charley's complacent mien, exchanging a tolerant glance. "Are you sure about Porter being in on this?"

"Stan, he is fine. I promise," Nick confided.

"He is your responsibility. There is too much riding on this for the slightest screwup. You see to it that he is kept in line, or I will drop him." Stan warned unblinkingly. He held his gaze for a moment, switched on the mic, and addressed the board.

"Ladies and gentlemen, I am Stan Duncan, president and CEO of *MoonCorp*, and I welcome you to sit down and be comfortable. We have a great deal to cover this morning. We are anxious to present our format for the next phase of *MoonCorp* Enterprises. I have met most of you, and those of you I have not met, we will get a chance to talk more at the reception luncheon after this morning's meeting." Stan surveyed the room quickly. A young Japanese woman raised her hand. Stan recognized her with a smile. "Yes, do you have a question?"

The woman said plainly, "Mr. Yokomoto's translator is not working correctly." A gray-haired Japanese man sat beside her, motionless with a blank stare.

The sound lady bustled from the back of the room with a replacement earpiece for Mr. Yokomoto, addressing the group cordially in Japanese, "Does everyone hear the translation?" A tremor of nods filled the room as she repeated the same in Italian, Russian, French, and German. Most of the members spoke English, save for about a dozen foreign delegates who received translations from a glass booth along the wall several yards above the floor, which housed a sophisticated translation computer.

"Thank you, Betty," Stan said, waving his hand to the light man also in the booth. Lights highlighted the front of the room, and the windows began to electronically tint, bringing focus on Stan at the front of the room. Nick and Charley sat in chairs next to the model. Night seemed to have fallen instantly on the outside, the room now ready for a professional presentation. Stan cleared his throat. "I would like to welcome some of the new members of our team, former science advisor for *TerraLuna*, Herr Robert Franz."

A lean balding man with a large smile and a light-brown suit stood and waved his hand as the group applauded. "Signor Michelangelo Moreni from the New European Space Capitol Group is here with us today."

A rather reserved man of sixty-five with piercing blue eyes stood and bowed slightly. "Of course, Pierre Etienne, president of the International Association of Hotel Owners . . ." A large boyish-looking Frenchman of around thirty-five stood and said chidingly in broken English, "No, no, monsieur. It is now zee Interstellar Association of Hotel Owners."

A round of laughter followed an approval of applause as the large man sat blushing at his own statement of fact.

Stan smiled and laughed along with the group. "Yes, *oui, bien sur*, Monsieur Etienne. It is my pleasure to introduce Mr. Yokomoto to all of you who currently head up the joint Chinese and Japanese coalition company Yokomoto-Chen Aeronautics that has all our appreciation for being here today with some new technology which will finally make our dreams of *MoonCorp*'s luxury hotel and convention center a reality." Stan began clapping as the entire group stood up and cheered Yokomoto. The Chinese woman stood with him, obviously representative of the mainland faction of the company. Stan regained the floor after a great deal of handshaking and friendly back pats.

"I know several of you want to be acknowledged as well. Yuri, I see you craning your neck back there. Let us welcome the foremost off-Earth energy specialist, Mr. Yuri Povlovich. Mark Sadler from the Lunar Construction Corporation and Ben and Francine Skylar, owners of the LINDY Space Defense Cooperative, are present. Let's see who else had invested at least ten million in the room."

A murmur of laughter now warmed the audience at a comfortable temperature. Stan changed to a slightly more serious tone as he noticed Nick and Charley ironically in the corner sitting upright in their chairs.

"I would like to introduce one of our most brilliant theorists who has been working on this dream of ours for several dedicated years now, Dr. Nick Nicholas, who will enlighten us with a new defense strategy for *MoonCorp*. Also, Dr. Charles Porter, who had devoted many, many hours in defense development and solar power economics." They stood, restraining themselves with dignity, adjusting from accustomed sophomoric activity, and receiving the end of the applause.

"I would like to begin with Mr. Yokomoto's new technology that has allowed us to commence. Please, sir, would you mind outlining the essentials of the system." Stan beckoned for Mr. Yokomoto, who rose with a slow dignity and made his way to the font of the room. Stan looked up to the booth and gave a nod. The translator controls allowed him to speak freely in Japanese while his voice was heard in English on the loudspeakers. The non-English-speaking guests adjusted personal volume from their hand held devices to comfortably hear the speaker.

"I thank you all for your support of our technology. We share a great dream that history will recognize as a radical step forward in space engineering. I have prepared a simple program that I am sure will reassure any who have doubts that *MoonCorp* will take the lead in interplanetary habitation. Would you please dim the lights?" he said, trying to avoid more applause.

The lights dimmed. The screen came alive with a simple picture of the moon. Yokomoto held a small control that changed the screen. Images of the moon from different angles in both still and motion pictures dominated the entire end of the meeting room.

"Essentially, history has provided us with the basic fact that the moon's surface is rich in silicon. I am sure we should thank Mr. Povlovich and his in situ lunar wall smelting technology that can easily transform moon strata into viable building materials."

He thumbed the control, and a wide vehicle gobbled up the surface of the moon and created vast flat slabs of pavement. The image switched to a clip showing the created vertical pieces being placed together as walls. The room rolled into applause, speckled with bravos and other kudos.

"This perhaps is a greater contribution than our new heavy-lift system that will allow us to transport these massive machines to the moon's surface in sections, easily assembled in low-G staging area. What we will do will decrease the building time and consequently bring opening day in less than one year. Previous technologies would not have allowed opening for at least six years."

Rapt listeners erupted in applause as Yokomoto paused from necessity. The image of the smelting machines changed to that of a round tank-like structure surrounded by six rockets supported by a platform. A view from above depicted a large cargo space nearly ten thousand square feet. The film illustrated the entirety of his description.

"These containers will be able to lift up to ten tons of equipment to within ten miles from the edge of the Earth atmosphere. A second ship launched from a low-gravity moon surface will be ready to take the ship beyond into space. A shuttle lock attached to a series of heavy-lift cable will descend to the rising container. This manned craft will lock onto top and take over the lift task from six rockets. Winches will raise the container to the underside of the freight ship and lock securely. The rockets will have enough fuel to be guided safely for water landing. Rockets are reusable, and it is estimated to save many hundreds of millions of world dollars. For this economic technology, I must thank Dr. Chen. Let us give her some recognition."

The crowd, utterly attentive, offered its appreciation as Yokomoto realized the translating machine was an amazing invention as he had been speaking his native Japanese. He poured a drink of water from the sweating silver pitcher, rainy pictures transmitted from the invisible stickers to a bank of monitors somewhere in the cool basement of Gerhard Steele's Texas headquarters. Steele sat quietly, taking notes.

*****

Haley Williams thought she felt light-headed from lack of oxygen. She tried to draw a breath and found it rather easy despite the traumatic landing near the garage door. FIDO came to an abrupt halt, and the quiet engines resigned skillfully. Through the observation window, she saw medics and technicians gaping at them. Dave's voice sounded a bit louder because the engines had stopped. "How are you two?"

Ed was completely calm and in control despite the circumstances. "Fine, Dave. Air locks all clear in one minute, thirty-two."

He continued the shutdown protocols and shot a nonchalant, fleeting look at his copilot who was nearly doubled over in her seat. She sat, unmoving, as she returned to clear thought. "The gauge malfunctioned, and I thought I was out of air when I actually had sixteen hours and twelve minutes of breathing time. Remarkable how a few bits of glass, wire, some light, and electricity made me feel so close to death."

"I've been closer," Ed chimed casually. The inner doors opened, and a collection of faces rushed FIDO, each with a separate assignment. Ed opened the hatch, and hands entered, pulling them out. Several jumper-clad men secured the holding tub that contained the bits of meteor in the forward bin. Ed and Haley were taken to a small room off the white-lit thin hallway for examination. As they walked off helped by many hands, Dave broke open his within and called Steele.

The familiarly smooth Germanic voice answered from far away.

"David, tell me the good news."

"We have it," Dave said with a relieved sigh.

"Excellent. Transport for the dead, wounded, and otherwise unfit to work is on the way. A team of repair specialists will be along seventy-two hours later. I will contact you later when the timetable realizes. Inform the key people in writing that their contract states they must remain for at least one cycle. Reconstruction will be the highest priority, and Earth-Leave will not be available for at least thirty days."

"Sir, many of them expect to leave when the next ship arrives," said David, remembering his promises.

"If they leave, it will be the end of their employment. Please see that my instructions are carried out, David. Also, I want that meteorite sealed and locked down. There will be zero access. Do I make myself clear?" he said with influence.

David paused briefly, then replied, "Yes, of course, Mr. Steele," and closed the phone.

*****

Time in a playground passes more quickly than in real time. Children called to go home are invariably cheated by some unknown evil plan that steals them away for washing, eating, and other unimportant necessaries . The meeting of the board of directors and investors for the revitalized *MoonCorp* hotel and convention center on the moon brought together people who had been waiting a long time for their chance to realize their dream of a big step in space inhabitation and enormous profit. They certainly will not want to go home early from this event.

The plans for the newly structured, average, consumer-friendly *MoonCorp* unfolded for most of the morning. Speakers presented new technologies that surpassed current operating procedures used by *TerraLuna*. These innovations thrilled all involved like a new playground in their new fantastic land, the moon.

Ben and Francine Skylar were called to outline the improvements for the LINDY system. Some of the guests dismissed their urges for lunch and continued to diplomatically quaff cold water, unknowingly refocusing the plastic cameras in the water pitchers. Stan ushered them to the front, and the sound lady fixed them promptly with microphones. Ben was more than middle aged. He was at home in his three-piece suit, obviously a smooth politician with a nurtured golfer's tan. Francine stood by his side dressed as a first lady should. A helpful stance communicated that she was not only a wife but also a contributing partner in scientific and financial aspects.

Ben cleared his throat briefly.

"Stan tells me that Francine and I open the meeting briefing you about the improvements on our defense system. It is the meat and potatoes of our decision to move forward. Speaking of which, there will be a delicious lunch served after a reasonable amount of time with actual meat and potatoes. That is the extent of my opening joke. I hope the meal makes up for what I lack in comedic talent."

Instinctively, the guests sniffed the air for hints of what might be for lunch. Pierre moved involuntarily, parting the air with his nose to detect the aroma of roast beef. A tiny sign of understanding spread across his face as he settled into his chair.

"We are still studying the tragic events that lead to the accident at *TerraLuna*, and our prayers go out to those families who lost loved ones. A computer simulation of the occurrence has brought us back to the drawing table for new ways to defend Earth and all edifices on any planet we inhabit." Ben turned to the screen and nodded as a depiction of the meteor hurdled toward the moon.

"As you know, the detection process is key in the laser defense system or LDS. We can detect possible threatening projectiles up to 7.2 light-years away and deploy laser cannon—equipped satellites to fly alongside and effectively break them down before they encounter our safe space. The center of some spacefaring media can be incredibly dense, and the chances of destroying them are slim. Yet with up to 70 percent blasted away by the LDS, the core is more susceptible to our second phase known as the CDP or centrifugal detonation pattern. A compact series of nuclear devices are released in pattern around the object, spinning it apart with great force in many directions far away from our defensible zone. The trouble with the *TerraLuna* meteor is that it came into range before our NMAT and NDS systems were able to detect and shave it down enough to incapacitate its destructive possibilities."

Ben paused, sensing that his wife wanted to contribute. "Francine will update you on our new technology that will further reduce the chance of falling prey to other such occurrences. Francine . . ."

Francine watched as the movie complimenting Ben's speech faded out. She began, picking up eloquently from where her husband left off.

"The detection mode divides local space into one hundred sectors. Any spacefaring media is detected and dealt with. We have theorized that this particular object may have come from another aspect of normal dimensional space. Scientists in our employ as those throughout the world community for years have suggested such "other aspects" to be wrinkles in time, wormholes and curving space effects among others, which could not have been detected with our current hardware. I can assure you that we have begun work on a new sensitivity docket that will give us a better picture sooner of what might be heading our way." An encouraged tremor of applause ran through the crowd. Ben and Francine bowed diplomatically, smiling broadly.

Ben resumed the conversation as the crowd quieted.

"We hope that what happened at *TerraLuna* was one in a trillion occurrence. Be assured that we will be ready for it happening again. I would like to take this time to formally announce our new bounty program. As most of you know, we sponsor an aggressive award program to encourage development of technologies that will improve Skylar Enterprises and forward the reach of off-world technology. Currently, we are taking a new look at laser lens technology. Delivering a more powerful laser punch will require a better glove." He shot a quick look at Francine, who seemed pleased with the metaphor.

"Our generators can now more economically use available power, yet the test lenses shatter before the generators can express their full potential. We will offer the standard ten-million-world-dollar prize to the company or individual who can develop a lens hard enough to utilize the new power output we propose to add to the LDS. Another area of importance is in situ oxygen development. Also, we are pleased to announce a special prize for breakthrough technology for the future of our Earth–Moon/Mars schedule. Fuel production from lunar mining and satellite power sources will save incredible amounts of capital and allow us to devote our resources to new Mars-based projects. I have packets for any here interested in the competition. Please see Francine or myself before you leave here today. Thank you, all. Go, *MoonCorp*, go!"

Skylar raised his fist high as a sign of unity. The crowd erupted, repeating in unison, "Go, *MoonCorp*, go!" Stan Duncan extended his hand and shook Skylar's vigorously.

"Ladies and gentlemen, we have much more to share with you today, so please, let us adjourn now and return in one hour. You will find lunch waiting in the reception area. Please join me in thanking our presenters, and I am certain that if you like what you heard this morning, you are going to love what is in store for you this afternoon."

*****

Two days of fishing did not erase what Pepe had seen earlier that week, no matter how he tried to explain it to his friends or himself. Others had seen the effect in the sky, yet no one wanted to talk about it. Pepe had contacted the news service, the *Celestún Watcher*, in town and explained his version of the event. They ran an article in today's news feed that read, "Comets fall in Yucatan."

Pepe enjoyed his predawn coffee as he read the article on his reader. It was a portable seven-by-eleven flat-screen about an half inch thick. The news was beamed in as it occurred. He always seemed to spill his coffee on it. Luckily his wife bought the waterproof model. The daily news also included so much advertisement that gave Paloma big ideas for spending. He did discourage her spending time with it.

Tico stretched before rising from his pillow bed, blinking sleepily at Pepe. Paloma was still in bed, and he prepared to leave carefully before she woke.

"Come on, Tico," he whispered.

The dog sprang up, took a few laps from his dish, and tagged along at Pepe's feet. Pepe, Paloma, and Tico lived about a mile from the shore in a simple, modern one-level white home with a new roof, of which Pepe was particularly proud. He always looked back at it when he closed the outer gate.

The morning sun had begun to lighten the night. The white roses lining the clay tile walk almost seemed to light the path in contrast. The pickup truck hummed on. They backed out to the road as the rest of the neighborhood slept with the knowledge that Pepe and Tico were off to work on the sea.

The headlights cut through the dusty, foggy air as the truck bounced its way to the shore. Similar homes with flat roofs and fenced-in yards marked his way to the end of the development. None of them had such a lovely garden as Paloma's. Of this too he was proud. Once past the turn onto the main road, he clicked on the radio to the local news station. The familiar theme song adjusted their minds to take in the latest news that they could talk about over cold *cervesas* with their friends at the dockside bar. The announcer began talking rapidly as the theme song's rapid beat slowly faded.

"Our top story this morning, a team from the University of Merida, Dr. Rene Sanchez, has begun plans to investigate the series of comets or meteors that fell into the Gulf of Mexico ten miles off the shore of *Celestún* earlier this week. Eyewitness accounts state that countless projectiles entered the sea at sunset."

"That was us, Tico," chortled Pepe. "We called that one in to the newspaper. You know maybe we had the best view, no?" Tico fussed in the front seat as if he wanted to talk back and managed a little bark. "Maybe we go down to the school and tell the professors what we saw? What do you think?" Tico barked again as they hummed along the paved road for another day of fishing.

*****

MoonCorp set wonderful lunch. Investors, board members, and scientists gathered at the buffet, finding their way to the twelve circular tables set with fine silver and freshly starched white linen. Hand-carved roast beef and fillets of tilapia entertained the group rather well. Freshly steamed broccoli, carrots, and zucchini tempted the most devout vegetarians. A variety of salads, breads, and desserts completed the lavish fare, leaving no appetite wanting for more. Charley and Nick were at the table where most of the empty chairs remained. They shot quick looks at those leaving the buffet to solicit their table. Francine Skylar, who seemed to have an answer for everyone, was walking to their table with a smile and a modestly filled plate of mostly vegetables. She was not a shapely woman. Wide-set hips and the sort of hair that bordered on the need for a stylist, her sense of business and science filled in all the gaps left by the want for pure simple beauty.

"Is this seat taken, Dr. Nicholas?"

"No, Mrs. Skylar, it's yours," Nick replied with extra congeniality to the billionaires. She took the seat, still smiling, and unfolded her napkin.

"I am very interested in your new defense technology. Benjamin and I were speaking earlier of why we have not seen an entry from you in our innovation contest. Does Stanley not allow you to freelance?" she offered, laced with incredulity.

"Well, actually, the work I do for the lunar project is considered property of *MoonCorp*. I signed a contract," Nick said flatly. "I suppose off-moon work isn't out of the question, but now where will I find time?"

Charley sat, noiselessly commandeering his rather highly piled plate of mostly roast beef and bread. The Italian Michelangelo Moreni, who looked to sit with the currently conversationally stalemated lunchers, interrupted their period of adjustment.

"Signor, we'd be honored," said Nick, who had heard that this man controlled the financial clout that originally financed Gerhard Steele's *TerraLuna*.

Moreni was tall and thin and most often seen in very expensive cream-colored suits. His thinning hair, stylishly combed, never left him looking bald in the negative sense. He was mostly concerned with money and did so with a sense of cultivated class.

"Tell me, Mrs. Skylar, have comprehensive technology entries been submitted geared toward using Martian ice caps for conversion to water or oxygen or perhaps ultra-condensed fuel sources? These topics are regular discourse among the European investors. Many millions are ready to be spent for new life support sources as well. It seems that today's off-world travelers would like an atmosphere."

He punctuated his statement by cutting a small bit of beef and elegantly forking it, keeping eye contact with Francine and expecting an answer.

She pursed her lips slightly, pausing with her eyes raised upward. Charley was not sure whether she was still chewing in very small movements or stalling to find the right reply.

"Signor, since Benjamin and I have become substantial stockholders, I, *MoonCorp* . . . we, let's say, have become less interested in hard fuels due to advances in solar efficiency like electrically generated water. Several insightful submissions, however, are on file. We feel that the establishment of our lunar hotel and moon bases are primary before any plans are put in place to establish a working presence on Mars. We do not want to put our horse before the cart," Francine said, feeling satisfied with her reply.

"Perhaps we could meet sometime to discuss these entries. The Europeans are a bit aggressively impatient for Mars habitation. It seems a rather more formidable goal. Between us, many of the European Space Capitol group are rather bored with lunar projects. Yet I see your point. We strive to be economical in my circles." He produced a card, offering it across the table. "Dr. Franz would be very interested in some input from your contestant's insights. Solutions by and large are very valuable to my investors."

She pierced some lettuce prudently. "I would have to discuss this with my husband and Mr. Duncan. Be sure, Signor Moreni, that I will bring this up at our stockholders' meeting," she said, politely attempting not to sound either sublime or suspicious.

"The European Space Capitol group would be quite attentive to any new advances that would help all involved in populating the stars much more efficiently." He rose with his plate. "If you will excuse me, I promised Herr Franz I would sit with him. He is alone." Moving with the ease of a wolf, he made his way through the crowd with information for *TerraLuna*'s former science advisor whose job was eliminated for undisclosed reasons. The slight genius sat at a table alone and craned his neck, seeing Moreni approach.

Francine Skylar needed to say something to ease the burn of the arrogant Italian as he left the table of Americans, a bit off-put by his controlling attitude.

"It appears that Signor Moreni must be involved when large amounts of money are involved. Anyway, Stan still holds that it would be to our mutual advantage to forgo the European usage fees unless absolutely necessary. Sharing profits is a new interest with Yokomoto-Chen for sure . . . What can I say, it all makes sense. Steele's interests are in Europe with the Europeans. I hate to sound political, but it seems to me that the ball is in the United Russian Nation's court. Where they place their allegiance and money is key."

She now appeared to have had enough lunch, took a long drink from her water glass, and placed it on the auto cooler as the lights dimmed for the meeting to begin.

"I have been meaning to get some of these glass coolers. I do so enjoy cold water." The lights dimmed and lit again, signaling the meeting was about to begin.

"I think we are about to begin again. I am very much looking forward to your presentation, Doctor. We hope to be encouraged by the soundness of your work." She rose, inspecting her suit for stains. Pleased, she made her way to the boardroom.

Nick turned to Charley blankly. Charley pointed his fork at Nick's plate. "Are you going to eat your bread?" Nick shook his head. The room thinned as the lights dimmed again.

The room was now filled with refreshed people, who began to settle as Stan Duncan approached his place and tapped his microphone.

"I hope you enjoyed lunch. Ladies and gentlemen, we here at *MoonCorp* are very ready to move ahead with full confidence of the Skylar's faithful investments of time, money, and faith in our purpose. Here now to explain in more detail our progress in lunar defense is Dr. Nick Nicholas."

The crowd applauded for Nick. Approaching the front, Nick surveyed the group, who appeared quite sated from their recent ingestion. Nick drew an extra large silent breath and raised his eyes to see a crowd that he was sure he could impress.

"Thanks, Stan. I would like to offer a quick overview of how the current defense system works and offer some additions that would ensure a next-to-nothing chance for another *TerraLuna* tragedy. Long-distance tracking systems can detect an incoming hostile body tens of light-years away. The first and most effective way of dealing with this is the LINDY's satellites at long distances, the rotating nuclear dispersal system CDP used for larger objects. The lunar defense system will be able to pick off smaller projectiles if they enter the moon's safe zone. For yet smaller bodies, I have developed an effectively strategic plan. I recommend that no edifice be built on any off-Earth location without complete coverage from my system. My defense system is in use at all times in the unlikely event that something slips into the gravitational pull of the moon."

Nick motioned to Charley, who started the holo-imager. It transferred their model into a hologram. Cameras in the ceiling transferred the model of *MoonCorp* into a three-dimensional image hovering over the center of the sprawling table. As the lights dimmed, the image rotated to give all a complete look.

"As you will notice here along the frame of the building, these tubular conduits are equipped with tiny holes." Nick pointed his finger pointer at the now-enlarged sections of the outer sections of the hotel. A large arrow floated to indicate the holes. Charley handed samples of the spiracle tubes to the members to pass around.

"Using the solar resource technology of Dr. Porter, here we have super-intensified the power from the sun as a power source. Since the gravitational pull of the moon is much lesser than the Earth, speeds of asteroids are much slower yet fast enough to cause damage. Each of these tiny spiracles creates an antigravity zone. Upon activation, a powerful solar-powered force is generated around the complex, creating a field of antigravity in a gravity-free zone. Momentum will be reduced for an average surface area of twenty-five hundred square inches around the tubes, lessening impacts by a factor of more than 9,000 percent. Most particulate up to fifteen inches across will bounce away into open space. Larger pieces up to ten square feet will be dealt with by the LDS local laser system. Dr. Porter will demonstrate the effect."

Nick turned to Charley, who held four tennis balls, two in each hand. He nodded, and bright light shined on the model. A hidden generator within the model began an unusual humming. Standing ten feet from the model, he began a slow windup and hurled the ball at the model. It bounced away as if it hit a strong pane of glass. The hum was the only sound as the audience sat enthralled. The model above the table also depicted the ball spinning out to the back of the room. A server ran along the back of the room to get the ball. Charley threw another, hoping to get the crowd to clap. It bounced, erratically hitting the table in front of Pierre Etienne. Nick regained the attention of the people and held his hand out to the ball girl who ran up and handed him the balls.

Charley waited for his moment and then announced with pride, "These tennis balls represent killer meteorites that would leave visible craters on the moon. In effect, the spiracle defense system would use radio-conducted natural sunlight to generate a field capable of surrounding *MoonCorp* with a shield that would, with Skylar's help, make the hotel safe from all spacefaring rock, junk, comets meteors, debris, what have you. We are proud to be responsible for bringing this process into realization for the new *MoonCorp*. Thank you."

The audience rose with hard clapping as Nick and Charley took unrehearsed and unexpected bows. Charley, with pride welling up from the audience's reaction, wound up a pitch and beaned another tennis ball at the model, giving them another round of the effect of the defense system. Smiles were on all faces, even Stan Duncan who was nearly hit by the reflecting ball.

A very small grin appeared also on the hard face of Gerhard Steele, his cuff-linked wrist moved to lower the volume of the exuberance from his console so many miles away.

CHAPTER 12

Steele's rooms were as dark as he could have them and still be functional. He hated natural light. It promoted workers feeling too carefree and frivolous—very unproductive and cautionary traits. Keeping with the four fluorescent tubes and austerely cold working environments made workers many times more productive; this was the bottom line to the unseen master paycheck signer. He was such a figure. You can't be friends with everyone. Yet irony was not an amusing thing to Gerhard Steele. Twelve banks of monitors fed raw footage into the recorder to be sifted through later. Seeing the elated expressions of the meetings members, most of them former participants in very similar caucuses of his own, simmered revenge hotly beneath his clenched teeth.

Most of these men would write off their business losses at tax time and think nothing of them. Their children played with toys labeled with the same company name as their anticipated dividend checks from the new fair-haired child that was to be *MoonCorp*. It was a good idea for Duncan to come out with a line of toys representative of the hotel, space planes and lunar rovers, at first only available for the children of the employees. If *MoonCorp* opened for business, there could be a brisk trade in the public market.

Franz and Yokomoto could have done for *TerraLuna* what they are doing for *MoonCorp*. He placed counter markers at various key moments in the video playback of the meeting and focused in with the turn of a large hand dial on the red face of Ben Skylar. He was the most traitorous of them all. Rather than be partner with the defense baron, he would now continue to pay rent for protection. He uttered an unintelligible curse under his breath and turned the dial to the fat Frenchman Etienne Pierre, who was going to provide the highest endorsements from the European marketing standpoint. There he sat with an involuntary grin brought about by an excessive helping of bloody beef. He winced, thinking of the money he spent courting that pig with rich dinners and rare wines.

Turning the dial, still maintaining his vast sense of composure, he found himself studying Michelangelo Moreni. This was the man he felt sure would cherish a loyalty cultivated by hours of discussion and planning. Not sure he would betray such a tenured trust, Steele shook his head, slowly scanning for some shred of deceit in Moreni's intentions. He would find funding for anyone who was willing to pay his interest; it was the nature of his need for respectability. Respectability and profit do not often make good bedfellows. It confounded his bottom line. Steele needed to act fast. If he did not emerge from the accident with some new angle, popular consensus will sway to the competitor.

Stan Duncan was a patient man, a politician. He had waited carefully for the right moment to unveil his defense initiative. He would not hesitate to sell the same technology for an unreasonably heavy price. Funding to rebuild what remained of *TerraLuna* would cost him more than he wanted to spend or borrow as his case may be. The dial brought him to Charley Porter hefting a tennis ball with kindergarten-like glee and then Nick Nicholas who was the brains behind the spiracle local defense. They were indeed new players in this game. Duncan had been keeping them deep in his pocket, tied to some sort of contract that certainly would give him exclusivity to their work. *I know how Stan works*, he thought to himself, squinting inwardly for some thread of a plot to lure them into his employ.

Yes, but Duncan has at least as many lawyers as I do, ready to pounce, he mused almost dejectedly. Then a wisp of a notion took hold of his naturally creative mind. He turned another dial to zoom in on Porter throwing a ball. *No ring? Nicholas too? Yes. These boys were so involved with Duncan's work that they had no time for marriage, a true symptom of terminal genius. They might be swayed or torn apart by money or no . . . Money wouldn't do it. They seem dedicated and devoted in their youth. Disgusting. Besides, I am sure Stan has taken care of their fiduciary situation.* He paused in his silent thought. *What about a girl, a girl to separate them? New defense systems for* TerraLuna *will be developed that are new and improved with their help.* Bright lights began to grow in Steele's eyes. He drew a careful breath and thought of just the girl; a hard grin crept its way across his face. Automatically, he opened his wrist phone and spoke his first word in hours: "Leslie."

*****

Leslie Davis was the subject of a song. She would never admit this even when men produced the lyrics. Being brilliant and beautiful gave her the right to remain unsatisfied with anything. At thirty-three, she was still a cute, natural blonde with a foundation of southern Baptist propriety that dealt with male propositions with the mental agility of a seasoned hypnotist. The telephone rang. "Hello, this is Leslie Davis."

"Leslie, this is Ger. How is my princess today?"

Her hospitable southern accent barely perceptible from her travels around the world returned a bit at the sound of his velvet voice. "Why, I am just as fine as could be. You have been a busy CEO to not call me. I was beginning to think you had found more fertile pastures to graze. Somehow, I knew you would be back. The grass is certainly not greener on the other side, I assume?"

"Leslie, you still know you are the finest flower in the garden. I might sniff a few here and there. Do not I always come back to the finest and most cultivated bloom?"

"I recognize that tone of voice, Steele. You are up to something, and you need me to realize some billion-world-dollar plan for you again. Am I right, sugar?" She adjusted the phone with her delicate, well-tanned, whit-fingernail-polished hand.

"Naturally. Need I remind you again of how excited I get when I am around that magnificent mind of yours? Gifted and gorgeous have one manifestation, and that is you, Leslie. Can you meet me later this evening at the office? I will have *Chez Sam Houston* cater something lavish for us. Seven o'clock at my private entrance."

"Steele, you truly do know how to treat a lady. I will be there." She closed the phone and, without a thought, went back to her magazine.

*****

Leslie took very little time to become glamorous. Natural beauty was first on the list of her becoming qualities. Pulling her fine, shining blonde hair into a swirl and pinning it skillfully behind her head accentuated her sharp features and clear expressive eyes. A light-blue wraparound dress and white silk scarves around her neck and hair undoubtedly raised her above the average looks she strived to exploit.

Steele was particularly vulnerable to her when she makes herself up. Grabbing her silver and white purse, she called for the lights to dim and left for the stairs to the garage. Her pearly white electric convertible with a full charge from the charging floor mat hummed on, and out she sped into the waning Texan daylight. Living twenty minutes from the city allowed her time to think of nothing. She was so involved with her research and diplomatic projects for Gerhard, so driving time was reserved for the simple pleasure of thinking about nothing.

Living in a world of what-ifs was the curse of a scientist and the gift of a genius. She would wait until the time was right to excite Steele, like an experiment. Steele was crazy for her, and though he was quite intelligent and liked to be thought of as such, she tried to never say or do anything to disturb the truth in that she was, by far, his mental superior. Respect was the bottom line in their relationship. She knew he was not committed to anything or anyone beside his obsession with the success of *TerraLuna.*

The special missions he sent her on did intrigue her.

Investors would not complain or ask questions when she arrived with papers to sign. Her being his proxy had added class to his business. She would be able to answer technical questions that appeased anyone with qualms about the veracity of the project. Whatever he wanted her to do now had to be important enough for him to call her at such short notice. Missions were always briefed at a sumptuous dinner.

It was simply his way of doing business. *TerraLuna* appeared around the corner with a glint of the setting sun sparking a glare that made Leslie tip her visor down and adjust her sunglasses a bit. She pulled into the rear parking lot, to the now unmanned security gate. Quickly, she passed her access card across the reader. With a beep, the screen flashed and announced in a friendly voice, *Welcome, Leslie Davis. Please proceed.*

The gate slid open, and she continued to a landscaped lot. *Chez Sam Houston's* delivery truck sat in the lot. Her stomach tweaked daintily at the sight of it. She remembered past meals there that had left her more than satisfied. She parked next to Steele's black Mercedes and made her way to the small silver door where again, the card allowed her access. The aroma of cooked chicken with wine and herbs pointed her toes in the direction of the elevator. She entered and yet again presented her card and touched the dark screen at the prompt to bring her to LL4. The doors opened to reveal four white-suited waiters with gloves looking up at her from beyond the glassed meeting room, momentarily removed from their preparations to catch a glimpse of her and then quickly return back to work. By the looks on their faces, she could only imagine what he must have told them. Steele swiftly came to her side and brought her into the meeting room with a kiss on the cheek and a directing squeeze on the arm.

"Dinner in five minutes." He nodded to the headwaiter. The small, efficient man nodded and began to direct the others to stir sauces and ready salads. He took her into a small meeting room lit only by opulent silver candelabras. Two settings across from each other at the center of a thirty-foot glossy black table glittered with silver accents.

"Quite lovely, Gerhard," she said as he helped her into the chair. He moved around the other side of the table as waiters, ready with salad and wine, began their service regimen. They sipped the wine and began the salad, quietly ingesting the mood and its excellence. He knew she was sensitive to atmosphere and was savoring the romantic finery in silence. Sharing several appreciative glances across the table was sure to increase his chances of success.

"This is really lovely. I know you have something special in mind for me to take care of for you. An appeal from you is always presented on silver," she offered and then ate a fork of salad.

"Am I that predictable? Is it so out of character to invite you over for a friendly supper? You know, there isn't another girl I would rather be with, don't you, Leslie?"

"If you weren't so charming, I might accuse you of being an opportunist. Yet being charming is sort of like opportunism, isn't it? Of course, it is. Whenever you want something, you use that old charm of yours . . . you opportunist," she declared, taking a sip of a nice chardonnay.

"Some would say that I know how to treat a lady," he said with a slight smile. Waiters approached with the aroma of lobster bisque that happened to be Leslie's favorite, and he was well aware of this fact. Her pointed blue eyes focused further on the rich, steaming soup. She was confident now that this was not going to be some routine check collection or document signature.

"I heard that *MoonCorp* announced a merger with Skylar today and that they plan on going forward with some new plan for their five-star hotel complex on the moon. I think that is a hard challenge after what happened at *TerraLuna*, don't you? Did Stan Duncan call you?" she said between spoonfuls of bisque.

"No. Stan Duncan is a very skilled strategist. He probably is waiting for a call from me, a call for help."

He continued eating silently. Waiters emerged again from the darkness to clear plates, and the distinct aroma of herbed chicken found its way to their senses. She knew there was something unsaid. Knowing that he would eventually reveal his hand, she gave a silent shake of her head and finished the last of the second course. She cataloged the lack of music to the seriousness of this plot. He romanced her, convinced her, and then paid her. She was reminded to let herself face the fact again that she could pretend to love him for the sake of social and financial security. She wondered if he thought she loved him. He never asked!

Her thoughts shifted easily to the steaming silver trencher of chicken breasts on a bed of wild rice that danced into the room with an accompaniment of two sauces, each bearer white gloved and expressionless.

"This is really wonderful, Marcel," said Steele, accepting a generous portion of chicken and rice. "I will take the mushroom sauce." Marcel made his way around the table to serve Leslie, and this was Steele's chance to start weaving his design. Leslie was a passionate woman and a bit more so than her fine endowment of intelligence led one to believe. Steele knew this to be the key to operating Leslie.

"Thank you. I will take the fruit sauce, Marcel." She smiled courteously, and Marcel took his leave. Another waiter was ready with a trencher of assorted grilled vegetables. He spooned them ample portions and left them in a waft of fruity sauce.

"Leslie, I don't want you to get the wrong idea about all this. I'll get to the point. Yet this time, there is more at stake for *TerraLuna* and for me." He continued to eat, coolly parting a quick glance to see if any of the waiters was within earshot.

"I need you to take a job of sorts at *MoonCorp* and retract some information that will be beneficial in completely securing our investors' confidence."

Leslie ingested his proposal with more difficultly than the tender chicken, waiting for him to say something else. She carefully swallowed and touched her lips with her napkin, trying to think of a response.

"There is good reason for me to believe that some of *TerraLuna*'s key supporters will be allotting more of next year's budget to other endeavors. *MoonCorp* now has the full support of the Skylar Corporation, which was at one time a mutual resource and, to some extent, still is. However, what my investors will soon learn is that local defense plans are underway to prevent similar *TerraLuna* accidents." Leslie came close to saying something when he stopped her with the wave of a finger. "The science behind this is something that Duncan will want to charge me for. Based on our new opening date, even if we get his new local defense program, he will have his accountants figure a price that will severely dig into our profit margin, which he knows will force me to raise my prices. We must turn a profit. I can promise so many points to the board before I look like a fool." Steele paused as a waiter entered with a water carafe and offered refills.

Leslie continued eating without revealing any discernible sign of an opinion to Steele's credo. She held his glance with a dispassionate evenness; Steele had trouble forecasting her response. He looked hopefully back at her to allow the good food to do its work.

Leslie had not finished her meal. However, she had had enough. Giving her full lips a final wipe and taking a sip of wine to compose herself, she looked squarely at him and said, "If I am caught, I cannot be traced back to you, right?" she said finally, laced with suspicion of betrayal.

Steele held her glance for only a moment and said straightforwardly, "Leslie, please try not to make me seem heartless. We will work something out. Naturally, I will want to remain anonymous. Any connection to espionage will be the end of me.

You know I pride myself on my sterling reputation. Get the information and we will fabricate an escape, a sick mother or something."

"You want me to steal classified data for you? This is a bit more serious than wearing a low-cut blouse in order to make some tough investors loosen their pen caps!" she blurted.

He reached across the table, took her hand, and stroked it with his other. "I said it was for *TerraLuna* and me. If you do this for me, I'll stop playing around, and we can be together. Having this hotel will be twice as satisfying if I had someone to share it with."

She pulled her hand away slowly, sizing him up. He hadn't promised fidelity before. She could love him, she could manipulate him, or was it the other way around? This was so much the truth of the matter. Romantic, true love of high school sweethearts growing old together never made pure sense to her. There was always some ulterior motive at play, familial tradition, financial security, peer pressure. It was her turn to have one. Being so scientific about matters of love never seemed to offer a solution until now. If she committed his crime for him, then she could not only share his high-profile life, but so with the solidity of a ring. Part of her licked her mental lips, yet another part kept savoring her own unique freedom.

"Gerhard, I love a challenge. You know that. I really hope you have this thing planned out to the smallest detail. I will not agree until I see the complete scheme, with backup contingencies. I've done a great deal for you, but I will not go to jail for you, Steele."

Marcel and his boys entered with a trencher of chocolate mousse.

"That I promise. But first let's have some dessert." Chocolate mousse would help to settle the indigestion that Steele caused. Leave it to him to provide a cure after causing the pain.

They spent some time not quite stalemated with the beautiful mousse at a meeting room table transformed into a five-star restaurant. Leslie attempted to conceal how nice she felt after the meal.

"Let's go down to the video room. I want you to see what we are working with." He came around the table to assist her. They made their way to the elevator. He pressed down. They found themselves entering the dimly lit hallway to the video room that was opened with the swipe of his universal keycard. He brought the computer online and snapped on the bank of a dozen monitors.

"Duncan has two wunderkinds that engineer most of the projects of any importance. They are certainly on the cutting edge of the local defense work. Here they are preparing to demonstrate the new defense system."

He turned the dial, and the screen zoomed in on Charley and Nick sitting on the right of Stan Duncan. She looked at them in a strange sort of way as if they were prey of some kind, yet she smiled briefly. This plot seemed to appear colder and impersonal than any of the other clients she had done for Steele.

He reviewed the other *MoonCorp* attendees, some of which she knew. She had to be careful not to make contact with any of the people she might have dealt with before. Fortunately, the people she knew would not be involved in the daily operations, yet she had to take note of people like the Skylars and Pierre Etienne who would recognize her and have questions. She pointed Dr. Franz and Moreni. Are they going to be briefed?" she said with concern.

"Naturally, Moreni should not be told anything outside of his detail. Dr. Robert Franz and I have had a falling out, of course. This offers us a bit of a problem. He will be involved throughout the process. I think, for safety's sake, we will take some precautions."

She darted a quick look at him. "What sort of precautions?"

"It seems that the former science advisor to *TerraLuna* with his new title at *MoonCorp* will be the fly in the ointment with whom we must deal. I would hate to have him recognize you. I have had a couple of solutions to this problem. We need to discuss this." He paused gently to prepare her for what he was thinking of.

"I think a disguise of minimal proportions will throw him off. Something as simple as dyed hair, some glasses, and perhaps colored contact lenses should do the trick. You will, of course, have a new identity, and the thought of an accent of some kind did cross my mind. You spent some time loitering in the theater department at that impressive university of yours, didn't you? I am sure we can devise something that will be sufficiently deceptive."

He stopped, looking for an answer without objection. Leslie looked at him squarely in silence for a moment. She turned away and sighed. "Gerry, I do not know. Is this really necessary? You want me to use an accent? Should I be Natasha from Kraplapastan, or would you rather Eunice from Great Britain? It seems so crude."

He suddenly engulfed her in his commanding arms and held her close.

"Leslie, you have to understand that I have been working on this for some time, and I am certain it is the best way to get what we need. No one will know we have stolen and then modified a top secret defense schematic. They will be impressed with our own technology. We will test it and possibly patent it before they know what hit them. We can install the local defense and have it running before they even break ground on *MoonCorp*. We can call it a final change that has not yet been installed. We are not beyond such technology. We will change it so it will be different enough and enough to make it uniquely ours. Alter a power source or use revolutionary conduits, anything. The beautiful part is that you can be involved in the engineering. You love that. I will also put you on the payroll as an associate engineer with a five-year contract. Regardless of what happens, you will be earning a number seven pay scale!"

Leslie relaxed her shoulders and buried her head in Gerhard's chest in a rare emotional episode for her. Knowing her compliance in silence, he held her and surveyed the screens over her shoulder with enhanced scrutiny.

CHAPTER 13

Pepe considered taking his faithful friend to see Dr. Rene Sanchez at the University of Yucatan at Merida but thought he should leave him at home rather than keep him in the hot truck. The four-hour drive from Celestún to Merida seemed much longer without Tico to keep him company.

His appointment was for one o'clock, and he was early. He parked in the university lot, which was nearly empty as the majority of the students were off for summer break. He ate his hand-packed lunch of a warm thermos of carnitas, tortillas, and a couple of orange sodas. His digital truck clock read 12:52 as he wiped chili sauce from his mustache and inspected his white shirt and green tie for stains. He made his way into the school. It seemed to him to be like a tomb with its waxed floors and tall ceilings. His footsteps fell solidly against the hard floors, echoing importantly against the tan-painted walls covered with Mayan art and bulletin boards.

The science department was on the second floor. He followed the signs and made his way up the stairs. A receptionist looked up from her crossword puzzle and gave him a happy smile. He entered the glass door, impressed at how sturdy the artisanship was, and smiled at the young girl of about twenty. "Hello. I am Pepe Fernandez. I have an appointment to see Dr. Sanchez."

"Oh, yes," the girl said, deftly sliding her summer crossword puzzle beneath a handful of file folders. "Have a seat and I will tell him you are here." She smiled again as she went to the back to get the professor.

Pepe squirmed his toes in the hard shoes he had not worn since the death of his aunt Estella. He adjusted his off-white suit that fit him quite snugly, wondering if he was gaining weight. He sat in the comfortable chair under the fluorescent lights, noticing the variety of unusual scents in the office. It certainly did not smell like fish in here, a sensation he did appreciate despite the fact that it made him nervous.

Dr. Rene Sanchez appeared from one of the back offices and made his way to greet Pepe, who stood and accepted his outstretched hand. He was a smaller man than he sounded on the phone, in his early forties, and dressed in a polo shirt and khaki shorts. Several gold chains appeared under his shirt. Pepe relaxed a bit, noticing a gold cross on a chain.

"Senor Fernandez, I am Rene Sanchez. How are you? Please come into my office. Would you like something to drink?" he said, guiding him past the desk and into the hallway

"No, thank you. I am fine." Pepe followed the professor, whom he thought would be older. He must be a smart man to be so young and a professor. They passed several doors and entered one that had a nameplate on the outside that read, "Dr. Rene Sanchez PHD, Astronomical Sciences."

Pepe made himself comfortable in the cluttered but organized office. The walls were covered posters and charts mapping the heavens. A bookshelf covered two of the walls stuffed with papers, magazines, and texts apparently related to his field of study.

The professor took a sip of his coffee and sat officially into his swivel chair.

"Well, senor, I am glad you have come to see me. As we spoke on the telephone, I am heading up the investigation of the occurrence in the gulf. Any information you can provide will aid us in determining what exactly happened. As you know, the Skylar defense system at the *TerraLuna* hotel shattered a large comet that had evaded their long-range sensors, and the remains seemed to have landed in our backyard, so to speak. Please tell me what happened that night."

Pepe shrugged slightly with a roll of his eyes and relayed the story of the night in question. During his retelling, Sanchez took a few notes, furrowing his brow as to determine what kind of a man Pepe Fernandez was, really. He handed him several snapshots to look at during the story, some of his boat; Paloma, his wife; the men at the packing dock; and of course, Tico wrestling with a small shark.

Perhaps he was a drinker. No, he seemed to be quite a sober, yet eccentric family man since he had referred to his wife, Paloma, six times during the story and his dog, Tico, at least a dozen. He was devoted to his business and seemed quite satisfied. Pepe finished his story with some questions.

"Senor, I was concerned that the comets were going to cause a tidal wave of some sort. We felt great waves swelling up, and there was quite a splash of the shore, but nothing serious. Why is this?"

The professor sat back a bit in his chair and said, "It seems that from your viewpoint, the comets were maybe ten miles out, you said? I suspect that they were a bit farther away than they seemed, or we would have experienced more devastation. Another possibility is that the waves were caught by deeper current and taken out to sea. The brunt of the impact was certainly not felt along our coastline.

"Another thing you had said," the professor continued, getting up to freshen his coffee cup, "was that the comets entered the water vertically." He motioned up and down with his free hand.

"Yes, they came straight down from the sky in groups. They looked almost like fireworks, a bright light with a glowing tail. Tico and I have never seen anything like it." Sanchez looked at Pepe for a long moment and then decidedly returned to his seat.

"Senor Fernandez, I am planning a scientific investigation of this event. The University of Houston is sending us the latest submarine camera equipment so we can see what happened to the seafloor due to the impact. How would you like to come and show us where this happened, as sort of a guide? We would be gone for about four or five days. Do you think you can spare the time away from work?"

Pepe drew a deep breath and let it out with a slight reverberation of his lips. "I can tell Paloma it is important if you really need me. Maybe she would like to go and visit with her mother and sister for a few days. I think she would understand. I would like to go very much," he ended, beginning to like the idea of a voyage for something more than fish and shrimp.

"Excellent. The submarine will be here next Tuesday. I was hoping we could use your ship. I am sure I can arrange for you to dock right here at the Yucatan Marina." He began to slide his finger along an electronic index screen built into his desktop for the marina's phone number.

"I would like to bring my crew along as well if it is not too much problem. You see, Professor, Tico comes with me every day to fish. He will not be a bother. He saw it too," Pepe offered using hand gestures to punctuate his speech as he became excited about the adventure to come.

"Sure, not a problem, Senor Fernandez. I will call you when the machine arrives, and we will make arrangements. I have another appointment to go to at three o'clock. I am sorry we did not have more time today. We will have plenty of time next week."

Sanchez stood up and escorted Pepe out of his office cordially. Pepe waved goodbye more than once as he left, revealing an uncontrollable smile brought on by sheer exhilaration at the prospect of going to sea for science.

*****

Ten days had passed since the incident on *TerraLuna*, and progress on the reclamation of the decompression areas was moving along swiftly. The majority of the east-wing guest rooms were salvageable. If the meteor had directly impacted the main atrium of the building, the damage would have been greater. Fortunately, it cuffed the edge, and the momentum carried it off in the wide outer band of the west end. Assembling the replacement, wall pieces for the upper tier of rooms built above the outer ring which served as a running track were digitally scanned and reproduced to fit into place at *TerraLuna*'s labs. The eastern part of the complex could be sealed off as it designed as a natural division from the larger central areas into the guest rooms. It actually was designed to allow for sealing sections that might sustain damage. The inner walls were able to function against the possibility of being exposed to the lunar atmosphere. Gravity control was in effect after an extensive survey of the structural integrity of the entire complex. A crew of six worked day and night, clearing debris, removing the crumbled outer modular walls. Most of the parts were designed to be interchangeable, making repairs easy.

A large cargo vessel had been launched two days prior and was due later in the day, fifteen days since the impact. Several specialty relief crew members were assigned to arrive and replace those scheduled to return after being on duty for a month. Very few would return because of the need for manpower to reestablish *TerraLuna*'s operation status.

Ed Zonic sat at his computer at his desk station in the reclaimed control center, reading a transmission from the *TerraLuna* corporate office requiring him to stay and supervise the repair effort. He sat, staring at the message, conflicted with the idea of having to stay and his sense of responsibility to the extra money he would receive. He still maintained that the construction system was too simplistic.

Ultimately, problems would occur, and he was needed to handle them. Apparently, Steele thought so as well. Before going down to get some lunch and running tests on the gravity generators in the emergency sealed sections, he decided to write Nick about the latest events over to the big blue ball outside his window.

Nick,

Hey, friend, how are you? How has the media bastardized this thing down there? I am guessing that they have blown it way out of proportion. We took FIDO out to reclaim a piece of the meteor and located it with metal detectors and infrared scanners. Steele wanted a chunk of it for analysis. It is an interesting mix. I took a hot amenities director with me, and we are seeing each other often. How are you? How is the love life? What does Duncan think about all this? What is new at the office? I have to get chow now. I am still alive and involved. Hell, it takes a near-death experience to get a date up here. Write back soon and not just when you need more solar photos. Out. Zonic.

Ed sent the transmission. He looked to the window, imagining the low band wave beaming toward Earth, when he saw Haley beaming at him instead.

"How about lunch?" she said with a tip of her head.

"Sure. I am ready now," he offered and walked to the dining area, fighting the urge to have a cigarette while he was with her. Avoiding social smoking was a dangerous sign that he cared about this person enough not to offend her by smoking. *Well, these things happen,* he thought.

*****

Charley sat inside the 750-foot hangar door inside from which the Yokomoto-Chen heavy lift system would load tons of equipment to transform the moon's surface into building material. Usually, brilliant economics was not a part of his scientific thinking. Charley had to admit to himself that it was a great idea. The afternoon sun baked dry the white cement desert that spanned the distance between the hangar complex and the runway and launch areas. It might have rained briefly that morning. Any sign of it having rained was long evaporated, leaving only the faint smell of ozone and fuel exhaust.

The launch base was virtually in the Mojave Desert about twenty-five miles southwest of the old Twentynine Palms Marine Base. Trucks leased by *MoonCorp* had been coming and going all morning, unloading parts of the smelter machines and Yokomoto's cylindrical lift vehicle.

Charley sat on a folding chair, watching the coming and goings for nearly the entire morning, with occasional trips for donuts and bathroom breaks. He could not put the thought out of his mind that he was a very small part of the operation. There wasn't anything important for him to monitor or supervise. Looking out as the trucks came up the service road after stopping at the checkpoint bored him. Therefore, he asked them if he could give tours to groups invited to observe the process. No one seemed to mind, and he was assigned a base handheld radio. However, very few tourists were allowed on the campus. He felt on the periphery of the project.

The radio crackled on as the familiar voice of the gate attendant alerted him that a group of doctoral students from the University of San Diego were on their way to observe our progress.

"Roger, gate," said Charley. Most of the technicians were Japanese employees of the inventor of the heavy lift machines eager to actualize the *MoonCorp* dream. He rationalized that his contribution would be appreciated after the hotel was wired for power.

The workers were concerned with preparing the huge squat cylinder. In less than two days, the shell of the vehicle was in place. They continued installing the booster rocket and delivery transfer mechanisms to ensure pickup by the gigantic ship that would also serve as quarters for the initial construction crew.

The Junk Colossus or JC was parked in the next hangar and was prepared to roll out onto the launch site early next week. It spanned two hundred yards long and seventy-five yards across. It was capable of carrying six containers from the edge of Earth's atmosphere. The manned connection pods cabled to the ship had a locking claw and magnetic seals to secure the container to the Junk Colossus. Charley wanted to sneak over to take another look at it when a van filled with students pulled up to the hangar door. He stood and consulted the video screen inside the door that was offering a list of security information on the five students and two teachers. With a roll of his eyes in recognition of some of the names on the list, he pressed the "print" button on the computer, and a list of the guests emerged from the bottom of the computer.

A light-blue minivan approached the hangar, and Charley straightened up to greet the faction from the university. Walking out, he motioned the van to park on the side of the hangar where thirty or so cars were parked along with several busses.

A small man with heavy glasses and the remains of a comb over maintained for years exited the vehicle with a large smile of yellow teeth that Charley recognized immediately as Dr. Winslow, his former chairman at the astrophysics department. He squinted briefly and approached Charley with his hand outstretched.

"Dr. Porter, I presume. Well, I must admit, I thought Mr. Duncan would greet us. I see you have worked your way into something of a majordomo. Be comforted that we are not carrying any luggage. I would have you carry it Porter. We left it at the hotel, lucky you. Front!" He smiled his trademark yellow grin when he thought he was amusing.

"Nice to see you too, Dr. Winslow," Charley said, quickly dropping the old nerd's hand.

The van opened as five students emerged and took in the sight of the grounds. Each carried some sort of note-taking apparatus, pointing and wowing mutely as they came.

A tall dark-haired man appeared from the van, whom Charley recognized as Bill Worth. They had been students together, and now he seemed to have pandered his way onto the faculty. Bill was a thick sort of fellow, always willing to do whatever it took to find the path of least resistance.

"Welcome to *MoonCorp*," was all Charley could muster. Bill Worth stepped up and greeted him with the same insincere attitude he remembered from his days at the university.

Charley regarded Bill's dedication as less than serious. To his surprise here, he was now assisting Winslow. *What a pair*, he thought.

"Charley Porter. How the hell are you? I thought you would have been out of here for the coast."

"No, Bill, I got a real job. How about you, back in school?" said Charley, feigning dumbness.

"No, actually, Porter, I am an adjunct professor now. Physics 101," he responded with pride.

Charley looked at him for an unusual silent moment and then addressed the group officially.

"Just for security reasons, I would like to scan all your ID badges and ask that you keep them in plain view at all times. My name is Dr. Charles Porter, and I am going to take you in to tour the facility. Please refrain from touching anything, and please stay with the group. At any time, please do not refrain from asking questions. I have the answers."

He turned to the hangar door, and the group followed him responsively. At the door, he arranged them to singly show him their badges. As he verified their scans, they filed into the building.

"Fred Finch, Gary Bannister, Hakim Touzanni, Selma Arcarla, and Dana Kim. Okay, a few more rules: What you see here is, of course, the property of *MoonCorp*, and as you have noted by your nondisclosure statements, nothing you see here is to be discussed with media personnel or competitive source of any kind. Such activity would disqualify you from attaining credit for this course. Throughout the next ten weeks, you will be a part of the *MoonCorp* project and will be given a specific job, which I am sure Dr. Winslow has worked out with Mr. Duncan. I will give you a general tour, and then we will break for lunch, after which Mr. Duncan will take you to your stations based on your dissertation subjects. That's it, folks. Any questions?"

Selma Arcarla said in her naturally sultry Spanish accent, "Yes, Dr. Porter. I have read your paper on the hyper-reflexive holo-imager. Did you ever make a prototype? If so, I would like to see it."

Charley raised his eyebrows, slightly surprised by the question.

"That question I cannot answer now, but perhaps later, we can discuss the matter privately."

Dana Kim turned to Charley, carefully meeting his gaze. The small, apparently half-Chinese woman made Charley take in a slow breath as she was stunningly exotic. Her eyes were a deep dark blue, something he could not recall seeing in an Oriental person.

"Dr. Porter, you must know that your papers are often referred to in our theoretical concept course at U of L? Perhaps we can talk later about the practical uses for the power relay system. It cost twenty billion to put into orbit, and we were hypothesizing what could it do besides a communication satellite. Really, what is its true operation? I mean does it work?"

Charley looked at her with setback eyes for a moment.

"Well, I can see we will have to reserve some time for some lengthy discussions as far as I am allowed to discuss such topics. For now, let's stick to our job at *MoonCorp*. Let's begin the tour."

The group followed him past offices on the left to the center of the hangar where the Yokomoto-Chen people, or YAMOCHs as he liked to refer to them when they were not around, were busying themselves walking in and out of the cylinders.

Yokomoto and Dr. Chen themselves were very involved with the doors of the cylinders as a group looked on. They listened in for a moment, not asking if they could watch.

Dr. Chen, slightly begrudged by the intrusion, agreed to explain to the students what they were doing. They walked through the tanks on platforms, noting the key construction elements and integrated design strategy to allow them to contain the heavy cargo.

Mr. Yokomoto was a bit disturbed. It was either from the intrusion or the mis-explanation the young Dr. Chen was offering. He bustled through his lab coat pockets and produced a headset with an attached mouthpiece. After adjusting the controls on the earmuff-like headset, he spoke quite rapidly into the wraparound mouthpiece in Japanese. His voice came out of the speakers from either side of his head.

"These six containers will be filled with machinery, supplies, and tools, everything we need to begin *MoonCorp* construction. The most important item is this." He led the group into the open hatch of the canister where dozens of large 270-gallon plastic reinforced containers were stacked.

"This adhesive, when in combination with heat and the smelting machine, will fabricate the actual walls and floors, building blocks of *MoonCorp* hotel." Waiting to get a reply, he adjusted a dial at the right earmuff which would automatically translate the questions of his listeners.

"Hakim Touzanni Jr., University of San Diego. What is the total tonnage that can be lifted into space?" the student said, not sure whether Yokomoto's receiver was on translation device.

"Anything will be able to go into the Junk. This is why we call it Colossus. Okay, we are very busy now. Come back later and you may help us load," the fatherly man said in his native tongue, translating his preoccupation with his work.

Charley led the tour out of the canister, not wanting to upset Yokomoto. As they exited, he noticed Selma Arcarla was near him again, and he did not think it was only by chance.

Selma Arcarla was making herself a fixture next to him as they left the huge tanks. He didn't want her to catch him dodging her attempts to gain nearness to him. Not having had much luck with women lately, or ever for that matter, it could be his imagination, but Dana Kim undeniably offered a pleasing glance now and again. This he did not imagine.

CHAPTER 14

Three days of meetings with engineers is more than adequate to begin production of the specialized conduits and generators required to maintain the protective force around the hotel. The great idea that had been wasting on Nick's shelf was now a major undertaking. Nick shook thoughts away of being able to save lives at *TerraLuna*. Political decisions between Stan and Gerhard Steele could have been made in the name of common safety. He promised himself that his latest technology would not comprise any basic benefit to humankind. Nick was not in this for power or money but rather to make a contribution.

Nothing pressing could be done at the office today. He told Eleanor he was going home to work. Before the noon hour was up, he was on the road again, involuntarily immersing himself in the dynamic of the solar cycle.

Pulling into the driveway and up to the mailbox, he put the car in park and removed several pieces of mail and, to his happy surprise, a small box from the University of Phoenix. This was awesome, another entry for his collection. The driveway took him into his private peaceful world. He frowned inwardly that he lived alone and remembered Ada for a fruitless moment, looking at the empty passenger seat. He parked in the garage, turned the car off, and collected his mail and briefcase, reminding himself that he had to press on.

He would sleep on Saturday, hopefully waking with satisfaction on tonight's work. After a healthy three-hour nap and a long shower, he ate a modest frozen dinner, filled a large cup of coffee, and made his way out to the barn with the package from Phoenix as the sun threatened to set in the late July sky.

He opened the security system on his wrist phone with voice activation. A sea of fluorescent light cascaded across the barn. Taking his seat at the computer, he started the system and then unwrapped the small box carefully. The clear plastic sample case was about the size of a box of animal crackers. The top contained a folded piece of blue paper. It read, "Gryllidae Phoenxiius Dragoonae." He pulled a top cotton pad to reveal a rock the size of a golf ball. Resting in the rock was the fossil of a small cricket with a very tiny head and unusually large legs.

The note read further,

Dr. Nicholas, we found this one in a recent dig near the Dragoon Mountains. We have several to spare. We estimate this to be approximately 400 million years old from the Devonian period and heretofore unrecorded. Good luck. I hope this helps in your study. H. P. Martin.

Nick flipped on his lighted magnifying glass on a flexible arm and took a closer look at the little creature. He got right to work on documenting and processing the latest addition to his vast collection of crickets found over great periods of time. After photographing and logging it in to his book, Nick took the specimen to the back of the bar where his lab tables, storage cabinets, and wide variety of instruments waited patiently for him.

Climbing on his stool at the high table, he began to scrape the fossilized creature into a paper cone. He added a clear solution from a corked flask into a centrifuge tube and then added the powdered insect. He set the tube into the centrifuge and programmed it to spin for ten minutes. To pass the time, he checked his message access.

He found several messages from colleagues, including a note from Martin and one from the Skylar group. Eleanor had mailed him a story about the object that struck the Yucatan Peninsula. He decided to open the message from Ed Zonic, realizing it had been more than a week since he heard from him. He read the message, clicked the respond button, and wrote a reply:

Zone,

It is good to hear from you. I am happy to hear about your love life. I cannot say I have found anyone to spend some time with other than my work. Be careful up there. A pregnancy in space might be problematic within artificial gravity-regulated areas. Can you imagine what it would be like up there without those generators?

We have begun work on MoonCorp. *I do not know if you heard, but the money took a turn after your accident. Skylar and Duncan have joined forces, and the Europeans want in. it is unbelievable how much support the project is getting. I may be up there before you know it! Next week, on Sunday afternoon, we will be heavy lifting the foundation machines, and I think you will be able to see the progress from the towers. See if you can't get some footage of the Junk Colossus landing.*

I brought Porter back in to help. Stan gave him the job of watching the hangar door. He is pissed. Anyway, I am glad to hear you are doing well. If you have a chance, get me a sample of that meteor . . . What would a note from me be without a favor? Help out a frustrated geologist! I would like to run some analyses. Be safe up there and keep me in touch.

Your friend, Nick.

Nick sent the message and returned to the centrifuge flashing a red light, indicating it had completed its cycle. He removed the tube and held it up to his work light magnifier. Specks of ancient DNA older than any kind in his collection lay suspended in the thick fluid; this was quite a find. He carefully poured the precious liquid in a fresh large petri dish and covered it immediately to avoid contamination. Carefully, he carried the dish across the lab to an environment conditioner, flicked the switch on, and opened the automatic door. A tray slid out, and he gingerly placed the dish in the slot and closed it with a sight push. He set the temperature and peered through the window at the latest addition to his rare collection as it baked gently to melt the suspension.

Satisfied that he could do no more, he automatically went to a tall metal cabinet, retrieved a flat metal box, and bought it to the worktable. It held seven glass spheres about the size of a baseball covered with a thick layer of protective foam. The glass was specially tempered to his specifications, with a thickness of close to half an inch. A small hole plugged with a cork waited in pristine foam packaging. He went to the cabinet and removed what looked like a glue gun.

Calm satisfaction came over Nick like a warm shower. He still reviewed the steps that he performed many times before. Today's addition aroused in him a mounting sense of becoming for he was closer to the final stage of the effect for which he was striving to actualize for nearly four years. Patience was more than a necessity for a scientist with designs on new significant discoveries; he reminded himself it is a discipline.

He remembered his doctorate chairman, H. P. Martin, said this to him years ago when he would come to his office with a myriad of questions with traumas of the failure of his attempt at creating substantial theoretical proof of his designs credible and well supported enough to publish.

Removing the possibility of failure was his daily grind. Repressed thoughts of disaster settled calmly below the electric threshold of imminent success. He suppressed the oncoming painful reminder that he was unable to share his work with Ada. She appreciated breakthroughs with a unique zeal that he missed terribly. Emptiness lived in him left by her premature death. Its reality tempered his work without consciousness or reason. Most of the time, he found her memory to be the will and purpose driving his research. Achievement was his personal therapy used to deal with honoring her life. He dwelled periodically on the possibility of moving on to meet other women but, more often than not, went back to work, unable to adequately resolve his loss.

Yet another trip to the cabinet produced a metal stand designed to hold several globes and a plastic-wrapped pair of soft sanitary gloves. Returning to the table, he placed the items carefully beside the gun stand. Wetness in his hands prompted him to reach below the table, remove a sterile towel from its protective wrapper, and clean his hands thoroughly. He pressed the button on the automatic Bunsen burner and set the flame low beneath the steel holder. He placed a flask from a rack at the back of the table onto the burner and loosened the cork without removing it to avoid a foreign material from entering the pure clear media.

As the viscous fluid began to swirl and become more fluid, melting its way slowly through the entire flask, he lowered the flame by two clicks. Satisfied with the heat level, he donned the gloves and placed the globe on the stand with the hole pointing upward and retrieved a wrapped glass funnel designed by his glass blower to fit snugly in the small opening.

The graduated flask holding the fluid was warming slowly with small wisps of steam escaping from around the top. Nick produced a wrapped beaker from a box beneath the table, placing it with the other components. Before bringing the fossil suspension to the table, he swirled the heating flask to equalize the melting. He opened the environmental conditioner and gently removed the warm dish. Moving with the skill of a surgeon, he measured precisely 120 ml fossil into the beaker. He replaced the remainder of the solution in the chamber. After measuring the proper temperature in the flask, he slowly added 225 ml of the warm liquid to the beaker and stirred the two gently with a glass wand.

He immediately poured the mixture through the funnel, filling the globe methodically, emptying nearly the entire contents of the beaker. He took the gun from the holder that had been heating the glass solder and primed it. A slow squirt of molten glass oozed out. He crimped it off onto a metal plate.

Replacing the gun, he consulted the temperature gage attached to the globe holder. It had about four minutes to cool. He opened the hermetically sealed thick copper wire nearly ten inches long. A mark two inches from the end indicated the insertion point. When the globe had cooled, he inserted the wire into the globe and tamped the molten glass around the opening, sealing it with minute taps from the wand. He added a metal receptor plate to the top of the glass, and satisfied it was sealed, he looked intently at the evenly suspended flecks of vital material with the eye of an artist.

*****

The thoughtful Mexican handed his world dollar card over to José for the pile of supplies at the marina store well before sunrise, mostly basic supplies for his journey, including flares, oil, lengths of rope of varying sizes, bottled water, snacks, and cigarettes. Pepe Fernandez could not spend the professor's money wildly and, of course, asked for a receipt. The trip to the Merida Marina was only about twenty minutes along the coast where Dr. Sanchez and some of his students were to meet him later in the morning with the remote diving unit from the University of Houston. Pepe assumed they must have been saving some money by having it driven down from Houston rather than traveling across the gulf. Every day, Pepe gassed up at the Martinez Marina. His friend José had worked there as long as Pepe remembered. Pleasure yachters as well as anglers frequented the old, yet well-preserved store. José accommodated all business in his usual likable way. Of course, the gas was less expensive here since he was a frequent customer. All in all, Pepe came here every day. Pepe and José had been friends since school, and now it seemed they would be friends into middle age as well. José put the items in a sack, keeping an eye on Pepe, who was looking down at the counter.

"Pepe, is this professor covered on your insurance? In case he gets hurt maybe, he will sue you. Be careful, my friend."

Pepe checked the receipt and placed it in his billfold carefully.

"José . . . don't worry. He is paying five thousand world dollars to charter my boat. That is more money than fishing shrimp brings me in one month. I figure it out. If he wants to do more exploring, he calls me because I am a good captain who knows the sea in this locality. I am paid each trip. I have to take a chance for my family and myself. Where would you be if your father didn't take a chance with this business? I will tell you. You would be working in the salt mine or picking cocoa beans. Fishing is good work, but it is time for something different before I get too old. You might be worried I stop bringing you free fish? Well, I bring you a souvenir, okay?"

José shifted the toothpick in his mouth. This was a rare occurrence for the aging shopkeeper. He pulled a long shock of dark, silver-streaked hair out of his eyes and looked intently at his friend, and with a hint of jealously, he reached below the counter and produced a thick shank of jerky. Placing it in the bag he was holding, he revealed his usual friendly smile and said, "Give this to mi amigo Tico. You know he is expecting it." Pepe left the store to embrace the cool, dark morning.

The trip was occupied with dreams of spending the money for things at home. Paloma would not be eager to have more electronic gadgets around, yet with some convincing, they could enjoy a new computer to make life easier. Tico sat peacefully with the jerky between his paws, gnawing appreciatively, giving a quick glance to Pepe to check on him.

Before the sun was barely lighting the eastern sky, Pepe cut the engines and glided his ship, *La Fresca*, into the small harbor where a flashing blue light would be as the professor directed. The beautiful, like-new boat had been Pepe's pride and joy for nearly a year now. It still received silent nods of approval back at home and at sea. Now was a chance to show her off away from her usual route. Two young men prepared to moor the boat, and Tico left his big piece of jerky to look over the side and see what was happening. Pepe tossed them the rope that was quickly tied to the dock. Sanchez was standing next to a pile of gear and supplies with his cup of coffee and a rather reserved demeanor.

"Senor Fernandez, these are my students, Enrique and Benito. They will accompany us and are very eager to learn about the impact for their studies."

"It is good to meet you," said Pepe, shaking hands. Tico gave a quick pair of barks making sure not to be neglected. "Oh, and this is my Tico, first mate aboard *La Fresca*."

They spent the next two hours preparing the ship for scientific exploration. After loading the gear and crate with the minisub. The boys donned wet suits, affixed some sonar readers to the bottom of the boat, and wired some basic computers to the ship's computer system. Since his was a newer boat with computer navigation, microchip-controlled engines, and satellite station, it was easily converted into a science vessel.

Pepe preferred the old-fashioned way to fish, yet he kept up with the latest gadgets. Within the hour, they consulted maps, and after a bit of a laugh over Dr. Sanchez having to take his coffee maker with a built-in grinder along, they were underway in the dawning day.

The colors of day were charmed back to life, while the shadows of night faded off into the crisp spray of the open sea. Enrique and Benito did not talk much, Pepe noted as they scrambled in boxes and checked instruments to prepare to catalogue data. They sat on the deck with their portable computer screens, always ready to consult. *They couldn't be older than twenty*, he thought to himself.

Computer screens offering the weather and satellite positioning were shrunk with the touch of a key. Pepe browsed his log to find his exact position on the night of the impact. It was easy for him to control the ship with the click of a computer, yet Dr. Sanchez stood nearby, awed by the integration of ship and computer.

Pepe paused and said to Sanchez, "This is the position where I saw the meteors. If you would like to press the Enter key, the ship will take us there. Be sure to hold on. There will be a slight change in direction."

Sanchez curled up his bottom lip, impressed with efficiency, and pressed Enter. A sudden, yet gentle lurch pulled the vessel a few degrees port. With forty minutes left before arriving by NavSys, the navigation system allowed them to spend some time preparing the sub for its mission. Deciding to counter Senor Fernandez's impressive demonstration, Sanchez asked Pepe to help him uncrate the sub and gave him a rundown of what it could do. The aluminum box was six by four by three. Its sides when unclipped fell over to reveal a yellow egg-shaped submersible. Various camera lights, detection devices, and maneuvering mechanisms surrounded its circumference.

"This is what we call *La Huevo*. I have borrowed it on many occasions. Before, they used to send someone along to operate it for me. Now I am a veteran. I am sort of its occasional captain. Have you ever seen anything like it, senor?"

Pepe Fernandez shook his head with the wind blowing his curly hair away from his face.

"No, Professor. It is amazing. Can someone go inside?"

Sanchez moved to the large end which was mostly a glass window looking into the egg.

"It was designed as a one-man pod, yet we have used it so often as a remote vehicle. Due to the recent development of high-resolution cameras and micro-halogen lights, we are able to get a better look from on board the ship with the monitor. No need to man it."

As the men discussed the winching logistics, *La Fresca* carried the busy crew farther out to sea. Pepe moved to the bow of the boat after switching off the automatic pilot and thought he would give them a bit of a ride. He opened the boat's engine wide and elapsed the remaining ten minutes of the trip in five. He stopped the boat as his NavSys reading reached zero. The boat bobbed in the somewhat-choppy water as the men looked out into the horizon.

"This is where I was when I saw the lights in the sky, Professor," said Pepe, reliving the experience. "I would say about six or seven miles ahead. It could not be less than that."

"Take us there," Sanchez said firmly.

Pepe moved into action, shifting the boat ahead with manual control. Excitement sprang from his belly as the distance meter on the NavSys brought them closer to answers from above. Before long, the few miles fell away, and Pepe put the engines into neutral. "This is the place," he said.

Squinting with the warming sun, Sanchez directed the computer to initiate sonar devices as Benito and Enrique tossed tethered mushroom-shaped readers into the sea.

"Senor Sanchez, we will get some initial readings and then conduct a section-by-section sweep in order to locate any major bioturbation in the seafloor," Enrique said.

Pepe nodded as if he understood and waited at the controls. The boys had removed their heavy coats, allowing them to maneuver the deck much easier in their white cotton pants and T-shirts. Nearly four hours passed as they combed a two-mile square where Pepe estimated the entry would be.

Tico had grown a bit bored without any fish to bring in and retired below to take a nap away from the noon sun. Sanchez and the boys wore wide-brimmed straw hats to protect them from the burning sun. They had brought an extra for Pepe, who declined. He produced a large red bandana and wrapped it around his head. He said it absorbed the sweat. They laughed together at Pepe's seriousness.

Sanchez, keeping to his screen, abruptly turned to the others and said after a series of rapid beeps from the sonar board, "Here it is. We have found the impact point. Come look and see where the sonar shows this drastic difference this area. Let's drop *La Huevo!*" Pepe placed the ship in neutral and readied the winch.

The long arm that usually dragged nets full of shrimp now lowered the yellow egg over the waiting sea. With the touch of a button, Pepe lowered it into the water where the boys unfettered the egg. It bobbed and tossed with the boys as they rechecked the cameras. They climbed back onto *La Fresca* and came to Dr. Sanchez's side, looking onto screens listing the egg's statistics.

"Our seafloor depth is 1,700 feet. This I why there was not very much wave activity, the depth was too great. Check your portables for readings," said Sanchez, indicating the waterproof computers.

Within minutes, the micro-halogen lights began to transmit pictures of the descending bathyscaphe. With a joystick control, Sanchez moved the egg farther into the depths. The pictures transmitted nothing for a good ten minutes.

Abruptly, darkness filled their screens. The boys sat cross-legged on the ship's floor and were suddenly facing a dark screen. "This may be one of the impact craters. I am going into the center. It may be deep."

Sanchez referred to the sonar screen, holding the sub at hover mode while he determined the depth of the depression. Pepe found nothing to do and asked if he should stop the ship's engines. Sanchez agreed with a preoccupied nod.

"I am going to get some cold water," said Pepe. He went below and closed the door, leaving the heat behind. Tico jumped around, waiting to be scratched as Pepe took a water from the refrigerator and plopped himself into his leather chair, immersing himself in the air-conditioning of his cabin. Pepe closed his eyes for what he thought was a moment and was startled awake by the sound of a splash. He went on deck to see what was going on.

Benito had spotted some sort of translucent strips that looked like a sea plant. Curious as to why they would be so far out, he grabbed a goody bag, slipped off his deck shoes, and dove into the water. He gathered several handfuls that smelled quite bad to him.

He looked overboard to see Benito in the water. Pepe went to the side and saw Benito swimming around with a net sack and collecting something that looked like brown kelp.

"What's going on?" said Pepe.

Sanchez remained fixed on the screen. "Senor Captain, come here and see this," Sanchez urged from the command station.

Pepe went to the screen to see an unusual sight. The sub had its cameras fixed on the seafloor where piles of what seemed to be exoskeletons shed from what appeared to be snakes or some kind of crustacean by the looks of the small legs. The body seemed to be too long to be a lobster. Suddenly, from under the debris, something scurried past the camera, disturbing the sand. Sanchez used the joystick to reposition the egg when they both stopped and starred at something quite amazing. A series of round white objects the size of basketballs littered the area. Something white moved, catching Sanchez's eye, at the corner of the screen. Moving the sub into a better position, centering the screen on another basketball, this one was covered with white ooze that moved with a gentle pulse. After a few seconds in the direct light of the sub, it became quite clear that the insides were hollow. Pieces of rock appeared in the screen every ten feet or so. At first, Sanchez thought they were spacefaring rock, but because of the large crater the egg was in, it was more likely that they were sections of rock blasted up from the seafloor.

"We have found some floating material. Come look, senor!" Benito held up the long, skinny material, treading water. Benito turned his head aside from the smell and stuffed them into the mesh bag.

Sanchez checked the recording icon to be sure that he was getting a record of this activity. Without warning, something large ran along the sloping seafloor. It could be a lobster or an eel yet looked impossibly like both. Sanchez and Pepe both lurched back in fear, realizing that Benito was still in the water collecting the floating skins.

"Benito!" Sanchez screamed to the side of the boat.

Enrique stood up and ran to the side of the boat, looking overboard for his friend. "Benito! Come back in! Benito?" said the young man, his voice cracking with fear. Enrique's head went from side to side. He turned back to Sanchez and screamed, "He's gone, Professor. He's gone!"

CHAPTER 15

"PORTER, THE CATERER is here with lunch," said the gate guard over the radio. Charley brusquely acknowledged the call, interrupting his detailed description of the solar energy transfer system to the students.

"Would any of you like to come with me to pick up the food?"

"I will," said Dana Kim immediately. Charley and Dana came out of the hangar to the service van used to run to the gate and back with minor deliveries.

Charley started the deep-blue cargo van. The air-conditioning blasted on full and instantly cooled the van as they made their way along the road to the front gate. Charley commanded the van with authority, not driving too fast despite his hunger. Now certainly was the time to get to know the beautiful doctoral student who had been displaying marked interest.

"So, Dana, where did you do your undergraduate work?" Sitting with her white sneakers propped on the dashboard in an unconsciously provocative pose, she looked at him offhandedly. "I studied at the University of Louisiana. I earned my MS in theoretical physics at the University of Alabama and now enrolled at U of San Diego for my PhD. Yeah, I know. I get around," she chimed, hoping there was nothing she said that would raise suspicion.

Stopping him from asking questions, she added frankly, "I know I am a sight to see. Have you ever seen a blonde half-Chinese, half-Norwegian girl with blue eyes and a bit of southern accent? I am rare! What about you, where did you come from originally?"

Charley responded indifferently, "Well, we Porters can be traced to English descent, however, recently from San Bernardino, California. Have you been to San Bernardino?"

She scratched her newly cut and dyed hair at the back of her neck and shrugged slightly.

"No. It seems that wherever I have been has been for school. I am sure you know what I mean. Science is seriously important to me. It may not seem so, yet I find myself practically unable to communicate with men, people for that matter, unless they know something at least as interesting as thermonuclear dynamics."

Nodding knowingly, it occurred to Charley that this girl talks an awful lot. Assured he knew what she was talking about now made conversation easier. Normally, the opposite was the case. Women rarely knew what he was talking about. He imagined her to be in her late twenties and apparently not married. Not wanting to show an overly eager interest just yet, he approached the gate and turned to her coolly.

"I know what you're talking about."

They laughed a bit and left the van to pick up foil trays from the waiting caterers who had become accustomed to the routine. Although it was usually expected for them to set up events, security restricted them from entering the site grounds. After the gate men filled their plates, Charley and Dana were back on the road to the hangar.

The smell of fried chicken and mashed potatoes emanated thickly from the back of the van. Dana sat in thought, staring out of the window, evidently with nothing important to say, when she suddenly asked, "Do you have a power relay?"

Charley swallowed hard, taking the van along the road a bit quicker now that his hunger was more insistent.

"I do, but I need the satellite upgrade to beam a modified solar wave to my unit to use it."

"So what's the problem?" she said.

"It is not licensed for personal use yet. I mean, I invented it for God's sake, and sure, there are some things the government regulates, and satellites are an issue, especially one that would eliminate the need for energy costs to the average earthling. Unbelievably, I have going on other exciting things. Did you get your work assignment yet?" he asked.

I work with the support distribution linkages: computer links with the valves from the rockets on the heavy lift cylinders. It is easy for me being a theorist. I know this territory is new, yet I want something I can sink my teeth into and be part of rather than checking for leaks and sealing valve couplings.

Charley neared the hangar and instinctively chose to help Dana with her problem, partly because of her fantastic mind (and body) and because of needing someone with engineering ability to Earth test the spiracle defense system.

"There is a possibility that I can arrange for you to assist on the spiracle defense test. You might find that challenging. I'll talk to Stan and Dr. Nicholas," Charley offered.

"That would be awesome! How new is this?" she said with restrained glee.

"It is the latest theoretical concern in practical production and very secret. You will be impressed. I know. But take it easy. I have to get you approved first. Saturday, we start construction with the lunar engineers. We'll be the fourth launch, so there is plenty of time to work out any bugs." He smiled at her excitement and parked the van in its spot outside the main hangar.

They unloaded the food and brought it into the break room. They placed the food on the designated tables and rang the lunch bell. Dana set out the plates and began to fill a plate for him which he found very kind of her.

"Are you available to see the JC liftoff tomorrow?" said Charley, munching a piece of chicken.

"Sounds cool," she said.

"That would be great. We roll her out at 0600 hours, and she is scheduled to take off at 0800. Let's meet here at 0745. We'll take the van and get a good spot away from the crowd," he added efficiently.

She winked at him, and he unconsciously winked back. Winking again felt a bit strange.

"Do you have something in your eye?" he said.

"Yes, I do. Excuse me, I need to get some drops." She left the break room and made her way to the women's lockers where she kept her purse. Throwing the door open, she bent to see if anyone was in the stalls. Seeing no one was there, she went to the mirror and looked at her left eye that was twitching uncontrollably, sagging and dripping mascara tears, which burned her eye.

She produced a device that resembled a small tuning fork with pointed ends and activated it, and it hummed, producing two blue laser points. She applied it under the eye, and her sagging round eyes angled up. A few applications brought the skin back to its oriental slant. After treating the other eye and washing her face, Leslie Davis reapplied her makeup and, within five minutes, was Dana Kim. *Not a bad job*, she thought.

*****

The forty-five-minute drive from San Bernardino to the launch site flew by for Charley. Daily stress about being alone usually flavored his trip out, but today was different. Today, he was occupied with thoughts of Dana. He coursed through his memory, listing a dozen girls he had been with since he left *MoonCorp*, none of them had anything relevant in common with him. Dana was engrossed in science. When most of his girlfriends had to be educated in basic modern solar energy, she knew about the power relay.

After months of hanging at Sneaky Petey's, seeing the same girls week after week, Charley wondered if they went with him basically because he was there, a familiar, nonthreatening figure.

Now, after meeting Dana, he felt insulted by the casual relationships that were invariably about his trying to bring them "up to speed" about how smart he was.

After deliberation, he committed to not jump into a relationship with Dana. However, she was obviously the kind of girl that would be turned off by procrastination. She might become disinterested. All things considered he would certainly make some sort of move after he had won her trust or before the job was complete whichever came first.

With twenty minutes of driving ahead of him, he decided to call Nick and see what was new. Taping a button, activating the wrist phone, he said, "Nick."

Charley put his wrist phone to his ear and waited for his friend's voice.

"Hello, Charley. Are you at the hangar yet?"

"I'm twenty minutes out. I haven't seen you in a couple. Have you found a way to travel faster than the speed of light yet?"

"No, Charley, I am too busy for that this week. I'll get started on that first thing next week." Nick laughed for the first time today.

"Nick, I wanted to call you and tell you that I am going to watch the JC liftoff with one of the doctoral students. This could be my earliest date yet. Anyway, I will be over right after, and I was hoping to bring Dana along for the local D test. What do you think?"

Nick paused for a serious moment to think. No objection came to his mind; the presence of a fresh mind might be a welcome thing.

"No sweat, Charley. It will be nice to show off to someone who can understand how it works for a change. Come over to the hangar after the liftoff. I will be with Stan and Yokomoto in the observation building."

"Roger that, Dr. Nick. Oh, while I'm thinking about it, did you talk to Stan about the free week on the moon, *for two* when this thing is complete. I'll need a vacation after three months of running the catering van."

Nick noted the sarcasm.

"Haven't had a chance yet. Don't worry, I'm sure he'll be okay with it as long as everything comes off without a hitch. So keep in mind those hitches that might get in the way, Charles. Nick out."

Charley pulled up to the guard shack and flashed his ID to the guard. "JC is taking off today. I hope you guys get a chance to check it out. It will be a sight to see."

"We'll check it out, Porter," said the guard.

He parked his car, entered through the side door, and then worked his way through the cool hangar where he found Dana mixing her coffee. She was fifteen minutes early; that is better than prompt.

"Hi there," he said.

"Good morning, Dr. Porter," she said with a powdered smile. "Good morning, Dana. You are one of those fifteen-minute-early types of people, aren't you? I like that you know. We had better get going to get a good seat. Bring your sunglasses," he added, reaching for the donut box.

As they walked out, a chill met them from the now-opened front door. Something about the silence enticed him as they strolled to the van. They drove around the back of the hangar to a spot with a clear view of the Junk Colossus right up to the chain-link fence designating the safe area. It was like waiting for a drive-in movie. To start, Charley had procured a top for his coffee and half a box of donuts. Positioning his sunglasses, he looked over to Dana, who was preparing her camera.

"Thirteen minutes, two seconds to lift off," he said, consulting a timer on his wrist phone.

Dana placed her coffee in the holder and tuned the radio to the top 10 stations. She looked at Charley, and their glances met with a silent exhale. She moved toward him and kissed him slowly without a shred of fear or hesitation.

Charley responded, not missing a beat. Exchanging series after series of fresh kisses, a natural pause came so as to savor the enjoyment of the newness of exploration. Charley forgot rules, guessing the point was physical attraction.

A loud siren heralding the imminent takeoff interrupted their embrace. Dana adjusted her lips from kissing Charley and placed herself into the seat. Within seconds, the jets below JC ignited and then raised the monolith and its cargo of tanks a short distance above the ground, hovering. It was the beginning of *MoonCorp*. It was a peak experience for both Dana and Charley, who found themselves holding hands as the majestic ship increased thrust to rise to the skies.

After a minute, it began its deliberate rise. It shook the ground building with a great force, shaking the van up and around, nearly launching Charley and Dan from their seats. With its trembling, the exhaust sent clouds of dust billowing about the area, blinding the windshield with dust and gravel. They looked at each other in disbelief for nearly a minute until the Colossus stopped far above the launch site at ten thousand feet. Its rear rockets ignited and shot forward and upward with intense force into the clear.

CHAPTER 16

Ed Zonic switched his computer screen from the cargo manifest to write a personal message to Nick Nicholas. Investing seven hours at the computer earned him a break, but he was not in the mood to run down and get a smoke and a candy bar.

Nick,

We have received our cargo shipment, it has been an engineering hell up there. We seem to have most things under control. The new personnel are under my feet, and the storage areas are filling with every kind of hotel nonsense you could imagine. I guess Steele wanted to send up as much as he could this trip. There is a general investigation being done later today on the meteor fragments supervised by some science team from Europe and Japan. I am going to try to get you a sample, but Dave has things pretty tight on the thing per Steele. In case you are wondering, yes, I am encrypting this message, so no worries there. The shift change lasts for about four days. If I can get a sample, I will get it to you via one of my trusted people who will not know what they are transporting, typical mule stuff.

We will all watch for the JC. I have programmed the cameras and secured the telescope with Simey's help. He is more excited about this than any of us. It should be here early tomorrow morning. Simey has volunteered to bunk in the control room to catch the landing.

Halley is staying another shift to restock the rooms. She is nice. Don't laugh. I am not the romantic type, you know that, Nick. Something is happening here, and I want you to know that it can happen to anyone. Keep ready, man; it could happen to you. What was it that Ada used to say all the time, "Life finds love" or something like that? Gotta go. Too gooey.

Zone.

Ed sent the message and then resolved to make the trip to the break room, preparing a cigarette as he went. Once Nick gets a girlfriend, he would be fine. Ed thought as he made his way down the hall and into the bunker break room where he propped his arm on the candy machine and stared at the selections. He mechanically lit the cigarette and spied the last *Payday* bar and, with a shake of his head, bought it, and hoped that the amenities people would refill the machine soon. He liked candy, but having it too often made him like it less.

MoonCorp's Junk Colossus hung in low Earth orbit, ready to receive the rocket-powered canisters. The multi-rocket rig that brought them nearly into outer space held the canisters still as the one-man tethered pods dropped from the bottom of the JC. The pilot steered his craft to land atop the canister. A guidance system directed the pod, and after a series of checks, the holding lock rig disengaged, leaving the canister to the pods to take them in zero gravity to the moon's surface.

Upon deploying the pods for six canisters, the massive cargo vessel, now not as heavy, reset itself for its next phase of the mission. A crew of about thirty cosmonaut engineers would make the JC their home for the next two months, laying the foundation as a base station for the greatest engineering feat in history.

Unlike the *TerraLuna* project where the entire bulk of the materials used were shipped via hundreds of small transport vessel sorties, the *MoonCorp* people planned only five missions to erect the hotel. The complex would be 25 percent larger and most definitely safer than its rival.

The first canister contained the paving machines that would turn the moon's silty surface into building slabs. The highest wattage of solar panels used on *TerraLuna* would be considered minimal emergency power in contrast to the radio power collection and transfer dynamic to be used on *MoonCorp*. The second canister contained the basic relay collectors that would immediately provide power to the smelters. Every machine that needed power would depend on the solar radio power transfer.

The collection satellite, as close as it possibly could be to the sun, attracts maximum raw energy. The radio systems special receptors are able to transfer this great power, almost as potent as the satellite experiences, using a radio signal. Without a doubt, this technology, developed by Charlie Porter and nurtured by *MoonCorp*, is pivotal to their success.

The third canister held hardware designed to secure outer wall sections to the foundation. Long poles to hold wall sections filled the canister as well as sealing tools and drills.

The fourth canister held vital veneering materials such as aluminum, Lexan, and rolls of protective lead sheeting to insulate the outer core. The fifth and sixth containers each held three rovers to allow mobility over the moon's surface. There had been little discussion as to the location of the hotel. A perfect spot near the northern pole offered optimum sunlight and exposure to Earth glow.

JC computer monitors signaled the canisters to land in a circular configuration. It hung in space for a system check and then fired its rear propulsion system and was on its way to the moon to land just to the south and remain until the first segment of the construction was complete. After a day's travel and all of an Earth night, the megalith found its way into the moon's gravitational pull. The JC coasted in like a graceful island in space slowly floating into place on the moon.

Using the tower cameras, Simey monitored the Junk Colossus floating gracefully in moon space. With a sarcastic tap of a screen, he relayed the live video to the open view screens throughout *TerraLuna*. "Here comes trouble."

*****

As Pepe was walking back to the *Hotel Progreso*, Dr. Sanchez called him with news that a car would be there for them at 8:00 a.m. A police car picked up Pepe and Tico right on time. Now full of the medicinal meal, they were as ready as they could be for the next day on the sea. The sergeant and his man took them in the odd-smelling police car with little ceremony to the dock. Soon Pepe stood outside his ship's door, for a moment wanting it to be the door to his home back in Celestún.

Enrique stood over the rail with one hand on his straw hat, searching the waves for his friend. Sanchez left watching the sub stats to join him. "He was right here near the ladder. Now he is gone. *Benito!*" he cried into the warm air.

Pepe came around and into action. He climbed the main hoist pole on a little silver ladder to get a better view. He reached the crow's nest and looked out at the sea thoughtfully.

"Do you see anything, Senor Fernandez?" yelled Sanchez from the deck. Pepe looked around before answering, not wanting to tell him no. He spotted the yellow-lined goody bag Benito had taken into the water. "There is his bag!" Pepe pointed about twenty yards behind the ship. "Its line must have snagged the ship."

Climbing down was considerably easier for Pepe. He opened a lock box in the side of the gunwale and removed a fishing rod. "Do you know how to use this?" he said to Enrique forcefully.

"*Si*, yes, senor," said Enrique.

"Fish that bag."

Sanchez looked to Pepe and then said, "We can use La Huevo to search for him. He has a chip. We must also grapple up a sample from the seafloor. Those rocks from outer space are becoming a hot item, Captain Fernandez."

Pepe looked into the small eyes of Dr. Sanchez and wondered what was really important to him, the boy or some rocks that might make him famous. Not able to answer his compound request to himself, he nodded and agreed to help the professor. "Okay, senor."

"Senor Fernandez, I have the bag!" exclaimed Enrique.

He hoisted the dripping bag across the deck. Pepe closed his nostrils and mouth at the wretched stench and then directed him to drop it into the live well.

Pepe called to the professor, "They are skins, molted skins like a snake."

"Stow them in the cooler," the captain directed Enrique, who obeyed, promptly refraining from breathing in the rancid fumes as little as possible.

Sanchez manned the computer and took the ship to the coordinates saved on the NavSys. The sea was not as cooperative as the crew was desperate. They reached the spot in twenty minutes. The sub was down again to view the seafloor. Choppy water lurched around the deck as they tried to find Benito through his ID chip embedded in his wrist.

Pepe went to the console next to the professor and activated the camera in the crow's nest to get a wider view of the area.

"I will send the sub on a grid pattern." Sanchez employed the sub on an automatic sweep.

All three men suppressed thoughts of the creatures they saw having eaten their young friend as the search continued. "What were those things down there, Senor Fernandez? Have you seen anything like that before?" said the young student.

"Enrique, these could be a variety of creatures, most probably some kind of giant sea arachnid. Way out here, they are too deep for us to fish and can grow very large. Sometimes when the food sources are low, they will attack anything, even each other. If they did attack Benito, I hope we will find him in time to give him a decent burial for his family's sake."

Sanchez looked to the captain with true admiration for Pepe's use of straightforward tact with Enrique. "You are good with people, senor. Do you and your wife have any children?"

"No. No children. Paloma and I weren't able to have any. We have Tico here. He gets enough attention for three children," he said, his voice devoid of humor. Tico, who was reclined in a shady spot near the helm, perked up his ears, knowing that his master was talking about him. He stood up and stretched his short legs, sensing his nap was over.

Pepe's mind began to tool on how to relay today's events to the authorities as well as to Benito's parents. It would not be so bad if they recovered the body, but it seemed unlikely. As the sub came closer to the central point of the impact, a surge of dread came over him of the thought of having to retrieve the half-eaten body onto the boat. He squinted to see something recognizable through the silt.

If he had been consumed or drawn away by a violent undercurrent, he most certainly was dead. Perhaps it was better if they did not find him, he thought momentarily. The dignity of a burial at sea might prove to less of a shock than a mangled corpse.

La Huevo reached the bottom and began to feed images of the seafloor. Rocks littered the bottom like the trail of a broken garbage truck. These samples were the focus of their trip. Did it have to be at such a cost? He rubbed his eyes to clear his thoughts when he saw something dart across the corner of his screen. The sub was within four revolutions of the vortex. More and more rocks and shed skins occupied his screen. Something white contrasted the dark mosh of sand and rock. The professor redirected the camera and steered it back to where he saw the white flash. Soon it came into view. A white milky mass of substance that coalesced at a thick core sat on the bottom, oozing into the surrounding water. He brought the camera's telephoto lens online. It appeared to be oblong and not quite six feet long.

A closer look verified that it was not resting on the bottom but rather floating a few inches from the seafloor. Backing the sub away ten yards and lowering to a parallel angle, he tried to get a better look. Sanchez pulled himself back from the screen in amazement to see at least four of the creatures he had seen before affixed to the bottom of the white form. Their legs clenched the underside and were busy emitting the viscous white fluid adding to the bulk of the object. The bodies from what he could tell were smooth yet segmented. The fifty or so pairs of legs moved rhythmically, securing the ooze to the mass. The heads seemed small, very much like an insect by design, perhaps like an ant. Sanchez knew they could not be any kind of a lobster he had seen before, especially since the tails were designed for swimming as in snakes or eels.

The creatures seemed very interested in their work to make something. It did not take long for Pepe to join him at the screen and less time to suspect that Benito might be at the center of the white mass.

"*Mi dios*," exclaimed Pepe. "What are they doing?"

"They seem to be making some sort of cocoon, like a spider does to a fly," the professor suggested.

"I am assuming that it is Benito they are covering with their mucus. We may assume he is dead, senor. This video will be proof for the police. I am going to circle it and get some video from another angle," Professor Sanchez said, using the toggle to direct the yellow egg around the milky mass of goo.

The sub began a wide circle, revealing the uncomfortable sight of a person as the new angle exposed the end of the body. Benito's foot could clearly be seen.

Several dozen smaller ones were scurrying along the bottom, jumping onto the group to join in. There wasn't enough of Benito for all of them. Smaller ones would fall away, not able to find a spot to grab on since the entire underside was dark with the larger ones all busy building onto the carcass that was growing to about six feet long and nearly three feet across. Several of the sea spiders launched themselves at the submersible, trying to attach themselves, squeezing their white sputum on the yellow egg. They could not seem to get a grip; the three stared hard into the screen at the virulent creatures.

"The smaller ones are trying to get to the sub. I am bringing her up and over," Sanchez noted, his eyes still fixed on the screen.

La Huevo flew sideways up and away, still holding the camera on the event twenty feet below. As it turned away, Sanchez saw a fissure slowly fill his screen. Rock pieces of various sizes were strewn around the hole's edge. Its diameter was indeterminable from the sub's angle. It ran along the rim, carefully keeping a safe distance. Swarms of creatures less than a foot long zipped and darted along the floor, testing their tails to swim higher.

Sanchez looked at Pepe for a moment to reassure him. "Senor Captain, I do not believe it would be in the best interest of our project to bring it on board. Do you agree?"

Either a pang of sadness or hunger hit Pepe's stomach. Whatever unwillingness he felt to abandon the boy failed to find words. The captain simply made the sign of the cross and gave a nod. "May he rest in peace and all the souls lost at sea."

Sanchez looked at the captain. "We should get a sample of the rock and move away from this spot. I believe we have enough video. *La Huevo* is equipped with a retractable claw that can reach down and take some rocks. We must have this analyzed."

He typed in a command, and a small claw encased in a mini egg-shaped housing emerged from the base of the sub propelled by a miniature motor, and rudders made their way to the bottom. A halogen light and camera guided it to the fissure's edge. The split screen now offered a perspective from the mini-egg's camera. It whirred its way into the depth.

The white bulk was now covered with at least fifty creatures. Most of the rock was alike, yet for every forty pieces, there was another type of rock, discernibly darker and more porous than the rest.

The sea bugs bumped and inspected the claw box as it came closer to the bottom. As they rammed into it, squirts of milky fluid shot out as if to subdue the interloper. Sanchez knew he had to act fast. Moving the claw over an appropriate-sized piece of shell to fit in the box, he spotted a section of rock that would travel easily within the housing. It opened, releasing the claw. It reached out, immediately retrieving the piece, and retracted it into the bubble-domed egg.

A flurry of sand blinded the camera. Sanchez wound the bubble back to the sub and then repositioned it to get a clear view of the second set of rocks. He enabled the second claw and sent it into the clear water. He clawed the more porous rock and, after a few attempts, scooped one in and reeled it into the pod. Another spasm of legs, heads, and goo tails sent the claw askew as it was trolled back to the egg.

Once the claws were secure with their booty in the plastic bubbles, the professor sent the command for *La Huevo* to surface. "Prepare to bring the sub on board."

Enrique cleared the deck. Pepe started the winch. It wound the cable into the spool. He checked the guide to be certain that it rolled evenly.

Twenty minutes passed before the sub made its way to the surface. Another twenty passed as the crew replaced the slimy sub into the aluminum box, snapping the panels closed, eager to get underway the rock and egg samples still clutched in the mini-pods.

Pepe moved with surety to the helm and started the engine. He engaged the pre-set coordinates for Merida Marina. *La Fresca* pulled them through the sea to the shoreline in the distance. Pepe looked on as Dr. Sanchez and the Enrique reviewed the videodisc of the events at the bottom. They were silent.

"Senor Captain, will we be home before it becomes dark?" said Enrique, breaking silence.

Pepe gave a silent nod to Enrique as the boat pushed into the sea. Once the ship came away from the impact site, the white floating blob hit the surface now nearly twenty feet long and five feet wide, with a hundreds of seething bugs affixed to their inverted raft. The ooze reacted with the sunshine and turned from a sticky fluid into a harder buoyant material much like a mixture of tree bark and Styrofoam. Steam fumed from the raft as it bobbed, an amalgam of coalesced sputum propelled shoreward, and the sun now began its daily journey into the horizon.

CHAPTER 17

Nick designed the plans for the spiracle defense system inclusive of multiple prototypes for demonstration and schematics for several test applications. This next test was on a much larger scale. Shipment of the test hardware arrived two days before the JC liftoff. Piles of numbered curved alloy pipes lined the floor, occupying nearly a third of the rear wall of the hangar. Nick walked the sea of pipes in five- and ten-foot lengths, inspecting the quality of the holes and ends that would be screw-locked together on the moon in the staging hall once the artificial gravity had been established in the shell of the building.

Estimates were running at a thirty- to fifty-day window before they could lay the pipes. He triggered his radio to call the transport crew to retrieve the test pieces to be placed into the hangar for assembly. Nick leaned against the wall, staring at the pipes that looked like a deck on some alien battleship he might have read about in some alien space novel. Habitually, he reviewed the system in his mind again, integrating proportional considerations. Technical problems did not interrupt his thoughts that now wandered into the gloom of loneliness. Love and family life was such a part of his plan for the future he now found himself not living.

Resolving that, he was married to his work, and these projects were his children which had helped him through the past few years. Now that he was drawing closer to the reality of the moon program and his DNA sequencing, he wanted so much to have the success with his soul mate. He replayed the scenes in his mind with a ritualistic exactness from that night ten years ago. He and Ada had been on the way home to his apartment after going out for pizza and a jazz floor show at Joey's club.

"Up a Lazy River" played on the stereo. Classy Jazzy had performed this tune, and he bought her a copy sold in the lobby. He had asked the band to sign her copy. She was thrilled when he produced it in the car.

Closing his eyes, he savored the remembrance of how she enjoyed the music, the atmosphere, and the food that night. The drive home was free from fear and worry of any kind. Being together with her had no effect that surpassed any empiric scientific breakthrough.

He looked at her, and they sang together with smiling eyes that reflected his indisputable definition of love. Where on Earth could he find that feeling again? Nick may not have known that he always made sincere eye contact with all people.

He needed knowledge to be understood by those to whom he spoke, free of doubt, and any questions must be settled directly. His stare became friendlier as his listeners communed with his thought process. This won Nick many friends with whom he spent long unscheduled hours. He was steadfast in believing this communication skill was nurtured during his time with Ada, a motivational force aiding him in his work, even now if only in spirit.

The car turned a bend in the road. He adjusted the car in his lane, not equipped with the guidance system found on the highway today. It would have brought him around the corner like a roller coaster. For a split second, he denied reality, meeting the headlights of the oncoming car with a gaze that looked like nothing less than anger. The car was in his lane and not moving out. The curve left him little room to escape collision. Turning the car to the right while braking bounced his blue Chevy against the other car, and it careened off the road into an unavoidable tree. Instinctively, he thrust his arm across Ada's chest. Nick relived the nausea that found its putrid way into his stomach that night. Her head slammed against the window, breaking it with an impossible thud, leaving her instantaneously limp.

The jazz played fearlessly in the night as blood moistened his head. He had hit his head on the roof of the car as it bounced up and off the road. The song repeated itself in his mind to this day when he remembered her. He loved her even as she sat dead and unable to respond to his pleas for life.

Up a lazy river where the robin's song wakes a bright new morning, where we can roll along . . . There are blue skies up above, as long as we're in love, we'll be up a lazy river, how happy we'll be, up a lazy river with me!

It was such a happy song. It was their song. She would have wanted him to think of her whenever it played, even now.

Nick roused himself from his dream, wiping the mist from his eyes to see an electric truck enter the hangar. He waved to the two men there to transport the pipes. He helped the workers load the material and rode along with them in the back to the hangar in the still-dark morning. Why did she have to die? Nick tossed his issue to the stars fading from the cool sky as day approached.

Just after eight, Charley appeared with his doctoral student. Nick was impressed with Dana's physical beauty and amazed at her clinical aptitude. He mentioned to Charley that he thought she was a rare find.

Nick welcomed questions from Dana about field generators, going as far as opening one to review the basics of their operation. Lunch came and went briskly for Charley, who loved his work just a shade above his food. He was proud of the power relay concept and spent a good deal of time with Dana explaining the reception and transfer dynamics. The crew and its designers stopped for a moment to recognize the significance of their work to the ultimate success of *MoonCorp*.

By two o'clock, the majority of the domed frame was complete. It stood twenty feet high and forty across with a depth of ten feet. It looked like a giant version of toy building set he had as a child. Nick instructed the crew how to set the screw locks and seal the matrix.

The power relay was ready to plug into the format. Installing the field generators that sat at each of the eight corners required template support, and double seals took the better part of the morning. It looked like the outline of a cube with a smaller cube on top. The shiny glass-like reception power relay box was designed to plug into the hub field generator that was painted red to distinguish it from the others sat in the lower base of the frame. Nick opened his phone and called Stan Duncan.

"Stan, this is Nick. I will be ready test within the hour. Get ready to be impressed."

"Nick, you know how important this is to us. I want to see it work before I start inviting others, especially Romanoff. I'll be there in forty minutes." Stan closed the line.

Nick stood at the control center, and after running a seal check that came up secure, he activated the local spiracle defense system that was able to operate in a wide range of gravity levels, including the Earth, moon, and eventually on any surface with varying gravities. It worked just fine. His wrist phone chimed with an alert he programmed to inform him of any special news reports. With a command into his phone, he turned the screen on the control panel to display the Central News Network.

A white-haired newswoman appeared on screen.

"Good afternoon. We bring you a special report from around the nation and the world. A team from the University of Merida in the Yucatan region of Mexico announced today that they will send a research team to seek out samples of the meteor shower that resulted in damaging Gerhard Steele's multibillion-world-dollar TerraLuna moon base hotel and convention center slated to open later this year. The world's foremost experts will meet to determine how the projectile evaded the Skylar defense sensors that track potentially dangerous materials in space. TerraLuna CEO Steele commented that new technologies are in development to prevent safety issues from affecting the grand opening of the first hotel on the moon. Also, this week, the MoonCorp company launched its first construction crew to begin the second or maybe the first hotel center on the moon . . ."

The hangar manager watched the news on his office television and snapped on the monitors in the hangars so that all could see. The hangar workers looked up in unison to the quadruple televisions suspended from the ceiling to take notice of the news report that continued to give details of their work to the world. When it was complete, a chorus of cheers and applause offered a sound not heard in the two weeks they had been there.

Nick witnessed Dana giving Charley a hug. Turning to not let Charley see him watching, Nick clapped louder and shook a technician's hand. The television stayed on after the show, which was unusual in the hangars. Nick reminded himself to contact satellite control to prepare to transmit the power wave to their coordinates. The amount of power needed to engage the local defense system required an enormous amount of energy that could only be supplied from the solar satellite radio power system. Nick radioed the hangar manager, telling him that they will need the hangar's ceiling door open around three o'clock. The receptors were located on the roof of the hangar. Nick hesitated from the idea to go up there and recheck the circle panels.

Charley appeared from the storage hangar in an electric truck, carrying five mannequins. "I have the test subjects, but they didn't come with any clothes. I hope this does not offend anyone. I had considered giving them old clothes from deep in my closet. I am fairly sure *that* would offend someone."

No one seemed to mind. Charley and Dana posed the figures within the lattice of pipe. They could not resist putting them in dancing positions, laughing to themselves while a crew of engineers sidled in came and went about their business of staring at the lattice of spiraled pipes. From the control panel, Nick lowered a net on a crane suspended from the side wall of the hangar. A cart filled with bowling balls was soon emptied into the net by the crew and raised with a winch controlled by a remote box wired to the wall with a power cord. The balls would be dropped seventy feet and theoretically not slam into the dancing guests below. Nick scanned the excited area for his boss, Stan. They were about ready to start the test when the chief appeared from the front of the hangar. He walked briskly to the test site with an assortment of investors, all in suits and taking in the wonders of the edifice. Stan greeted everyone with a smile and handshake in hopes of a successful test. He made his way to Nick on a ladder, checking the field generator boxes.

"Dr. Nicholas!" he called from below. "*The safety of our guests is our most valuable asset.* How does that sound for a slogan?" Nick looked down and, without words in his involvement, gave Stan Duncan and his team an encouraging thumbs-up.

"Those balls look dangerous," Stan said, calling up.

"Actually, Stan, we are not sure where the balls will land. Stand around at your own risk. They should fly outside." Realizing he had drawn a crowd, Nick opened his wrist phone and said, "Intercom hangar." His voice was not live for all to hear. "Everyone has parked his or her car in the third hangar lot? The safest place here is in the lattice. Would you care to step inside?" Nick offered without smiling.

"Nick, we paid for those mannequins. Let's make them last. Why don't you run a test without them first?"

"I was hoping to join them myself. Does anyone want to go to the moon and see what it is like to survive a meteor attack?" Nick announced to the crowd that responded to him in silence. He climbed down the ladder and made his way to the control panel.

"Stan, how are you going to get people to make reservations if they have reservations of their own as to the safety of the hotel?" Pierre announced, always trying to be controversial.

"I am sure this will work. You saw the prototype at our meeting. This is the same technology, only larger. Charley, get your cameras ready." Nick held his ground as Stan tried to gather his response.

"I would rather you not be inside when those things fall," the Frenchman said with an attempt at finality.

"I have to be inside. The control cord is not long enough. I am not going to stand against the wall to witness my success. I want to be in the center of it all. If I was not 100 percent sure this would work, I wouldn't do it. What do I have to lose, my life? Oh well. I must live life, and I won't do it against the wall!"

Nick was encouraged by several grinning crew members, his friends with resolution that all would be safe. He held the control box to release the bowling balls attached to a cord and then walked into the lattice with the mannequins, and nobody was going to stop him. Stan took a long look at him, scrutinizing his change. What could have made this quiet genius shift so abruptly? Whatever it was, the look in his eyes bordered on anger. Not having seen Nick get angry, truly he did not want to experience it now.

Stan looked at Nick with his best fatherly mien, and realizing that there was no chance to sway him, he nodded officially. "Have it your way. I hope you won't be offended if I ask you to at least wear a hard hat?"

"I'm okay with that. I suggest that everyone pull back to the side of the hangar. Theoretically, the balls should bounce straight up. I do not foresee any problems. Yet *safety is our most valuable asset* here at *MoonCorp*," Nick directed to the crowd.

A technician approached Nick, holding a yellow hard hat, which the scientist effused, followed by Charley taking his place at the control console.

"The satellite will activate at three o'clock and stay on as long as you need. Burt says hello. I have programmed the camera banks to make a recording of the experiment from different angles," Charley shouted from the control console after several unsuccessful attempts to tap into the intercom system. Dana giggled a bit, and the other students and technicians began to gather at the far end, donning helmets as they went.

Within fifteen minutes, all systems being operational, Nick gave the signal for everyone to be well out of the way. He slipped between the mannequins housed by vertical pipes holding the net control attached to a wire and reaffirmed quietly his belief in his prototype.

"You may start the video, Dr. Porter," Nick said into his wrist phone.

Charley Porter started the video and then consulted the control console for an indication that highly concentrated radioed solar energy was indeed being sent to the receptor panels on the roof. Its sound was firm and present through the thin metal hangar walls. All in attendance were awed at the presence of such a fierce force.

"Radio satellite power is being received," Nick said through the intercom. "All system go! We are at full reception capability. I think that may be too much power. Dialing it back to four points, Dr. Porter."

Nick made an adjustment and then scuttled to the center of the structure, striking a pose with one hand on the shoulder of a female mannequin, and explained to the audience, his voice resounding in the hangar.

"The field generators are calibrated to operate in our atmosphere, and they are adjustable to perform in a variety of gravitational situations, making them useful anywhere in the galaxy," Nick said, deliberately choosing his words carefully and speaking clearly, knowing that it would be televised as part of an advertisement for the company.

Nick called to Charley, not at the control console, "Activate the hub field generators!"

Charley paused dramatically and started the machine. A hum shook the entire lattice as solar power surged through the system. The others in the room felt a breeze from the spiracles and saw bits of paper and dust swirl around.

Offering a five-second countdown, coddling the box in his hands, he pressed the button, and the net released the balls. They fell with a velocity that would surely break through any roof he could think of. A ball about to hit the lattice immediately shot up with a greater velocity than that of its falling. A second ball shot up as well and hit one of the other falling balls, slamming it up through the open roof of the hangar. Another ball ricocheted and flew toward the front of the hangar, bouncing and rolling to the feet of the onlookers. The crowd spread forward to see where the balls went. A few of them were still flying through the open roof, then falling back into the antigravitational field being held aloft by the spiracle field. A loud thud startled Stan. It must have been one of the balls landing on the roof. The remainder of the balls had landed in the field beyond the hangar and created mini craters. Nick stood among the mannequins unharmed and unmoved. Charley looked to Nick, who gave him the "turn it up" signal. The bowling balls held aloft by the stream suddenly shot up and out into the field. Nick gave the "cut off" signal. Charley switched off the system and ran out to meet the others who were cheering with amazement.

Nick was pleased and called everyone to attention. "We have a successful test. Yet we may want to have another. Can anyone think of something larger we can drop at it that can go a bit faster?" The group quelled. No one said anything.

CHAPTER 18

Arpit Patel never imagined that his skills as a forensic scientist with an MS in physics would land him a job on the moon. He was making more money than any of his coworkers at the Dallas City Morgue, where he had worked for three years. Luckily, his uncle had done some electrical consulting for Gerhard Steele. Without this connection, he certainly would be assisting in autopsies today rather than diagnostic analysis for *TerraLuna*. Any material needing to have its components broken down fell to him. Finding a job in a crime lab was his dream. Yet his current position made him re-evaluate this dream. This experience was undoubtedly the luckiest thing to happen to him.

That he was one of the youngest people on the *TerraLuna* staff did not intimidate him as much as resolving to maintain a decidedly low-key attitude out of sheer amazement that he was hired. He was bursting on the inside. He was famous back home. Being of average height and weight and having small brown eyes and nondescript black hair, he really regarded himself as ordinary. Unmarried, he found his job experience to be quite exciting. Most of the women on *TerraLuna* were smart and effective, seemingly easily turned on by Earth glow.

These natural tendencies in women fascinated him. Yet Arpit's attraction to women had practical limitations. His family trying to arrange a date or even a marriage seemed barbaric to him. Dating free from his parents and sisters was a great adventure for him—in a word, liberating. Passing the physical test to gain entry to *TerraLuna* was not hard. He had been active in track and field. Women spent time with him with hopes of intimacy, which was a credit to his good looks. Yet jumping into bed with every woman he spoke to was not his style. It was only the thrill of possibility that made him one of the more outgoing persons on *TerraLuna*. It sufficed.

He was aware that he would work for much less than some other professional candidates, which was a major influence in his appointment. Not giving much attention to the details of the terms of his employment, he continued his trip to the vault to retrieve the asteroid sample, pushing his aluminum cart along the hall of the laboratory wing located down the corridor from the administrative department on the far west side of the complex. His passkey allowed him access to nearly all the research and development areas, including the quarantine bays where the extraterrestrial finds were kept.

He opened the door into the room, flicking on the lights as he entered. The room was empty, save for a long metal table. The walls were lined with lock boxes of all shapes and sizes able to store the most valuable commodities of *TerraLuna*. He did not know what was in most of them. The west wall comprised one large door leading to the largest of the containment areas. He wondered what that might be used for: giant alien ships! He fumbled through his white lab coat for his glasses and handheld computer. It was programmed with the location number and access key of the sample he was asked to retrieve for today's initial examination. Arpit scanned the keycard, authorizing it to open the sample box.

It had been close to a month since the accident, and much of *TerraLuna* had been rebuilt. Lately, the staff had been more interested in viewing the *MoonCorp* project from the observation lounge than any other activities. It had become the place to meet others. A refreshment station was brought in to accommodate the ten to fifteen people found peering out at the reconstruction at any given time.

Arpit located the number and wheeled the cart to locker number 17. He slid the card and the red "Locked" light changed to green. Inside was the three-by-two aluminum box locked with a similar slide mechanism, its red light glowing. He put his key away, feeling the six-inch sample canister and some jelly beans in his pocket.

The surveillance camera's red light blinked, acknowledging his presence. Motion detectors activated the cameras to record the comings and goings in the room. He would have to palm a sample later, a more dangerous time to do so since he would be assisted when he opened the box in the lab. He dared not try it now. He hefted the box onto the cart and left the room, trying to seem unsuspicious. Ed put him up to this. He liked him, but his girlfriend occupied most of his free time, which from what he gathered was not much anyway. Video games were their thing; he played alone lately. Zonic promised to pay him a neat sum for a souvenir of his adventure at the crater. He had said that when he told the story back on Earth about the gauge malfunctions, he needed a bit of the rock that nearly cost him his life to make his story more effectual. It was only a meteorite sample.

The rocks shook along in the box. The sound, along with the rattle of the cart, made for a noisy and nervous trip to the laboratory. No one was in the lab. Arpit honed in on the camera's red light in the corner that had begun taping once he entered the room. He would have to do it when they had the sample out before he brought it back to the locker. It should not be difficult to do; it was rather more difficult thinking about it.

A moist sweat had begun to dampen his collar. It was seven fifty-six. The others were due to arrive at eight o'clock. He activated the diagnostic machines and prepared the various tests that were to be performed this morning. Footsteps could be heard in the hall. Soon Pat Beck and a girl he did not know entered the lab quietly. They nodded quickly to Arpit and prepared their pocket computers to take notes of the analysis.

"Thanks, Arpit. I hope you have the right one. We want number 17 . . . and you have brought number 17!" the tall blond man of about forty-nine said with the slightest spin of clinical sarcasm. "This is Becky Morris. She will be assisting and taking notes for her dissertation. She won't miss a trick!" He slapped Arpit hard on the back and moved to the diagnostic machine to see that it was already on.

"Hi. Nice to meet you. I'm Arpit Patel." He offered her his hand, which she shook politely. She took an extended moment to replace a strand of her dull blonde hair that had fallen away from her bun.

Arpit thought one egocentric blonde-haired person was hard to deal with. Here he was with two, and at least one of them was not going to miss a trick. For an instant, he toyed with the idea of not taking sample if the opportunity did not arise. He would simply tell Ed that he would have to tell his bar story with some other rock and pretend.

"I think we are ready. I would like to run a general density scan first to see what sort of metal we are dealing with here. We assume most spacefaring material is comprised of metal. Mr. Patel, would you open the case, please?"

Involuntarily, Arpit focused on the streamline slope of his nose that gave him some kind of credibility. He nodded silently and passed his keycard through the slot. Red light changed to green. They were each snaking their hands into special rubber gloves that came up past their elbow.

They reminded Arpit of the gloves used by cattle breeders to inseminate cows. He moved to the drawer and put on a pair for himself, fighting nausea.

"Becky, I think we should wear some breathing protection."

Three of them placed a blue and white rubber-coated mouthpiece and nosepiece that Arpit thought looked like an athletic supporter. Upon placing it over their mouths, an automatic seal formed, allowing them to work and speak while the tiny electronic filter cleaned their breathing supply.

Gloved and masked, Arpit opened the container to reveal several chunks of rock that, if reassembled, might have the volume of a softball. Arpit instantly sized up a segment that would fit in his tube and serve well as a conversation piece for Ed.

"Arpit, that top drawer has a tray and the one below it some forceps. Bring those over, won't you?" Pat said with a brave level of command, trying to impress the girl.

Arpit and Pat removed the pieces and placed them under a device that radiated a light and displayed data on a screen adjacent to the scanner. Pat adjusted several dials, explaining the process to Becky.

"This device can perform X-rays, infrared/temperature, density, and even a new version of carbon dating. Do you believe that office people used carbon to make duplicates with paper back in the last century? At any rate, our version of the carbon dating test will determine the age of the sample without the mess."

Arpit was amazed at how fast he spoke. Getting women must be a cinch for a fast talker. Becky hung on his every word and watched him arrange the samples below the yellow light. The density scan was over within seconds. Data began to file onto the screen; the three of them closed in to read the data bathed in the glow of the computer. Becky was the first one to speak as the men reviewed the information with concern.

"It's not solid," she said plainly.

"I'll have the computer design a 3-D," Pat said, tapping the console above the viewing area. As the computer drew a three-dimensional schematic, Becky took notes and prepared to download the information onto her pocket computer. When Becker wasn't looking, she took a quick snapshot of the rocks. This was something the marginally wholesome woman did, thinking he wasn't looking. She was not told to take a photograph. Arpit decided not to bust her. He waited to see what else she was going to do. Maybe he would ask her out. She was sort of rude—in a dumb sort of way.

The computer diagram indicated that here were various hollow places within the largest piece. Arpit took the forceps and turned one of the smaller pieces (not the one he was planning to steal) so that the broken side could be seen in the magnifier.

"These pockets are consistent with some platinum metal groups. We should be able to determine what kind of metals are here and the nature of these cavities."

Becky took initiative at this pause in her findings to stick her computer in the side of the console and press the button to download. Within five seconds, the data was stored, and Arpit followed. Pat stared up from some manual notes he was writing with his electric pen and then took a copy for himself.

"Okay, the mineral analysis test will help us determine the electron configurations of the varying metals that are present in the sample, assuming that these metals are available in our periodic table. We could very well find a new element that would make me famous. How does the element Beckium sound after Patrick Beck?"

He offered with sincerity.

"Not Patium. That sounds like something you spread on fancy crackers."

Becky laughed immediately. "Beckium. It sounds great. It's my name! Perfect."

Not amused, Arpit stopped Pat from changing the test dial, pointing to the data screen.

"Look here. The pockets are less dense, and there is something in there that has a very low-density rating. The point is it is hollow. The two blondes exchanged looks with appreciation at the young technician's foresight.

"Maybe we can call it Armptium, after you," said Becky with a smile.

"My name is Arpit, not Armpit!" he said, protecting some old wounds from reopening.

"I'm sorry," she quickly apologized.

Yellow light changed to orange as the scanning machine hummed an altogether different tone. Mechanical movements within the machine allowed new testing elements to be brought into place to determine the configurations of electrons. The screen wiped out and restarted. Soon list of numbers began to line the screen. Arpit checked his computer to translate the numbers into recognizable elements. The computer would do this eventually, but he decided to show off to Becky that he could do it faster. She was mildly impressed.

"Iridium and osmium seem to be the main components, with traces of rhodium and several other metals that appear in atomic numbers without names yet." Arpit offered his screen to Pat for approval. Taking his handheld computer and comparing it to the numbers lining on the monitor, Pat furrowed his brow for a long moment without saying anything and then bluntly handed it back to Arpit, who continued to cipher the translation for his own satisfaction.

"It could be Beckium . . ."

Footsteps were heard in the hallway. Arpit knew it had to be Steele's board people wanting to get a firsthand look at the sample. The door opened, and a slight Japanese man in his late twenties and a barely taller Yugoslavian entered, both looking as if they spent most of their days in classrooms.

The academics entered with an importance that accompanies absolute mastery of field. Pat broke away from his thoughts of naming the new elements and greeted the two men.

"Dr. Nogishi, Dr. Meleyev, so happy to have you here. I think you will find our testing so far very interesting."

The men fell quickly to positions at the monitor and then were briefed by Pat. Arpit stepped back to allow them to review the information. Obviously, Pat took control of the experiments to be able to take credit for anything that was worthwhile in the findings. They found throughout the day that the most interesting test concerned the small pockets in the large piece that seemed to contain a very low-density material. Pat instructed Arpit to scrape the surface of the smaller rock for suspension documentation.

Arpit removed the pieces and brought them to another station for processing. The next test involved drilling into the large section for a sample of the material within. Pat Beck commanded the machine while consulting the instructions for its use on his personal computer. Arpit was alone with the smaller bits as the rest gathered around a drilling machine that held it fast while a tempered drill bit eased slowly into the space chunk.

The sound of the drill seemed to charm the scientists. Arpit saw his chance in their preoccupation. This would be a good time to palm a sample.

While arranging the pieces of rock on the tray, he pulled one into the palm of his sweaty hand and held it there for a few minutes, hoping the cameras had not taken notice of the theft. Drilling continued for another couple of minutes, and Arpit battled the sweat from revealing his fear. He moved over to the group, casually placing his gloved hand into his lab coat. He dropped the sample and looked on to see three broken bits on the floor. Pat worked fervently through the rock, hoping not to break a fourth.

"These bits cost a thousand world dollars each," said Pat, beginning to turn an even bolder shade of red.

"Mr. Steele will be happy to know as much as possible about this rock so that we can prevent it from destroying this nice hotel. I am sure he can afford it," said Nogishi. His laconic partner nodded in ascension, offering a tiny smile.

The drill dipped deeper into the rock. Bits of metallic jetsam were contained in the cubic plastic housing that encompassed the vice holding the rock steady. After a few minutes of careful drilling, the bit sunk deeper without breaking.

The group held their silence with a sense of devotion.

Without warning, Becky gave a shriek as the bit fell the distance of a half an inch into the rock. Pat stopped the drill. Excitement billowed in the wide eyes of the onlookers. A murmur emerged as a whitish gray liquid welled over the edge of the hole made warm by friction. It oozed over and spilled out, dripping along the sides of the rock.

Pat stopped the drill and called for Arpit.

"Bring a sterile liquid suspension kit and a collection tool now!" Arpit moved to the supply drawers and found the items Pat wanted and rushed them to the drill site. Pat unlatched the small plastic kit, took a small spatula-like tool, and began to collect the liquid. He instructed Becky to open the small, flat dish containing a clear, viscous material to keep the sample from drying out. Pat placed the scant drippings into the dish and continued to get all he could. She covered the dish. Arpit instinctively started the electron-hyper microscope. Soon the magnification levels on the screen accessed by the lab computer's screens listed higher and higher until silent awe was the only description of the atmosphere in the fluorescent-lit lab.

"It's moving," said Meleyev, the first thing he had said since he entered the room.

CHAPTER 19

It wasn't a usual day for Pepe and Tico. Who could possibly imagine this happening to a poor fisherman and his dog? Rather than the calm of the sea, they were met by the buzz and odors of the city of Progreso. The local police could be seen waiting for them at the marina. Feeling unsure, Pepe phoned Paloma for the third time today and told her the police were waiting at the marina with their lights flashing.

After shaking many hands of people he did not know, Pepe, Tico, and Professor Sanchez drove in the police car into the crowded downtown area to the police station. News vans were in the parking lot. Dreading to have to talk to reporters, which led to being on the news, Pepe tightened his shoulders as he pulled into the police station parking lot. They bustled into the police station where Pepe signed a waiver stating that his findings were to be property of the university and some other legal things he did not quite understand; from what was explained to him, it was a nondisclosure agreement. Looking out of the glass window, he recognized the young news reporter Dahlia Morales from channel 2 news loitering professionally in the lobby outside Sergeant Aroja's office.

He turned to the balding man with an unreal potbelly tucked in his stretch pants.

"Senor, must I talk to the news lady? I do not want to say anything for the public. I am sure Dr. Sanchez can take care of that."

Sanchez was fixing himself some coffee, overhearing Pepe's fearful tone.

"It's okay, my friend. I will talk to Ms. Morales. You and Tico go to the hotel. Go out through the back door. It is only a few minutes' walk down the street. I will keep her occupied. I reserved a patio room so you can take Tico outside when he needs to go."

Pepe shook his hand vigorously and looked to the sergeant, who nodded a dismissal. It was nearly two o'clock as Pepe left the station through the back door with his overnight bag, came around to the side of the police station, and untied Tico from the bicycle rack where he waited patiently for his master. Some students were waiting outside in support of Dr. Sanchez. Pepe walked on with his dog, hoping they didn't recognize him.

The *Hotel Progreso* was only ten doors from the police station. They walked past a food cart, and he decided to come back after he checked in and bring back some steak burrito for dinner. He thought to himself as they strolled unfamiliar streets now basking in the afternoon sunlight. It was rather busy with small shops and an occasional corporate computer store. The summer pedestrians of the little town were busying themselves going home among the rows of closely placed buildings, hoping to enjoy the cooling evening.

An occasional electric car whirred by, playing local music, mostly driven by young people. Progreso was a coastal town, and many of the youths surfed or attended the University in Merida. A group of teenagers were standing on the stoop of a sweet shop, playing soccer with a crushed milk carton. He passed a young couple that was making a fuss over how cute Tico was, which was bound to happen as Tico was a cute little dog.

After checking in, they walked to their room and unpacked a few things he brought from the boat. He would have been happy to sleep on the boat, but Dr. Sanchez and the police sergeant insisted they stay at the hotel on them. The room was simple and clean. The large bed took most of the space in the room. The curtains matched the floral design of the bedspread. The sliding patio doors led out onto a railed cement area of about six by four feet. Tico ran out and inspected the area. Realizing he hadn't eaten in six hours, he washed his hands and face and went out to buy some food.

Pepe couldn't help feeling like a tourist in the bustling little town. His thoughts often turned home to his comfortable chair and smiling wife. He would walk to the marina before dawn and be underway hopefully before the sun rose. His eyes rose to the steam from the food cart taking him a bit faster while putting the unpleasantness out of his mind. Pepe ordered enough food to fill two bags, deciding to eat back at the hotel. Soon he and Tico were reclining on the bed with an array of burrito, rice, beans, gazpacho, and some orange sodas.

After their feast, Pepe felt sleep rapidly approaching. He forced himself up to let Tico out and brushed his teeth. The air was cool on the patio. Looking up to the clear sky, he wondered about the meteors he had seen that night and how they related to the strange absence of shrimp. Anyhow, it was something to toss across his mind while he tried to get comfortable enough to sleep. Sometimes it was hard for him to sleep right away, but not for Tico; he could sleep very easily. Pepe thought it would be nice to be able to knock off like that whenever he needed. Pepe turned down the stiff bedding and tried to get comfortable. The hotel could try using some fabric softener, he noted as sleep rather easily overtook him. Tico curled up at his master's feet and was already fast asleep.

*****

The morning in the lab passed quickly as the team documented line after line of information on the rock and its secret center. Arpit involuntarily popped some of his jelly beans when no one was looking. After one thirty, Becky Morris suggested that they should take a break. Agreeing quickly, they readied themselves, but not before Pat warned them. "Steele wants this classified, and I am sure that there will be no problem with that. This discovery will have ramifications. Any release of information will be handled through official *TerraLuna* channels. Is this clearly understood?"

Each of them nodded, now ready for something to eat. "We will take an hour."

Arpit's imagination ran away with thoughts of being caught with a sample of the top-secret rock. The sooner he got it to Zonic, the safer he would feel. Pat locked the lab, and they made their way to the cafeteria.

As they walked briskly along the white fluorescent corridor in silence, Arpit's face was beginning to flush. Pat looked at him with a look that might have been suspicion. He nodded briefly and continued down the hall. Calling Ed now was out of the question. He would have to wait. The rock scratched in his pocket. He dared not look down. He imagined it to be protruding like a boulder out of his pocket. He took a deep breath and composed himself as they entered the lunchroom.

Most of the noon lunchers were gone. leaving less than a dozen people to their meals. Arpit had hoped to see Ed in the room. He was not there. They ate together occasionally at the same table, but not today. Arpit did not expect this much tension. Steele must know this meteor was different, and he was right. The initial analysis led them to believe that the rock's strange liquid pockets had biological properties. A find like this would have the scientific community beating their desks for a report.

Pat Beck would most certainly want to take credit. Arpit was sure Meleyev and Nogishi would try to exercise their influence to do the same. The young Becky Morris sat across him and was not a bad-looking woman who could handle herself in social situations. In fact, she looked for social situations. Arpit would not mind getting to know her better today if his stomach wasn't so nauseous.

Arpit's thoughts began to wander away but seemed to fall back into the cleavage of Becky Morris when his wrist phone rang. "I need to take this. Excuse me."

He shook his head visibly, clicking open the phone. He pulled an earring silencer on a retractable wire at the back of the phone. He clipped it behind his ear. He strummed the taut wire the reverberation field spread, emitting a path of purple light across his face, muting his conversation to those around him.

"Arpit Patel," he said professionally. Listening to the voice of Ed Zonic made a muscle twitch in his neck.

"Arpit, this is Zone. Are they with you still? Do you have the sample?"

"Yes and yes," said Arpit, not trying to be funny.

"I am still working. I will not be able to have lunch with you today. I am just finishing now. How about dinner? Why don't you come and pick me up at my room at six? We should be through by then. I will call you if we run late."

Laughing again to conceal his nervousness, he said goodbye and closed the phone. He undid the earring, and the wire retracted back into the phone.

Becky quickly broke the silence. "That ooze in the meteor sample has me wondering if any other phenomenon such as this had been documented. None comes to my mind. Have you seen anything like this, Dr. Nogishi?"

"Not to my knowledge. I plan to search the data nodes on the subject tonight. This goes far beyond the microbial fossils found on Mars. My inclination is that this comet might be from such a distant sector of space where the condition of its natural origin is unfathomable to us. It is intriguing, to say the least, that it is with properties familiar to our own."

Pat, who had been on the phone and also using a muting device, closed the line and addressed the group. "I think we should get back to our analysis. Mr. Patel, we need to be sure that the security of this find is not compromised. I will accompany you to secure the samples when we have completed testing. Mr. Steele wants me to take all precautions."

"We may be wise to take some tests on how the sample reacts to heat and cold," Nogishi said, now certain he had finished his lunch. He collected his tray garbage and rose to go back to work. The others took his lead and filed their trays to the trash receptacle and made their way to the lab. Arpit collected his tray as he re-rationalized the level of risk of getting caught with the sample now that Steele was tightening up security on the rock. Fears would have to wait until Ed Zonic came to his room at six.

He remembered his friend Maury back on Earth at the morgue who was safe and satisfied with his job without any possibility of danger. Punch in and punch out, Maury had his garden and model trains to occupy his time. A simple life once seemed pointless and mundane, now he would change places with the old coroner if he had the chance. There was no turning back, nowhere to run on the moon.

A group of security personnel approached them in the hall. These large unsmiling fellows came along in the repair vessel to increase security, apparently increasing tension as well. The men passed suspiciously. Arpit swallowed as quietly as possible. Soon they were back in the relative safety of the lab. The rock seemed to pulsate in his pocket, but it was instead damning evidence beating out a rhythm in his conscience.

Meleyev and Nogishi spent most of their time with the liquid sample, running a variety of test that would occupy most of the rest of the day. Pat and Becky continued work on the metallic identification and general constitution while Arpit assisted both teams. The extensive tests required photos and sealed samples.

Arpit prepared various pieces in a clear sterile gel sealed in cubic glass/polymer containers. These jars would withstand seven hundred pounds of pressure and had an electric lock in the top of the lid openable by a tiny pass card the size of a razor blade.

Pat performed sodium, radiation, solubility, and granular fortitude tests with Becky. Arpit spent time with Steele's scientists as they examine the liquid found in the rocky pockets.

"We assuredly find a biological nature here. This is our assumption to proceed with our thesis, Dr. Meleyev." Nogishi directed the computer to auto-focus, showing small tubular organisms. He was a man of few words, choosing them with excruciating exactitude.

"They appear to be from our perspective some sort of bacterial strain, yet I am not convinced until we dissect and run acidity and protein tests. Mr. Patel, would you prepare for these? We can do them simultaneously. I will conduct the protein testing, and I'm sure Dr. Meleyev can run an acidity test."

The Yugoslavian looked to Arpit with intent for the first time, genuinely not a trusting person who might suspect he had pocketed some of the rock, Arpit thought as he broke their glance and moved to another part of the lab and prepared the experiments.

Moon day was unlike day on Earth. *TerraLuna*'s fluorescent lights, powered partially by a ground-mounted solar farm and a small nuclear reactor, controlled atmosphere and gravity surrounded by the starlit galaxy with periodic views of Earth and created a new format for time. Hours spent in the lab removed the scientists further from moon reality and back into a normal Earthlike frame of mind. This was the philosophy of off-world psychologists, that after the initial thrill of being on another planet subsides, people will proceed instinctively with their Earth-life habits.

Becky Morris was able to detach herself from extraneous thought better than most people. This quality made her an ideal candidate for *TerraLuna*'s student program. Since the apparent apathy and misdirection of the world's governments to take effective fiduciary advantage of space at the turn of the twenty-second century, *TerraLuna* and now *MoonCorp* have created a network of interested organizations, predominantly universities, to fuel progressive space exploration with work/study people. These things just couldn't be done by individual countries' space programs in the past. It was simply like most government agencies, very fiscally mismanaged.

Becky had been selected from thousands of applicants. Inclusive of her recommendations by some prominent figures in the scientific community and her extraordinary good looks, she was invited by Steele to spend some time on the asteroid analysis team. She was called when needed. It was a viable program. In line with Steele's style, she kept making it known that she was capable and beautiful, two qualities she understood men appreciate.

It was nearly four thirty when Meleyev finally sat on the aluminum stool. Sitting promoted blood to settle in the rear end, in effect slowing blood flow to the brain. He lived by rules like this but rarely spoke of them to others who almost expected a lecture since the man never sat unless he had to.

"Dr. Nogishi, Mr. Beck and I believe we have come to some conclusions about our mystery liquid." The others gathered at Meleyev's station and peered into the monitor.

"My analysis shows a 94 percent probability that the nature of the liquid is biological and a 90 percent probability that it is seminal in nature. If you look here, we see these prominent elements of the sample dissected and processed to reveal not only genetic structure but also consistent with our concept of spermatozoa. Unlike mammalian sperm that resembles a tadpole, this material reflects a lower form of life much like that of an insect."

The group stood soundless for some time, allowing them to formulate the next pertinent question in the style perhaps of one of Meleyev's students. Nogishi came around from the silence with what he regarded as a logical question. "Why is the male sexual material locked in an asteroid?"

"Is its design consistent? Where are the ova?" Meleyev continued carefully. "We may have interrupted the most amazing mating ritual encountered anywhere."

"This is most intriguing," Nogishi added.

"Where are the parents?" Arpit added with some concern.

"The levels of radiation present in the sample and the ingenious coating acts as some sort of preservative to keep it potent during its long voyage in space," Nogishi offered.

"...To Earth?" Meleyev countered.

CRICKET HOLE

CHAPTER 20

Nick felt subtle shifts of his devoted attention turn from the spiracle defense project to details of his other experiment. It would be at least a month, maybe two, until the spiracle skeleton would be built around *MoonCorp* shell. After several meetings with engineers to review the virtual location, both that would essentially put him on the moon to supervise the assembly, he had time to pursue his sequencing project. He had spent most of his time at the hangar the past week. Now the activity there involved routine shipments of material and personnel. The work there now was not his.

Charley didn't mind his job. It kept him out of the bar and near his new girlfriend. The JC deliveries were scheduled for one per week. Stan and his management team were eager to execute construction after years of setbacks and delays. The team was sensitive to the designers' vision and responded to the careful steps of actualizing their design with a surety resembling devotion.

Appreciating the lull in the need for him to be at the hangar, he was able to arrange with Stan to slate time to work at home. He thought taking a personal break might even his nerves. Being at home eliminated excuses to postpone his long-standing experiment. Nick stood silent in fear that it would work this time. Fear of success could be a more trying ordeal than fear of failure. Where would he go with this breakthrough? He cycled through faces in his mind of people to whom he could introduce his work. All seemed to be ready to bastardize his invention. For now, Charley was the only one who knew. He needed security. The right to use the power of solar sequencing would remain his. Nick needed this as well. Its potential for misuse bothered him for some unknown, haunting reason. He didn't trust anyone and barely trusted himself. He would keep it under wraps. This conclusion seemed to end his thoughts each time he took his fanciful concept climbing onto the next step toward actualization. It excited him and yet devastated his every sense he could not stop; was this addiction?

A calm acceptance ran through him, rationalizing science as a viable form of addiction in contrast to other more defeating varieties he had encountered. Admitting his tendency to function maniacally for high levels of achievement heralded his starting position. There was no other answer. He had been here before.

His blue eyes seemed to shrink and harden with purpose. Previous thoughts of going out for a show or a meal were now floating away out of the realm of options.

When his phone rang at his desk, he shifted his tightly focused eyes slowly to the phone, wondering who could interrupt him at this mental nexus.

"Hello, this is Nick Nicholas."

"Dr. Nick? This is Dana Kim, Dr. Porter's assistant. How are you? We have been so busy here, and since it is Friday, Charley, I, and another intern were thinking about going out tonight, and we would like you to come with us. Do you have plans for the evening?"

Nick smiled unconsciously, now feeling a bit younger.

"Hey, that sounds like fun. However, Dana, I was going to do some work at home tonight, so no, I do not think I should put it off. It is important."

Charley Porter took the phone from Dana and said, "Nick, this is Charley. When was the last time you went out? I cannot remember. Remember that new holo-club, Boombier's, we saw under construction outside of Crestline? Well, it is open now, and we want to go tonight about nine o'clock. Do not tell me you have plans because I know it is not true. We'll meet you there. What do you say, pal? Selma Arcarla is coming, and I wouldn't want her to feel like a third wheel," Charley implored.

"Okay, all right, Porter you missed your calling. You should have been a salesman. It has been a while. I'll meet you there at 9:00 p.m. I will work at home today. I cannot remember the last time I had a beer. See you."

Nick placed the phone in the cradle, finding himself staring at his peach/orange walls at the spot where the plans for the spiracle defense system used to sit, wanting to have another project completed, waiting for approval. He had grown accustomed to the secure, if not smug, feeling it gave him.

It was nearly 11:30 a.m. He gathered his things and secured his briefcase as his computer shut down with a voice command. After closing the window, lights, and blinds, he left the office, stopping to tell Eleanor he would be working from home today if anyone needed him. He knew she liked to have lunch with him from time to time, but it could not be today he told her with a scant apology.

The sun was indeed hot this July, and there was no relief in sight, not a cloud in the sky. The drive home temporarily cleared his mind of habitual calculations. He would work today and go out at night. That was normal, he thought. *I could use a bit of normal.* Soon, he pulled the yellow Buick into his familiar rural driveway and ran the routines of checking the mail and securing the security systems. No problems today.

After a brief hot dog lunch, Nick started his lab, welcoming the familiar smells and sight of his workplace. The experiment had been untouched for over two weeks, and he was anxious to begin again. In his side workroom, a gurney was tucked under a long table covered with a blue plastic tarp. He carefully pulled the tarp away to reveal his collection of glass globes arranged single file order in a long aluminum frame. There were thirty balls in all, placed in custom indentations along the frame with numbers designating their position. Below the gurney were four metal boxes of varying sizes with electric power cords attached to them. Nick went into the back storage area of the lab to find some surgical tape, scissors, soft gloves, and the last globe prepared from the latest four-hundred-million-year-old Dragoon sample. Taking his time, he renumbered the glasses to including the latest sample that reordered the array.

A device resembling a movie projector sat at one end of the gurney. This was his new holo-projector. It was a long time coming for its first test run. Slots between the machine's mechanics and its long tubular lens housing held six lenses. Six six-by-six filter boxes were connected to filter the power from the solar radio energy. The lenses were carefully covered with a clear computer feed mesh substrate. Nick removed the boxes and replaced them with a new cube of filter media. A tangle of filaments with drops of silicon solder on the final lens represented the changes that Nick hoped would modulate and direct the focused sun power correctly. He slid the prepared lens comfortably into the slot. *It was as easy as that!*

The opposite end of the frame held a holo-reflective enhancer. The end that faced the globes was an open pane of tempered glass nearly two inches thick. Several mirrors arranged at angles behind it as well as photo dimensional actuators were poised in the steel housing at the end of the string of lenses.

Nick took a long drink of his soda as he circled the device, inspecting the alignment. Nodding to himself, he went to the back lab and wheeled another tarp-covered cart to the work area near the end of the globe frame. The long table was uncovered to reveal what resembled an oversize coffin-like box with high sides and a jet-black film affixed to each of the six sides, the outside made of the same thick glass as the reflector. A viewing port on the side allowed him to look inside through a small door also covered with black film.

During the next two hours, Nick connected three computer relay stations with the main nodal computer able to perform the thousands of individual commands required to realize the desired effect of this experiment. Three screens monitored the chronological evolution of the sun, the accompanying cricket change calculations, and the operation status readings that would keep him apprised of the experiment's vital data. Charley was originally supposed to be here for this test, but it wasn't meant to be, he supposed. He didn't assemble the sequencing project the night he was there because it would have taken longer than he expected and they had to present the spiracle defense the next day. Now Nick hoped the addition of the Dragoon fossil and the new imager and filter would produce a hologram by interpolating the additional span of time to the matrix.

It was almost three o'clock. He had only to test the holo-imager before the experiment could receive power from the satellite relay. He spun on his heel. He was ready to call his friend Burt at satellite control to ask him to send him his solar relay linkup. He used the wrist phone to call Burt, who was more than happy to hear from his old friend.

"Burt? Nick Nicholas here. How the heck are you man?"

"Just fine, buddy. It is somewhat slow today. Do you need some sun today, or is this a social call?" the older man said, laughing at the other end behind some cool jazz music.

"Well, Burt, you know I like to talk about world politics, but today I am in kind of a hurry. I need you to open the wide collection sails and patch me into the program

I sent you a couple of months ago, number 653 in your system. It will come to the lab at home, setting 3218 in case you forgot."

"That collection range is pretty thick with flare material right now, not to mention the X-radiation. But don't worry, the sails can handle it. We haven't brought her to that configuration in some time. It will take me about forty-five minutes to get that ready for you. I will download the cycle counter so you can keep track. Do not forget you are still invited to little Burt's birthday party," the man injected kindly.

"I will make an effort. If I cannot for some impossible reason, you make sure to look out for a delivery from California Holo-Clown van. They owe me a favor for increasing the clown party parade from two to thirty-two. They got a great deal on my old holo-imager. I can send them my image from the barn here. I'll be there at least ionically,' Nick promised.

"Okay, buddy, I will get on it. One more thing, Nick. Do me a favor. Have a nice day!"

Nick went directly to his main terminal and activated the big screen to display the solar radio power cycle program. It was forty-one minutes until the satellite was in place. Burt was a good guy, he thought, and was going to make an effort to go to the birthday party. Before he went back to check the holo-imager, he rifled through his desk to find some licorice. He chewed thoughtfully through half a pound of candy during the next forty minutes, reconfiguring the steps, connections, and functions of the system with respect to the holo-imager, and retooled data mesh feed and new filter. He recorded the configuration after he was sure it matched his schematic. This was, of course, a formality since he had it committed to memory; he was assured his good habits were at work.

A sudden beep coming from the computer made him look up with a start; the satellite was in position, and power was available. The solar sails were now in place, and he would be able to tap into the rarefied solar power essential to the success of this project. He stopped himself a moment, fathoming the research and painstaking effort that had gone into the arrival of this moment. It truly may be one of those peak experiences. He had a sudden desire for champagne but thought he had rather wait to determine if it did indeed work. It took numerous experiments such as these to get a small distance forward; it was the bump and grind of the empirical scientist.

Nick rechecked the holo-imager at the end of the array of globes. This was the most expensive piece of hardware next to the super computer. He took a low flow air hose and blew dust away from the inner workings behind an access panel. It was able to bring state-of-the-art resolution to the items being transferred into three-dimensional holograms as well as handle multiple subjects, sound, motion, and incredible color range.

This one was made to his specifications at a respected high-tech firm in Germany. He tried not to remember exactly what he paid for it, but he knew it cost much more than his house. Nick routed the power from the collector on the roof of the barn into the system from the heliographic modulator box that he had affixed to the wall near his desk. The cable was nearly six inches thick and very heavy. It was important to regulate the immense power without blowing the equipment. He had been through eight heliographic modulators, and now he had one that was able to handle the specialized amount of wattage—theoretically.

He started the modulator box with the setting at the lowest possible level. A vibrating hum ran through the concrete floor of the barn that made his toes squirm, feeling the power surge into his devices. Nick leaped to the computer screen to note the chromospheric emission reading and then ran the solar history program, looping it to replay the solar flare patterns he had spent so many hours finding and recording.

His contention is that the sun's cyclical pattern and the intense energy of the magnetic fields would fuse the common structures of the cricket genome sensitive to the effects of the solar flares over the centuries. In union with the holo-generator, theoretically, he should be able to imagize a three-dimensional rendering of the insect as it was at the time of its existence. The world of holograms a thriving business, but with this technology, the ability to imagize true pictures from the past would be a stunning breakthrough.

The second terminal serving as an operation station and relay recorder to the nodal computer awaited the commanding code. At the projection field container or PFC, he made a minor alignment and then closed the lid.

Now at the end of his licorice bag, Nick stood at the operation terminal and set the automatic globe reader at the newest ball, tenth in the lineup of thirty, and entered the coded sequence. An electric slide reader moved along the bottom of the line of balls to the tenth one and stopped. The computers began running their courses. Being at this juncture before reminded him of the ruined modulators from past tests; he routed power from the heliographic modulator box to the terminal. It was holding.

Taking a breath slowly, as poised and prepared as he could be, he raised the power and sent it through the system. The cable from the modulator box rolled and squirmed from the generator and through the globes of centuries of cricket cadaver dust. As it passed through each of the globes, a different color swirled and glowed some blue and some yellow, red, purple, green, and orange. Nick stared in awe. He enabled his wrist phone's audio mode, set it to record, and documented the experiment.

"July 17, 2168. My eightieth experiment with solar genome sequencing has included a new specimen from outside the Phoenix area approximately sixty-five million years old. The glass samples are displaying rainbow colors, differentiating themselves. This has not been observed until the addition of the new specimen."

He clipped closed the phone transfixed by the colors in the line. There must be some sort of prismatic effect perhaps from the new enhanced imager. *It pays to buy the best,* he thought. He noted that the power level was off from the previous experiment by .0083. Not sure if that was making a difference, he recorded it with a tap on the keyboard and made his way to the projection field container.

Light passing through the swirling globes would enter the holo-imager through a manually operated control. Nick liked throwing switches rather than typing commands anyway. *Here we go,* he thought, moving the toggle switch to the "ON" position. The imager sucked the light with a shake and instantly processed its program. Light moved from the lens array into the front of the container, moving mechanically with rays of blue and white. Nick opened the phone and dictated.

"The prismatic effect seems to have been coalesced in the imager, presenting a unique shade of blue. This is unprecedented. It is a new range of light. It should enter the PFC with a range of colors or at least pure white. I am sure this is a new phenomenon. For now, I will call it *infra-blue light*. It should not exist, but it does."

He walked around the PFC to see if any light was leaking from the film he had applied.

"A section of film has come away on an area at the end of the box. Photonic impulses from the reaction occupy the box. Movement was visible!" he said with a raised inflection of his voice. "I am coming around to the view door. I am donning protective goggles."

He affixed the large goggles hanging on a hook and then slowly opened the door. The inside of the box was completely filled with light; the hundreds of holographic imagers were pulsing in many shades of blue, some very curious. Nick stood basking in the new blue light, a cricket unaware of its observer, simply being alone, enjoying a warm bath of computer-generated blue sunshine.

It moved casually among the grass and pebbles. The eerie blue-and-white, movie-like scene had incredible clarity. The upper end seemed to glow brighter from the imager end, representing a sun-like effect from the end of the box.

He engaged the wrist phone recorder, and not moving his eyes from his incredulity of success, he said, "We have an image . . ."

CHAPTER 21

Nick stood looking at his blue friend while attempting to fathom his achievement. After at least fifteen minutes, he decided that it should be recorded. With a couple of simple strokes from the control computer, the built-in recording mechanism began to document the hologram of a cricket "living" from the DNA re-sequenced with high-powered sunlight, dated at sixty-five million years ago, originating from the cricket fossil of that period. Satisfied that he had reached a substantial pinnacle, it was time to test another specimen. Nick directed the holo-imager to power off so that he may reset the designator to another position, highlighting the suspended material in another globe.

The blue and white lights faded slowly as did the noise level in the lab, leaving the PFC dark again. The next specimen was determined to be roughly fifty-nine million years old. He enabled the procedure again, and soon, the black box glowed, encasing another sample of blue three-dimension pictures. From the movement within the light, Nick tensed in anticipation that the program's second test had also proved fruitful.

Setting the recorder in motion quickly, he went to the view door and opened it with childlike accuracy. His widened eyes beheld another cricket scurrying about some stones highlighted by a light source recreated by the holo-imager. It was certainly smaller than its six-million-year older cousin, yet its eyes and legs seemed larger. Nick watched the creature for a long time, wondering if he should disassemble the imager to find why it was monochromatic. He opted to test each of the samples before fudging with the machine.

After slating at least three hours to complete the full test, he needed to call Charley and tell him he was not going to be able to meet tonight. Nick powered down the imaging system and reset it to the next media-filled globe. He snapped open the wrist phone.

"Hello, Nick. If you are wondering what to wear, I am going in jeans. No big deal."

"Charley, I have used the solar sequencer today, and for the first time, it worked! This is an absolute breakthrough. I am just beginning the confirmation tests and recording the results. I am not leaving until I have completed a full battery of tests. You go on ahead. I know you want to see her tonight. Call me later if you can. If you don't score, get over here and see this. It is like nothing you have ever seen. Give my regrets to Selma and Dana, but try not to say anything about this yet. You are the only person I am letting in on this until I have run a full series of tests, so do not say anything to anybody. Are you still there?" Nick said, realizing he might be rambling to dead space.

"Nick, don't worry, Selma doesn't feel good, so it will be Dana and myself, and that is fine with me. You know that sex is the only thing that is keeping me from coming over to check it out. I'll call you later." Charley hung up.

Nick was soon back at work, peeking at images from life in the past. He began to muse about creating a video presentation featuring the various creatures. Closing his mind to the fear of whom to show his amazing circus of crickets, he continued documenting his findings with precision. Nick had anticipated logging in worthy data for a very long time.

After thirteen viewings, all of which were fairly consistent, something halted Nick's procedure cold in its tracks. The image of a cricket from 201 million years at first seemed very much like the others. Y201 million cricket sat on a flat rock and was soon joined by a fly. It then landed on the same rock, paused for several moments, and then flew away about its business. What? How could a fly be in the image? It was amazing enough that the faint surroundings were present in the representations. He deduced that the sun and its relationship with the genome were so specific that it identified the conjugal phenomenon of its environment over its lifetime, which was also able to be imagized. Microscopically, molecules forming grass, rock, and wood were actually present in the original fossil. The fly perhaps was fossilized, along with the cricket. Nick recalled the sample collection and wondered how he could have overlooked the fly's presence when dissecting the petrified corpse. Looking to the image revealed the absence of the fly. Where did it go?

Nick held the knob of the door between his thumb and forefinger and, in his confusion, moved the door a tiny fraction, when to his utter amazement, the cricket darted off the rock and disappeared into a small hole. It was gone. He refocused his glasses with a turn of his head and crunch of his nose. The cricket was no longer being imaged, but the misty surroundings remained. A long, empty thought came and stayed. Answers to this anomaly did not flash in his mind. It stood open like a field of grass. Rather, answers to new questions scrambled to take their place. Movement was amazing enough, but the definition of depth was remarkable. Where did the cricket go? Moving with nothing more than instinct, he took the long rubber gloves from the desk, trying to surround the concept itself with unsettling torpidity.

Approaching the PFC with a new sense of unfamiliarity like a well-trained dog with an uncharacteristic menace, he reached slowly inside. The oscillating shafts of light hit the glove, and unexpectedly, more shafts of light completed the image from another angle. The imager shone the strange new hue of blue on the glove despite his blocking the rays. It was compensating for the obstruction, still maintaining the image and brightening the glove magically. Turning his head gradually, he found a new respect for the technology he designed. It was not supposed to do this, but it did.

Not wanting to form assumptions before the deed had been done, as well as the mounting thrill of discovery, urged his hand forward to the holo-image of the rock. Touching it gently, briefly, feeling its harness confirmed something beyond his expectation, unrivaled by any sensation he could recall. It was real. He touched it again to assure the sensation. Nudging it couldn't hurt. He pushed the rock, and it seemed to have the properties of a rock its size in reality, yet an augmented light machine was artificially generating it.

No, no, he chided himself in retrospect to the research he toiled with for such a long time. Colleagues may have branded his thoroughness as pedantic. The scientific method appears to have paid off with a jackpot that would identify him to the ages. Holograms did not have weight. So maybe it was something more than a hologram, something new.

Closing the valve leading to notoriety unbounded, he continued poking at the images in the PFC until he found the cricket hiding in a shallow hole. Careful not to harm it (as if he could), he retracted his hand. It looked at his glove, and suspiciously unafraid, it ran out and sat upon the smaller rock, seemingly enjoying the pseudo-sun's warmth. Nick noted the behavior and continued to arrange the pieces of the puzzle. It would appear that he had brought this little creature out of its eternal hibernation, and it seemed grateful in some insectoid way. Acting instinctively (which he thought the great scientists did all the time), he shyly reached for the little fellow to come to his hand. It crawled on, and he held it up, feeling like a father for the first time or perhaps something more.

"I'll bet it feels good to be out of that rock after millions of years, doesn't it, little guy?" Nick said aloud.

Satisfied, he put the cricket back into the blue grass. *What could be the exact cause for this to be happening?* he thought. Not being able to identify the exact answer to a question actually led to the answer of another question. A conglomeration effect of the sequencing, the power source and the computer generator had an effect that added up to something far beyond the sum of the components. He adjusted priorities to include experiments to see what else might happen in the remaining samples.

Stopping himself momentarily before another period test, he picked the rock its size, tossing it lightly in his rubber glove. He tried to pull the rock out of the PFC. As the rock came near the edge of the sanctity of the box, it abruptly fell out of his hand and onto the light-imaged grass. *It makes sense that it could not leave the box as it could only exist through the power of the emitters,* Nick thought. However, he interacted with the cricket and the rock. This needed some explanation. The most advance holograms had interactive programs, yet they were based on recorded response data. Giving credit to the new imager did not hold the answer to questions now presenting themselves.

For the rest of the day and into the night, he continued testing. Each had an image of a cricket and was able to interact with outer stimuli. Most interesting were the tiny burrows into which the crickets retreated. They gave the image of a depth that seemed incongruous to a normal holographic projection.

At this point, Nick realized that he was dealing with dimensionally relevant change. This effect redirected his focus of observation and experimentation of the solar genome sequencing study to newly actualized realities in an entirely separate quantum.

He had tested thirty of the thirty-three samples, and he had put dinner off long enough. He went to the house, naturally locking the barn, to order a meal from the compu-meal 2200. It needed to be filled soon. He liked the convenience of having a delivery truck fill it every three weeks or so. More so, he liked the idea of not having to wash dishes or shop. Aunt Dolly's meatloaf and mashed potatoes with green beans sounded good despite the fact that he avoided it for some time. A cola in his big glass completed the meal. He ate in silence, forcing himself not to think about crickets during his meal.

Feeling full of stomach and empty of mind as to his next step in the experiment, he opted for a quick peek at the news and maybe a short nap before going back to the barn. Taking the remainder of the soda into the sunken living room, he ordered the television on and to the Central National News Channel. The news channel was airing a live special report on the Yokomoto-Chen mission that had made headlines.

Yokomoto and Chen had spent billions of world dollars developing heavy-payload space vehicles. New trends had been focusing on lighter weight, less expensive systems using alternative fuel systems. However, the YC group took the best technology of these pioneers of private space development and combined them with heavy-lift vehicles. They were heralded for being the first (and only) company to actually capture an asteroid from the belt between Jupiter and Mars. Amazingly, they had sent a variation of the new Junk Colossal called the ATLAS into the asteroid orbit. After matching speed, it maneuvered itself in front of the object, locking stakes into the carbonaceous chondrite, thereby avoiding damage from the blowback of the tail by engaging the thrusters. It was not only able to create a new orbit into low Earth orbit but was also able to land the eight-meter rock back onto the ATLAS and land dozens of them in China.

The rock was mined for precious metals like platinum and traces of gold. These metals were of extreme value and made YC enormous amounts of money. The iron of the first captured asteroid was used to create a monument at the Yokomoto-Chen Space Industries headquarters outside Shanghai. The statue was an iron rendition of the first Junk Colossal launched in the early 2140s. CNN was covering the unveiling of the statue as a lead-in to report on a new mission designed to capture another planetesimal.

"Using a refined ATLAS craft designed to convert the kinetic energy from its wake into the propulsion engines of the ATLAS as sort of a recycled fuel, YC was planning another trip into the asteroid belt between Jupiter and Mars," the newsperson said.

The film resumed, and Nick noticed the president of the United States of Korea, who, for years, had wanted to join in the Japanese and Chinese partnership for space-based technologies development, was sold on the idea of selling its arsenal of nuclear missiles to YC. The bombs were used to eject the asteroids from their orbit. It was the first time a world government had handed over authority of the use of nuclear devices to a private organization for scientific use. It made sense since the private sector technology company was able to generate so much more money, as profit was the goal, rather than misdirected bureaucracy. Korea's government was able to devote its strong world dollar profits for humanitarian causes in the Orient.

The world changed in the year 2100 in so many ways. The most important change was the world began to use one currency. It lowered prices on so many inflated items and was called the financial renaissance.

Communication throughout the world was opened wide since now from Korea to Kansas, everyone spoke the same language that of the world dollar. Of course, the United States, having the most powerful currency, endorsed itself and established the New World Bank with ten million branches across the globe. It took some time and politicking, but it was in place for business in 2100. People across the world found that when they spoke a common financial language, they did not want to talk of wars and social injustice but rather a discourse of solutions based on easier availability to the things they needed.

The United States of America realized that its cities and towns were not being rebuilt because of lack of capital. Entire city infrastructures had crumbled away in areas. With the new system, they were engorged with cash. They used this cash to buy and develop vast areas of private property and rebuild neighborhoods, reselling them to the public at an affordable price. This put more cash in the American pocket, and soon, private corporations took over the project, leaving the government free to expand its financial reach.

This reach went far into the creative minds of corporate innovators eager to keep more and more of their wealth. As the system was further, instituted goods could be purchased without any money exchanged. If you had the minimum amount of capital, say, ten billion world dollars, everyone else with that same amount collected similar business benefits. A point matrix was established where a corporation could obtain goods from similar companies without the exchange of world dollars with the understanding that the transaction was for equitable items used frequently. Profits were gleaned along the economic lines. The thought was to keep their money and exchange nearly all they needed, thereby not touching their principal. The acquisition of points became the cutting edge in the business world. It you did not have corporate points, you would pay in world dollars. Point deals were on the rare side, while ordinary world dollar transactions were common.

Stan Duncan, the YC group, Skylar, and Gerhard Steele used both regularly. Most people were not aware of this esoteric process and probably did not care. In combination with the World Bank and the corporate point system, America kept peace in the world with a new weapon, financial clout for a greater populace than even its own citizens. War was obsolete by 2100. War made less sense than opening food processing plants in starving countries funded by the World Bank. Nuclear power now solely used for energy would soon be replaced with the eventual use of solar radio energy. Nuclear innovations were used for sculpting the heavens for the benefit of the people of Earth.

The YC Corporation had several missions slated for the next five years designed to mine the asteroid belt and sell these raw materials for an ever-widening array of uses, causing more profit to be funneled back into its growing deep space projects. Finally, the human race was onto something.

Yokomoto came to the podium equipped with his strap-on translator and gave a rousing speech to his audience of employees, shareholders, and media. He certainly had captured the hearts of the people who, for many decades, had been yearning for a space program doing something to help people. His company employed large numbers of workers in various locations, including facilities for refining the celestial raw material.

Nick thought of the prestige of which he really was very much a part. He did not like to bask in glory like Yokomoto or even Duncan and Steele. There was too much work to do. However, when he thought of it, he did spend lots of time with the people of YC, and they were one of the most successful corporate leaders in the world. It was amazing to Nick that he had almost no recollection of a time when governments actually sponsored space programs outside some regulatory agencies. It seemed normal now that most government's sole responsibility was humanitarian services. There was a time when people had to pay for health services and taxes on their income. Incredible, he thought, how the release of so many governmentally moderated services had allowed the national economy to flourish to the point of being able to establish the world ban. That was America. He felt a surge of patriotism in his chest, or maybe it was indigestion.

The news show ended with mention of the YC Corporation's association with the *MoonCorp* project. Nick sat surprised as Stan Duncan came to the podium and took a quick bow. "That's my boss!" Nick said aloud.

It was nearly 8:30 p.m., and Nick felt sleep to be an inevitability. Rest stimulated his imagination, which was now postulating possibilities for the next stage of this remarkable discovery. As he drifted to sleep, blue crickets sat in the sun, enjoying their new freedom.

*****

Charley Porter found time to put together a pile of articles crediting him for his scientific contribution, with intentions of putting them in an album. They sat in a box. For several years, the pile grew to include clippings from magazines and science journals sent to him from friends and relatives still without organization. Knowing Dana would be interested in seeing his progress, he purchased a photo album and put it in the box. Nervous about being on time for his first date in at least six months, he forgot to bring it along to the restaurant. He thought about dressing up but settled for jeans and a new sport shirt and deck shoes.

He spun his silver sport out of the parking garage and cruised along the hot highway to pick up Dana. She lived in a nice apartment about fifteen minutes away. He made it there in nearly thirteen and a quarter minutes according to his digital gauge. As he pulled up, he saw the door open and she was in the car in moments, wearing a very sexy green flower print dress and white shoes.

"Hey, Dr. Porter, how are you?" She smiled.

He looked admirably at her slim body find a comfortable position in his leather seats.

"I am great. We are going to this new restaurant called Boombier's. It has the latest in holographic entertainment. I've been waiting for it to open for some time now. It is just outside of Crestline. We should be there at 8:57 p.m. Our reservation is for 9:00 p.m. They have a holographic floorshow."

Charley routinely checked the auto-drive gauges, taking the sport along the automated highway with satellite assist. The drive was relatively uneventful without being uncomfortable. They listened to the radio and tapped to the beat while she checked out his car; he noted her shape yet again.

The clocked ticked 8:57 p.m. as they pulled into the nightclub as the hot sun refused to release its hold on Crestline, California. An impressive neon sign still off because of the brightness of the day radically spelled BOOMBIER'S. Charley looked forward to seeing it on when they left; it would look cool against the dark night. The music stopped abruptly as Charley turned the car off. The lot was rather full. He thanked himself for calling ahead to make reservations as he held the door open for Dana Kim.

A tall woman with long curly blond hair greeted each person with a handshake. Her long legs were visible in the slit of her sequined black dress. Charley was not sure if it was her big brown eyes or her large motherly breasts that welcomingly drew the men to her outstretched hand.

"My name is Christine. Welcome to Boombier's." Charley shook her hand, and entered the beautiful foyer centered with a fountain flowing with lighted green-colored water. Statues of voluptuous women greeted the guests from their friendly positions along the wall. Ornately carved marble chairs and benches lined the path to the main room.

Beyond the small group of twenty or so patrons waiting to be seated, Charley and Dana could see the garishly decorated stage above the large dining room. It reminded him of the ancient Wild-West-style show platform that came out into the audience. Waitresses were clad in fluorescent pink-and-green hot pants and wildly colored stretch tops and moved briskly among the tables with a cheery quickness to and from their admiring customers. A strip of LCD material was sewn in above their shoulder blades. It advertised their names, drink specials, and of course, salad dressings and soups available. It was a novelty Dana saw nowhere else. Another hostess with a clipboard seated them after a few minutes.

They sat at a dark sturdy round table for two. Dana craned her neck to take in ornate, if not gaudy, gilt dragons, large animal statues, and maritime paraphernalia, all overseen by four large antique chandeliers.

"This place is awesome, Charley."

"They have this democratic way to choose which performers will be seen. We use this voting link here to pick which shows we want to see before, during, and after dinner. All the performances are complete with band, singer's dancers, and special effects. It is supposed to be phenomenal. Let's see what we have to choose from."

He scrolled the selections set in a small screen in the center of the table.

"We have country classics, modern jazz, blues legends, rock and roll anthology, classical highlights, new wave expo, and crooners. What do you think?"

"I like country, of course, and wouldn't mind seeing the blues show. What about you? I place you as a rock-and-roll kind of guy," she said flatly as the waitress came over to explain the voting and take their drink orders.

They opted for the country, blues, and crooners. They would not know which show would appear until the votes were in and the evening progressed. The atmosphere was electric in the club. People were talking freely, both old and young, and having a nice time as lively techno swing instruments kept heads bobbing and toes tapping. Dana Kim found herself looking at Charley from Leslie Davis's perspective for a moment. She truly liked him. Was this man attractive to her because of his attitude toward his work? Or was it the work itself? He did have an appeal that maybe most nonscientific minds would not appreciate.

Putting Leslie Davis away pointedly, she reminded herself that she would have to maintain her cover at least until the spiracle defense system was in place. She had ample information for Gerhard Steele but wanted the actual plans for the field generator boxes. She was not sure she understood the process enough to recreate it without the schematics; it was Nick Nicholas she actually needed. Neither of them would actually say how it worked even as she skillfully asked the proper questions in the most provocative way. Charley Porter would be her path to the designs. She felt quite sure also that under different circumstances, she might be able to get along with Dr. Porter.

The music changed to a light blues riff, creating a pleasing atmosphere in the restaurant/theater, supporting her friendly gaze with Dr. Porter. A spotlight suddenly interrupted it on stage, accompanied by a fanfare. A tall silvering-haired man in a tuxedo walked into the light. He was greeted with ample applause.

"Ladies and gentlemen, welcome to Boombier's. I am your host, Cardamon Cartwright, and tonight you will be thrilled with the latest holo-entertainment and the finest food this side of New York. If you haven't heard, we operate on the democratic system here in Crestline and at Boombier's. I hope that you will enjoy yourselves and tell your friends. We have a number of shows from which you will choose. By popular vote, we will have three performances that can only be described as unforgettable, so close to reality you will have to come again . . .and don't forget to tell your friends"

From the stage right curtain, a large white tiger strolled onto the stage. It glistened occasionally, denoting that it was a hologram created by the imagers throughout the building. It walked to Cardamon and sat at his feet. From stage left, a large lion sauntered over and sat at his left. The enthralled crowd filled the room with "oohs" and "wows."

Cardamon took the opportunity to sing an old swinging standard about being out on a Friday night as the stage began to fill with bears, gorillas, a hippopotamus, an ostrich, and finally, a huge elephant and giraffe. The began to rock and sway to the music all having a wonderful time with the audience, happy together.

"I told you this was going to be great," Charley said through his big smile. Dana looked at him and for the first time forgot she worked for Steele.

CHAPTER 22

Pepe was woken by a strange gurgle. At first, he thought it was his stomach. He heard it again now louder, and it was most definitely coming from Tico, who rested unsettled between his master's legs.

"What's the matter Tico? Do you have a stomachache? You need to go out?" He threw over the thin printed bedspread and rose with a stretch to the still dark morning, finding an odd feeling deep in his belly as well.

"Uh-oh, Tico, I think we might have got hold of some bad meat last night."

Pepe quickly opened the sliding door and let his dog out and then made a more than hasty retreat to the washroom. As he sat reviewing the unreal events of yesterday, rubbing his forehead, sweat appeared on his hand. *Do I have a fever?* he thought. *It is not time to be sick.* After a few minutes, he heard Tico barking in the small patio. He washed his hands, face with cool water, and let the dog back into the room with a gust of cold air.

"It is cold this morning. Okay, come in. Are you feeling sick too?" he said, checking the dog's eyes and smelling his breath. They drank some water to settle their stomachs.

"I think you are sick like Pepe. Come on. Let's go back to bed. We no fish today . . . Oh wait, Dr. Sanchez will not be happy if we tell him no."

They crawled back into bed, sporting more gurgles and groans. Pepe fished on the nightstand, catching the remote control module to watch some television to see if their adventure would be on the news.

Finding the news channel with some effort, Pepe watched a commercial for the new Earth surfer personal hover disc that allowed people to float ten inches above the sidewalk at speeds of close to ten miles per hour. The commercial featured four teenagers with their feet secured to a twenty-inch disc. A cord strapped to the leg and along the arm led to a control pad worn on the fingers. They whipped along a park path, having a great time. The commercial ended with a number to use to order and the byline "Surf the Earth."

"I wonder if they make one of those that can hold Pepe. It would have to have a very great power source. I think we stick to walking and fishing. What do you think, little Tico?"

Tico looked at him and licked his lips, resuming his position for more rest. The local news appeared, and Ms. Morales was seen at the police station giving her report about the growing interest in the offshore activity from earlier that week. Advertisements for documentaries about meteors followed. It was certainly a growing interest for those who wanted information. Maybe it would make their little town famous.

Pepe hoped he would be able to conclude this business and get home today. He hated to sail when he was not feeling well, much less if he was going to fish for rocks. He opted to take a couple of hours rest and see how he felt. Finding a comfortable position, he tried to fall back asleep. The news continued while his eyes closed. Listening to the rest of the news in darkness comforted him, and since Paloma liked to stay awake and watch television while he slept, it reminded of being home.

"*MoonCorp*, in conjunction with the Skylar Corporation and Yokomoto-Chen Technologies, has begun construction of a second lunar-based hotel and convention center. I am here with Yuri Povlovich, the chief lunar excavation engineer, whose lunar paving machines are seen here pulling up tons of moon rock and dust, smelting it into large slabs of building material that will eventually constitute the majority of the hotel. Mr. Povlovich, could you tell us something about how this machine works?"

The slight Russian with the winning smile was seen in his white shirt and piercing blue eyes before a video chart that started with a wave of his hand.

"Thank you, Ms. Morales. We see here the moon is comprised mostly of soft silica, rock, and a variety of meteors and ejecta from centuries of bombardment. What our machines will do is agitate great amounts of this material so that is it loose and manageable. The next step is the collector device that draws the material into the smelting chamber. This is done with a combination of suction and matter conveyors. The sizes of the slabs we will make are variable. Most of the slabs will be ten by thirty feet long. The smelting chamber uses a combination of heat, pressure, and an adhesive to create one of the most durable and compact materials known to man, rivaling the strength of some granites found naturally on Earth. The smelter will roll forward and, in this case, actually leaves the slab where it will stay as a section of the foundation. Other sections used in the construction of the walls will be left in the cooling area over here. The cranes here will lift the cooled pieces into place to create a very safe and efficient structure. Once the building is in place, we have a special buffing machine that will polish the surface, making it very smooth and quite attractive." He ended his presentation with a smile and a nod.

"Mr. Povlovich, do you think that this material might be available here on Earth someday? May I have a house made from moon rock?" Dahlia said.

"Well, I would welcome the business. We would need to colaborate with Dr. Yokomoto and Dr. Chen to see if we can work something into their busy schedule to transport slabs back for you. I don't think it will be soon, but someday you might be able to order a house made from the moon."

Pepe and Tico drifted back to sleep. They dreamed not of living in a hotel made of moon rock but rather of their simple life in Celestun with Paloma and something nice roasting in the oven.

*****

Pepe knew after another hour's sleep that he hadn't lost his stomach flu. The sun was up, and the sounds of the day starting only made his stomach feel worse. Cars were starting, and people were heard on the street going to work. Dr. Sanchez had not called him. Anyway, it was a new day.

Pepe would have to eat plain rice with creamed chicken gravy, his mother's remedy for a bellyache. It wasn't what he normally had for breakfast, but it always did the trick. He remembered passing a diner last night that should be open for breakfast. It would be worth the trip to talk to the proprietor and ask him to make his special remedy. Tico looked like a walk would be out of the question. Pepe scratched his furry head.

"You stay here and sleep. Pepe will be right back with some rice to settle our stomachs. Be a good boy. I won't be long."

A quick shower and shave refreshed him but didn't cure sour stomach. Soon, he was on the street heading to Philippe's diner. It was just before nine o'clock. People milled the streets about their work. He entered the small diner his mind fixed on the remedy. The manager was happy to make a special order for the large out-of-towner.

"It would be a few minutes," the young man said.

Pepe sat and enjoyed a cup of coffee and the local news while he waited. This shop had the newsreaders built into the tables as most coffee shops did. These were particularly clean during the tourist season, free from food smudges and fingerprints. He wondered for a moment why they still called them newspapers since most paper news sources were not used for fifty years. The ecologists loved this as trees were not destroyed for the manufacture of paper on a large scale. Alternative recycling provided a paper-like material that published some books and periodicals.

Modern electronics had a great deal to do with the saving of forests that now produced much more oxygen for people to breathe. Pepe thought it was a good idea to save the trees. There was a lot less paper used in general now than there was when he was a child, which meant less litter in the streets and parks. Pepe turned the reader on and selected the item about Benito, adjusting the contrast to accommodate the bright morning sun streaming in through the large plate glass window of the diner.

The door opened, bringing in the smell of fish from the seaside street, a smell that reminded Pepe that he should be at work. Turning, he saw a small man in his twenties who apparently knew the manager already preparing a cup of coffee for him.

"Philippe, how are you today, my friend?"

"Good, Gus, really good. What's new?"

"Well, we are getting a late start today because the boat needs to be cleaned. As usual, the coffee they give us tastes like crap. Could you make me a chicken torta today too? I will bring it back. I only get fifteen minutes for my break because there is more work today."

"Sure thing. Say, Gus, you smell especially fishy today. Did you forget to take a bath?"

"No. We are cleaning the outside of the boat, and it is covered with some slimy shit. Chavez says a whale gave birth near the ship. I just nodded, but I haven't ever seen any whales out there. Maybe sharks were screwing near the boat or a giant squid took a dump. I don't know! All I know is that it smells like a big dead fish, and I have to clean it up."

Pepe half-listened to the foul-mouthed and fish-smelling man. He noted an unusual odor, even to him being around it all day every day. He crunched his brow, took a sip of coffee, and continued to read the local news that had included a picture of his boat featured in the story of Benito's death. A blurb mentioned his name as captain. Pepe sent the story electronically to his account. He pulled his world card, swiped it on the table terminal, and punched in his number. Moments later, Paloma's dear face appeared in the table.

"Paloma, darling, it has an adventure. Let me tell you what has happened to me . . ."

He relayed the events of the last two days to his worrying wife, who looked at him understandingly with occasional shakes of her head. He told her he did not know when he was going to be home, and that he and Tico apparently had food poisoning. She told him to get some rice and chicken gravy. He assured her they were making it for him now. He asked her to read the article he sent her and that he was going back to the hotel to rest with the specially prepared remedy. He spied the manager approach with his food.

"I love you, Paloma. We will be back soon when this is all over . . ."

*****

Charley and Dana ate, drank, and laughed, enjoying the music and spellbinding atmosphere of "La Boombier" until sometime after midnight, having a final drink before heading out into the early summer morning. From the smiles on the patrons' faces as they wiped their world cards, it was evident that they would be back. Dana collected her purse, and they nimbly stumbled out to the car.

"That place was fantastic! We must come again!" she said, finally getting in as she groped for her seat belt. Not able to get it to click, Charley reached over and found the belt and strapped her in, once again finding himself close to her face, and, taking his chances with proximity, grabbed a kiss, which was welcome.

"I love holograms. I wonder what they will be like in a hundred years," she said, unconsciously taking the visor down to check her makeup and artificial eyes in the mirror.

"What will we be able to do and experience with an interface system? I would like to see a virtual reality system interfaced with holograms to send a deep space mission that can be experienced from Earth. Then space encounters could be transferred into holograms for generations we can 'BE' in deep space or build a city on Mars and then go home after our shift is complete. What do you think, Dr. Porter? Can it be done? And if so, will you hire me to work on the project?"

Leslie was testing him. She knew this technology existed and wanted to know if he was aware of it; she queried with still taut and smiling oriental eyes and some sincerity.

"You know, I have been doing some experimental work with holograms at my lab. I should show you my latest effort. You will appreciate it more than most."

He started the car and put it into gear, heading toward his lab, not mentioning that there was an adjoining door to his apartment. They turned onto the highway in the starry night. Soon, Dana realized that they were not heading to her place.

"Are we going to the lab now?" she asked, sporting an intoxicated schoolgirl inflection.

"No time like the present. You're not tired yet, are you? Because if you are, I can take you home," Charley asked with sincerity.

"No. I am always up for holography," she said, her voice trifled with excitement.

After fifteen minutes, Charley pulled into his parking lot, turned off his car and went out, seemingly all in one motion, happy to show her his lab. She got out of the car, inspecting the building with a question.

"This is your lab?" she said, following him up the stairs.

"I also have an apartment here . . . so I can be near my work. You see, there are other people as dedicated to their field. Come on in."

He brought her down the hall to his apartment door, tapping on it with his keys.

"This is the apartment, and this is the lab," he said, putting the key into the door. They entered the apartment-turned-lab, and the lights revealed what looked more like a movie studio than a laboratory. To the right, a raised stage peppered with holo-emitters from above. A control panel connected to several computers sat on the left of the stage. Storage cabinets and recording devices made up most of the room, along with a lighting control station and various and hanging spectral imagers. A state-of-the-art multi-speaker audio system was spaced among the holo-emitters as Charley liked music with his holographics. Dana looked around with awe, not saying much of anything as she digested the potential of the laboratory Charley kept at home. He was more complex than he seemed.

"The other room there is for storage of some of the lenses and projectors I am not working with now. I might have to rent another apartment if I want to grow my collection. For now, this space suits my purposes."

He went to the control panel, flicked some switches, and started his computer.

"Let me show you my apartment. It is right through here. Do you have to use the washroom? I do."

He walked to the left side of the large room and went through the door into the washroom. She followed along, taking in his rather dark and certainly messy rooms. It was normal for the most part. Couch recliner, TV trays and trash, a large television. The kitchen was strewn with the remains of weeks of takeout. It did not look like he used his kitchen for cooking but rather a bureau as the countertop was strewn with mail, loose change, receipts, and various things found in pockets. The toilet flushed, and he was heard washing his hands.

"Watch out for the golf balls," he said, returning into the living room. "I think it is important to keep your work close to home. It is indicative of devotion to your science but not in a fanatical way. Some people leave their work at work, and some take their work home. I just go through this door."

She did not laugh as much as he expected her to and excused herself to the washroom. She turned the water on to cover the noise, retrieved the skin puller from her purse, and applied the purple laser light tip under her eyes to tighten the skin and maintain her disguise. She used the toilet, washed her hands, and returned to the living room. Charley was in the lab, and after a quick sniff at old burger wrappers and chicken buckets, she moved back to the lab to find him at the computer, preparing a program.

"Sorry for the mess. My maid is on hiatus. Come here, I think you will like this."

He brought a chair next to his stage. He lowered the lights and started some romantic digital music. With several clicks on his computer, he created a young lone female dancer wrapped in a light tan billowing material. She danced gracefully, spinning and changing upon the stage using her long hair in the highly artistic dance. The detail was frighteningly real to Dana. She looked at her eyes, and it seemed as if she was looking back at her. She stared to be sure, but it must have been part of the program.

"How do her eyes work? It seems like she is looking at me."

"In a way, she is. I have installed an optical sensor that is now tracing your eye patterns. The computer is matching her eye movement to appear to follow yours. It wasn't difficult. It is what I do. I am an innovation guy. Because patents make the man!"

"That computer is different. Is it devoted to holography only?"

"I do other work on several computers. I like to keep this terminal exclusively to operate the display. Here, look at this."

The dancer continued her interpretive dance. Dana felt too comfortable with Charley again. Not ready to admit to herself that any feelings for him would alter her mission, she sat still, enjoying the holography. The way things were going, she had to consider the possibility of spending the night. It was nearly two o'clock. Leslie Davis stopped Dana Kim once the thought crossed their minds and reminded herself that this was the first date, and while Dana was willing, Leslie was weak. All romance aside, the holography controls computer was the only one in sight. He must have a portable or use a terminal at *MoonCorp* to store pertinent information about the lunar defense system. She hoped it was not excessively encrypted. This was her worst fear.

As the dance ended with the woman doubled over in a sitting position, Charley looked to get a reaction from his guest.

"That was nice. What else do you have?" she said plainly for fear of appearing to be excited. She did not want to give him the wrong idea. Besides, the sight of his kitchen was very much a turnoff.

After some adjusting, he made the dancer disappear and the lights faded to black and then came up again to reveal two sparsely leaved trees with several birds perched in the branches. Chirping and songs were heard as the birds flitted and hopped between the trees.

After a few minutes, he accompanied the image with some baroque classical music. Charley stood, took Dana by the hand, and walked onto the stage. She came with some trepidation but soon felt comfortable with the touch of Charley's hand on hers. He raised her arm and instructed her slightly to hold her arm out and keep it still. He looked at the birds and, nodding, a blue jay gave a distinctive call and flew from the tree and landed on her arm, eyeing her with the reality optical communication. Charley nodded at the cardinal (tapping a handheld remote), and the bright red bird flew over to join the blue jay on Dana's arm, adding its song to the soft music. Her naturally smiling face beamed even more at the fantasy as several birds landed along her outstretched arms.

"This is really cool. I could be entertained here for hours. However, Charley, I really do need some sleep. I have been really pushing myself. It has been hard to sleep lately. I think my summer work schedule is catching up with me. Would you take me home? I hope you have more of these programs. I can't get enough of this stuff. Maybe we can get together on Sunday afternoon so I can be awake to enjoy these incredible holos. It is so much more real than the stuff you see at the malls and bars," she said, regarding the large hawk that had flown to her.

"You should see what Nick has in his lab. It makes this look a kindergarten project."

She looked at him squarely. "I would really like to see what Dr. Nick has to top this."

Charley knew at once that he should call Nick and that he shouldn't have said anything to her about his work. She wants to see what he is doing, and Nick will not want publicity.

Hot notions of her spending the night cooled slowly as he found a light jacket to wear on the ride to her place. Charley got the idea despite his genuine desire for her, he did not want to ruin a good thing. He knew they would be together, only it wasn't going to be tonight.

CHAPTER 23

Arpit Patel was beginning to catch the odors of the foreign scientists busy at work all day. Something unusual tweaked his nose. He did not intentionally smell them. Maybe it was the foods they ate or personal hygiene products from other countries they used that defined them as not familiar. He was sure he did not smell very fresh either from sweating about the ejecta sample in his pocket that would certainly get him fired if discovered.

They wound down the experiments at just after 6:00 p.m. Arpit wondered if Nogishi, Meleyev, and Pat Beck would keep him in the loop on the next phase of findings. He imagined that this was where his talents as a politician would come into play. Nothing was said to him about any tests other than the usual *be quiet about this* he heard in one form or another as many times as they felt necessary. He got the idea. Pat, who was either tired or wanting to be alone with Becky, shut the main analysis screen off and turned to Arpit.

"Those samples will have to be placed in the vault, Patel. Dr. Nogishi will go with you. He may be briefed on the locking procedures in the event that he will need to do some additional tests. Go on now and show him how to put them away. Good work today."

Pat dismissed his young assistant without a handshake and turned to the young female student waiting silently behind him.

Arpit nodded and began to wheel the cart with the silver lockbox out of the lab and down the hall with the ripe-smelling diminutive doctor following close behind.

"I think today's work was most exciting. This will change our perspective on interstellar geology big time! You are good in the lab. Are you planning to go for a doctorate?" said the doctor. Arpit realized that the entire day, neither of the foreigners spoke his name.

"No, sir, not at this time. I am still unsure about what field in which to specialize. There are so many to choose from. I have time, not much probably, but I want to be sure."

Arpit forgot about the rock for a moment as he truly did not know what his next career move would be. He opened the security door, describing the procedures for Nogishi. He assumed that Beck would give him a key; he was not going to give him his. After the doctor was re-briefed, Arpit parked the cart in the room, locked the door, and made his way to his room; checking his watch, he quickened his pace. It was 6:25 p.m. Zonic would be there in five minutes.

Soon, he was behind his door and feeling some relief; he opened the silver sample tube and placed the rock inside, screwing it tightly. His mouth was dry as was his body. He went to the refrigerator, took a bottle of water, and drank nearly the entire contents. He would have had more, but his mouth and throat felt constricted and frigid from the icy water.

Two sharp raps at the door sent him to answer it directly.

"It's Zonic."

Arpit let him in and handed the capsule to him instantly.

"Zone, those guys were all about security on this thing, and I know why. I could have lost my job if they found me with it."

"Take it easy, man. What do you know? What is this thing?" Zonic said, putting his hand on the young man's shoulder, calming him slightly.

"Well, it is radioactive, it is from another star system, and it is biological in nature." Ed looked at him for the complete story and was certain he was getting just the basics. Arpit stopped, adjusted his glassed, and looked away.

"What else, Arpit?" Ed said slowly.

"Drs. Meleyev and Nogishi are quite certain that is not merely a rock but also internal scans and tests prove that it is a mode of transportation for some sort of—you're not going to believe this—alien sperm." Arpit realized immediately that he was sworn to secrecy. He continued.

"No one is supposed to know, so don't say anything. It can be dangerous if handled, Zone, so whatever you do with it, use gloves. Better yet, do not touch it at all. Have it encased in plastic or glass."

"Sperm? This rock has sperm inside? I promise that I will keep it on the down low, and I will take precautions. Thanks, man."

Ed took a world card form his jumpsuit with a five hundred and a globe printed on the front and handed it to Arpit, who took it and was suddenly relieved that the deal was done.

"You want to get some dinner?"

Arpit was not hungry. He was also not good at stealing and pretending to be innocent. He gave Zonic a nervous shrug and the hope of him leaving as soon as possible, taking that incriminating rock out of his proximity. "No, thanks. I need a shower. Remember, nobody knows," said Arpit.

"Nobody knows."

*****

Nick slept for the better part of ten hours, and his dreams were unmemorable, but he was sure they were not as fantastic as what he stumbled across in the lab. He awoke calmly, looking at his watch from habit, not really caring what time it was, and rose with a stretch and resume his work. He went to the bathroom, brushed his teeth, and gargled; these things should be done before he went to sleep, he thought in passing. Taking another coffee from the Compu-meal 2200 machine, he took himself across the gravel yard to the barn.

The night was clear and not quite cool. The stars were out tonight in abundance. Stopping, he looked up and gazed at the heavens, hoping to get lucky and see a shooting star. He basked in the starlight orchestrated by a symphony of crickets, some near and others far, feeling certain that his childhood fascination with these insects had brought him to the discovery of a lifetime.

Satisfied with his personal absorption of solar reflection, he continued the walk to the barn. He opened the door and turned on the lights, assuming Charley was doing well on his date and would call eventually.

With three samples left to test, he still had no idea how to present his findings. It seemed that any venue would bastardize the beauty and power of the accidental effects of fossil-enhanced imaging or whatever he would eventually call it. It occurred to him that he needed to test the parameters of the ultra-dimensionality aspect of this phenomenon. He was on the phone in no time. Burt was surprised to hear from him so early but accommodated his request for solar access.

Soon, the machines were humming again. He was on the thirty-first sample, wearing his gloves and goggles for protection. This cricket sample depicted the creature in a wetland's atmosphere. A mist floated in the chamber to test the wet air. Small amounts of condensation formed on the glove. The small cricket sat patiently on a twig.

He pulled his hand away, and the water fell off into the chamber. Entering the box again, he pressed his finger into the mud. It responded. An indentation formed in the odd-feeling, less-than-normal-density mud; water seeped in the hole. After recording the data of the sample, he reset the machine to view the next globe. Scratching his face, not worried about his need to shave, he started up the imager and peered into the box. Cricket number 32 was much larger than most and seemed to be the most mobile. It ran around, apparently searching for food under piles of fern fronds. Something was different in this time. The holo-image seemed to intensify around one corner of the PFC. Light shone an odd shade of blue. Nick set his camera to take ten automatic photos, one every ten seconds at a telephoto level, bringing images into frame twenty yards away.

Nick heard his heart beating a bit faster taking the camera to the computer and placing it in the cradle. The computer snapped into place and then collated the photos in single flash. Ten fuzzy photos revealed a landscape of blue leaves and trees.

The resurgence of sun power combining with the records of the cricket cycle seemed to have expanded the details of the cricket biota to include even a wider area that originally expected. He did not expect any of this. A still image would have satisfied him plenty. The question that remained was that of parameter. How far would the imager image? He knew what had to be done and was not sure if it could be avoided. He had to get inside the box himself and look around; it would mean exposing his body to the possibly dangerous light-emitting configuration. He had to cover himself completely, and the thing that wouldn't dismiss itself from the small list of possibilities was a wet suit he had in the basement.

Leaving the machine running, he ran back to the house and into his basement, where he found the old wet suit he used to snorkel with from time to time. Leaving the flippers and tank but taking the mask and gloves and a good pair of firm soled slippers, he crunched his way back across the gravel and began to strip. Soon, he was covered from head to toe with black rubber, complete with gloves, boots, and protective orange-lensed goggles. Disregarding his comic appearances, he took a step stool to the PFC and opened the coffin-like lid. Standing on the stool for a moment to maintain his balance, he stepped into the box and then brought himself to a sitting position in the far end of the PFC.

He noted the warmth of the light and was concerned that the imager, having cycled upward, exerting adjusted power levels over a period of a fifteen seconds' time, might cause an overload. Amazingly, the system was somehow accommodating his presence in the PFC. He sat in the bathtub of light. He took the lid and closed it slowly, taking a supine position. Pulling his body up, he saw a most amazing view.

The orange goggles blocked some of the blue light, realizing traces of color to his brain. Nick squinted to make out the unmistakable image of a forward-generated light source: the coffin remained pulsating with many shades of blue light.

He moved carefully to adjust himself, not to disturb the cricket that appeared between his legs. Nick forced himself to observe without drawing conclusions initially. This was a skill he had developed for some time, finding that jumping to conclusions often led to omission of important data.

With the aid of the orange goggles, the sun source color had changed to a dull yellow, and leaves seemed to take on shades of orange, red, and brown. Propping himself up on his elbows to get a better view and misjudging his balance, his hand slipped and met the blue wall of the PFC. Nick felt the side of the coffin give way. He drew his hand back and was certain he had breached the wall. This prompted him to stare with all his ocular power. His glasses pinched his face under the goggles. Adjusting them, he could make out hazy images of uncertain coloring in the light. What effect did the light have on the walls of the cabinet? He placed his weight on his right side and slowly moved his hand to touch the light, when to his utter amazement, it pushed past the light.

Expecting to touch the box less and less, his hand pushed into the swirling blue wall. For a moment, he thought his hand was going beyond the wall. He had to be reaching out the peek door. Yet as he moved it to and fro, he knew that the image system was creating more than a holographic reproduction.

It exerted enough intensity to actualize much more of the surroundings of the sample regardless of the physical parameters of the PFC. Nick raised his leg, meeting rubber boot to wall, his hand passed through; likewise, his foot disappeared into the light.

He kept a cool head, remembering a rule of progression in scientific experimentation to not take a step forward without reviewing previous steps. Upon review, the next step was quite logical. He rolled his body completely over slowly to the left and passed beyond the light. He was now lying on the leaf-covered ground, staring up at the sun in what appeared to be a very real forest.

For a few minutes, nothing made more sense to him than staying still and looking straight up. With a new sense of confidence, he acknowledged a transition into alternate reality. He looked to his right to see a six-sided oblong box of blue light, oscillating gently and eerily in a small open knoll sparsely strewn with trees overlooking the gentle slope of a hilly forest. The air was fresher than any air he had ever smelled. His lungs welcomed the euphoric cleanliness that soon spread the entirety of this body and mind.

"Unbelievable," he said aloud, and after he spoke, the first words in the new world he was instantly aware of sounded of life in the sky. He could not see them at first but heard the most incredible birdcalls and squawks, not unlike parrots or macaws, only dominantly louder and accompanied by smaller chirps and songs that sprang sporadically from the trees above. Finding the instance to sit up, Nick beheld a world from the past.

Recalling the age of the sample being over fifteen million years redirected his thinking. He had found a time machine, and he was not looking for one. He felt a sudden dual sense of lack of forethought and luck. There were too many variables entering his mind.

He spun at the sound of a loud call that was not a bird, maybe a monkey of some sort. This confirmed to him that it was a good idea to return into the light and see if he could get back. This was important. He laid back after taking a long look into the primordial trees and then rolled to the right, finding his body meeting a more than slight resistance to the light; nevertheless, he penetrated it and found himself back inside the blue light-drenched box, hopefully yet in his pole barn laboratory.

CHAPTER 24

Michelangelo Moreni inspected his shoes whenever he was on an elevator. Making a point not to talk to people in elevators was another rule by which he lived. Any conversation carried on in an elevator never amounted to anything more than superficial banter. The things that people said in an elevator aggravated the Italian because it was always insincere. Why do people feel the need to say anything to perfect strangers-in an elevator?

If it was about the weather or how fast or slow the lift was, he usually ignored conversation with a smile and some feigned European miscomprehension. Seeing someone you were acquainted with was another matter altogether. A "good morning" or "hello" was aptly sufficient, for the sake of decency.

He finished checking out one shoe for scuffs and dirt and then moved to the other. The doors opened to release several socially uncomfortable office workers off to their floor. His light gray tailored suit accentuated his lean build, standing nearly a head taller than the other three people in the elevator adjusting themselves in the available space. Never placing his suitcase on the floor in an elevator was another rule since it usually carried world cards valued at costs higher than that of the entire building he was in at any given time. Being the chief liaison between the European Capitol Association and a variety of space-based organizations had not been his job for long, yet dealing with large transactions was something that he had been doing now for nearly twenty-five years.

A young woman was trying to carry on a conversation with a young mail carrier, who was apparently used to idiotic discourse. The woman was talking about the temperature in the electronic shading canopy in the parking lot and how it gave her child a cold.

The bell rang, heralding another floor. He had several to go to arrive at Gerhard Steele's penthouse offices. His left hand was gloved and wired to a tiny yet effective power source taped to his side. The palm and inner fingers were equipped with a metallic fabric that when activated would deliver a shock capable of disabling the largest attackers. The pointer finger was armed with a laser lens that could sever bone in one quick burst. Diplomacy was rather his style, but the European Capitol Association made him wear one. Luckily, he had not had the opportunity to use it, but it brought him a sense of ease to have it in case his charismatic diplomacy failed him.

A hacker would have to be of international class to be able to steal and transfer the value of a world card in his new leather briefcase for *TerraLuna* today. It could happen in an instant. He needed to be prepared.

His thoughts turned to Steele, who was receiving reconstruction funding for *TerraLuna* built into the contract as disaster insurance. All insurance companies contest paying huge sums of world dollars and reply with a counter offers. This contract was clear and fair, and settled upon by tough Texan lawyers expecting not a murmur of nonconformity.

The association funded several organizations looking for capital for space exploration. *TerraLuna* was easily approved because of Steele's solid reputation but more importantly because it was very well organized, for the first year projected substantial profits, securing the integrity of the loan. However, since the accident, there had been a 26 percent cancellation rate, alarming everyone involved.

Since the accounts and details of expenses were established as an open charter with the Space Capital Association because of the lack of precedent of a hotel on the moon, Moreni was aware that Steele might want to negotiate new terms for repayment on the initial loan. He was prepared to talk but had little slack to offer the project that had come under scrutiny now that safety issues could cost the SCA insurance capital and reputation.

As he realized his shoes were clean, he looked up to see the light settle on the fortieth floor. The mail carrier and his friend left together, still talking about some nonsense. A woman with a graying Dutch boy haircut and teeth too large for her mouth angled her oddly shaped body away from others, apparently sharing his disdain for elevator babble in her own way.

The elevator stopped on the forty-first floor, and she exited after giving him a quick glance and smile that he returned silently. Now alone to make the final ride to the fifty-second floor to meet with Steele, Moreni felt a twinge of desire for coffee and hoped Steele had some fresh cookies as well.

The elevator decelerated to the fifty-second floor and released its passenger to the plush offices of *TerraLuna*. A bespectacled woman seemingly very young for her position sat at a large desk, meeting Moreni's glance as he walked in across the steel gray carpeting of business headquarters.

"Good morning, Francesca. How are you today?" Michelangelo offered with extra charm, knowing she liked his accent.

"Very well today, Signor Moreni. It is going to be a hot one today. Can I get you some coffee? We have iced or hot," she said, already standing.

"Yes, I would very much like some. Hot, please."

"One teaspoon sugar and a touch of cream. I remember. Have a seat, and I will tell Mr. Steele you are here." She went into a room to the left with Moreni tagging his eyes along her bottom reflexively.

He took a comfortable seat at the windows overlooking the cityscape of Houston in the distance, tugging at his glove to ensure he hadn't activated it. The weapon had a very safe "off" mode; he found some calm by checking it from time to time out of habit. The haze of the early hours lifted slowly as cars eased their way to their daily destinations.

Steele emerged from his office, walking in his usual ultra-erect fashion, extending his hand to the Italian.

"Michelangelo, Good morning. Did Francesca tell you we have some fresh cake today? I will have them set out in my office. She has your coffee there. Let's go in." He smiled and, with his left hand, directed him into his office. Moreni, still holding his briefcase, allowed himself to be led into the German's hospitality and took a seat on the leather sofa. The mahogany coffee table held a silver tray containing some familiar Italian cookies designed for dunking as well as a small white cake that he suspected might have a cannoli filling. Steele had done his homework and undoubtedly wanted something.

"This is a surprise. I love biscotti. How did you know? Did you call my secretary?" he said, taking a small taste of the cookie.

"I am trying to thank you for all you have done to help us," he said, taking the coffee.

"Well, there are perks to high finance. I won't deny they are usually very nice. Thank you. How are things going on the moon?" he said before a sip of hot coffee.

"The repairs are nearly complete. The next transport is due to arrive later this year, after Thanksgiving, and it will have hotel operation staff, as well as myself, on board to prepare for the grand opening. You will be attending, I hope? I have not seen your physical confirmation. We really must see the doctor. It is a requirement, of course, but for you, being in such good shape, I am sure it will be a formality."

"I am having some trouble with the wife, Gerhard, to tell you the truth. She is very . . . traditional and frankly is concerned about being able to breathe and motion sickness. Needless to say, she has some issues with space flight. I have shown her the safety video. Perhaps with some more coaxing, I can convince her to come." He finished his cookie, not revealing all his wife's concerns. She hated Gerhard Steele.

"We should have her in for a weekend to tour the simulator. Once she takes a ride on the mock transport, her fears of the nausea of the space place will disappear faster than her first glass of champagne during the simulation, which is followed by a gourmet lunch. She will be on the moon, and it will seem like a luxurious afternoon at her favorite restaurant. You will talk to her about this. I am looking forward to having both of you there. It is important."

Steele looked at the moneyman, hoping he would be excited about the free trip to the moon.

"I will talk to her. Most certainly, it will take some coaxing, but it is not out of the realm of possibility. Gerhard, you will forgive me. I have to catch a flight, and I cannot stay too long. Shall we come to business? I have a world card here from our insurance division."

He opened his briefcase after sliding his right pointer finger over the lock sensor reading his fingerprint and then entering the combination behind an automatically appearing panel. He produced a file folder containing a gold holo-signer and a platinum world card with the insignia of the Space Capital Association icon of the solar system, designating the earth and moon color green, glued to the inside of the folder. He placed the three-by-seven-inch plate on the coffee table and tapped its screen. A holographic sign pad generated a line and an X. Steele read the settlement terms of the damage to *TerraLuna*, hovering in holographic script three feet above the table.

Steele presented his finger after only a moment of professional hesitation. The sum seemed sufficient to cover the cost of the repairs, considering the premium; it wasn't such a bad deal. He signed his flamboyant signature into the field. Moreni removed the card from its glue and handed it to him with a receipt.

"Thank you, Michelangelo. Before you go, you must have some of this cannoli cake. I had it sent just for you. I know you will love it." Steele deftly took a silver knife and sliced a wedge of the white confection. Before Moreni knew what was happening, he was holding the plate with raised eyebrows at the aroma of the fresh cake.

"You do know how to treat the Italian. This is certain. Thank you." He took a forkful of the cake and nodded his approval, while Steele cut himself a slice as well. After a few moments of enjoyment, Steele found his opportunity to bring up some new business.

"Michelangelo, I am sure it is not secret that people are taking our accident very much to heart. The Skylars have taken a great deal of care in the defense of our hotel. You know more than anybody that as Benjamin brought most of the major watchdog organizations, he created the most comprehensive COTE system anywhere. Any 'celestial object threatening Earth' is detected and eliminated. In most cases, millions of miles from Earth. His dealing with objects threatening the moon has won prizes in the scientific community.

"We are developing some new technology that will help us defend the perimeter of *TerraLuna* so that a second assault will not harm our investment and our guests." Moreni continued, eating his cake in silence, readying himself for the pitch. Steele was going to ask for more money. He kept listening to the consummate salesman, allowing him to make his proposal. The German's talent of getting whatever he wanted was established by his excellent communication skills and executed with practical terms. He nodded understandingly, allowing him to finish.

"What we have in mind is a local defense system that is currently being researched. This program will allow a sort of field of force to be generated around the complex design to deflect any potentially damaging material from space. What we are looking for is probably another 375 million to make it happen. Naturally, we will need to refinance the entire loan with a higher yet reasonable payment. With the projected profits from *TerraLuna*, we could increase our monthly by, let's say, 30 percent. I believe this increase in security with our new defense model will, in fact, lessen the need for such as, let's say, excessive insurance premium. To completely realize our financial goals for the first year based on projected return business and referrals, we will be reorganizing our advertising strategy, of course. However, the beauty of it is that with this local defense, we can be sure of the complete safety of our guests. Could you set the ball in motion on this? I would like to begin sometime before the end of the month."

Michelangelo Moreni finished his cake and washed it down with some coffee with sufficient pause, making Steele wait as he sorted the brass tacks of the offer. Wiping his lips with an imported linen napkin, he caught Steele's gaze squarely and explained to Steele's alacrity in a tone not unlike that of a priest responding to a question of gluttony.

"Gerhard, you must know that we have entered an arrangement with *MoonCorp*. Stan Duncan had spent months organizing this team that consists of Yokomoto-Chen and the Skylars, among others. Accommodating their financial needs has put the SCA in, shall we say, a fiscal freeze. Not that the answer is no. We foresee no problem with *TerraLuna*. The asteroid was a freak. Skylar thinks some sort of spatial rip that allowed it so near so fast. I understand it was a one-in-a-quadrillion chance. I will have to bring it to the board. I cannot authorize such a loan during this period of growth on the spot. I will draw up a prospectus based on your proposal, and I will pitch it for you. Although I might suggest another avenue even if it is somewhat bias to our clients at *MoonCorp*." He paused again, dangling the jewel before the anger-prone German.

"What sort of avenue are you talking about, signor?" Steele said, keeping control.

"Stan Duncan's people have already developed a local defense system that works. I saw the demonstration, and it is incomparable to anything I have seen. I am not sure of the dynamics. They did not explain them. You might save some time and money by giving Stan a call and working out some sort of trade. Work out some points with him. Trade services or vehicles for the technology. Of course, Gerhard, the SCA or I do not propose to mediate any such deal. You are my friend. Stan Duncan, shall we say, has had his share of setbacks. I cannot say how he would respond. Though I remember a time when he decided not to proceed with his hotel until he solved the local defense problem, among others. This does not reflect a degree of financial ethics and insight that we at SCA appreciate. Frankly, *MoonCorp* had some troubles financing before the Skylars, and YC added their wealth to the project. We decided that with these two super companies backing him and with a more than reasonable degree of assurance of the new defense system, the project merited our attention. You see, we have invested a great deal in a sure thing, and, Gerhard, I am afraid it will take a measurable increase in the area of COTE safety to affirm any funds for *TerraLuna*, insurance payments notwithstanding. I suggest you take your hat in your hand and call Stan. See what you can work out in terms of price or trade. In the meantime, I will tell my wife that you are concerned with her comfort and safety." Moreni finished his coffee, collected his briefcase, and then consulted his watch with finality.

"You are right. I really should give Stan a call. It is unusual that *he* has something that *I* need! I hope he is of a mind to negotiate considering that I am his only competition." He laughed slightly. Steele quietly regarded his predicament in fear of what he would say if he were in Duncan's position.

Moreni extended his hand, knowing that he had placed *TerraLuna*'s chief executive in a humbling position that was well deserved.

"Work together, and forget about the race or the glory of the first hotel on the moon. You have already won that fight. The building is there. However, I would advise not opening it without local security. You are the first hotel on the moon, yes, but you cannot afford the risk of being the first fiasco on the moon. Good morning, Mr. Steele."

Steele looked after the moneyman after he left for a moment. Instinctively, he pulled at the world dollar card, separating the dab of glue from the cardboard folder. With a few precise steps, he took it to his desk, tapped the computer screen build into his desk to access *TerraLuna*'s bank account, and scanned in the money transfer, depleting the card in the process. As the yellow-green light of the card display dimmed to zero world dollars, his eyes narrowed as did the options of what sort of lunar defense this money would buy.

*****

After Pepe and Tico gorged themselves with the binding rice with chicken gravy, a short snooze was in order as the rest of the morning warmed into a sweltering afternoon. The plan was to go to the marina and prepare to set sail and be home for dinner if Paloma's remedy had its effect.

They woke just before one and set out for the dock. The streets were nearly empty, save for some electric bus passengers waiting in the cooling booths on the corner about a block from the hotel. They made their way to the dock where a commotion was taking place. Several of the boats along the perma-painted white pier had people milling about them with cleaning brooms and buckets of some sort of antiseptic-smelling solution.

Pepe approached one of the boats and stopped to see what the matter was. The boat was a bit smaller than his was. The sides and underbelly as far as he could see was covered with some kind of whitish or clear jelly smelling like dead fish.

Even with Pepe's lifelong resistance to the smell of fish, he couldn't help but cover his nose. Tico sneezed and walked away in a funny circle to get himself clear from the odor. Pepe approached the boat and called to the sailor wearing arm-length blue-green rubber gloves, using a mop to scrub the boat.

"Hey, what happened to your boat, amigo?"

The small deeply brown-skinned man squinted from over his bandanna covering his face and under his straw hat.

"We do not know. I think we might have had an attack of whale barf or jellyfish. Sometimes the tide brings millions of them in, but I don't think so. I never saw anything like this." He continued to wash the boat, the antiseptic cleaner apparently not working so well to remove the slime. Pepe waved to the man and started toward his boat, hoping he would not find the same condition on *La Fresca*. Unfortunately, Pepe found that the same goop that had infested most of the other boats he saw along the dock was surrounding his boat with a sticky ring and a stinky smell.

"This is awful, Tico. We are sick in the stomach as it is, and now we have to have this smell to make it worse. I bet this has to do with those deep-sea bugs we saw."

A queasy feeling presented itself again in Pepe's lower intestines, bringing a wide roll to his eyes. They climbed aboard, and Pepe unlocked the cabin and went into the small washroom, where he kept some medicine for indigestion, and took three tablets, washing it down with a swig of water.

They sat on the couch for a moment to rest. He thought of starting the ship's engines and run the air-conditioning system. He closed his eyes to collect his thoughts and quite naturally opened his eyes with a notion he did not like. He grunted resignedly and reached into his dungarees and pulled his phone from the back pocket. His thick fingers tapped the professor's phone number at a very early hour.

"Hello, Professor Sanchez? This is Pepe Fernandez. I think you might want to come to the dock. You remember the white stuff we saw on the seafloor, the stuff that was on"—he lowered his voice—"Benito? Well, you should come now and see. It looks like the same white slime that is all over the boats at the marina! It smells like death."

Sanchez listened motionlessly in his usually swiveling, swiveling chair.

"Senor, where are you now?"

"I am on my boat. The other boatmen are scrubbing it off with disinfectant, but it is thick and is collecting along the dock." He paused for some kind of answer from Sanchez.

"I will come there in an hour. Meet me at your boat at around nine o'clock. Try not to touch it, senor. I will bring sample collectors and some gloves and other gear. Goodbye for now."

Pepe closed the phone. Tico was snooping around the cabin, trying to find one of his toys or a bone, not as worried as Pepe now that he was back in a familiar place yet aware that his master was upset. Another gurgle from Pepe's stomach prompted him to spend some time in the bathroom and catch up on the news. The vid-screen he had installed across from the toilet really came in handy sometimes. He crouched forward, examining the news from Celestun and the nation and international sources.

Before long, he thought that rather than starting the engines to cool off, they should go back to the hotel and wait for the professor there. He secured the cabin and settled back to the hotel. Other boat owners were out on the dock scratching their heads, trying to make sense of the phenomenon in the marina. Pepe spotted a local police car pull up into the parking lot above the dock. His pace quickened to avoid talking to the police, melding into the crowded street.

The indigestion pills seemed to be taking effect, but it was probably the rice that was doing the trick. The walk to the hotel was uneventful. *Thank goodness,* Pepe thought. They walked into the cool lobby of the hotel, and Pepe almost came to a halt at the door when he saw the newswoman, Dahlia Morales, standing at the front desk, talking to the clerk. The clerk saw the fisherman and his dog and abruptly, with a pointed finger, referred the local celebrity to their arrival.

Morales turned to them and offered her a large painted red smile surrounding large teeth, altogether a frighteningly big mouth. She approached him with an outstretched hand.

"Senor Fernandez, how are you today? I am Dahlia Morales from Mexico One news." He politely took her hand, which she pumped generously, still smiling at him. Pepe, unable to speak for fear of talking to the woman, nodded and offered an attempt at a smile. "I was hoping to ask you a few questions about the events at sea a couple of days ago concerning the death of Benito Juarez. It won't take a few minutes."

She took his arm and led him to the couch in the lobby next to a window overlooking the street. A slow ceiling fan whirred noisily above their heads. As they sat, Morales scratched Tico's head, who did not mind the attention one bit, quite unaware of his master's fear of reporters. He sniffed the new smell of her brightly colored print dress and young legs and then found a comfortable spot on the rug.

"Did you happen to see that jellyfish infestation at the marina? I have never seen anything like that. Do you charter your boat for parties, senor?" She started into the questions.

"No. Not usually. I fish only-no party."

"Dr. Rene Sanchez hired you to take him on sort of a rock hunt earlier this week."

Pepe looked at her after a period of pretending to inspect the lobby's decorations and then said, "He was looking for rocks from the sky."

"You helped him find these rocks?" she said in a tone not unlike that used when speaking to someone who was hiding something.

Pepe would have liked to tell this woman off with some fancy word like "patronize," of which he was not quite sure he knew the exact meaning, but he nodded.

"Yes, we found some rocks that had fallen into the sea near Progreso. He is a respected authority on the subject, you know. You should really speak to him."

Dahlia made notes on her handheld screen with a plastic stylus. "It is very sad about the death of young Senor Juarez. Can you tell me in your own words what happened that day?"

Sweat started to form around his eyes, not from heat but because of nervousness and maybe food poisoning. "There was something floating in the water, and Dr. Sanchez wanted Benito to take a goody bag and collect it. It was a kind of skin like snake's shed. The water was a little choppy, but Benito thought it was safe. He jumped in. I saw him collect the skins and went back to work. The next time I look in the water, he is gone." Pepe, still unaware of the sweat wave building on his forehead, looked directly at the woman fixed by her gaze, hoping he would be excused to go back to the room and lie down.

The reporter was inwardly impressed with herself that she had taken the time to meet with Senor Fernandez. Nowhere in Professor Sanchez's statement did he mention anything about snakeskins. He had said that he had gone into the water, implying that it was for a swim to cool off.

She wrote *snakeskins* on the screen, tilting it to prevent him from looking on.

"Ms. Morales, I really must take Tico back to the room. He is not feeling too good. Is there anything else?" he said, which to him was a polite attempt at asserting himself.

"Yes. What can you tell me from your experience? What is that white slime on the boats?" She looked squarely at him, her stylus touching the pad.

Pepe felt his throat stiffen as he recalled the creature's grasping legs as they tried to snatch the underwater camera on La Huevo.

"It could be a whale or dolphin sperm from a pack that was mating. That can be pretty thick, you know. Or maybe . . . jellyfish? Sometimes a collection of whale barf . . .," he said with half a chuckle, now feeling the need to reach the washroom himself. Tico wined a bit, thinking it would be impolite to bark in the nice lobby.

"Okay, Tico, we go out soon."

Dahlia Morales reached into her bag and offered Pepe her card.

"Here is my number, senor. In case you would like to tell me anything else about your trip with Senor Sanchez," she said with vague suspicion. Pepe shrugged and smiled.

"I don't know what else to say. It was an accident. He hit his head or had a seizure. For all we know, it could have been a shark or a barracuda. I will watch you on the news tonight, senorita. You are very pretty. But now Tico and I have to take care of some business. *Buenos días.*"

Pepe rose, and Tico followed his lead immediately as they both walked oddly to their room.

CHAPTER 25

The idea of calling Stan Duncan turned Steele's face and neck red. He went to his adjoining bathroom, removed his coat, opened his sleeves, and placed his cufflinks and glasses in a silver dish on the counter. He washed his face and hands and rinsed his wrists with cold water. This calmed his nerves, allowing him to think clearly and compose a proposition for Stan Duncan. It was suspected by pundits that *TerraLuna*'s groundbreaking inception and financial clout delayed *MoonCorp* nearly two years. Investment capital on that scale found favor with his company and left Duncan waiting for an appropriate opening. He had won the battle of preeminence but now had to arrange diplomacy that required nothing short of begging for political mercy, at need for additional defense technology.

He stared at his well-preserved mien, nearing fifty. A smile skipped to his face to compliment his classic good looks. He dried himself with a fluffy gray towel and rolled his sleeves down. After replacing his cufflinks and glasses, he combed his hair, finding himself searching for some way around the problem. Leslie Davis had infiltrated the company quite well. She had reported gathering some essential information but had not managed to copy actual blueprints. He hoped that the defense system could be applied when *MoonCorp* was distracted by the excitement of their success. *If he disguised Duncan's plans as his own, could they ever know?* He thought. Finally, he put the comb back in place. After tamping away his faint wrinkles with an electronic skin puller, he was fully refreshed. Grooming had a stimulating effect on his imagination.

He stumbled upon the issue of distraction. What could be distracting enough for *MoonCorp* to not be suspicious of his new defense initiative if the grand opening wasn't enough? If only he could stop that, then they would be devastated. A slow surge of darkness crept across the soul of Gerhard Steele. Sabotage? Did he want to go that far? It would double his profits. He would be the only commercial venture on the moon and the second to Yokomoto-Chen for off-world profit. Crossword puzzle answer for "Moon Hotel"- *TerraLuna*. *It would be the only answer!*

Remembering again why he needed to win—a woman—made him nearly lose the composure he had attained. Not satisfied with that motivation, it came to him— *the other woman*. His in-reserved uncharacteristic riff was abruptly interrupted by a familiar sound. He heard the outer office door open. He finished in the washroom and entered his office to find his secretary slicing a piece of the cake he had ordered for Moreni.

"This cake is really good. It's so fresh tasting. They must have made it early this morning," she said, tasting the cake.

"Take it home with you," he said flatly.

"The clinic called and has passed you, again. You are clear for the trip. Also, the flight coordinator wants to know if you will be taking a guest, and if so, she will have to make an appointment for an exam."

She ate some of the cake, looking to her boss with a discerning smile.

"What do I have to do this afternoon?"

"There is nothing planned. Yet we have the list of things that need your attention."

"Let's meet at 1:30 p.m."

He nodded her away. She gracefully removed the tray and left the room. He followed her, closing the door behind him, leaning against it, deep in thought. He looked to his desk and thought that showing interest in Stan might be the first step, if not completely honest, to resolving the defense issue. His simple swivel chair was designed not to be comfortable. This was ironic since his office offered modern conveniences and comforts many people did not have in their homes. Staring at the phone, Steele knew the price for Duncan's defense system would be huge, but how huge? Steele felt not the slightest bit of guilt for the schemes he hatched to win investors. Whatever seemed to hinge on the result of this call, it had to happen. He needed a price. He rang Stan Duncan.

"Hello, this is Stan Duncan."

"Stan, how are you? Gerry Steele here."

"Gerry, it has been quite a while. It's too bad about that accident. How is it coming along?" Stan said without a hint of sarcasm. Of course, Steele often heard sarcasm when others spoke, inventing it for himself.

"Well, luckily, we have insurance. I suppose it could have been worse. If it had happened with a hotel full of guests and a direct impact on the atrium, we could be completely ruined. I am getting some pressure from the investors, pressure for safety."

There was a brief silence to allow him to receive the gist, and then the German continued. "I understand your golden boys have designed a local defense in case old Ben Skylar's space defense misses a bogey. How is that coming along?"

"We tested it a couple of days ago, and it is effective actually. It may change the outer aesthetics of the complex, but it is worth it. We predict that in addition to Skylar, it offers . . . complete invulnerability against any foreign object down to the … well the testing is going to need to continue in situation of course. Yet base on the model I am working toward having our insurance premiums actually *lowered*."

Steele gave a friendly chuckle that served as a bridge to the reason for his call, now hating the position he was in. "Reason I am calling, Stan, is to congratulate you for getting *MoonCorp* on track. I understand Moreni, Skylar, and Yokomoto have more than a minor interest in your hotel these days. It takes some politicking to make that happen. You have done a great job, and I am proud to have you as a lunar neighbor. What I am interested in is your feelings about sharing your local defense matrix with

TerraLuna. Being the only neighbor on the planetoid has its advantages, and I am willing to provide our vehicles and services at any time. We could get some mileage from our CPs."

"Thanks, Gerry. It is good to know that you are there in case we run out of tartar sauce or cocktail napkins. That goes without saying. Let me explain this to you. Our prospectus accommodates us with a complete list of equipment, supply, transport—you name it. We are self-sufficient, have to be. However, When it comes to our proprietary trade brand…if you are interested, I suppose I can give you an estimate to install our local defense array on your hotel. Could you transfer the specifications to my screen?" Stan countered with the agility of also being a seasoned salesman.

Gerry paused slightly at the suggestion of sending his schematics, but what harm could it possibly do? He fingered through his computer on the desk, and within seconds, Stan was surveying the blueprints of *TerraLuna.* Steele sat quietly, almost out of small talk, and entertained a series of wordless, perhaps contrived murmurs from Duncan as he adroitly calculated the cost to outfit *TerraLuna* for defense.

"Gerry, our system is based on radio-powered sunlight. This technology is not yet patented, but as you know, once it is, we hope that the world's energy problems will be over. You will need that system and the relay collectors installed. The field generators and piping for a building your size and the labor for full operation would have to be added. Of course, we will need to send this to our engineering department, but Mr. Steele, if you will consult your screen, the estimate is sort of a base price. It will start at three billion world dollars."

Stan sat reviewing his estimate that Steele was able to see on his screen. What Stan couldn't see was redness flow from Steele's neck to his face.

"That is going to include maintenance, of course. I really hope that price includes a lifetime warranty as well," Steele negotiated feebly, still in the early stages of shock.

Stan Duncan continued imperceptibly, loving how the honesty of his proposal was certainly getting on the nerves of his old adversary and perhaps bump him out of the ten billion Corporate Point Club.

"Naturally, Gerry, we stand behind our product. It will take some time to produce the pipes. They have to be specially manufactured, and the generators are built in our labs. The satellite time, of course, we will have to charge by the monthly, much like a home utility bill, but I am sure that will not amount to much more than a few hundred thousand or so a month, which includes power for the entire complex. You can sell your nuclear generators or keep them for backup."

Steele cringed inwardly. The power base currently installed cost him more than the building itself. "Is there any way the defense system could be integrated with the nukes?"

"Well, we disregarded that after the radio power was so much more economical and safer. I would have to ask my engineers. I can get back to you on that. So what do you think?"

Stan offered with satisfaction that finally had the great Gerhard Steele in a corner. Duncan knew that those funds were going to be hard to come by, but Steele was the kind of man who could create the urgency to raise funds for anything.

"I would have to know if there is some way to transfer the power from the nukes to the matrix before I do anything. If it is not possible, I suppose the solar radio is the only way to go. I will have to speak to the board, of course. I thank you for giving me a starting point. I will get back to you sometime before the end of the month. Send me itemizations. I am planning a trip to *TerraLuna* the first week of August to prepare our opening. I will send you a prospectus. You should come up and see us. Thanks again, Stan."

Steele hurried off the line for fear of exposing the anger that was mounting within him. There was a time when three billion wouldn't be a problem. However, having to abandon the nuclear power facility was out of the question. It was waste on a monumental scale. He had a suspicion that this solar radio power thing was ready for some time and didn't mention it as a way to force *TerraLuna* to the undue expense of the obsolete nuclear source. That was a cruel trick even for Duncan. He knew *TerraLuna* would pale from the need for the radio-powered defense technology, or maybe the accident was actually an act of sabotage. This was why he had to have a sample of the meteor. He had to know.

Sitting back in his small chair to think, his face red again, needing to be rinsed, he hoped the system could be used with nuclear power. If that wouldn't work, he would give Leslie Davis more time to get him what he needed from those two, Nicholas and Porter. Her success would up the stakes considerably in his favor. It was the most economical alternative he had. There will always be a way to pass it off as his own technology.

His fingers numbly tossed unwillingly across the keyboard to his financial page to the line that brought him to a cold stop. Paying Duncan's fee for defense and power in world dollars would compromise the ten billion that kept him in the bartering game of corporate points.

*****

The Mexican day lingered in its usual sultry way with most of the inlanders going about their business of keeping cool and tending to everyday affairs. The coastal community, however, was more than concerned with the appearances of the slimy residue that in addition to clogging the docks and marinas was washing up on the sandy shores. Local police sergeant Aroja was unaccustomed to these sorts of events. His daily activity confined to local thievery and some domestic crimes. Mostly, there was a lot of fabricated milling around. Physical activity defined by Aroja was limited to the realm of simple lifting, usually carrying free boxes of steaks he would get from his brother-in-law, who managed a local slaughterhouse.

He and his men found the day exhaustive, erecting signs indicating that the public beaches were closed until further notice. The sergeant finally was resigned to drive and let the younger, leaner officer put the last sign up while he sat in the air-conditioned car, logging in his daily report.

Armando Ruiz had worked for the city of Progreso for nearly two years and was not sure of what else he could do to get a promotion. He was sure of two things, that he would have to accomplish something unique, like crack a murder case (there had been but four years to date), or impress Aroja with efficiency. One thing was sure, if something didn't happen, he was not going to stay long in this town. He wanted to get five years in, which would be a viable bargaining chip to apply for a job in Mexico City or maybe Tijuana. He drudged his way up the sandy ravine with posters under his arm, a staple gun in one hand, and a handkerchief in the other. As he approached the car, he saw his boss busy with his touch screen propped against the steering wheel, the top of his belly coming uncomfortably close to the wheel.

He opened the running car and was greeted by a surge of cool air. "Sergeant, that goo is along the entire shore. Some of the stuff dried and looks like that Styrofoam material they used to make coffee cups. What are we supposed to do?" He unceremoniously swabbed his forehead.

"Some people from the university are coming this week to run some tests. We have had a couple of reports of children touching it, causing inflammation on the skin. No one is to come in contact with it until we get the okay to have the city clean it up. That's all I know. For now, we have to patrol the beaches."

He raised his eyebrows with authority and logged an entry onto his touch screen, expelling what was certainly more routine bad breath. Armando turned his head away instinctively and caught sight of something on the shore. It looked like a large fish had washed up on the beach. "Sergeant, look over there!"

The fat cop turned and squinted simultaneously with the urgency of his years policing and saw what seemed to be a five-foot shark that must have recently washed up.

"Okay, let's get a picture of. Grab the camera and one of those body bags from the trunk."

In a minute, the young officer and the old officer were taking the ravine down to the shore to see why a shark would be so close to shore, especially since the DNA nets made it impossible for them to come near for fear of horrible electrocution. It was an amazing concept that offered a serious charge based on certain generic configurations. Whales, sharks, even pesky jellyfish steered clear of the public beaches.

The sweaty duo trudged their way through the whitish sand, each sporting sunglasses that were able to allow protection from the sun without darkened field of view. Their vision was that of a normal partly cloudy day while the blinding sun continued its reign on the hot sand below. As they came nearer the animal, they saw it was a shark. A quick lurch of the animal put them on guard. It was still alive and might bite. It was covered in the thickening glue that was suffocating the animal, covering the gills and around the mouth.

Aroja drew his gun as they carefully approached the dying shark. It writhed not so much from suffocation but from pain. In fact, it was bleeding into the surf perhaps from a wound on its underside. It lurched, sending the fat sergeant rather high in the air for a man his size.

Armando came around the side of the creature, careful not to step in the goo, and gave it a kick, rolling it over on its side. The body lunged three feet inland, exposing the underbelly as it landed. A parasite nearly two feet long was affixed to the bottom side of the shark. Four needlelike protrusions at the head were stuck into the shark's body, while the legs frantically propelled the shark back into the water, all along exuding a viscous white liquid that appeared to cause the nearly dead shark some final bursts of pain. It flopped back two feet and then another two feet. One more flop and it would be back in the water. It hissed in defiance as Armando fumbled with his camera to take a picture. Sergeant Aroja fired two shots. One missed, riveting into the sand, and another hit the shark in the head. Within the next determining moments, the insect had made its escape with its quarry and was gone.

"Did you see that thing, Sergeant? It was carrying the shark! I have never seen fangs like that! What was that thing! I didn't get a chance to take a picture!" He stood brewing frustration that there wasn't anything he could do, holding the camera and bag with futility.

"I do not know, Armando. I do know it would help us to catch one and get it to those electric net people for a DNA sample. Hopefully, it will keep them away from the beach."

He turned toward the safety and cool of the car with defensive thoughts of his young granddaughter being dragged away by the strong propulsion of the bloodthirsty bug. Her picture clipped to his visor, he recalled how she liked to play on the beach and was certain that the creature would have no problem with a thirty-pound baby if it could do that to a five-foot shark.

*****

Pepe limited himself to the prepared meals Paloma had stored in the small freezer on the boat, now eating only a little at a time, hoping her home cooking would gradually restore his system from the street food. Tico slept most of the time, but Pepe knew he was getting restless to get back to work. Not barking at a shark in more than three days upset his schedule. He was a worker as was his master. The little dog did not understand why their routine changed, but he trusted Pepe and tried to make the best of the situation. It was close to four o'clock, and he readied his returning appetite for some baked fish and tomatoes that he would reheat before meeting the professor at five. He and Tico got themselves together and made the walk to the boat. Passing the burrito vendor on the way, he had the notion to give him hell for selling bad burritos. On second thought, he noticed a bakery across the street and decided to avoid the cart and buy fresh bread to have for dinner.

Most of the shelves in the small clean-smelling store were empty, yet several cakes, cookies, and loaves remained. A lady almost as wide as she was tall in an ill-fitting dress was giving her order to the young girl behind the counter, while her similarly chubby, short daughter was watching a boy a little older than her, who may or may not have been her brother. He was fishing in his pocket.

"I have some candy for you. Do you want some candy?"

The little girl stayed close to her mother, yet her eyes ballooned at the sound of the word "candy." Nodding shyly, her attention turned to his hand as he drew it from his pocket.

"Yah!" he yelled and thrust a large rubber bug into her face, scaring the girl somehow between her mother's legs.

"The bugs are going to get you!"

The girl behind the counter reprimanded the boy and then apologized to the customer, who simply wanted to get home and have dinner. The lady and her daughter left, and Pepe ordered a loaf of bread. Looking past the counter, he saw the boy standing in the doorway, crawling the lifelike toy up the doorframe. He looked at Pepe and showed him the bug with a bit less ferocity, not intending to scare the big man but rather to show him that the bug was real-looking. Pepe nodded with a tiny smile and headed to the marina now, reassessing his own fear of sea creatures with teeth on land.

The bread reached the ship with a few bites taken away. Pepe took Tico in his arms before climbing aboard for fear that the little dog might fall into the slime bath below. Normally, he would jump on board; he never fell. He peered over the pier to see a larger amount of the goo slopped around the boat now than earlier that day as it sat in the water. Quickly, within the better-smelling safety of the cabin, he prepared dinner. Gratefully reminded of home, Pepe was soon sopping up tomato sauce with the fresh bread.

A plastic sign was being stapled to a light pole across from his berth by a slim police officer.

"ALL BOATS ARE RESTRICTED FROM LEAVING THE MARINA UNTIL THE HEALTH INSPECTOR AND MAINTENANCE CREWS HAVE REMOVED THE BLIGHT FROM THE AREA. A LOTTERY WILL BE HELD TOMORROW AT 2:00 P.M. TO DETERMINE THE ORDER OF CLEANING AND INSPECTION. PICK UP YOUR TICKET AT THE MARINA OFFICE. FEES WILL BE WAVED FOR THE DURATION OF THE CLEANUP. SORRY FOR THE INCONVENIENCE.-MANAGER."

Pepe shook his head in disgust and knew he would have to tell Paloma, who was already angry with him for being gone three days. He had not the slightest idea how long it would take them to sanitize nearly seventy boats currently moored here. He took a thoughtful drag of his cigarette and returned to the cabin with a shrug of his nose at the bad fish smell, only to be greeted with the much less putrid smell of his wife's cooking. Suddenly sick of fish, he sprayed the cabin with some air freshener, sat on the couch next to his dog, and waited for the professor.

After a fifteen-minute catnap, Professor Sanchez was heard calling from the dock. Pepe roused himself and hurried to the door, opening it to a surge of hot rank air. The professor was standing on the dock with an older woman shorter than he with her graying hair pulled back in a bun. She didn't smile at all and held a perfumed scarf over her mouth and nose.

"Senor Fernandez, this is Professor Sophia Alba. She works in the biology department at Merida. I thought she would be able to help us."

"Come in where it smells a little nicer," said Pepe with a welcoming smile.

Sanchez helped his colleague onto the boat. They went below glad to be out of the sun.

"This is Tico. He will smell you once and won't forget you after that. He is very loyal. Please come in and sit down. Can I get you something to drink?"

Pepe took three bottled waters from his refrigerator and handed them out without objection from his guests. They sat on the couch, eyeing Pepe's comfortable cabin silently, noting how neat and decorous it was for a fishing boat. After a brief silence, Dr. Sanchez began with an excitement Pepe had not seen since the discovery of the rocks when they were at sea two days ago."

"Senor Alba is a specialist in marine biology. We have had several calls from people in the town we saw on the seafloor. We will be staying at the hotel to investigate reports that I am afraid may be connected to what and conducting some tests. I know you want to get back home, but we were hoping you would stay and help us. You are familiar with the terrain, and your boat is well suited to our study. The fee is small, yet we are facing a phenomenon that is dangerous to the community and make the history books." Sanchez took a swig of his water, keeping a fix on Pepe's eyes to communicate his sincerity.

"I told my wife I would be gone for two days. I suppose four days is not so bad if . . . we are paid. She misses us very much. I suppose she will not be mad if I tell her it was that important. She gets nervous when her boys are off and may be in danger. We can handle ourselves, of course. Dr. Alba, what are those things we saw?"

"Senor, that is why I have come. From the video nodes I have seen, it is hard to classify, but it seems to be in the family of arthropods. This is a large class of animals that includes sea insects. It may also be in a larval stage like a dragonfly or mosquito. We do not know. Our goal is to capture one for observation. From what we can tell, they are parasitic and carnivorous, two traits that make them dangerous to the populous sea life and toward humans. You have ample storage for fish on board the boat and nets, I assume?" she stated, assuming Pepe understood some of the academic language.

"Well, this is a state-of-the-art fishing boat. I paid for it from catching fish. I know what I am doing, senora. I am a fisherman all my life. What worries me is that sticky substance. It is safe to be around. We saw how it"—he paused and looked to Sanchez for approval. The doctor nodded his understanding that he had told her about Benito—"stuck to Benito. It was like a cocoon. I do not want that stuff wrapping around my boat!"

"It seems to be gathering around the shore and the docks. This is why we need to set sail tomorrow before the condition worsens. I have taken the liberty of arranging your boat to be cleaned first tomorrow for our journey. We plan to capture one of the insects. Secrecy is vital at this stage of the game. Do not talk to anybody. I will have to address the press and the sergeant of the police. I would like to have some facts to present to them. We are the official word on this project."

Pepe looked worried and hoped they did not notice. He scratched his dog's head and stared off for a moment of reflection. *How did I get myself into this situation?* he thought. A part of him wanted to ask them to leave, but that would be rude. Sanchez had been fair to him, and obviously, this was a major happening. *It is the right thing to do,* he concluded to himself, now ready to address the academics.

"I will help you. However, as I do not like too much attention, please let me stay in the background. Tico and I do not like too much commotion. We are ordinary fishermen. However, I will help you find out how to deal with this problem because it will help the people feel safe. It is the right thing to do, and this I will explain to my wife."

Sophia stood and shook Pepe's hand vigorously. "Thank you, senor. We will have an expedition together that someday may be a documentary or video thesis for Enrique, who will be joining us. Leave the politics to us. They are not important. What is important is that we get one of these creatures and find the truth. I have a team at our lab at the university documenting the DNA sample from the she skins Benito was collecting. By next week, we can program its genetic code into the electric nets. We still have so many questions, and we will try to conclude our business as soon as we can so you can get back to your wife."

The over-fifty biologist was smiling more now, and Pepe enjoyed talking with someone who was so dedicated to her work. He nodded simply and, when she had finished, was eager to begin.

"Is there something I can do to help?" he inserted.

"Well, actually there is. From what Rene has told me of these creatures' habits, it seems to me that we have to acquire some kind of bait, something large and bloody. We thought you could help us by icing a calf that we will pick up from the slaughterhouse early tomorrow. Do you have an ice machine on board?"

"Yes, I do," Pepe said, offsetting the fear of him and Tico becoming a meal for these nasty things.

"Good. Dr. Sanchez and are going to discuss the trip over dinner. Would you join us?"

"We ate already."

"You must come along anyway, we will take a drink. Do you know of any good restaurants in town? I haven't been to Progreso in a few years."

Pepe paused for a moment and said, "No, senora, I cannot say that I do."

CHAPTER 26

Leslie Davis kept her simple furnished apartment free of any decorations. Anything that tempted her for a long-term stay was ushered out of her train of thought, including things like houseplants and spices. Her meals were eaten out at family restaurants or brought in plastic bags from local fast-food purveyors.

This upset her regimen of good eating as well as her attention to her shape. She wasn't going to stay for more than a couple of months. Her cover was to finish the summer with *MoonCorp* and leave at the end of August to return to class. This was what she was expected to do. It seemed like a neat enough arrangement to her. Her deals with Steele's clients usually ended with an unexpected disappearance.

She woke from her night out with Dr. Porter, thankfully without a hangover. Most importantly, she found him unobjectionable to the idea of having her in his apartment. Gaining his trust was never a problem. The information she needed was probably stored on his holo-control computer at his home. The computer was likely dedicated to his experiment. It probably would not be at *MoonCorp*, or simply existed on a data node.

The simple five-room apartment in a complex of about forty individual units was located in the southern edge of San Bernardino. She rarely saw any of her neighbors, and that suited her situation quite well. The media desk allowed her to shop and communicate, but she refrained from most normal activities of Leslie Davis. Storing any information concerning her findings at *MoonCorp* was not a good idea. She kept encrypted notes on a data node in a locked drawer disguised as a letter opener. She kept a student diary and other school items in the drawer as well.

After being undercover for three weeks, her reports were anticipatory. Leslie was admittedly eager to contact Steele with some progress but was dissatisfied with the completeness of their data. From what she gathered, the system was dependent upon the solar relay system that would be difficult for *TerraLuna* to recreate. Since Charley Porter was responsible for its inception, stealing those plans from him was her secondary objective.

That he would keep them in his computer at his apartment was logical. She would have to have time to locate and copy them onto her disguised data node. Not wanting to harm him but willing to drug him, she took inventory of the tools she would need for the task. Opening another drawer revealed an outfit of pink satin shorts, and a matching midriff top was the first check on the list. The data node/letter opener, an empty brown bottle of fast-acting sleeping powder, and some smelling salts completed her arsenal. Certain that finding her way to his apartment after work was inevitable, she gathered the things and placed them in her small duffel, ready for when the opportunity presented itself.

Taking a moment, she sent a message to Steele, including her daily report, to his private secure address. Stopping herself before shutting off the computer with a memory of past affairs with Gerhard Steele left her fingers poised on the keyboards. It was four years ago when she had applied to the *TerraLuna* Corporation on the recommendation of one of her doctoral professors who knew Steele and his affinity for young blond-haired females. He had once said that he was convinced that blond women were the most effective people of Earth. Knowing how to get what they wanted, he called the first skill. This appealed to him. Applicants were required to provide a photo. Her academic record was superlative. Her athletic physique and Barbie doll looks raised her application to the top of the list.

It wasn't long before she was hired as a research assistant. The job was exactly what she had hoped for, an opportunity to work at the birthing of new technology. Being dedicated and attractive worked well among scientists. She was entrenched in a project to minimize the size of artificial gravity generators. Coworkers not accustomed to working with beautiful women were finally able to be near a flawless woman, satisfying their egos and improving their effectiveness. It was like their lucky day, every day.

Leslie was, of course, aware of the effect she had on men. Later, she concluded that Steele manipulated her natural talents like an old trusty tool. Her control of the wandering eye (Leslie's own terminology) simultaneously kept workers at bay and satisfied them.

One day while finalizing her gravity modulation prototype, Steele stopped by to see his favorite employee in action. She deduced later, from his continuous obsession with cameras, that he likely had been watching her regularly in his screening room. A suspicious, knowing glint in his eye caught her attention when he spoke.

"I see you have risen near the top, much like in school. I am proud of you, Leslie. I would like you to see me in my office today at 3:00 p.m. I have a new project I would like you to spearhead for me."

He smiled his standard political smile until she agreed. Later that day, she sat in his office surrounded by the cherished opulence of his position.

"What I have in mind for you now is more of an ambassadorial nature. You have an excellent rapport with men . . . people. I have business in Italy with the European Space Capitol people this week. A brand-new investor is on the fence, ready with investment money. Doubt in the veracity of our latest science is the nature of his trepidation." He paused, studying her face clinically.

"I am not sure what you want me to do, Mr. Steele," she said with enough coyness to make Steele adjust his chair.

"I need you to take our plans for the gravity modulation generators and convince him to sign this contract based on the laurels of our work. Do you think you can do that for me, Leslie?" he said, nearing a tone of challenge in his voice.

It was his maneuvering of her ability to manipulate others that intrigued her so deeply. She could not call it love. It was more like sensual management. Over the next year and a half, thoughts akin to professional prostitution lurked on the outskirts of her Baptist sensibilities, where she fiercely kept them at bay during her repeated associations with parties interested in *TerraLuna*'s vision. They both knew that the modulators were still being tested but secured funding anyway.

Excitement like this was addictive. The commitment involved represented something unspoken she had always wanted from men but was nowhere to be found in her dealings with them, yet with Steele it was ever present. By the end of the first year with *TerraLuna*, she spent more time convincing the signing of financial agreements, committing huge sums for the company, than on her lab work. Long afternoon strategy meetings evolved into long lunches and eventually romantic interludes with Steele. He satisfied her with physical pleasure but moreover with his eloquent use of power. He utilized her personal skills, which yielded very exacting results, in the billions.

After the third year of being not only a senior engineer but also his main emissary to social and business liaisons, another woman appeared, and suddenly, she was important in Steele's workplace. The young raven-haired socialite was a niece of a major financial connection whose hiring deal was politically based and romantic. Leslie had a bad time dealing with jealousy since she was quite unaccustomed to the feeling.

One day she had decided to stop and see Steele to update him on a new development in the poly-clear panels. Steele was in the midst of a wild lovemaking session with his black-haired beauty with red lips on his black leather couch. She backed out of the office and suspected that he saw her but could not be sure as she went to the elevator, finding jealous tears dropping on her lab coat.

She had stopped sleeping with him for close to a year, yet the small jobs continued along with innuendoes of rekindling their relationship. She had never told him that she saw him in the compromising position and had blamed the cessation of their affair on fear of having their relationship interfere with her career. She tried to avoid him after that, but as time passed, the diplomacy missions were less frequent and more mundane. *TerraLuna* was born. She felt more like a midwife than a mother.

During this time, she had several boyfriends, most of whom were nice, but none of them made her feel the way Gerhard Steele made her feel. Working on the actualization of *TerraLuna* had strongly occupied her time, and longing for the satisfaction she had sampled with the president occasionally crept back into her day's routine of meditations. Lately, she rejected offers for holo-movies and dinner, finding sanity in solitude and research. She wondered if he was serious now about being together. Leslie could not find time to analyze his actions and arguments.

It was nearly six o'clock Thursday morning. She tuned the music station to play top 40 hits and stripped out her underwear as she went to take a shower, leaving her blonde pony-tail in place. The shower was shorter than she liked but wanted to get to the base and have a donut and some coffee before her loading task began, hopefully having time for Charley to ask her for a date. Ultimately, she wanted the entire ordeal to be over. She dressed in dark jeans and a low-cut purple top that accentuated her small, yet well-rounded breasts more than usual, hoping to entice Charley to try to occupy her weekend at his apartment.

She applied her makeup and stretched her eyes before pulling a brush through her hair, leaving it partially wet. Topping the outfit was a pair of purple-tinted sunglasses. She was Dana Kim again.

Soon, she was on the highway into the desert, her duffel on the passenger seat of her rented economy car. She felt like a student but truly missed her luxury car, gourmet food, and library at home in Houston. Young Dana Kim felt it was going to be a good day anyway.

*****

MoonCorp's progress was as swift as it was accurate. For two years, the plans did not lie completely dormant but were revised and reviewed for the eventual prompt erection of its version of a five-star hotel on the moon. Camera crews were on hand, documenting progress, and would be used in promotional marketing structured to optimize the willing guests to experience lunar vacationing. Lately, the most popular form of recreation at *TerraLuna* was not tennis under Earth glow or swimming under the stars but the eastern observation deck that oversaw the construction of their friendly rival. Telescopic imagers presented the show on a limited media band. A bank of monitors displayed many angles of the construction, yet most of it could be seen with an ordinary pair of binoculars.

Zonic and Haley stood side by side at the window, Haley settling her hand in the back pocket of Ed's jumpsuit. The past few weeks had been the most romantic time Zonic had experienced in recent memory. Adult romance was something he had always imagined during the tumultuous teenage dating years. He scrolled quickly through his list of girlfriends and did so with rapidity, not wanting to relive the things women do not like about him. Granted, his flaws were appreciable, but the real reason he was single was he did not have the patience it took to keep a woman.

He had always liked the idea of a soul mate and resigned himself to keep looking for a woman who had the same intention. Years passed, and he found it was harder than he had imagined. Love and marriage seemed to also be a financial arrangement that he was not prepared to bankroll. Once they started asking about how much money he had, the flames of love were doused. The definition of a turnoff was his bank account. As a result, spending time on his career was the only love available for many years. He still avoided those commitment discussions with Haley, happy to enjoy learning about this amazing woman.

So far, Haley knew he made more than her with *TerraLuna*, and she was fine with that. Haley was content with a man who was not about pressuring her into marriage or sex or both. Indeed, she appreciated Ed Zonic, the man of quiet mystery. Haley was enamored with his instinctual command of any given situation. His rugged readiness under pressure comforted her, filling the empty places within her. Haley Williams was not the kind of girl who wanted to be relied on by men. She termed herself as a competent subordinate.

She positioned her hand amorously deep into his pocket. He took a breath that felt like a sigh. *That was something I haven't experienced until now,* he thought. They watched as the vertical wall sections were welded together with a superheated torch that filled the tiny spaces between the thirty-foot tall and at least two-foot thick modular pieces. Tall cranes held them in position with titanium cables as silver-suited workers spotted and calibrated the assembly. The entire foundation had been laid only four days since they began. It was a remarkable process, creating slabs of compressed, superheated moon rock.

Another machine scooped the rock into cylindrical columns reinforced with asteroid iron alloys. These columns were seated in the foundation and would support the second level of the complex. After two weeks had passed, the nearly complete outer walls encompassed most of the two hundred yards square. Work would begin on the second level by the end of the month. *MoonCorp*'s insignia was proudly emblazoned along the sides of the bright yellow mechanical smelters as well as the helmets of the workers. It was an efficient crew using the finest mining machine ever built, fueled by circular onboard solar radio panels.

As the lovers surveyed the moonscape, sunlight highlighted the moon's powdery gray surface, exuding into an organic extension that rivaled *TerraLuna*'s sleek line, which wasn't very far away, by design. The silent interlude was interrupted by the familiar ring of Ed's wrist phone. He eased his arm off Haley, who seemed to coo with disappointment at the loss of his touch.

"Zonic," he said quickly.

"Ed, this is Tom. We are going to set the specs for diversion of the B2 in a few minutes, and Dave wants you to be here. So kiss your girlfriend goodbye and get on over," Tom said, nearly overstepping the line with Ed sporting a goofy giggle.

"No problem, Tom. I'll be there." Ed closed the phone.

Tom stopped for a moment, expecting to get a snappy and sarcastic comeback, referring to his lack of sexual contact. However, there was nothing of the sort. He sat at his console in the reclaimed control room. All were elated to be out of the bunker and back to business. Simey cleaned the bottom of an upside-down bag of potato chips while fixed on readings of the second bogey coming from the same sector as its nefarious partner. Dave, busy on his phone, paced the floor of the command center. Tom was genuinely concerned that the second bogey, while slower, might have a similar tenacity. Dave finished his call, looking around for his chief engineer.

"Did you call Zonic, Tom?" said Dave, managing stress.

"Yes, Dave. He is on his way."

Ed entered the room before Tom could finish his sentence. "Zone, we are going to send *The Motivator* out to nudge B2 away from our safe space. As we want to deal with that thing as soon as possible and as far as possible, we are preparing *Motivator* now. You are the most proficient with its operation. I want you to operate." Dave tested his authority.

"Dave, we have half a dozen pilots here twiddling their thumbs. I have responsibilities. Can you give one of those flyboys a chance?" Ed countered.

"That's just the thing. These pilots have flown freighters, tugs, and shuttles. None of them has a fraction of the practical experience you have with *Motivator*, Ed.

"Steele and I are not prepared to jeopardize *TerraLuna* or mankind for that matter by not sending our best man. So take a compliment for once and familiarize yourself with the parameters of the bogey." Dave's stress level seemed to be holding steadily. Ed saw he was serious and relented an objection.

"Okay, Dave. Thank you for the compliment. I would be more than eager to save *TerraLuna* and mankind. Thank you for the opportunity. One question: what is the pay for saving *TerraLuna*, and what, if any, is the bonus for saving mankind?"

Dave squared with Ed's nearly smiling eyes. "I'll talk to Steele after you nudge the bogey."

Simey thought it an appropriate time to bring some tension-relieving statistics into the conversation.

"We redirected the satellite telescopes when we were in the bunker. It has been traveling full speed, and the LINDYs have been relaying precise data. Ed, take a look at its telemetry reading from our satellite telescope closest to B2. Does anyone have an objection to calling it B2—*Bogey 2*? Good. It is smaller than B1 and traveling at a slower speed. It is coming from the same sector as B1," Simey said, wanting to keep it simple rather than rattling off a series of numbers. They usually made Ed nervous.

"Travel time? If we launch today, when will we see B2?"

"Calculating the payload of thirty-six hydrogen bomb fuel, thrusters, and factoring the absence of a manned crew, I would say inside of ten days, two hours, and thirty-two minutes. Fifty years ago, this trip would have taken three years. Thank your local antimatter propulsion researcher. The critical part is landing while matching speed. The satellite will give us a better picture once it is in a better position to determine the texture of the surface. This is where our piloting skills come in handy. If you totally freak out up there, we have the magnetic tether guns installed. That could help if there is a lot of blowback or the surface is rocky or unstable. Like I say, we will know more as better pictures come in."

"How soon can *Motivator* launch?" Ed asked, now more interested in the mission.

"We can get her off before dinner. We can use your input. *The Motivator* is easy to launch and navigate. It is the landing and deployment part that needs the skill of a veteran pilot. The sooner we program her and run some system checks, the faster we'll be on our way."

Simey and Ed headed down the stairs and into the outer ring of *TerraLuna*. Supply crates were being unloaded from the transport ship that had sidled up to the outer wall along the northwest side of the complex.

"Hey, wait up, guys," said Tom, running to catch up with his coworkers.

"We ride again," Simey said like an old cowboy.

Ed rolled his eyes, unseen by his partners, as they began a walk nearly a fourth of the distance around the outer ring. Simey ran ahead and hopped into an electric cart parked against the wall.

"Why walk when we can drive!" he said happily, swiping his card, starting the vehicle. They climbed on with Tom in the back and drove the rest of the way to the bunker access where *The Motivator* was kept.

As they went, occasional workers passed both in carts, some towing supplies and others waking about a variety of task as the hotel was scheduled to open by Thanksgiving. Soon, the large access door came into view. Tom consulted his handheld computer to locate the codes for operation and swiped his card in the machine that usually hung on his belt. The computer downloaded the access codes into his card, and he handed the machine to Ed, who swiped his card likewise.

Simey unclipped his card from his shirt and handed it to Ed. "Would you mind validating me, Ed? I can never get enough validation, you know," he said, attempting humor.

Ed swiped Simey's card as they pulled up next to the large metal door. Tom inserted his card and pressed the "OPEN" button, and the gate-like door began a slow ascent. Simey walked in first, activating the lights with his card. The crew spent the next hour uploading and switching on the various systems. The large room was divided into three sections, each coordinated from a console in an alcove in equal thirds within the room.

The first alcove left of the door was the system's alcove that monitored the integration of the entire system. Next over was the holographic interface, the most impressive part of the room. Essentially, it recreated the cabin of *The Motivator*, complete with pilot's controls, view screen, communications, and of course, the chair. From this point of view, Ed would be able to control the ship millions of miles away. The holographic imager would interface Ed's being with the control pad on the ship. He would essentially be on *Motivator* while sitting on the moon. This gave the pilot the sensitivity needed to make difficult decisions for distant missions. Ed wondered why Skylar or Chen hadn't yet sent one of these out into deep space for a trip that would last several lifetimes.

Knowing them, they probably have it on the table or on the way in secret to exploit the wonders of the universe. This model's success or failure would help them design better ones. For the most part, the pilot (or pilots) would be needed for takeoff, perhaps navigating dangerous space, conflict, and of course, the sensitive job of redirecting an asteroid from an impact course. The computer could handle most of the other basic functions. It was developed to reduce risk to human life in deep space.

When it was first installed, they conducted demonstration programs with some of Chen's top Chinese pilots. Several pilots, including Ed Zonic, piloted a simulation sortie consisting of everything from flying asteroid fields, contact with aliens, docking and landing, sensitive maneuvers, to, of course, communication with other environments.

To the surprise of the gathering of impresarios, Mr. Zonic scored the highest after settling an alien civil war by exiting the ship (holographically) and resolving the dispute, teaching the opposing factions not only the concept of "shaking hands" but also the rudiments of the game of baseball.

As Ed Zonic typically treated excessive congratulation with an introverted stare, the celebration lasted only a short while. The third section of the room trafficked the radio and satellite functions that checked the physical monitoring of the ship as most of the actual travel time was conducted without manual control. A technician was assigned to this console at all times. Between the second and third sections, another large door led to the hanger containing *Motivator* itself, an oddly efficient ship streamlined looking somewhat like a spider able to cling to the curvature of the cool side of an asteroid able to exert enough power to alter its course.

Simey and Tom had spent some of their free time in the simulator that for them was the ultimate in video games, of course they were practicing for the real thing, which made it even more cool, and now they were prepared to staff the consoles with earnest.

Ed slipped his card in the reader and opened the door to reveal the ship. It wasn't as large as he thought it should be. He was many things, but he wasn't a designer. The vehicle was round and squat, offering optimal attachment and mobility on the surface of the bogey. The top held the variety of bomb tubes some designed to deploy while the craft was clutching to the surface with its complicated array of bendable walking legs. Other explosives were meant to be planted in a spiral pattern while the globular-shaped vehicle crawled along, fixing the next bomb in position. If the bogey was too large to be motivated away from impact trajectory, these devices were left on the surface and then detonated once the saucer had disembarked from the asteroid. The spiral pattern of the bombs ripped the planetoid apart. Various sample-collecting units were installed to bring back rock, metal, and gaseous representatives to better understand and document the potential benefits of the specimen.

The men embroiled themselves for most of the day in reviewing and testing all aspects of the mission. Dave had sent several technicians to review *The* Motivator's systems. It was nearly three o'clock when Dave rolled in a cart with some food for his devoted staff. It was clear that he had the right people on the job as their dedication was tireless and certainly commendable.

He watched them coordinating the project like three brothers on Christmas morning. For a moment, Dave forgot his stress headache brought about by his last conversation with Gerhard Steele and enjoyed delivering lunch.

CHAPTER 27

Sleeping less didn't affect Nick's energy on tap. He forced himself to take a break from the lab. Sitting fitfully in his easy chair, he searched the media computer for some ideas on how to approach latest problem.

Scanning the various documentaries and Hollywood movies dealing with prehistoric environments was easy as his entertainment feed package offered hundreds of titles. Over the decades, people found equally innovative and simplistic ways to deal with their imaginations and fears concerning dinosaurs, among other things.

Next to war titles, monster movies were the most prolific topic on filmmaker's minds. Some used simple tools like spears and rocks, which come in handy when you were fresh out of shotguns, tanks, and missiles. Soon, Nick changed his search to documentaries relating to more factual theories about the environment, ecosystem, and politics of creatures he may encounter when exploring his new world.

A wild idea came to him to read some of the twentieth century's best fiction that pitted men against giant lizards, but as this would consume too much time, he opted to take notes concerning the subject of a documentary. Perhaps he would write his own account of actual events in the cretaceous period and win himself a Pulitzer. From what he could ascertain, the most dangerous creatures were the large carnivores that had great senses of hearing and smell. Knowing the habits and location of the prey formally was third on the list; the prey lived with an impending sense their hunter.

Nick had ordered some specialty camouflage paints and another wet suit, planning to disguise himself to blend with the local trees. It would be helpful to devise a means of escape quickly if the occasion arose. Offensive weaponry was another issue. If he had to kill something in self-defense, contrary to popular belief, it should not have a dramatic effect on future events as the dinosaurs vanished around sixty-five million years ago. Mass extinction would not miss one hungry, futuristic man-eater, as Dr. Nick hypothesized.

Modern laser pistols designed to stun a criminal seemed to have replaced the popular gunpowder and lead bullets of the twenty-first century. They still existed, but the nonlethal great-grandchildren of law enforcement clearly required justice over murder. The explosive laser guns existed and were illegal but accessible with a special permit. Being so expensive, they found themselves in the possession of serious gunmen, military personnel, and terrorists. Having both along would be a good idea,

Nick thought. Finding them should not be a problem for Charley as he had clandestine connections. For the right price, these weapons could be had.

The objective was basic reconnaissance, documenting the terrain. Nick planned to show Charley his findings, but it would have to wait in line for, behind his new girlfriend and new job. Keeping this device a secret gave him a creeping feeling he did not trust. He faced the reality of sharing his findings, not only for notoriety, but also for safety.

It was nearly eight o'clock, Nick messaged Stan Duncan and updated him on some adjustments for the defense matrix based on some additional space he wanted covered on the east side of the complex. Stan encouraged Nick to work at home. Nick spent most of that time in his lab with the holoimagers and cricket samples, yet still found time to do his job for *MoonCorp*, ensuring the defense system would work.

He was excited about using the Virtual Location Bot (robot) or VLB that would put him virtually on the moon while still at *MoonCorp* to survey the installation and oversee adjustments. He could make the trip to the moon but felt uneasy going through the protocols and red tape. Using the VLB would leave him his evenings free to work on the next phase of his exploration of Earth's past.

He paused a documentary where a tyrannosaurus rex was chasing some lesser beast. He took his keyboard remote from the coffee table, allowing him to access his communication computer in his television, and sent Stan Duncan another message, of revised schematics, to accommodate slight changes to *MoonCorp*'s defense spiracle defense.

Nick needed to leave the limited comfort of his chair in search of answers to the myriad of questions shooting through his mind that could only be answered by another trip into the box. Cameras were on his mind. He had several in a drawer in his bedroom and soon was milling through them for one suitable to take with him into the past. he selected a smallish black model that stored four hundred digital photos and had remarkable telephoto capabilities, allowing him to focus a picture from ten yards with decent clarity. It' was also wearable like a headband This would come in handy if he needed a picture of something that he wanted to keep at a distance of one hundred yards, and it is hands-free. Taking the camera into the living room, he plugged the system into the wall to charge.

Breakfast would be a good idea, but first, he had to call Charley to confirm that he would be there tonight to affirm that indeed he had come across the invention of the century.

Charley should be in his car on the way to the base.

He activated the number on the wrist phone.

"Dr. Porter here," he said, lowering his car radio.

"Charley, would I neglect your phone calls when you are in line for the Nobel Prize for physics? No. Here I am with the prize nearly wrapped up, and you are out chasing tail. Are you free tonight? I need you here to verify that I am either a genius or very lucky."

"Well, I have been in demand lately. This girl knows her stuff. She described the VLB technology as a viable solution to problems where I had not thought could be applied. She is also good kisser. I had her in my lab the other night," he said proudly.

"Did she stay the night?"

"Actually, not. It may or not be soon. She has a moral backbone, and I do not want to rush her. So yeah, I can come over tonight after my shift. It has been somewhat routine lately, lots of loading support column reinforcements. How about six? You buy me dinner."

"No problem. My machine is ready for you. Say, Charley, do you still know that gun guy? I may want to purchase some EL guns," he said casually.

"EL guns? What the hell for? How do you find time for illegal hunting and the Pulitzer? You know that stun lasers work better on boar. They drop right over, and the hides are intact. Or are you planning rubbing someone out?" he asked with half sarcasm.

Ignoring his last comment, he said, "Well, actually, I need one of those guns too. I'll explain later. Get here as soon as possible. You will not be sorry. Out here."

Nick closed the phone and finally acknowledged his hunger. He programmed some pancakes and read the news as it appeared in the center of the kitchen table. Pressing a button under the ridge of the table raised the tilted screen to a comfortable reading level while he enjoyed his pancakes and coffee.

A story caught his eye concerning an infestation of some kind of sea insect in the Gulf of Mexico. Clicking on the video clips, he saw an interview with the local police identifying the creatures as scorpion-like. He recalled having read that many centuries ago, scorpions and crickets shared common ancestors. His slimmer partner was posting a sign designating the local beaches closed. The female reporter continued the story with the admission that there were many unanswered questions and that a Dr. Sophia Alba, a marine biologist from the University of Merida, was on her way with a team to determine what could be done to abate the pestilence.

Nick viewed the remaining footage and returned to the story. It mentioned that a student on an expedition to retrieve samples of the broken asteroid that fell into the gulf mysteriously disappeared. A Dr. Rene Sanchez, also from Merida, conducted the search. Nick stopped and tried to recall how he knew these people. Perhaps it was a paper he read on geological components of space-faring rock. He had read such a paper and was quite sure Sanchez wrote it.

He had not only been able to determine its age and composition but also attempted to ascertain originating regions of space and proximity to other celestial bodies. Slowing his intake of pancakes, it occurred to him that his friend Ed Zonic was procuring a fragment of the same asteroid that had landed on the moon. This connection made, he filed the news line and logged into the communications file to write Ed a note. *This would be a stimulating compare-and-contrast experiment!* he thought. He used the tabletop computer and pecked a note to his friend Ed.

How are things going up there? Are you still working on those free tickets for me? I was wondering if you had procured that sample you promised to me. MoonCorp is coming along well. Though I am sure you could tell me a lot since it is being erected outside your eastern wall. If you have any photos, feel free to send them out. How's the love life? Knowing you, finding time for picnics and long walks is proving to be difficult on the moon, but I am sure you will improvise. My defense system will be up there soon, and I will be on the VLB. I'll be there at least robotically. Let me know when the package will arrive so I can expect it. Cheers!

Nick Nicholas

Sending the message with a tap, he wondered when he last saw Zonic. Memories of him sent him back to a bar they used to go to together to get drunk and talk engineering and theory. Nick liked Ed because he would tell him point-blank if the ideas proposed to him had any chance of being built. He was good at the nuts and bolts aspects of "practical physics," which were not words Zonic liked to use. He said they reminded him of science nerds who were afraid of playing softball with real men.

Nick liked to hang around with Ed sometimes as a thankful rest from his pal Charley, whose chasing women, attempting to impress them with various science-based bar tricks, wore thin after a time. Charley liked to tell Nick of his exploits with copious women, while Nick blushed inwardly, his fidelity to Ada safe and immutable.

Charley and Zonic met only a couple of times; they never really hit it off. Nick guessed their personalities were similar in that they appealed to a limited number of people, each other not included. Neither of them was big friend makers, although they were both what one would call loners. He was able to deal with them separately, but together, it would take an exhaustive amount of mental juggling to supervise their esoteric minds and egos. Balancing these friends helped Nick keep order in his personal life, and he was satisfied with the arrangement.

It was approaching nine o'clock. Several experiments came to mind all at once when he first found the doorway into the past. The mists of mystery and wonder cleared rather swiftly for him. Being of a scientific mind rather than an expressive one, he was able to waft aside the romance and intrigue and get down to documentation. The most important thing to do after verifying each period accessible was to record a photo and video album of each era. He would do this, keeping a close proximity to the PFC conduit back to the present time in case something went wrong. In the event of danger, he could literally slip back to 2168 and turn off the machine.

Of course, Ed would prefer him to stay and fight the creatures. Charley would want to set the place up as a one-hundred-thousand-world-dollar-a-day safari to the paying customer's choice of periods. Nick rose from the table, moving away from the thought of commercialization. He could record video with his head cam accessory and take photos, taking approximately ten minutes to complete a circular panorama of decent footage.

Now properly motivated, he went to the bedroom and collected his charged camera headband and went into the living room, then out into the warming morning. He crunched across the gravel to the door and soon was past security and booting up the lab for a morning's jaunt into the past.

A quick call to Bert activated the satellite feed, and naturally, isotopic rich sunlight was fed onto the concentrated solar array. Concluding that working backward would give a viewer a feeling of suspense, moreover, he wanted to encounter the more dangerous time with some backup. He had wanted to paint the wet suit in camouflage colors, yet he hadn't the time. The earlier years called for guns and protection. They could wait.

The latest sample in his collection was a mere one and a half million years old. Research told him that it was around this time that humans first appeared, thanks to potassium argon dating of bones found in several locations by early archeologists. Nick had planned to start here in his documentation.

Setting the machine's designator to align with the first sample on the bottom of the stack of globes, Nick typed the "ON" command, bringing swathes of blue light into the box. Donning his wet suit, it occurred to him that it would get more use in the past than it would in the future. Of course, the time to come was the future, yet he would actually be in the past. The irony of the situation brought a smirk to his face as he zipped the suit. Gloves followed, and then the tinted goggles, and finally, the protective rubber shoes.

A black plastic trash bag filled with his camera, a compass, a handheld voice recorder, a pocketknife, smoke bombs, and a lighter was cinched off under his wide black canvass belt. Nothing else came to mind, and he wanted to travel light. Nick climbed into the box, carefully taking the supine position as he closed the top of the box. Wavy blue images dilated his eyes slightly. Nick rested for a minute to calm the adrenaline rush. He was glad to have installed his contact lenses. Wearing his glasses under the mask would most certainly have been uncomfortable. These new lenses had a tiny processor that helped his eye focus faster in changing distances. They worked well, but he liked wearing glasses for some reason; maybe they made him see a shade more interesting.

As ready as he needed to be, he rolled forcefully against the side of the field, remembering the pressure it took to pass into the dimensional rift. The ancient sun had warmed the tall grass now forming a flattened mat on which he found himself. The oblong blue box glowered to his right like an alien intruder. Finding himself in a grassy, advantageous position, he stood slowly to survey the area.

He was in a large field of grass that rolled around him in all directions, climbing gently, rolling hills nearly half a mile away. Not wanting to waste time in awe of its purity, a typical scientist tendency, he quickly removed the plastic bag and fished out the headband camera. Its elastic band fit snugly above his goggles. An eyepiece on a flexible arm nestled before his left eye. A small remote to start, stop, and control the telephoto feature was fixed to the band with polystix. He could stick it to anything, and it would stay, and it was reusable—great stuff. He took the camera out, flipped on the power, and put the cord around his neck. Next from the bag was his voice recorder with a bendable microphone. It too was politicked to the headband. Now hands free, he lowered his goggles and took a new scan of the sunny, windblown grass. The air was remarkably fresh. He enjoyed some deep breaths before he activated the head cam. Moving slowly, he took a few pictures before recording his vocal date on vicinity 1, one and a half million years ago.

"I stand in a field surrounded by gentle hills half a mile away. The fresh-smelling grass is being blown by the wind. It seems to be summer. I stand in what seems to be near the center of a small valley. The sky is without clouds, and the sun is in the two-o-clock position."

He stopped recording and took a couple of still photos with his headband digital and then stopped to listen. Nothing but the wind in the grass found its way to his craning ears. Though still covered with the protective rubber cowl, he enjoyed the sound's authenticity.

He turned completely around and surveyed very much the same in the opposite direction. As he was about to turn, movement in the grass some sixty yards away caught his attention. At first, it looked as if the wind blew a section of the grass, but after focusing his camera on the area, he saw something perhaps grazing, standing still, maybe some kind of cattle-like animal. It was then he heard a faint groan; movement jostled the grass around it. He documented the vision on his voice recorder and then adjusted the camera to greater telephoto to see what it was. Through the camera lens, he saw an animal resembling a buffalo, only much larger than ones he had seen before. It wasn't grazing but rather on its side, its breathing labored. He clicked a few pictures. Something had wounded it. Enhanced telephoto revealed that a stick had broken off in its side. Blood soaked its thick coat, and rather vicious flies swarmed around the beast.

For a moment, he considered approaching the animal but thought better of it after another sight crept in on the horizon. Moving laboriously through the grass was a sight that remained with Nick until the end of his life. A pair of primitive men was lumbering over the horizon, holding crude spears. Tangled hair and gruesome teeth made their way into the auto-focusing camera lens. He adjusted the head cam to capture a frame of both the beast and encroaching hunters, apparently looking for their wounded prey. The primitives seemed to not notice Nick's presence, yet they continued in his direction, running with a sidestepping gait that made Nick take a fast look back at the blue band of safety waiting for him a few feet away.

After nearly ten minutes, he had an amazing amount of data. Now that the job was done as planned, he felt the need to leave, oddly threatened by the proximity of the ancient men. Crouching instinctively to avoid detection, he eventually found a safe but uncomfortable position. The men were nearly thirty yards from the buffalo. It sensed their presence and bellowed another guttural groan, perhaps more keenly aware of its demise.

Nick continued filming, hoping to capture what might be the final kill. His neck and legs ached from holding the awkward position. The men began to yell and wave their spears, now sprinting through the field, wildly sniffing a path to the downed animal. The yelling intensified. He moved the camera's eyepiece, better framing the event. The shouts were nothing short of orgasmic at the prospect of finding their prize. The beast caught sight and suddenly rose with a surge of panic and began running away from the primitives toward Nick's position. Once it stood, it was clearly the largest buffalo he had ever seen or imagined. It looked as large as an elephant. Several sticks hurled at the beast passed closely near Nick's position one stuck firm, pricking its thick fur. After running ten or twenty yards, it fell, again its leg severely hindered from the crude spear, preventing movement. More shouts now closer rang chills along Nick's spine as he rotated his camera and intently recorded a play-by-play information, describing the events like the old wildlife shows he was transfixed by as a child.

"The hunting party is shouting as loud as possible in celebration of their kill." He noted.

The jolting chills along his spine repeated as he took flurries of camera shots as the pack fell upon the downed beast, punctuating their shouts with multiple, finalizing stabs of their spears. They kept their distance warily from a charge or a kick. All their careful attacks did not stop the blood spray from saturating their hairy bodies and splattering the surrounding grass. Nick lost count at thirtysomething stabs that hit the animal.

Caught up in the action, he paused instantly when a new sound made its way to his senses. It was from behind. He spun around for the first time, now not carefully monitoring the camera, to see two other hunters not twenty yards away uphill, perhaps late joining the kill party, but now upon spotting the strange frog-like being, charged him at his entrenched position. Wild, bulging eyes and fanged teeth horribly highlighted the second pairs' yelling as they traversed the nightmarishly short distance. Nick froze for a moment, his mind racing to the locate the PFC. He focused inwardly on his inventory of equipment, stunned in his place, cursing silently at the nonthreatening size of his pocketknife.

CHAPTER 28

La Fresca had been moored all night in the special boat-cleansing stall near the marina. Four men had spent nearly an hour power washing and scrubbing the length of the vessel using large mops and hard brushes on ten-foot sticks early the next morning in the glow of halogen lights. Clumps of dried ooze floated in the water around the boat like wet white T-shirts littering the surrounding water.

The dock looked like a lonely trail leading into an unfriendly nothingness in the pre-dawn darkness. The sound of the other boats flopping in the waves gave an eerie sound to the ordinarily common sight. When Pepe and Tico arrived at the dock, Sanchez, Alba, and young Enrique were waiting outside the marina with stacks of equipment and supplies, including a canvass bag that Pepe guessed was the calf Sanchez had spoken of the other day. Exhaling deeply, he approached the fearless crew with an outstretched hand. They all shook, somewhat chilled by the morning breeze.

"You are all so early. I thought I would be the first here. It is good to get started before the sun rises. I always fish better that way. Let's start loading."

The student complied without pause, helping Pepe lift a long plastic bin into the boat. The others nodded and got right to work as well, the wind whipping their windbreaker jackets against their skins. Within twenty minutes, all but the calf was loaded. It took all four of them to carry it on board. Pepe ordered it stowed in the ice hold to stay fresh. After loading, they were a bit winded. The two academics busied themselves with installing the monitoring computer program into Pepe's system by the small halogen built into the navigation center. Pepe's system would now be using the DNA location software programmed with among many other species, the shed skin sample, of the creatures to narrow their search for a specimen.

Pepe, now without a task, decided to make some coffee and perhaps cook some eggs, fish, and potatoes for breakfast. Before the sun rose, the smell of breakfast crept out onto the deck. They all enjoyed a meal while discussing their plans at Pepe's small table. Essentially, the goal was to attract the creatures to the calf and raise it with the hoist, capturing one of the insects with a specially designed catch stick, much like those used to retrieve snakes using a pull cord wrapping tightly like a noose. Pepe would operate the hoist, Alba and Enrique would operate at the cooler, and Sanchez would use the catch stick. Sanchez hoped it would be a routine exercise and was eager to begin.

Pepe checked his watch and roused his crew to begin the voyage to the general again to the area where the creatures were first spotted. Within ten minutes, *La Fresca* was coursing into the dark sea with only the faintest sign of dawn approaching the eastern sky.

Sanchez busied himself with a small box and conferring with Alba. Pepe switched on the autopilot, coursing the ship to the DNA-guided location, and walked across his deck to see what they were doing.

"What is that?" Pepe said eyeing, a twelve-ounce vial of clear liquid.

The diminutive Alba raided the vial to Pepe's eye level, swirling it.

"This is sort of a tranquilizer. We will treat the water in the cooler so when the bug hit the water, it will relax and not fight. We do not know how it will react to capture. To be safe, we want it to be dissimulated."

She uncorked the vial and poured the contents into the plastic-lined metal box three-quarters filled with seawater.

Sanchez began assembling the catch stick, adding two-foot extension pieces as he spoke.

"I hope I can get a good grip. If it falls on the ship, I think it would be best if you use your baseball bat as soon as possible." The professor nodded to a weathered hardwood bat hanging on a leather cord outside the cabin door.

"I think you might have the most experience in clubbing dangerous creatures."

Pepe tilted his head slowly in assent, remembering the sharks that happened into his net. Most of them could be gaffed off into the sea, yet some of them were too big and liked to snap. A good blow to the head was enough to stun or possibly kill them before they took a bite.

"Yes, of course, I will be ready with that bat, but I also carry this."

Pepe lifted his blue-and-white T-shirt, advertising his favorite beer, and produced a stun pistol, its battery indicator registering "full charge available."

"This will neutralize up to two hundred pounds, and if I miss, it won't put a hole in my ship."

"A stun laser pistol is great to have," said the marine biologist.

"I only use it in an emergency. I want the creature undamaged."

Pepe nodded, putting the pistol away, and returned to his helm, feeling the thrill of fishing rise in his heart as the sun was now above the horizon. He consulted his instruments and called back to the crew. We should be there in about fifteen minutes. He opened the hatch to the ice room and walked down the stairs where the calf sat on a pile of ice chunks the size of sugar cubes. He unzipped the bag to reveal the hind legs. He took his knife and slit the ankles of the beast where he would thread the steel hoist cable. Pepe called up to Enrique.

"Enrique, bring me the coil of cable with the hook on the end."

The boy scrambled into the ice chamber with the coil and handed it to Pepe, who immediately secured the hind legs of the calf with the foot-long hook.

"This should draw those devils."

They tramped through the bloody ice and up the stairs. The two professors at the navigation console were tracking the location of the sea bugs based on their DNA pattern programmed into the sonar system.

"Sonar is bringing us to the most probable location. The computer responded and offered, constantly updating coordinated and approximate time of arrival."

"No problema, Senor Captain. We have an 82 percent lock. We will be there in ten minutes."

"Enrique! Man the hoist, green button down, yellow button up, red button stop! Let's get that cow in the air!" Tico stood on deck, his ears perking up at the sound of his master's voice, ready to help in any way he could. Enrique followed the captain's orders and was soon conversant with the operation of the hoist.

Sanchez and Alba watched as the captain gave the order to raise the bait. Enrique pushed the green button, bringing the calf slowly away from the ice hold. It flopped to the edge and soon hung parallel with the side of the ship. The console began beeping. The screen prompt flashed, indicating "stop engines."

"They're here!" Sanchez shouted. He took another three steps to the hoist.

"I will let it sink to the bottom. Be ready. These things are fast," Pepe said in a serious yet excited tone.

"Be ready to hit the yellow button when the strike indicator sounds," Pepe said, slapping the calf. He produced a circular oversize pill-like sensor and cable screwed it just above the hook.

"Hoist up!" he called.

Enrique hit the green button, raising the calf above the boat's gunwale. Pepe commandeered the hoist, swinging the carcass over the side.

"Hoist down!" demanded Pepe.

The winch lowered the cable and continued to lower it as the calf disappeared below the surface, bringing the carcass into the deep.

The eyes of the four shipmates passed from one to the other, each ready with their task, all primarily braced to snare prey. Pepe knew more than any of them that fishing could be a tedious waiting game but felt that the bugs would be on the calf quickly.

"I remember ten years ago before I had this ship, I was on the crew of the *El Mosa*. We fished all day and night until the hold could carry no more fish. You think this waiting is bad. Some days we would not have a single fish, but we stayed out in the sun with no wind. The ship had ventured far out past the gulf into the deep ocean in hopes of finding a school to take home. At last, the bell rang, and we started the nets into the ship. The nets were lowered, and we began sorting out the fish. Then one of my crewmates, Juan Ortiz, gave a shout. We turned to find his hand in the mouth of a huge barracuda. He thought he could grab it and throw it back, but it took his hand and would not let go. Pulling him away from the pile of fish and lifting the huge monster onto a table while he screamed is a sound I will never forget. You see, the barracuda has curved teeth that draw the prey into the mouth. I took a machete and chopped one fast chop in the midsection of the fish. Blood was everywhere, and the devilfish kept biting and sawing at Juan's hand. When it finally stopped moving, we went to the mouth and began unhinging the jaws from his wrist. One man held the fish's mouth open and another pulled his arm from the mouth. The arm was without its hand. Juan screamed one last scream and fainted as a fountain of blood shot in the air, landing back on his chest. With some effort, the hand was retrieved, but that day, we lost our crewman. He had died from a seizure at the sight of the loss of his hand."

He stopped his story abruptly to inspect the condition of his listeners. His tale kept Sanchez, Alba, and Enrique still and silent, each internalizing the fear and pain of Juan Ortiz.

In the silence, no one was looking at the cable that was being pulled toward the perpendicularity of the water, soon followed by a siren, indicating activity at the bait.

"Fish on! We have to get even with it, or it might snap the cable. Push the yellow button, Enrique! Now!" he shouted over the siren.

The cable slowly wound around the spool, bringing the bait and whatever was on the end into the haven of the deck of *La Fresca*. Sanchez reached for his catch stick and opened the loop, looking to his friend, who was ready to open the four-foot cooler. They each wore thick green gloves given to them by Pepe so the white goo would not harm them. Time passed tensely, only as fast as the cable wound about the spool. Pepe pulled the boat around, evening the draw on the bait.

A yellow mark designated the last fifty feet of cable. It wound around somehow slower than the rest, when suddenly, a great jerk sent the cable off starboard, altering the course of the boat. Pepe reached into his shirt and produced his stun pistol, ready for trouble. He half-ran across the deck, taking the baseball bat from its nail, and pushed it into Enrique's hands. Pepe checked the system to make sure it would hold, hesitating to release the cable to prevent tearing the hoist from the ship. It seemed to be holding. Soon, the bait would reach the surface. The tension brought them all closer to the side of the boat to get first sight. Ten feet from the surface, a white mark appeared on the cable, and Pepe broke the silence.

"Here it comes!"

As the final feet ran into the spool, the end of the cable twisted and jerked with threatening force. Then the top of the hook appeared, and the legs of the calf rose to reveal an unexpected sight. One solitary insect clung to the carcass. It was nearly as big as the calf itself. Four fangs burrowed deeply in the throat of the bat, and the hundreds of legs moved to and from menacingly, exuding more of the white poison. It had a longer tail than before and seemed to resemble a centipede with a broader body, looking like that of a lobster. This creature reacted to the light yet did not want to release its food.

Its body was reddish brown with the legs turning a dark orange nearer the ends. It hissed, reminding them of a roach, and spun, pulling down, trying to break the calf free from the hook. Sanchez brought his stick into the face of the creature and managed to grab a few of its legs in the loop. He pulled lightly at first to test the strength of the creature. Sanchez knew after a few tugs that the creature was much too large to pull off. It wriggled its way out of the noose.

"Senor, it will not let go! I think you should shoot it! Maybe it will loosen its grip! Shoot!"

Pepe did not need much else. He fired two blasts.

Bolts of yellow light pulsed from the gun. One hit the calf; the second flew off into the air. The creature was instantly aware of the firing and seemed to release the ferocity of its grip for its own safety.

Squinting through the gunsight, Pepe let a blast go that glanced the creature near its head. It shook loose, writhing spastically in the air. Splashing in a frenzy of grabbing legs and fangs, it immediately vanished into the sea below. The men clutched the side of the boat to catch sight of the beast. The water soon calmed, and nothing was there. A sudden creak scared them all. It was Professor Alba closing the cooler.

"I think we should have brought a bigger cooler."

*****

There is more than one way to eat a sandwich. The operations team at *TerraLuna* opted for the quick bite method, paying more attention to their work than the food. The flight schedule for *The Motivator* had to be rechecked before any of them would think of eating in the cafeteria. Blastoff was slated for 7:00 p.m. Earth time. Simey was naturally at his seat of the system's coordination section. Tom manned the automatic functions, setting them within mission parameters. Ed operated the control instruments, running simulations for landing, firing an assortment of explosives, and studying their effect on a mock subject that best matched the current information of the B2. Data stream telemetry reports offered hourly updated information.

Simey took some time to put together a simulation constructed from the latest data, frustrating Ed as the results did not indicate they were able to remove the threat. Behind the crew at their consoles, workers were diligently preparing the craft itself with fuel and live nuclear explosives. Mechanics inside and out tested every function from the most vital to the very basic. At six o'clock, a system's check would be performed, transferring all operations to their prospective moderators.

Ed's headset hummed with Simey's voice.

"Captain Zonic, our records indicate that three out of the last four missions have resulted in failure. Why don't we give it a rest and get ready for a blastoff sim? The program that you really need to practice with will not be ready until after she is well on their way. I am entering the blastoff and primary navigation program to fly this thing out of the solar system. Of course, we could do it automatically. It's really up to you." He waited for Ed's response in silence, something he was used to with Ed.

"Roger that control. I think this program is altogether full of an inordinate amount of your all too tricky special circumstances. It is challenging but also a pain in the ass. Switching off sim, standing by for standard blastoff. Let me know when you are ready."

"If I can interject here . . . I think that considering the time frame we are working within sticking to a basic format is advisable. The automated system is chock-full of self-compensating hardware. The computer will handle most of the quirks and problems. You know I appreciate your puzzles, Simey, but I suggest we stick to the telemetry. We do not want to make our captain nervous. Remember, he has the nuke deployment control," Tom said, evening the balance of the trio.

"Roger that. I will file the special circumstances. I am sure both of you will be referring to them eventually even if for entertainment purposes," Simey said with confidence, planning to play the programs himself later to see if he really did design them with excessive difficulty.

Ed knew the blastoff sequenced backward and forward. It used a standard control format. Protocol required that the captain make three simulated takeoffs for the record, each containing minor probable fluctuations for which to compensate.

It was after five. Before long, the alcove was darkened, and a curtain was drawn around his cockpit to block out glare from the continued activity in the center of the room. A screen displayed an image of the ship taxiing along the launch site. He prepared his focus as did the fasten seat belt sign. Tom introduced the sound, movement, and holographic functions to the simulation, putting Ed into a very realistic situation in his command chair. A platform on ball bearings tilted, recreating motion.

"*Motivator* is cleared on basics. Final system check is under way."

Tom paused as the automated program ran several thousand micro-checks. After nearly a minute, he returned to the captain. "Micro-check complete. Initiating final go releases to command center.

"Begin program sequence on your mark when you are ready, Captain."

Tom referred the manual controls to Ed's console with a tap of his finger on the touch pad. Lighted touch panels, as well as push button and level switches, lit up for Ed. He finally relaxed in his chair now that he had control of the ship.

"Control accepted. Thank you, automation." Ed surveyed the panels one more time, ensuring his mastery of the features of the ship.

"Engaging primary lift engines. Navigation check. Cameras check. LINDY wingman riding along control check. Set lift off at T-minus one minute on my mark . . . MARK."

Adding a bit of drama to encourage his fellow space farers, the clock began counting down from one minute. Rumbling increased as the blastoff engines gained sufficient force to push it away from the moon's gravity.

Simey and Tom, truly eager from the preparation exercises, kept a close eye on as many functions as they could at one time. The final countdown brought them to the edges of their seats, unsuccessfully controlling their natural exuberances.

"FIVE, FOUR, THREE, TWO, ONE . . . BLAST OFF!" Ed counted and took the craft off the pad and into space, leaving a cloud of moon dust obscuring the screen for a few moments. Slowly, the bomb-laden spiderlike saucer rose to the stars.

"WE HAVE LIFTED OFF" could be heard in the headset, as well as from behind the curtain, in the direction of Simey's station. Ed gave a brief sigh at the sound, taking it in stride while scanning the panel for problems.

"Engaging manual radar feeds live from satellite. Engaging micrometeorite shielding, retrieving liftoff gear. All systems go. Preparing for antimatter drive . . . Ready in three minutes on my mark. MARK. Directing sector course entry 6525 from database to navigation control. Entered and received, we have all systems go. *TerraLuna, Motivator* requests base systems. Okay confirmation." Simey and Tom took their cues to send their validations of their automatic and coordinating reports to Ed's console.

"Roger, *TerraLuna*, we have all green lights. One minute until deep space antimatter engines employed. Stand by."

Ed kept his familiarity at bay, executing his tasks by the book and to the letter. His thoughts were actually away, balancing time between Haley and the inevitable arrival of the wonderful Mr. Gerhard Steele. Ed was sure that Dave would make a big deal about the fine work his men exhibited in dealing with *TerraLuna*'s accident. Naturally, Ed would shake his head, accept a pat on the back, pose for pictures and maybe a certificate, but when it started to look like Steele wanted to make small talk, he was useless. Ed stared unfixed, preparing several escape routes from chitchat that would not offend his esteemed boss.

"Antimatter drive in FIVE, FOUR, THREE, TWO, ONE. Engage!"

The platform tilted dramatically, bringing Ed into an angle position. Satellite cameras that would offer a variety of real-time images noting the ship's outer visuals switched off, replaced after a moment with a slow pan of a camera, revealing Simey at his console.

"Thank you for flying the *Motivator* . . .," he said with an attempt at surprise visual humor.

Simey shut the system down, and after a break, they would do it again. At seven, they would take off live. The simulation would be quite similar, yet the sound and movement of the actual space ship would be radioed into Ed's control module, along with the actual view screen relays. That was the most stimulating aspect for Ed. It was better than the reality of being there.

CHAPTER 29

The brief coolness of the morning winds still chilled the crew of four as they stared at the bloody calf suspended over the choppy sea. Sanchez, with little to say, consulted the sonar. The rest, apparently waiting for his direction, looked to the water, not suggesting anything. Capturing one of the insects alive now seemed impossible given their size. Bringing a live specimen onto the boat was a danger none of them wanted to face. Alba now was more optimistic than the rest, trying to find some answers in solitude in a corner of the boat. She was making notes of her findings, sketching a picture of a bug from memory. She was struck with an idea and went to Sanchez immediately to consult privately.

"There is a way we may be able to drug one of them long enough to seal it in the cooler. You tell me if we have a chance. What if we injected the calf with the tranquilizer and dropped it into the sea? As it sucks the internal fluids, it will ingest the sedative. We then bring it aboard, put it into the cooler, and head for shore. What do you think, Rene?"

She looked at him for a long time as he reviewed the plan in silence. He eventually looked to her and said, "Yes, it could work, but we are going to have to be careful. The last thing I want is another fatality caused by these things. It would cause very much trouble. I have enough as it is with the media."

Rene Sanchez admired his colleague and, from experience, was always charmed at her active creativity. "The more I think about it, the more I like it. Do you have an injector and enough tranquilizer?"

Without speaking, the little professor went to her case and produced a large injector and twelve bottles of the clear liquid. She dared a smile that Sanchez returned professionally.

The others looked on, aware that something was happening, and soon, the plan was announced. Pepe now seemed more anxious to catch one rather than getting home. Enrique nodded his agreement, feeling the onset of retribution for his friend's death. Pepe and Enrique pulled the bar over the deck of the ship and lowered it, bringing the calf to eye level. Alba inspected the holes made by the fangs of the insect. After recording some data and taking a few pictures, she began to inject the tranquilizer into the jugular of the calf. The needle dug past the hide of the creatures with much less ease than the fangs that would be nearly an inch across based on her measurements of the punctures.

Sanchez went to the DNA sonar tracker, its search parameters set for this specialized prey. "They are still right below. They are waiting for us to feed them." He nodded to Pepe, who directed everyone to wear the long rubber gloves for protection.

The bar was lowered, and the cable fed the injected calf to the deep. While they waited, the day began to offer more heat than breeze. Enrique wanted to take his shirt off but thought he had rather wear a life preserver for protection in case the creature really preferred the taste of the blood of students to fishermen, professors, and dogs.

It took nearly ten minutes to lower the bait. They waited expectantly for a quick hit. The creatures had grown now to offer problems that they did not expect to come into play. This put them all on edge. How big would they get? Waiting for a strike, Pepe's silent hopes simmered as he held the ship idle as the sea's undercurrent slowly dragged the calf into the infested area, the cable taut and still. Enrique and Sanchez fussed with the canvass bag, trying to optimize the opening to insert the creature if the cooler was not big enough. They tied a handkerchief through the hole in the zipper to more easily close the bag once the creature was inside. Alba held her camera around her neck with her finger ready to shoot. She had been documenting the preparations and was ready as she would ever be.

"We are coming into a high concentration up ahead. Enrique, let about twenty feet of cable out. I am heading the boat opposite to the current. We should get a strike in no time."

Pepe slowed the boat, inviting the uncomfortable silence to occupy the deck. He turned to Tico, who had been running around, soliciting some scratching, and told him to go below. The dog responded, aware that his master was concerned for his safety.

All eyes were on the cable where it slit the water. A series of jerks all at once moved the cable. They each tensed at their posts separating the water's movement and glare from the sun when a huge jerk rocked the upper bar.

"Fish on!" Pepe yelled.

Enrique hit the yellow button. Cable filled the spool, dripping seawater into the boat. Expressions of anticipation and fear stretched the crew's faces. Sanchez re-gripped the bat, and Pepe had his gun on the outside of his shirt tightly against his belly. More cable entered the spool. Eyes ran furtive checks from the water to the colored depth markers along the line. One hundred feet between them and the hopefully drugged creature.

"Slow the cable! We want the drug to have time to take effect!" Alba yelled, taking on some authority. Pepe adjusted the speed of the spool at the controls. It rolled in at half speed with mechanical surety.

The next five minutes allowed the crew to review their jobs, and they were ready to see one of the creatures again. Deep-seated fears individually nurtured by everyone on board turned into tensely focused adrenaline-fueled readiness. What would happen if they couldn't find a way to stop these things and they simply overtook the ship? All were ready to fight for their lives as the presence of the aliens permeated the surface of the gulf.

The social aspect affected Sanchez most of all. Would these creatures migrate onto land? Was this state one of a series of metamorphoses? Might the area be devastated, and the people living on the shore forced to move inland. These questions hinged on their ability to study its anatomy and behavior; and hopefully an exploitable weakness.

Sanchez shifted mental gears upon seeing the thirty-foot marker appear above the surface. He moved forward to get a good look. More cable entered the spool. The calf finally broke the water, and there fixed to the carcass was another bug of about the same size as the first. Alba thought it looked larger. She snapped several pictures as Enrique stopped the winch, leaving the motionless symbiosis of calf and insect dripping and swaying.

"It's not moving," Enrique said, breaking the silence.

"I think it worked," said Alba, helping Sanchez with the long pole. Rene paused, pointing the pole at the creature. With a quick breath for luck, he poked the calf, and the creature remained motionless. As smiles filled across the faces of the crew, the boat began to rock and sway from what felt like a large wave hitting the boat. Their smiles left as fast as they appeared. As the cable continued to pull the bait upward, a sudden splash of water sprayed the deck, knocking Sanchez and Alba to their knees. Once the water cleared, they saw three or four of the creatures had attached themselves to the carcass wrapped around, pulling and wrenching it from the hook. Several others swarmed and sprang with ferocity around the lower third still submerged. As they looked on in horror, the bar suspending the calf began to bend. Pepe manned to the controls, guiding a stunned Enrique clear of the gunwale for fear he would fall overboard.

The soaking wet captain hit the green button, but it would not respond. Four bugs pulled and tore at the one immobilized bug that must have taken a good dose of the tranquilizer, trying to wrench their brother into the water. Pepe assumed the huge splash had affected the control. The winch was not responding, or it may be the sheer strength of the creatures.

Looking with a new anger at the monsters, meeting their black eyes for the first time, he reached for his pistol and began shooting them. Upon impact, the startled creature careened off and fell into the water with a tangle of legs, fangs, and spray. He fired multiple shots until the second fell into the water, followed shortly by the third. The last one had it fangs embedded in the calf, its body convulsing with manic hunger, sucking the remaining fluids within, unable to remove itself from palsy. He paused to take in the sight and to allow a recovering Alba to take pictures. The frightened creature began to exude viscous white fluid in spurts, claiming its prey. Alba and Sanchez watched as the tranquilizer took effect. To their surprise and horror, the feral creature seemed to be fighting the drug and began to fling itself from side to side, attempting to tear the calf from the hook and escape. White goo covered the beast, and some dripped off into the water. Sanchez looked to the others, still waiting for the creature to stop moving.

"Just let it be. The drugs should take effect anytime now," said Alba, studying the creature.

The monster persisted in pulling at the calf, emitting a high-pitched screech combined with a menacing hiss. She thought this was what a cockroach would sound like if she were small enough to hear it.

Suddenly, the insect gave a massive pull, and the calf's legs tore away from the hook, crashing into the water, saturating everyone. It swam away with its prize, leaving a slightly bent hook and more than slightly bent egos of the academics. A trail of bubbles followed into the deep and soon was replaced with unaffected water.

Pepe shook the water from his hair and turned a dejected head away from the sea, sickened by its sight. He noticed Tico peering from behind the cabin door, trying to avoid getting his feet wet.

"It got away, Tico," he said under his breath, but the dog heard him.

"Enrique pulled the bar in. I think we should move away from this spot for now," he said more audibly and then went to the helm.

"Why didn't the tranquilizer work on the second one?" Sanchez entreated his colleague.

"It seemed to be fighting the effects of the drug. I do not know. I think we should go back to the hotel and regroup. I do not feel safe out here. These things are growing, and they seem fiercer now. We are not equipped to handle this, Rene." She looked at him with intent.

Sanchez responded with a quiet nod and turned to the captain's general direction.

"Captain Fernandez, let's move away as soon as possible!" he shouted.

Pepe emerged from the helm without his usual affable demeanor and addressed the crew.

"The boat will not start. The water has shorted the controls just like the hoist. I will fix it."

A moment of silence passed, followed by another wave, hitting the boat, unsettling their stances. Pepe grasped the gunwale, stabilizing himself, his eyes wild, looking over the side. The boat rocked in the swells, and he saw the water teeming with the creatures bumping and biting at the boat. Gaining balance, he called to the others.

"Everyone, get below! Now! Sanchez, please take this gun and cover me."

Enrique, Alba, and Tico filed into the cabin and closed the door. Pepe took a deep breath and noted the stench of the creatures' spetum in the air. He reached for his toolbox with an angry grab and began work to try to repair the controls as Dr. Sanchez kept guard.

*****

The last choice Nick remembered being able to make was whether to dodge the rushing primitive or to run. Unfortunately, as his mind and body debated, a rushing force tackled him. The man pinned Nick and menaced his grotesque face upon him, complete with drool and unimaginably stinking breath. Others were approaching from two directions. Nick reminded himself of what one should do when attacked by bears. Nick played dead to avoid any conflict that would result with him being on the end of a stick. It applied all its weight on Nick, maybe hoping to crush or smother him. Nick instantly reverted to scientific inclinations, noting briefly that anthropologists would be very interested in his discovery of the behavior of prehistoric man if he made it back alive. It was trying to kill him.

The man stood, leaving the lifeless rubber-clad alien still in the grass, presumably dead. Closing his eyes, Nick listened to any sound that might give him a clue to first determine what they were doing and second if they were familiar with the game of possum. It gave a primal call of victory at the apparent kill. After a few frightening moments, he thought they might spear him anyway. So he opened his eyes just below a squint and saw four men standing around, more interested in the nearby blue light than the odd-looking creature. The largest one gestured to it with his spear, giving a loud and repetitive shout as if trying to convince the others he knew what it was and that it might be more important than the funny frog-like man. One of the others shook his head and tried to raise his voice above the others to express what he thought it might be, sounding a different word repetitively. The others listened, trying to decide so as to have an opinion or at least take a side.

They seemed to be satisfied to let the two argue after a time, calmly enjoying the strange and beautiful color on each other's faces. Nick felt their almost childlike behavior to be at first comic while truly primal, a rarity in his world. Resisting the temptation to take a picture, thinking rather it would be a good idea to work out the logistics of making a mad dash for the box light and then shutting the system down in the lab; he could end this episode with a few touches of the keyboard.

After a short argument, attention returned to the strange man in the black suit made from a smooth hide. One of the nonargumentative men walked over, reached down, and touched the wet suit material, softly pulling his fingers back with an expression that could only be defined as affirmation. He liked the material. *Useful,* he might have said.

Through squinting eyes behind the goggles, he noted that their conversation involved more physical attributes than any modern man did. They waved their arms, stamped their feet, pointed, and shook their heads to punctuate their meaning as it the "words" they spoke were subordinate to demonstrative gestures.

Soon, the anger subsided as the leader decided what to do. Nick felt himself being lifted and thrown over the furry shoulder of the largest man. Nick felt the rock hard back, ascertaining the man's strength. Frantically, he keyed in on the small grotto of flattened grass made by their recent activity, falling away in the distance. After a good fifty counted paces, Nick was placed in the grass next to the nearly dead buffalo, whose stench was a relief from that of his bearer. Still keeping his eyes all but closed, he was barely able to see in general what was happening. He saw one of them close in on his face mask, inspecting it with thick rough fingers that smelled intensely of feces.

Composing himself to avoid movement required a great deal of control. Somehow he was able to feign unconsciousness, and this appeased the foul-smelling being. A fly of some sort he had never seen landed on his hand within his fuzzy squint. He kept up the guise of unconsciousness yet focused on the black plastic bag tucked in his belt.

Closing his eyes to a sudden awful final gasp of the buffalo, he reviewed the contents of the bag that most certainly did not contain a gun. (This item would be included in the next trip, if another was to be.) Feeling through the plastic, he found the lighter. He had brought a smoke bomb. Nick felt for it and then guided it to the top of the bag, all along keeping his fixed gaze in the men now more concerned with the giant buffalo.

As their conversation subsided, Nick maintained his possum position. The fur-clad pair joined the younger set in the initial dismembering of the buffalo using some kind of sharpened rock as a hand tool. They worked together in silence with a notable amount of skill and an exorbitant amount of blood. Intermittent spurts saturated their bodies, yet they continued to work unaffected. If they had searched him, they would find the pocketknife to be a big help in skinning. *This might yet happen,* he thought with a flurry of fear and resumed his slow task of inching the smoke bomb and lighter to the top of the bag while keeping a squinting eye on the captors. Nick cringed at the sound of the men pushing the hind leg of the beast, attempting to break the leg out of its socket. The larger two held the body still, while the others pulled with tremendous force, finally cracking the leg away. They immediately began scraping and cutting the surrounding flesh, eating greedily as fast as they cut it away. Nick had the lighter and the cylindrical smoke bomb at the top of the bag. He tucked his legs up to his abdomen and slid them through the gathered opening of the bag with a minimal amount of activity. Soon, he had both items on the grass next to his right side hidden under his arm. Nick resumed his state of stillness. Looking again to the men busy at work with the spoils of the day, he felt a slight shift in luck. A small bird landed on the tip of a bloody leg and thigh piece of the giant red-stained buffalo. One of the men noticed it and stopped his work, walking slowly to it as not to scare it away. His bloody face glowed with grotesque glee at the sight of the tiny bird.

Nick found himself engaged with the frighteningly exaggerated display of sentiment. For a short time, he concluded that it was, from his perspective, a bizarre expression almost like a kind of madness. The duality of these people was remarkable. They shifted quickly from rage to adoring appreciation with, shaking him deeply. logical progression. Instinct in its rawest form is easily the most fantastic form of entertainment. Nick enjoyed an academic moment, and then common sense took over. *If ever opportunity presented itself to escape, it was now!*

With a slow motion, he brought the bomb and the lighter to his chest and lit it. Only after he was sure the fuse was burning well did he stand. Facing the men for an instant, a surge of confidence glared at them with hard fixed eyes, an expression they might understand challenged their essential core.

The man looking at the bird turned to see Nick standing. All the fear and surprise he could muster connected to the very pit of the man. The hairy brute took a giant step back and then mustered a rallying primeval yell at Nick.

The bomb shot a jet of thick white smoke, making his captors disappear. Hoping not to see any more of them, he held the stick out away from his body and took a few steps backward as smoke filled the space between them. He began a run back through the grass.

Sounds of confusion and anger fell behind as Nick sprinted along in the direction of the box. Twirling the bomb as he went in a circular motion to maximize coverage, he counted fifty steps back to the point of arrival. He found the trail they had made. The smoke had surrounded him. He came to where the box should be. It was not there; too much smoke.

"Damn it! Son of a bitch!" he spat aloud.

Smoke surrounded him. He had to keep moving, not really wanting to leave the smoke bomb. Running off to a clear side, trying to get a glimpse of something remarkable as a point of reference, he soon caught sight of the buffalo untended by the butchers, which meant they were in pursuit, behind him. He aimed himself to where he thought the box would be. Shooting a glance in a line angled away from the beast from where he was lying, he calculated the box to be thirty degrees from his current position. Counting a quick yet accurate fifty paces while avoiding the smoke, he found his bearings ran, noticing the remains of the path he made earlier. Nick searched the grass for some light to lead him back to the safety of his lab. Nothing.

Hard sounds followed him. Large arms lapped through the grass, grasping at the smoke, hoping to grip the escaping prey. A few more strides and he should be where he estimated the box would be waiting. *It wasn't there!* A frantic search for some clue left him nearer to the search party and further along the life of the bomb that had begun to emit less and less smoke.

He took a ninety-degree turn, hoping he was correct on the distance but askew on the angle. He found himself making another circle, something he did not want to do.

Trampling grass, now with no distinguishing elements to guide him, Nick zigzagged along, hoping to stumble upon the grotto. The grass was tall and difficult to navigate. He had to stop and look, wincing in fear of a sudden collision in the smoke. He turned and looked around, now running amok.

Panting uncontrollably, he veered around back to the buffalo. Looking up at the sun now in the two-thirty position, Nick remembered where the sun was when he arrived. He drew an imaginary line, calculating the forty minutes present in the past, and started toward open grass as the final spurts of smoke coughed out of the stick.

CHAPTER 30

Leslie Davis never thought of herself as one to avoid physical exertions, but after loading the massive heavy-lift canisters all day, a slow ache settled in the small of her back. She wouldn't seek out any heavy lifting after this job was done. Three o'clock came and went with Charley stopping to see her on the hour. He could be seen sneaking a peek in her work area more often than that. Two hours yet to go before the day ended. Charley seemed more than his usual upbeat self today, Leslie thought as she took a piece of candy he had given her earlier. Tonight might be the night to allow herself to be swept away to his apartment.

Steele was scheduled to leave for *TerraLuna* at the end of the month, and she had entertained thoughts of going with him, but he had not given her any commitment thus far, typical for Steele. She pushed a box on a conveyor belt to Fred Finch, one of the interns, who pushed along into the carrier for loading. Finch frequently offered her enticing glances that she avoided with skill. She behaved pleasantly, vaguely aware of his immature approach, exactly the right attitude for him. He was not sure what to do.

As the loading continued, she began to feel like she had years ago as a young girl helping her parents clean the small garden in the yard back home. She must have been eleven or twelve when it occurred to her that her family was not rich. Unpleasant realities of life weighted her dreams of having a beautiful home with a fountain in the yard and a pony in the stable. Beautiful summer dreams of how she would decorate the house filled her head now and worked their way to her chest, settling there, giving purpose to her work. Her striking attractiveness and quick mind would be the means to her ends.

Now years later, she felt as if these goals should already be actualized. Doing this job for Steele was a choice she had not doubted until lately. After it was done, she prepared herself for his adopting an entirely amnesic tone of this experience. At the least, she would get the raise. Actually being Mrs. Steele was an issue actively repressed with the heave of another box onto the conveyor belt.

Charley appeared from nowhere with two glasses of lemonade, offering her one with a chivalrous extension.

"Thirsty?" he said, twirling the glass at Dana Kim.

"How did you know?" she said, taking the lemonade, drinking it immediately. "You know, you have been so nice lately. I think I will let you take me out tonight."

She took another drink. "Without asking, the answer is yes. Dr. Porter, I would be honored to accompany you to dinner."

Charley looked at them with newly focused eyes. Then the thoughts of a date passed out of the realm of possibility, remembering his promise to Nick.

"Well, there is no doubt that I want to take you out, but tonight I cannot."

Dana stopped for a moment, not ready to believe what she thought she heard. It had an unfamiliar sound to her like a refusal.

"Well, Dr. Porter, what could be more important at dinner? What would happen to us if we did not eat?"

"You don't understand. I promised Dr. Nicholas I would meet him tonight. We have some engineering work to do, and I have been avoiding him to spend time with you. You *have noticed* that spending time with you has risen on my priority list? I need to be at his house this evening. If it were not for him, I would not have this job. Tell me that you understand."

Leslie kept her eyes fixed on Charley, simmering an idea that this might be her opportunity to see what Nicholas had been working on at his lab. She coyly began to invite herself.

"Now that you mention it, I haven't seen Nick around the hangar lately. How is he doing?"

"He's fine, I think. He has been working at home. I need to confer with him on experiments that requite my insights before we install the defense system. I am sort of a sounding board for this work. You know how insecure scientists can be."

"I have an idea. What if I come with you? I would like to see what he had been working on. I have a ravenous taste of cutting-edge technologies. Think of me as an objective third party. I had expected to do more here than load boxes with self-entitled genius wannabees. Please. Please, Charley, take me with you. This could be exactly what I need." She entreated his face with her natural yet augmented beauty.

Charley shifted his stance and fidgeted, knowing that Nick would pitch a fit if he brought her. He had explicitly wanted zero leakage concerning the project. He reexamined her pleasant visage that bordered on poutiness. Trying to find words, he began with a disappointed tone.

"I wouldn't expect to drop in. That would be rude. At least call him and see what he thinks," she said with a sexy twist of her lower lip.

"Okay, I'll see what he thinks." Charley opened his wrist phone and turned the band to accommodate his hand and said, "Nick."

The automatic dialer rang Nick's phone. He stood allowing the phone to ring ten times, and when he didn't answer, an alarm ran along his sensibilities. *Nick always answers his phone.* What would prevent him from taking a call?

"He isn't answering. That's odd. Dana, please, I need to go there alone. I will talk to him tonight and see if I can arrange a tour. We are working on some sensitive functions, and I cannot jeopardize exposure in any way. Please tell me you understand and that you will have dinner with me tomorrow." He dug his earthy brown eyes into hers with sincerity.

Dana accepted the situation, and yet it fueled her curiosity even more as to the nature of Nick Nicholas's project. Making a mental note to pursue the invitation to see his lab at a later date, she took a final drink and called off the entreaty, feigning an acquiescent tone. "Sure, that's fine, Charley." She handed him the empty glass and returned to her work. "Thanks for the lemonade."

Charley was relieved that Stan had not yet asked him to work late at the hangar. He observed that his boss was pleased with *MoonCorp*'s progress yet did not want to press his luck by telling him he couldn't stay tonight if he asked.

Five o'clock came, and with Stan nowhere in sight, he punched the clock and headed for his car with failed hopes to stop for a beer to kill some time before taking the trip to Nick's. Soon, Charley was in his car, putting the windows down to exhaust the heat buildup throughout the day. He started the car and selected instrumental jazz to take him past Sneaky Petey's, where he planned to eventually enjoy the long overdue beer. He half-waved to the security guard with whom he had never quite hit it off and entered the serviced road, leaving *MoonCorp* behind for today.

Moments later, Dana Kim pulled up in her rented car, welcomed more warmly by the guard than Charley. He waved widely with an uncontrolled smile, which Dana returned with an effective amount of playful interest, keeping her political agenda in mind as she rolled away, following Charley at a distance.

Glad to be in the car, she tossed the idea around of following Charley at least to find where Nicholas lived. Her communications with Steele were scant though inclusive of pertinent information of late. She needed something he would be able to use. She hated the feeling of not being in favor with Gerhard. Trying not to accept his propensity for using others (herself included), she toyed with the notions of being the prominent scientist and devoted wife of the powerful man. Now was her time to make this happen. It felt right as if her years of passing up marriage offers had led her somewhere better. This was it. Why else would she disguise herself and follow people to steal information? Not wanting to intellectualize her emotions, she entered the highway, keeping a safe distance from Charley's silver sports car.

Bustling along the highway, Charley entertained the possibility of taking Dana to Sneaky Petey's. Showing off his foxy girlfriend to Sam and Duke would stretch jealous smiles across their beer-soaked lips. Most of his thoughts that were not of beer or Dana during the drive settled on Nick's experiment and why he had not answered the phone after two more tries. He was nearing Sneaky Petey's and gave a hollow look to the plain building he used to frequent daily as he drove by with reverenced deceleration.

After sex and beer dropped from his immediate gratification options list, he was able to focus on what he had seen at Nick's lab last week, reviewing his list of questions that would be expected of him. What had Nick found with high-intensity filtered radio solar power and the holographic imagers?

Charley turned the car onto the local road, leading to Nick's house with Dana Kim keeping less than a half-mile distance. Her car, as most available for the past few years, was equipped with front and rear cameras, allowing telephoto images of distances along roads to assist drivers in finding street names and unfamiliar roads. She kept him on the screen centered in the windshield, noting the distance digitally logged along the bottom left corner of the picture inset into the windshield. Adjusting the camera to focus on the street sign at which he made his turn, she committed it to memory—Westheiser.

Charley pulled into Nick's driveway tumbling along the unpaved road slowly with paranoiac steadiness to avoid paint chips from the gravel concentrated along the road. He parked the car near the pole barn aware of the presence of the use of radio solar power system, as the air was scented with energy.

After parking his car he stepped along the gravel with excitement; he could feel the emanations from the energy being pumped into the lab. Quickening his step to the door, Charley experienced suspicion of danger. He opened his phone's memory bank where the access code was stored. His phone also allowed him access to the grounds under the security system.

Charley entered the code and threw open the door, welcomed by the near shell-shocking pulse of power in the room. Instinctively, he noted that he should stabilize this surge. What was all this? A project he had not told Nick he was working on. He ingested the situation and searched the room for his friend.

"Nick? Are you here?"

Drawn by the blue light's alien glow, he moved to the black box, holographic imager, and globes as to pieces of a new puzzle. *Where is Nick?* He thought that Nick may be in the house. Where else could he be? It was too dangerous and certainly too foolish of a thing for Nick to leave operational.

He pulled himself from the ongoing functioning of his genius friend's experiment and jogged across the gravel to the house and went in, calling his friend's name repeatedly. *Not here? Where could you be? I had better turn off the power in the lab, or it could overload.*

Charley saw Nick's car in the garage. He called again into the basement and then continued his jog back to the lab, hoping he could remember how to disengage the power grid.

Dana arrived shortly after Charley had entered the building. Parking her car off to the side of the driveway behind some trees afforded her the element of silence when she was ready to leave. Tucking her keys in her jeans and leaving her purse in the car, she made the two-hundred-yard walk to the house ju. If need be, she could duck off deeper into the woods. If Charley left, her car would still be far enough off the road to avoid being noticed.

Her white sneakers took her closer to the house and the now visible pole barn. Even from her distance, she felt the vibration from some dot of power source. She thought it too great to be a simple air conditioner, dismissing the idea that anyone would need to be that cold. As she approached, it was certainly emanating from the pole barn. She guessed that he might serve as a laboratory for what must be a large-scale project.

Closing the gap between her and the barn, Dana noticed Charley's car parked at an angle to the side door. The house seemed a decent size for one person, the shrubs were overgrown, and gravel was the only decorative element. Signs of a onetime flowerbed between the garage and the front door reminded her of the painstaking hours her mother spent primping and pruning their garden back home in North Carolina. The ground maintained a natural incline to the pole barn, and she approached it from the west end with intentions of circling it in hopes of finding a window or open door.

Crunching through pine needles leaves and twigs, with careful steps, she made her way to the far end of the property. The humming intensified with her approach. Electric exhaust flavoring the early evening air lent an odd tone to the night's events.

The end of the barn had no window or door. The side facing the woods was sheer, save for a service ladder leading to the roof, the source of the powerful vibrations. Wanting to get some information quickly and leave, she made her way up the ladder to access the roof.

After an easy climb, she found herself on the roof of the pole barn. A large square section had been removed, and a hard, clear plastic sheet was set in the opening, along with a ten-by-ten solar collection grid supported by an aluminum conduit that led into the barn. Below the plastic sheet, she could see several unfamiliar instruments hanging along a lattice of aluminum bars. A hatch was cut in the plastic and what looked like another ladder leading down onto some sort of circular metal platform. Cables and buffer connection boxes led to a control panel. She studied the inside of the lab, avoiding the temptation to climb down before using her phone to take some photos.

Dana crouched to avoid the hot metal against her skin. A door closed at the house, and immediately, she lowered herself to avoid being seen. Charley walked with purpose across the yard to the north side door and entered the barn. Dana repositioned herself to see what he was doing. She held a position that would not expose her to Charley, who was inspecting the machines and computers buzzing away with unusual energy. She found that lying on her stomach for short periods was the best way to keep her arms and legs from blistering from the searing roof.

Charley made his way back to the lab, wanting to have a clearer sense of what Nick was doing. He tried to put it together. The generator was connected to the computer containing the featured program. The power was apparently being pumped in from the radio panels through the holographic imager into the black box. The blue light drew his to the small door on the side. What was he generating? *Let's take a look,* he thought. Charley took the small knob in his hand and pulled the door open, revealing the grassy blue scene. Initially, he was impressed with the detail of the image; perhaps the solar energy was so intense that it somehow forced a dominant blue spectrum. Interesting. It had movement and depth as in a panorama. Something about its color was beyond the simple three-dimensional objects usually created holographically.

Charley pulled himself away from the box and began concerning himself with the power grid and its tolerances. At the control computer, he accessed the power status, and it appeared to be functioning above normal parameters. It needed to be shut down soon. It may overheat. So many questions were struggling their way to the front of his mind, but one beat all the others there. *Where is Nick?*

*****

Nick was struggling. First, he could not stop asking himself why he had not come better prepared. Second, what would he bring next time he came into the past, *if there would be a next time*, and last, where was the PFC?

His smoke bomb was spitting its last puffs, and movement in the grass by the confused Neanderthals was heard some forty yards away. They would certainly soon be aiming their sniffing noses in his direction. His senses reeled nearly out of control when all at once, an idea hit him. The sound of the power generator was very loud. In the midst of the sights and confusion, he hadn't stopped and listened. He pulled the cowl from his head and listened, meeting the limits of his natural hearing. He thought he heard a hum behind him. Turning and taking a couple of steps put him out of the diminishing smoke cloud, yet he did hear something. Slaloming through the grass, he tuned his hearing to the electric buzz of the generators.

The early men of the field were fumbling about, slapping the grass with their hairy arms, seemingly trying to put out a fire they could not locate. Nick, in a pinch, agreed (thinking as a primitive) that seeing smoke would imply fire. Nick shook off his limited knowledge of this period. He was not sure if they had learned to control fire. Perhaps they had, knowing it was important for them to try to put it out.

While the grass was being checked for a potentially dangerous blaze, Nick zeroed in on the sound while scanning the grass for some kind of light. As he scanned the area, the last of the smoke cloud was winded away across the field, dissipating to nothing. The men would not be confused for long; Nick thought now would be a good time to find his way home.

Charley stood at the control panel and began the shutdown sequence, first finding the power control screen and then trying to remember the order of commands. He paused at the timer. The power had been in use for just under five hours, a dangerously long time, he thought. Nick had initiated it at 1:07 p.m. Initiating the command to close the system was as easy as one keystroke on the keyboard. The generator slowed, the noise reduced, and the blue light began to dim. Once the system was off, Charley took the stairs from the command console hurriedly, starting for the woods to look for his friend.

CHAPTER 31

Enrique looked into Pepe's refrigerator for something to eat. He was tempted to heat some of the frozen homemade chili but waited until he had the chance to ask the captain. Sanchez and Alba were huddled around their portable computer, sifting through information that might help them determine what could have made these insects grow so large. Sanchez knew that there had to be answers to their questions and that they would not be found in the database of science journals. The coincidence of their appearance after the meteor fall haunted the logical conclusions of the professors' mind. Alba refused to believe that the creatures had originated in space and continued to look for some terrestrial data on radiation exposure or growth hormones that may have been dumped in the area. Sanchez had the skins sent to a bioanalysis lab. He was certain they would not find a match. He had sent an electronic message to download the information as soon as possible. While they were waiting for Senor Fernandez to fix the boat, a beep on the professor's computer alerted him of an incoming message.

"Professor Alba, I have the information from the bio lab. They have sent me the results of the test. This will help us," he said hurriedly, taking the tablet computer and accessing the message. He scrolled through the charts and DNA arrangements to the bottom to find the technician's conclusion. It read,

Dr. Sanchez,

> *We have arranged the structure of the chromosomes of this creature. At this time, our records do not find exact matches conclusively identifying the specimen. It appears to be an arthropod yet exhibit characteristics of several species. Initially, it resembles a centipede yet has a number of sequences that are much like the Pycnogonida class or sea spiders. The only living relatives would be the horseshoe crab. Yet the majority of its genomic content suggests it is not a crustacean. However, it does show indices of size of an ability to grow at least nine feet long as in the eurypterid or sea scorpions. They lived between 500 and 230 million years ago. Outstandingly, the creature that it most resembles in terms of numbers of genes matched is the Tardigrade. These creatures are tiny, measuring 0.004 to 0.02 inches long. You can find up to*

185,874 per square foot. They are known for their strange ability to enter a state of cryptobiosis, where they retract their legs and grow a double wall around itself, capable of remaining dormant for decades. Their life signs are barely detectable. In this state, they are known as TUNS. Tests have been performed, revealing that they can survive exposure to extreme temperatures, toxic chemicals, and even radiation. They have a taste for dead animals and can be quite voracious in groups. Theoretically, they can survive space flight. It is not conclusive that you have found a very large tardigrade, but it certainly will be classified similarly. I have included DNA graphs of the aforementioned species. I hope this information will help. Good luck.

They studied the text and accompanying materials in silence, digesting the information conflicted by the desire to capture a tardigrade and retreating to safety while the captain continued tooling with the computer, trying to reinitiate the ship's controls.

Pepe found the damaged keyboard that prevented him from entering commands. The engine could be started, yet the only way to transfer controls would require another computer interface. This had not happened before. Certainly, he would have the ship reconfigured to allow for total manual control once he got back to Celestun. The keyboard operated with a traditional press key system. Pepe favored this style over the touch-activated keys simply because his large fingers had some difficulty on the small flat board. No one made a waterproof press keyboard. His wife wanted him to wrap it in plastic from the cupboard, but he did not like the idea. He paused to look out over the sea, trying to think of a way to help them back to shore. The keyboard was partially disassembled in an attempt to dry it out. He feared that the damage was deeper and beyond repair of simple blotting dry with towels. Then Pepe had an idea. He went below to find the professors pouring over a computer.

"Dr. Sanchez, please bring your computer. I think it may help us to get the ship back on line." He took the tablet computer topside and began sorting through the tangled mess of cords to find the right jack wire from his box of spare computer accessories in hopes of wiring it to the ship's hardware.

Without warning, the front feeling legs of one of the insects began to climb over the gunwale with searching eyes and antennae, testing the deck for signs of food. Pepe took action with his gun and fired of two shots, sending the creature splashing backward into the sea. As he checked his gun's ready light, a thud hit the boat from the opposite side. The others below felt the boat respond to the impact. Each of them retreated to the privacy of their fears, looking to the door for the captain. Two more hits unnerved the crew further.

Pepe searched for any sign of more uninvited passengers. Realizing it was time to defend the ship, he reeled for the cabin door and went halfway below, the gun still in hand.

"Everyone on deck, these devils want the boat! Get a weapon!"

Enrique found the bat, and Sophia familiarized herself with the long pole. Pepe entrusted a gun into Sanchez's hands and then inspected the back of the portable.

"You know how to use this?" said Pepe, flipping the safety off.

Sanchez nodded. "One of them tried to climb on board."

Pepe rummaged through the box of cords and plugs, not finding one that fit it into the computer port.

The three shipmates formed a circle in the center of the deck, facing the sea, ready to defend themselves. Pepe fished through the box with his left hand while ready with the stun pistol in his right. A series of impacts jolted the crew, scaring them into a higher level of readiness.

Readiness turned to preparedness upon threatening sounds of scraping and scurrying of the insects crawling along the bottom of the boat.

"Senor Captain, do you need some help?" Sophia called across the deck, tuning from her watch for a moment.

Pepe remained at work, waving her over. "I can defend the ship better with two hands. Senora, come help me find the right cord!" Alba joined Pepe at the ship's helm to forage for the right cord as he fired laser bolts at the attacking creatures.

Just then, with a shocking thrust, one of the insects sprang out of the water and landed on the deck near Alba, flailing its mandibles. The creature seemed to have a wider body out of the water, flattening itself on the deck in a defensive position. She screamed uncharacteristically, putting the pole between her and four hungry fangs poised to attack.

Enrique responded in a flash and charged the unaware insect, bringing the bat over his head and pummeling the beast on its rear quarter. It hissed with poison and astonishment, recoiling to face its assaulter in a pool of white gum.

Several of the legs were damaged, writhing involuntarily. Enrique brought the bat back, ready for another swing. Alba gained control of the pole and stuck it directly in front of the fangs, startling it back along the gunwale. The creature spasmodically found itself surrounded yet made it over the side and away.

Enrique was breathing heavily, his hands clenching the bat with anger and adrenaline. He searched the area for something to bash. Nothing came into view. The boat rocked and swelled indifferently in the water.

Pepe turned to witness the attack, but it was over before any reaction came to mind.

"Be ready, my friends! They won't give up so easily!"

Alba continued her work, furiously searching the ill-managed box tangled cords. All eyes flitted about the edges of the boat. All ears listened for the now deafening hissing noise that had become the signature herald for the growing insects.

Sanchez, Pepe, and Enrique stalked the invisible yet imminent attacks, keeping a ready guard still in their circle at center deck. Silence never seemed so deadly to Enrique. He shook his head, tying to disbelieve the experience, but when he regained his senses, his attention was drawn to something floating in the water nearly fifty yards out. It floated white and long like a giant surfboard. Before he could alert his shipmates, several insects were crawling around the top and then back into the water.

"Look there! Something is in the water!" he said, barely avoiding a crack in his voice.

The others turned in unison to the direction of the floater. After a minute or so, it rolled and tossed in the sea, revealing a telltale tail of a whale. Alba suspected it was a calf being effectively processed by the bugs. Most of the creatures covered with the white bug cocoon remained submerged while the creatures spun their goo web, making the body float. As it tipped its sides at the waterline, the grasping legs of the bugs affixed to its underside.

"How is it coming, Sophia?" Sanchez called.

"I have not found the right cord!"

"Rene! Look there!" Sophia called, pointing beyond the entrance to the cabin. An insect had crawled on at the front of the boat and now was looming near the captain, trying not to be noticed. Sanchez hurried to the captain's side and fired the gun multiple times, hitting the creature square in the face, sending it stunned into the sea.

"Thanks, Professor," Pepe said, patting him on the back.

"Keep them off the boat. Hit them in the face if you can."

Another pair of bugs appeared from either side of the boat. Alba screamed inwardly at their ability to attack from two fronts at once, defining their social interaction more clearly.

Enrique charged with the bat, sending one into the water, grasping at air after three furious meetings with the ash stick. The second immediately squared off with its opponent.

Sanchez and Pepe faced the other, flattening itself and rearing its fangs, poised to leap at any opportunity. Pepe gave a mighty scream and pierced the creature with the fiberglass pole. He put his weight against it, forcing the bug against the side. Sprays of white and orange blood foamed and spurted around the jerking body. The bug's body was stuck on the end. He dropped the pole, almost leaving the rubber gloves with it, feeling the strength of the retreating creature. It was not going to fit in the cooler. It shook loose from the pole and considered another attack yet, after evaluating its wounds and the fierce look of determination in the eye of the captain, leaped overboard.

Enrique squared off with the last one. It dodged his blows and thrust with its fangs. Soon, he was using the bat to parry the attacks rather than to attack. The creature backed up for a moment, finding its footing on its hind legs, and then flung its entire body to the student. Enrique fell back, losing his footing yet keeping the bat between him and its front legs that had wrapped around his wrists. He shimmied his hands along the length of the bat, forcing the top of the bat at the fangs that reached and gored wildly for his throat.

Not able to keep both feet stable, he fell backward with the creature fully on top of him. Pushing against the insect was a most horrifyingly new sensation to Enrique. He had known insects quite differently until now, feeling its physical strength. It was a sensation laced with hunger. Enrique, not wanting to have his internal juices replaced with white insect goo, fought the many clutches of alien fangs and legs, large and small. With a lunge, he flipped over and was now on top, using his knees to crush its lower section while turning the bat horizontally, putting pressure just below the head. Goo appeared in defense from the creature now hissing and coughing.

A new sound fell upon the ears of the defenders, that of the half-barking, choking, and hissing sound as it writhed impossibly for escape. Sanchez stood by with the gun, allowing his student to overcome the beast.

Enrique vented anger and soon exhibited poise in overpowering the bug. He knelt hard on his victim, punctuating pressure and bat with grunts and expletives, leaving the insect countering only with involuntary twitches and jerks.

Sophia Alba inserted a plug that finally fit from the tablet to the ship's controls. The screen flashed a "standby" prompt. Pepe's laugh could be heard outside his loud nasal breathing at the sound of the computer ping.

Sanchez stood to regard the vanquished with nothing less than gall and then placed a fatherly arm on the boy's shoulder and said, "Let's get this one into the canvass bag. Good job, Enrique. You receive the grade of A. I will speak to the self-defense department about your extra credit."

With a buzz, the ship's engines started. Pepe and Alba engaging in an elated "high five."

As the boat came alive, its captain's laughter louder than the engines, Rene and Enrique packed the lifeless insectoid body into the canvass bag, securing it with a pull tie.

Pepe took inventory of the situation back at the controls, nearly ready to power the boat to shore. He put it into gear with relish, smiling wide at the notion of escaping danger. They slipped ahead with the surety of the Proturbo diesel engines.

La Fresca had moved nearly a mile away at a spirited pace that raced with Pepe's heart. The crew had settled the bug into the ice hold and was at the task of cleaning up the deck when an alerting beep turned the captain's smiling head to Sanchez's portable computer that operated the boat. A prompt flashed "low battery."

*****

Nick crouched in the grass, not sure what he was doing for a moment. Soon, he realized he was hiding, a natural instinct he had not experienced in quite some time. The hunting party still tried to find the source of the smoke, buying him some time to find his portal to the future. He crawled away from the noise using his energy to refrain from panic and now his sense of smell to try to locate electrical emanations from the PVC. He heard grunts and calls from a 180-degree span and kept himself away from the group sniffing along as he went on all fours. Humility fell away comfortably when one's life was in peril. He nearly welcomed the feeling as he scrambled along like a dog trying to find his way home.

Pausing in the grass, he wondered between quaffs of air how death would end his pain. He could unite with Ada even if simply by being as nonexistent as she most certainly was. Thoughts of heaven offered to paint the ceiling of his scientific mind. He believed in an afterlife and communion with God and departed loved ones but could not find as much blind faith as he could answer through science.

Instantly, he recalled the accident with Ada as the last time he felt that his life might end. He reminded himself of the fact he had survived to live a life, though now less tainted with reminders of guilt, loss, and loneliness, still one that left him separated from the simplicity of one of life's basic relationships. Feeling even further removed from normalcy, he confronted a very exhilarating cause to press on—continued existence.

After a few moments of resting his ankles, still aching, he put aside notions of futility and continued to scramble, congratulating himself for having grown emotionally since the crash. Dying now would only magnify the tragedy. He took a new direction and all at once found an area where the grass compressed. He stood slowly, remembering the scene he had first witnessed upon entering the field. It wasn't far off, not disturbed by the men. However, the box was not there. Where did it go? Had the power failed somehow? Had he run the system too long? Burt might have had some trouble, but what would make him shut down the system? He sat putting his hands between his knees and sincerely reconsidered death as an unavoidable option. *Bad science, Nick*, he thought.

After beginning the shutdown sequences as prompted by Nick's recall program, Charley stepped down the steel staircase and went to inspect the hologram in the box as the blue light began to diminish. How Nick had kept this from him was unimaginable. Touching the sides, he pondered for what function it was created. It was then he caught sight of a cardboard box on the floor next to the black coffin. Two flippers were sticking out of it and a snorkel. He stood over the box, not finding a mask or the suit. On the floor was a pair of shoes and Nick's blue jeans. Charley realized quite suddenly what was going on. Nick had gone into the chamber. He threw open the box to find the last glimmers of a blue holographic scene dimming from the emitter. Without another thought, he raced to the control panel and commanded the program to reinitiate. His mind sped at amazing speed, trying to find a way to restart. He did not know if the power link would automatically sever upon deactivation or if he had to call Burt at the satellite relay station to turn it on. Checking the screen, it was still offering power. He was in luck. After a few moments, he decided that before he would screw this up, he would try "UNDO" the last command. This function had come in handy during mistake situations when he entered multiple commands on complicated programs. He isolated the command list and pressed "UNDO" before it had finished deleting itself.

A surge of light reentered the coffin, and the horizontal stack of glass globes began to glow again. Sure that he had started the machine, he ran to the box shining light throughout the lab. He closed the lid and opened the small door. A grassy area appeared in a blue mist. Sitting huddled with its back turned was a human figure clutching his knees. *There he is!*

Charley called to his friend with frantic glee.

"Nick, is that you? Nick, can you hear me?"

For less time than it took to blink, Nick turned, pointing his skinny nose in Charley's direction. He was trying to say something, but sound no traveled from the hologram.

Charley knew that a normal hologram could be adjusted easily to amplify the sound with the use of a reactive soundtrack. But what kind of projection was this that allowed his best friend to exist in this dimensional anomaly?

Nick stood in amazement when the light reappeared; he repositioned himself on his back next to the perimeter of the blue rectangle. He motioned to the box with his hand. The last thing Charley saw before he closed the peek door was a dark fur-clad figure jumping into the area of flattened grass.

For a few moments, Charley stared at the box. What was that other guy doing? It seemed as if it was attacking Nick. He waited several nervous seconds when the top of the coffin flew open and Nick stood. He was out of the coffin and on the portable staircase in seconds flat, letting the lid fall with a whack. Charley stood in amazement as his gasping cohort stood yet doubled over, breathing heavily, unable to speak. Charley came over and instinctively gave a visual assessment of Nick's condition. He seemed okay.

"What . . . ?""Nick, are you all right? What the hell did you do?" Charley demanded impatiently.

Nick waved his friend's assertion aside, making a weak trip to the stairs and then to the control computer, his slender frame taking the stairs frantically.

"Hold that thought."

He interrupted the power inline. Within seconds, a steady hum of power began to wind down and away; the blue light dimmed. Nick sat on the small stool with his head buried on the keyboard.

Aware that his friend would want some explanation and knowing a flood of question would ensue, Nick lifted his head and said pointedly to Charley, "That was supposed to be a surprise! Don't ask any questions. I will explain. What you saw was my image within a holographic scenario that has been revised or reconstituted to include a dimension of time and space created by fossil remains. The solar research I have been working on has proven a new solar cycle spanning many thousands of years. I have tapped into this cycle, and once it coalesced with the fossils and the holo-imager, I found a new dimension, Charley, and the most important part is that there is more than one of them. I am sorry I did not tell you sooner. I could have used some help actually, but I wanted to keep a pure train of thought. I wanted to show you before, but there wasn't enough time. Then I received a new sample that somehow tied the whole thing together," he said, now more composed and somewhat relieved.

He was amused with another concealed thought. Nick raised a quiet finger and began typing a new involvement at his computer.

Charley watched the usual humor interlaced with Nick's persona now affected by his experience. Nick reduced the formula to an equation that needed to be recorded. Pure calculation merged with theory and chance to create something unique and provable.

Raw science kept them friends. Awe of this new, pure power kept them awake for hours in conversation that led to an assault of formulae on a wall-sized holo-display and an antique blackboard. To Nick, there was nothing more engaging. Charley knew he had to allow Nick to run the course to complete his stream of consciousness.

Silence was the best way to deal with him at this juncture as Nick faced a problem without an answer.

"I was in another time for nearly six hours! It was by my estimation just over ten thousand years ago. I was actually there. You saw me . . . 'in' it, didn't you? You must have. I lost the blue box. I have to know why it stopped . . ." Nick consulted the information on his screen and then slowly brought his nearly maddened gaze to that of Charley's.

"You didn't happen to have shut the system down manually, did you, Charles?"

Charley realized that his associate had been looking for an explanation for the shutdown. Nick waited calmly for a reply.

He paused for a moment to gather his words and then began to explain simply and innocently as Nick watched him listening intently.

"I came over at 7:00 p.m. and found the system running. You weren't around, so I thought something had happened to you, and I wasn't sure if the system would be safe being on so long, so I turned it off."

Nick gave a sigh of relief that still bore traces of anger, finally allowing himself to sit.

"Well, at least there isn't a glitch in the system that turns itself off while I am having lunch with a pack of freaking Neanderthals!" Charley remembered the other person imaged in the box, opting to wait to ask him about that later.

"Well, I don't know if they were actually Neanderthals. I will have to consult my database given that I couldn't ask them. They wanted to subdue me, save me for later," he said with a huff and then looked back at the globes, wanting some understanding.

"Calm down, Nick. You obviously have stumbled across some breakthrough technology here. Just take it easy. We'll go through it step by step," Charley said.

As Nick explained the events of the day, a cautious Leslie Davis undercover as Dana Kim lay flat in the shadow of the solar panel on the roof of the lab. She absorbed the conversation to the best of her abilities; her body became accustomed to the heat of the roof like a reptile. After the better part of an hour, she felt the men concluding their conversation. Not wanting to leave a syllable of the events from the black coffin unheard, she bargained with herself to remain another five minutes that eventually led to ten and then fifteen.

Knowing that she heard most of the details from the questions Charley had posed to Nick about the transition of Nick's research into a physical alteration of reality beyond the confines of holography, she knew it was decidedly the right time to leave. She shimmied backward to the ladder, nearly missing it, falling to her exposure, if not worse.

Finding her way down in the darkness, she paused and listened for any sounds outside the lab. Nothing. Stepping as lightly as possible, she made her way toward her car in the final throes of daylight. She walked along the gravel road to where the trees broke to reclaim her car. The halogen light that beamed from the pole barn onto the area in front of the house no longer helped her see her way. She cursed her unpreparedness for not bringing a flashlight, groping and tripping along the road.

Nick stopped suddenly in midsentence as his wrist phone that had not been operational in the other world rang a shrill alarm, repeating itself again and again. The prompt on his screen read, "Intruder Alert."

CHAPTER 32

The following two simulations went more routinely than Simey had planned. With twenty minutes until the actual liftoff, the ship, now out on the launch pad, the activity in the staging room died down considerably. Most of *TerraLuna*'s people were in the observation room. After several days, people began to pay less attention to the rapidly growing *MoonCorp* project as it grew several miles from the lunar pole.

Ed became fidgety in the command chair, now too ready to take off. Once he had set the *Motivator* in the deep space stage, he would be spending a minimal amount of time at the helm. A roster was set up for "pilots" to sign up to have a chance to monitor the ship. The trip was monitored by remote systems so there would not be actual piloting to be done until it neared B2. For the three days of travel, twenty-nine pilot trainees would sit in the chair.

Fifteen minutes until blastoff, Simey's voice echoed through the complex in his most dignified mission control voice. Dave and Tom entered through the tall dark curtain to find Ed in the cockpit, turning casually in the swivel chair. Other virtual ships had seating for a copilot and passengers, but Ben Skylar and Gerhard Steele had opted for a single seat more appropriate for the concentration required for this ship's particular purpose. It was still a matter of some debate.

Ben Skylar was on the video screen to have a last-minute pep talk with Ed concerning some pine points for blastoff.

"Now, Ed, I realize you have done this many times, yet no one has flown more of these missions than me. I designed it. With the moon's gravity as it is, you will, of course, have the one-eighth gee of the moon to adjust to, but of course, the computers will do the math. You shouldn't have any problem. However, it will feel different from an Earth launch. The switch to deep space drive is the juncture that can cause problems. I suggest that you perform a microsystems check before you engage the antimatter engines, solely as a precaution. We do not want a glitch that occurred during liftoff to rear its head after you are clipping along near light speed. Understood?"

"Yeah, Ben, that makes sense. How often should the antimatter engines be checked along the way?" Ed asked, hoping to find the real reason behind an automated feature he was concerned about.

"You do not have to worry. Simey has installed a self-cleaning program that will constantly keep the injectors free from any heat-generated residue. If it makes you feel better, you can activate the control reminder feature to update you when the cleaning cycle begins." Ben's image nodded as Ed bound his way to the program and activated the feature.

"It all looks good. I like to keep abreast of the minor details. Say, Ben, when is the ribbon going to be cut on *MoonCorp*? It is more popular than Friday night at the movies up here," Ed said with a chuckle.

"We plan on decompression sometime after the first of August. Take care of my A-Driver, and I will set you up with a free week." Skylar smiled beneficently.

"Yes, sir, I am motivated now. That will be a week for two, right? You know I have been practicing my lunar racquetball. I need some real competition. You still play, don't you?"

"Oh, I play, and you can be sure I will arrange it so I am there when you stay. Ben Skylar lives for a challenge. Take care. Ed, you seem ready for the countdown. Call me if you have any questions. Skylar out."

The screen blipped off, leaving Ed to resume his checks of systems. Dave and Tom looked on in place of Skylar on Ed's screen.

"I think you and Ben have everything in hand," Dave said, not in jovial spirits. "We still have a potentially Earth-threatening object that you need to stop."

Tom's face replaced Dave's, finding a smile. "Bring me back a souvenir."

"Five minutes until blastoff. All personnel, confirm station final check." Simey's disembodied voice boomed rather loudly. Dave crossed to his console and lowered the volume as Ed switched his screen to display function readings.

"Five minutes until blastoff mark. Engaging liftoff engines and primary functions package." Ed spoke into the flight recorder after tapping the appropriate switches.

The rumble of the simulated cockpit, its sound and movement package tuned with the actual *Motivator*'s functions, sharpened his focus. A clock ran down time until liftoff. At the designated intervals, he initiated the grouped functions readily termed as packages. At the three-minute level, all takeoff systems were waiting for the final countdown.

The clock made its inevitable count to blast off. A tense undertone was felt throughout *TerraLuna* with the impending liftoff. If something went wrong exploding the ship laden with many dozens of nuclear bombs within one hundred thousand miles of the moon's surface, it would destroy both *TerraLuna* and *MoonCorp* in one cataclysmic boom.

Ed replaced those thoughts with those of Haley and the new forms of expression entering their relationship. After tonight's mission, he would probably get some of that hero sex that Simey and Tom talked about. Another thought briefly passed his mind. The mule that Nick Nicholas had sent to deliver his rock sample had not yet approached him. Ed supposed he was waiting for the right moment; he had not been the most accessible person lately.

The clock turned from three digits to two. Simey cleared his throat, taking a long drink of water rather than his usual cola. He found that running the risk of burping during a mission control announcement would create a stigma that would take a long time to live down.

The ES or environmental simulator geared up a notch in preparation for liftoff, offering a rumble in his seat. Ed braced himself slightly, his hand on the ignition lever. Simey began the countdown with not more than the usual drama.

"FIVE, FOUR, THREE, TWO, ONE, LIFT OFF!"

The ship rose with ease in the low moon gravity. Its legs, drilling apparatus, and bomb delivery systems all tucked neatly below and along the sides, covered with protective panels for the high-speed, A-drive trip. The ship took to the moon's atmosphere like a white swan to a dark lake. Ed thought it was a beautiful thing. The multiple screens offered cycling views from *TerraLuna* and from the ship itself.

The workers at *MoonCorp* stopped their diligent work to view the takeoff. The diligent laborers worked four shifts a "day" by Earth time. Construction on the inner support system needed to be in place before construction of the roof could begin. Preliminary defense system installations would not begin for a few more weeks. The low gravity of the moon increased the workers' productivity, as low gravity made work less demanding.

In earlier phases of moon construction, the problem of dealing with the extreme temperatures prohibited full day and night activity. The radiant solar electricity transfer system cultivated by Dr. Charles Porter provided enough power to maintain temperature.

The suits are designed with a wiring system, able to convert sunlight falling on the surface of the suit into its own electric energy generator. It sorted the solar energy to the variety of sources function in the suit. The walnut size "batteries" spot the suit like "polka dots." The valuable power nuts were later collected and used to power any one of a hundred devices.

A computer that used the "solar nut" system was in the hands of Yuri Povlovich, the chief in situation engineer of *MoonCorp*. It was time to change the nut. Walking into the shell of *MoonCorp* to avoid the glare of the early evening sun, he reached to a fully charged nut affixed to his suit for a replacement. He transferred the nearly spent battery into the empty notch, securing it with a double tap for charging, and then continued his rounds of inspection on the load-bearing slabs of moon rock that would define the larger rooms throughout the complex.

A lunar welder piecing together two wall pieces seemed to be doing a fine job. The clock on his computer flashed a reminder of the *TerraLuna*'s *Motivator* liftoff. He tapped in the nearest worker's suit number that was printed on his helmet, activating the inter-suit intercom, as he was inspecting a lower connection.

"Bobby, all of you, take a break and check out the Skylar that's taking off."

He paused through his tinted faceplate and stood with a bounce, turning to the opening in the walls where docking bay doors would be, and looked up to see the ship.

Skylar had sponsored many missions to adjust the trajectory of NMOs and NEOs, but Yuri had never seen one from the surface of the liftoff. Others had not been alerted. Yuri tapped his "all call" feature, linking him with all the personnel at the site.

"Okay, everyone, listen up now. If you look in the direction of the *TerraLuna* hotel, you will see the ascent of the *Motivator*. For you new people, this ship deters and destroys space material, keeping us all safe."

Some of the workers outside the JC began to wave and take pictures with the camera built into the gloves on their suits. Yuri gave a warm Russian chortle.

"It is no use to wave. There is no one on board to see you. It is an unmanned craft."

Ed completed the micro check, and it cleared with a green light. "Taking A-Drive online," he said into the recorder.

"Antimatter engines engaging."

After the *Motivator* reached one hundred thousand miles above the surface, a change in the color of the light, emitting from beneath the ship, was noted by the *MoonCorp* band. Antimatter engines started sending *Motivator* into a ball of white light, cascading heavenward. Its momentum gained, and within seconds, only a faint tail remained as it tripped along at near light speed.

They stood like white pins, motionless against the gray lunar surface. The only movement was from the smelter machines that shot up some moon dust as they idled in waiting. Yuri Povlovich looked up with the others. "Let our blessings go with her."

His chair lurched several times. *Motivator* used breakthrough technology only a few years old to send it into space faster than any machine ever created by man. The imager's matrix duplicated the shifts and fluctuations onto the cock pit, giving Ed a near firsthand experience that was better than any amusement park ride. It was by far more exciting than the simulators because it was really happening thousands of miles away. As Ed enjoyed his ride, a prompt beeped on a secondary screen. It read, "FASTEN YOUR SEAT BELT."

*****

Enrique watched the calf's distance from the ship increase with clinging bugs sitting like piratical passengers along its back. He was sure they were out of harm's way when a frantic call from the captain for Dr. Sanchez shot through the warm mist of the nearly noon sun.

"Dr. Sanchez! Please come here!" the captain yelled over the ship's engines.

The professor was also watching the ambushed calf bob and fade into the distance. He came to the captain immediately, his face full of questions.

"We have a problem with our computers' battery. It seems to be running low. Tell me you brought a power cord," Pepe entreated. When no words but empty eyes met the captain's flustered visage, Pepe took him by the arm and showed him the LOW BATTERY prompt.

"Your portable is allowing me to operate the ship. If the power source depletes, I will not be able to enter commands to the ship's computer. Are you sure you do not have the power cord in the bag below? Please, would you check for it now?" Pepe impressed the urgency with a level of conviction he rarely had the opportunity to use.

Sanchez nodded and muttered, "Yes, of course." He made his way to the cabin to search his computer case for a power cord. It was not there. He folded his hands momentarily in the bag, squeezing his eyes shut for a moment to find some glint of inspiration in the darkness of his own mind. Opening his eyes without an answer, he saw Tico looking at him with an astutely puzzled expression for a dog.

"What can we do now, little friend? Do you have any ideas?"

Tico whined, perhaps wanting to go on deck to see his master or perhaps to take a leak.

He returned topside empty-handed.

"Professor, I hope the manual controls will work once I unplug the computer. We will not be able to use the sonar or the satellite navigation. Many of the other ship's functions will not be available as well. I can still steer the ship. I have a noncomputer directed compass."

Pepe transferred the control to manual and unplugged the computer, handing it to the teacher like something that was suddenly unnecessary. Sanchez took it in his arms and delivered it back into its case, vowing to always carry the cord when he traveled with the computer. The ship continued without a hitch. *La Fresca* trounced through the sunbathed blue waters with eagerness. Most of the trip was made in silence, the captain trying to give his passengers a good ride despite the circumstances of the morning. All were glad to be in some measure lost in the exhilaration of the ship as it comforted them a safe and speedy ride home.

After the better part of an hour, Pepe called Jose at the marina to tell him of their estimated arrival time.

"*La Fresca* to Progreso Marina. We will be docking in about a half hour, my friend. I have been fishing, but I cannot bring you any free samples today."

Jose paused with mock seriousness.

"Now, Pepe, you should think of your friend more often. You know I take care of you and Tico. I always like the fish you bring me. I look forward to it as do my wife and kids."

"Yes, but I do not think you will want this fish. It is more like a cockroach than a red fish. You will see when I get back," Pepe replied, feeling better now that he spoke with his friend; a smile found it back to his large face.

"Okay, you are the master fisherman. You know what is best. I have berth number 1 waiting for you. Good sailing!"

Jose placed the microphone back in its holder and, not missing a beat, picked up the telephone and called Ms. Morales, who had transferred one hundred world dollars to his card earlier that day to call her when *La Fresca* called in for a berth. Jose did not think Pepe would mind.

Sanchez, Alba, and Enrique did what they could to straighten the mess on board, feeling it was the least they could do to help Pepe, who had risked his boat to accommodate the expedition. Tests that had been planned for the trip home had dropped from the itinerary without question. Recuperations from their ordeal logically took rank from any tests the professors had in mind. Sanchez's computer was packed away, so they resorted to making notes of the encounter on small handheld devices during the trip back to Progreso Marina.

The last minutes of the trip came and went surprisingly fast for Professor Alba, who had been engrossed in organizing notes and anxious to dissect iced specimen in the hold.

The Progreso Marina came into view. Gathering her things, Alba would make her exit from the boat briskly. The brisker, the better, she thought as she collected her equipment, stacking at the side of the boat.

Sanchez, upon seeing the marina, realized that it had been too long since he had a cup of coffee and wondered if the girl in the snack bar wouldn't mind brewing him a fresh pot. Despite everything, he congratulated himself for returning with a decent specimen. Having to explain how a computer battery rather than some large bugs nearly thwarted his excursion was a tale he would rather not have to tell.

As the boat approached the berth, Sanchez tensed as he spotted Dahlia Morales waiting for them. He shot a look at Pepe, who turned away with uneasiness, still unwilling to give an interview. Sanchez gave a reassuring look to the captain, knowing he would have to represent the crew to the media.

Pepe began to fathom the end of this escapade. It was something he needed to give some spice to his tedious daily routine. In a way, it was sad to see it end, yet thoughts of his wife's commonsensical demeanor defined the unavoidability of his return home. It wasn't such a bad thing. As escapade once in a while, he thought, could be a good thing.

He knew she would say something predictable like "Do not make a habit of it, Pepe!" Well, he conceded privately; she was right. Enrique followed Alba's lead, helping her gather their things, subconsciously wanting to indulge his feet to some dry land. He had kept an attentive eye on the waters, holding the baseball bat during the entire trip back. Deep beneath his large brown eyes, there was still some rage to be released for taking his friend Benito. He wondered if he would have the pleasure of smashing one across the face before this plague was over. Deep down, he knew somehow it was not over.

CHAPTER 33

Leslie Davis sped along the dark highway, her heavy breathing falling away into the cars' momentum in an involuntary attempt to equalize her rapidly beating heart. Her eyes had begun falling back into their original shape, mascara and fear incoherently dripping down her cheek. In a billow of road dust from Nick's rural driveway, she noted that a car wash was in order tonight. She was entirely unaware of Dana Kim as she made her way to the safety of her apartment. Her thoughts repeatedly returned to the conversation she overheard on the hot roof of Dr. Nicholas's laboratory. He had created something that all scientists would trade in an instant for a lifetime of theorizing. Mentally filing the new information as she was trained to left her trembling with excitement and jealously.

A car came into view. She found specific emptiness in its oncoming headlights that would remain unfilled; something she could never know. Deep within the reaches of the void was the irrevocable truth that it really wasn't her place to feel that way. It belonged to Nick Nicholas. In an attempt to forbid herself to imagine the vast potential of his creation, her grip tightened on the wheel, forcing dark tears from her eyes.

Her portable phone rang, jarring her. With one hand, she fished the phone from her purse on the passenger seat and answered.

"Hello."

"Leslie, this is Gerhard. How are you?" he said in a comforting tone as if he knew she was upset. He listened searchingly to silence for a very long moment.

*****

Charley was ahead of his friend out the door, taking a rechargeable flashlight from its perch below the security panel. Nick was behind him, half an eye on his watch that localized the alarm signal. The filter was effective for not tripping the alarm for wild animals. At last, he felt his money was well spent. A real intruder was a great way to test the new perimeter detection system, yet Nick had more pressing projects in mind, making it a bother if anything.

"Down the driveway and a bit into the woods," Nick directed.

"What else does it tell you about him?" Charley called back, making his way around the trees along the gravel road as it sloped gently away against the loose forest.

"It is a general detection system. I could have had satellite imaging as well, but I didn't think I needed to treat my property like a prison, or to spend a lot of money."

They were taking the gravel road at a half run, the flashlight illuminating huge swathes of trees and road at a time.

They stopped, periodically checking the woods, the light nearly turning them day, lit in periods of high-intensity floodlighting.

"Nothing here," Charley said, continuing along the road.

"Look, something is moving over there! Further ahead!"

Nick directed Charley's arm to where he thought he saw some movement. A small dark figure was dodging its way along into the woods.

"That is a wolf or is it a deer? Now I know I should have bought the deluxe model."

"So what does that thing tell you?" Charley demanded, trying to catch a breath.

"It creates a profile. I will access it."

Nick stood on the road in the glow of the whitish light of his wrist phone, activating the profile program. Charley inspected the woods and adjacent field with the flashlight.

"Whoever it was, they seem to be on a solo mission. It shows one subject. Nick, check this out. These are slim tire tracks."

The woods revealed telltale tire marks skid a path to the road. He carefully surveyed the area for any clue to the identity of the stalker, staring dumb at the ground, reviewing his good reasons for not becoming a police officer. He looked back at Nick sanding still in a pool of phone light.

He doused the light and took a deep breath to prepare himself for the days to come now that his secret work was revealed. *A time machine in the lab,* he thought, *was not in the plan for this week.* "This is the life of a scientist," he said silently.

Turning to rejoin Nick, something caught Charley's attention, nothing visible but rather fragrant, a hint of a perfume. It wasn't flowery but rather a spicy scent. Not thinking much of it, he continued meeting Nick in the road lit by the cell phone.

"The profile says the individual was 5 feet 2 inches with an approximate weight of 115 pounds. The satellite infrared is all we have."

He activated the phone to show Charley a replay of a white blotch instead of the expected red, orange, and yellow ghostly infrared image walking at a fast pace from the lab through the forest, getting into car, and speeding off.

"It looks I have a spy in my ointment. This must have been during my time in the box. It took its sweet time recalibrating my signal once I returned. Unless he was too close to the lab for the satellite to . . ." He paused, remembering the service ladder and the heat-intensive collection dish that might have masked a person's heat signature.

"I think he or she was on the roof. That explains why the sensors did not pick up the heat signal. The warm collector panels confused it."

"Maybe the deer stopped to take a leak, then got back into the car with the skinny tires. Does the satellite continue tracking once the subject leaves the grounds?" Charley asked, watching the replay again.

"It could with the deluxe package."

"I think you had better upgrade in light of what I saw in your lab, Dr. Nicholas."

They walked back to the lab, digesting new information. Nick was ready to open another chapter in history.

"You know this is the biggest can of worms we will ever open," Charley said, his imagination tinged with adventure.

Nick looked at him, remembering the boyish wonder he tried to preserve in his work.

"Yes, I know. There is a lot we can do, but there are things that will kill us in there. I plan on a section-by-section video log. I need protection. How soon can you get those guns?"

"We can get them tonight unless." Nick checked the time. It was close to 8:30 p.m.

Charley was on his phone and, in a few seconds, was ringing Seth, the gun dealer, who usually did business after normal business hours.

"Seth, this is Charley. How is it going? Good. I was hoping to get a showing tonight on some ELs an SLs. We are planning on a boar hunt, and you know how nasty those things can get at close range. We are heading to Texas next week and can use some backup. Is it okay to come over now? Great. We'll be here in half an hour." Charley closed the phone.

"It's cool. We can go there now. He lives about twenty minutes away."

"Let's do it."

Nick and Charley shut down the holo-systems, leaving the computers in sleep mode, and locked the barn. Within a few minutes, they were speeding along the highway scarce of cars, along their way to Seth's small country house outside Colton, California. Charley drove fast, not thinking about the radio rather for a chance to talk about the time machine.

"How far back can you go?" he said after a silence.

"The oldest sample was dated at four hundred million years ago."

"How near to our time can you go?"

"The Neanderthal era is roughly ten thousand years ago. Anything after that would have to be developed with more current samples. Archeology always fascinated me. Most of the samples were collected at modern digs or from private collections. I expect I can extend the range based on later era samples. Do you know any zoological geologists that I don't know?" he said inquisitively.

"I met a few in Mexico. Do you have any samples from there?"

"No, I cannot say I do. We should look them up and see if they have any newer fossils."

Charley passed a sign stating that Colton was seven miles ahead.

"I know that exploitation is not your game. There is, however, an idea I have been kicking around about how these chapters in time might be able to win us that ten-million-world-dollar endowment from Ben Skylar."

He shot an enterprising look at his passenger, who met his glance with the onset of unnerved suspicion. Nick said nothing but offered silence as an admission to at least hear the idea.

"What if we had the forces of nature over time help us to super condense one of his laser lenses to be able to withstand higher energy outputs for the offensive satellites? If we planted a lens and then returned after a million or so years of geological pressure, we may have a carbon diamond hard enough to offer superior accuracy and power conductivity, an ultra dense lens, a ten-million-world-dollar lens," he said with clarity.

Nick tossed the idea against his mental wall and, in a moment, challenged him back.

"How do you propose to retrieve the diamond after the million years take a bulldozer in the PFC with you?"

"No, we plant the lens in the past and then return to the spot the next day with dynamite, and we reap the benefits of the eons. We would have the location with the use of a simple platinum beacon and maybe attach it to a cable to make it easier to find. Sounds like it could work, doesn't it?" Charley looked away to the road with his idea before solidification by his friend's approval.

"Write a proposal for Ben and Francine telling them you are going to use a time machine to reform one of their three-million-world-dollar lenses. Let me know what they say." His sarcasm bit at his friend. Thinking twice, he continued.

"No, don't. Charley, listen to me. Yes, it is a good idea . . . that needs some work. Tell them you made a breakthrough with a new experimental pressure system, something you cannot go into great deal about, and see if they buy it. If they do, we can past a plausible theory together. It very well might work, and then it probably would not bastardize the integrity of time and space. However, before we go on with this experiment, I want to document each segment of time so we know as much as possible about what we have to work with. It shouldn't take very much time. I do not have much because next week, I need to spend time with the virtual bot. They are almost ready to install the defense grid."

Nick retreated into his organized sense of personal authority concerning his work, sitting quietly, satisfied with his schedule statement. Charley knew it was his friend's way of dealing with the true grandness of the scope of his discovery.

*****

"Well, actually, it has been a tiring day, but I am fine, thank you. I think I have found the computer that likely has the defense plans, so in that respect, it's been a good day." Leslie said, fighting back the cry in her voice.

"Fantastic. Do you have access?"

"No, not yet. I will in a couple of days. I followed Dr. Porter to Nick Nicholas's lab. It must be there. As I was leaving, they came out and may have seen me, Gerhard," she said, struggling to keep an even tone.

"Leslie, you are upset. Why don't you pull over? I can hear that you are in the car. I have an idea that might settle you. Can you pull over?" His serene tone was laced with proposition, something she had learned to respond to uniformly. She pulled into a gas station parking adjacent to the road and turned the car off with new relief.

"Okay, Leslie, I want you to listen very carefully to what I have to say. I know this charade has been somewhat of a pain in the ass, but now new issues have arisen that make your part in this even more important. I will spare you the bullshit and get to the point. I want to offer you an incentive, a bonus. At the end of the month, I am expected to make a visit to *TerraLuna*. I want those plans before I leave. Once you have retrieved the information we need from Dr. Nicholas, whom I suspect if he had the world arranged by his lights would gladly give it up for all to use, I will take you with me as my guest to the moon. Would you like to go to the moon with me, Leslie?" His romantic voice found its mark as he gripped the phone closer to her ear.

"Why, Gerhard, that sounds like a most enticing date. You certainly know how to motivate a girl," she said, her fear now subsided.

"That will be the deal, Leslie. It will be our beginning. You must understand how vital those plans are to our success. Dr. Nicholas might also be convinced to lend a hand in the end. I know you are aware of his extraordinary talent."

"Yes, I think I am."

Her voice trailed off as an unmistakable silver car raced past on the highway. It was Charley Porter and Dr. Nicholas. She scooted down in the seat to avoid being seen.

"Leslie, the sooner the plans are with me, the sooner I can make your *TerraLuna* reservation. We can be swimming in the low-gee pool a month from now," he said, feeling her hang on his carefully chosen words.

"That sounds wonderful, Mr. Steele," she said, patronizing him gently.

Leslie, knowing that this gas station was the only thing between Dr. Nick's house and the San Bernardino limits, seriously entertained the idea of going back to the lab.

Stopping for a moment to establish clarity in her plan, she started the car and pulled out onto the highway toward Nick's house, specifically to the computer in his barn.

*****

Charley considered a proposal from the Skylars lucrative enough to let him borrow one of the lenses without supervision. Some plans needed to be devised that would be adequately impressive. As he composed the design, he thought it might go over better if both of their names were on it. Nick had him beat on the credibility chart. He would tell Nick later after he had ironed out the details. Another two miles along the road, Charley slowed to a mailbox shaped like a large mouthed bass. "This is the place."

Charley wasn't sure if Seth had a legitimate job and never really cared enough to ask. The extent of their friendship was bullshitting and drinking together at Sneaky Petey's. He pulled into the paved driveway lined with oaks and willows.

A light on the side of the house surrounded by a rather extensive plasti-wood deck welcomed them with a bachelor-esque sort of warmth. They got out of the car and walked to the front door. It opened as they took the steps. An outer screen door pushed open, and there was a thin mustachioed man with thin light brown hair of average build not yet thirty years old. His dark brown eyes seemed a bit deeply inset, Nick thought, for such a young man. His tank top and jeans probably were the only thing the guy ever wore, Nick guessed, trying not to be too cynical.

"Hey, Seth, what's new, man? It's been a few months. You're looking well." They shook hands vigorously, exchanging smiles.

"This is my hunting buddy, Nick. Nick, this is Seth."

"Good to meet you, man. Come in, fellas. Beer?"

"Actually, no, Seth. Thank you. We have some girls waiting for us back at the house. I believe the party starts once we get back. You know how it is." Nick gave him a wink and a nod.

"I see. This will be business only tonight. You'll have to call me up, Charley, when you get back and arrange some planned partying. Bring me a tusk?"

He motioned for them to sit on an old cracked leather couch that sat in front of an impressive large stone fireplace in the far end of the sunken living room. The real-wood paneling was a suitable backdrop for the myriad of rustic decorations, including boars' heads, mounted fish, rural paintings, and a variety of old hunting and fishing weapons—strictly bachelor. He walked over to a locked closed door and opened it with a small key.

"You know, Charley, I enjoyed seeing you bullshit with those college girls before you went on your trip. You sure have a way of getting fine birds to take down their guards. Yes, sir. Do you remember that dark-haired girl from Columbia? What a fox. I know you have a thing for those Mexicalis too. I bet you had your share when you were south of the border. I got the postcard, but this is the first I have heard from you. I know you are a busy holographic designer man and all, but you have to remember your friends. Next trip, I'll tag along," he said, retrieving a large plastic case from the closet. Putting the case on the large real wood coffee table, he opened it, displaying four illegal electronic guns for inspection.

"What is a man if he hasn't got friends?"

*****

Leslie made the trip back in less than fifteen minutes, parking in the same place next to the open field. Half-running to the pole barn, taking the ladder with some familiarity, she was now looking down on the dim interior. The protective rain shutters were still open, venting heat from the lab, pouring out into the night air.

The circular platform sat nearly fifteen feet from the ceiling. She adjusted her bag, stowing it on her back, and climbed in to a hanging position. After a pause, she dropped onto the platform with a resounding "pling."

She stood still for a few moments, letting her eyes adjust to the darkness. To her surprise, the computer at Nick's desk was active. She opened her bag, taking her skin puller out, activating it into a makeshift flashlight. In the low light, she began work at the computer, accessing the enormous file system. Scrolling through the various entries was a task she had no time to try. Clicking in search mode, she typed *Defense System*.

The computer worked for a moment and then listed a series of ten entries. Taking the data node from her bag, she placed it in the drive and began copying the files without opening them. She offered herself a moment of criminal thanks that Nick had not enabled a security system, since alarms were not going off. As the computer worked, she looked around the screen-lit lab, fathoming the other information stored in the huge node cabinet, its red lock lights oscillating randomly.

This was it. She was stealing for personal advancement. After a brief emotionless encounter with guilt, laced with integrity, she took the data node from the drive and put it into her purse. She sat back for a moment, wondering if she would be happier being a part of this life with Nick and Charley, concerning herself with integrity and true scientific empiricisms. *Well, not today,* she thought.

Automatically, images of swimming in the moon pool and perhaps being chief science engineer of *TerraLuna* found priority. Her dilated eyes caught her flashlight reveal a sign near the door, interrupting her thoughts. Replacing the chair as it was, she walked to the door where a box was affixed to the wall. SATELLITE SECURITY was printed on the front.

A rush of fear hit her stomach. She turned the knob on the door. It did not budge, dead bolted from the outside. She made a careful sprint to the platform stairs and grabbed the bottom of the hanging ladder, pulling her up onto the roof. A quick look back at the lab and then onto the road beyond; everything was calm. She took the ladder down and made a fast jog back to the safety of her car, listening gratefully to the territorial chorus of crickets resounding in the dark woods.

*****

Charley and Nick listened to Seth for ten minutes as he unfolded his pitch for the guns. It really was not necessary, but it was no use trying to stop him. He was intent on asking questions that they both answered without a shred of resistance with the goal being to expedite the transaction to further the experiment. During the spiel, an odd white cat walked into the room. Its fur was speckled with blue, yellow, pink, and green flecks. It peered into the room, gathering information without drawing attention to herself. It sat in the doorway, sniffing around an empty pet bed. Seth noticed the cat and reached for a remote control from the mantle. He pressed it, and a holographic hound dog appeared on the bed. The cat ran away out of sight.

Charley observed the scene and remarked, "How long have you had the Gen-Al cat?"

"Oh, that's Confetti. I've had her for about two years now. They tell me that the genetically altered cats can live up to twenty-five years. I always hated when the cat died when I was a kid. Roy Boy there is all light. He is a good watchdog if I remember to turn him on. I had him linked into the security system. Blink! There's a dog."

Seth turned to the guns. "I can get you all four for two thousand. I'll even throw in the case." Nick and Charley exchanged a quick look, and Nick gladly handed over two one thousand WD cards.

"You will be satisfied. Any maintenance issues I can cover right here at the ranch—"

During his guarantee, an alert beeped incessantly from Nick's watch. Charley placed a gun he was checking out back into the case. He turned to look at his friend's watch. It blinked red lights, and display once again read, "INTRUDER ALERT."

"He's back," Nick said in a sotto voice to Charley. "Seth, we have to go, man. Thanks a lot. We will call you if we have any questions. Let's go, Charley."

Dr. Porter closed the case and followed Dr. Nicholas out the door, enjoying a quick tousling of the hair on Roy Boy's holographic head. He had planned to put the guns in the trunk, but in light of new developments, he slid them in the back seat.

"This time he won't get away. I am calling the police," said Nick, intensifying the brightness on his wrist phone, and then opened the band to place a call. Charley put a hard foot on the pedal and soon was nearing top speed back to the lab.

CHAPTER 34

La Fuentes was a medium-sized hotel with sixty rooms and nearing seventy-five years old. It had been well over a month since the Mexican Gulf had experienced worldwide exposure with the arrival of meteorites. Progreso, Mexico, with its average tourist business, was hoping the celestial event might bring visitors to perhaps view another show in the sky.

Since most of their business was in the winter hence minimal attendance, the second smaller swimming pool was left drained and gated for the season. If the summer guests wanted to take their kinds to the beach, it was only a ten-minute walk.

With the current concern that sea insects may infest the beaches, the manager of the hotel decided to have his custodian begin filling the second pool since the beach customers would come to the hotel for a swim. It needed to be cleaned of leaves, debris, and the myriad of unusual dead insects that sought refuge from the heat. The precious fresh water collected there in small amounts provided them a last desperate drink. Escape from the pool was rare. Possibly, they sensed water would rise from the bottom. They waited for it and then died.

His name tag that was coming unstitched said Manny, though he was referred to as Manual at home. He carried a shovel and bucket of plastic bags to the pool, thinking about the weekend. The workday was beginning as any other. As usual, the pool was covered with grasshoppers, mayflies, dragonflies, and a variety of other creatures with which he was not familiar. Without ceremony, he took the stairs holding the shovel and bucket in one large hand. His breakfast still hung in his belly. He resolved to drink more water in the morning to help him digest, but he was always in a hurry.

After the third step, he felt multiple constrictions around both of his legs. In a flash, the constrictions turned to mobile pain, rising along his back. He dropped the shovel and bucket, gripping the handrails, and began moving up the ladder, craning his neck to see what impossibility could be causing this attack. From the corner of his eye, he saw mandibles attached to a huge insect. Finding some speed, he moved one rung up the ladder, shaking with miserable failure against the impossible beast. Manny's efforts brought him up another rung. When he turned again to see that his attacker had crawled up the entirety of his body, he winced as four goring teeth plunged into the back of his neck, tearing and sucking the janitor's throat from both sides of his head. His failing attempt upward to another rung resulted in a scream for help, but his vocal cords were suddenly not intact. Overcome with fright, he fathomed a weak swoon, accompanied by a warm wet strength covering his body, now devoid of control. The smell of dead fish infused his senses. In a final attempt to survive, he reached back to hit the bug, but as he released his hand from the rung, the creature pulled with a force, tearing his other hand from the rung, sending both of them plummeting backward into the empty pool.

They landed, Manny first. The creature seemed mildly affected by the drop and, after a beat, continued consuming his bodily fluid while excreting milky-white juice from its sides. The rest of the hotel slept, basking in the very hot morning.

*****

After that day on the water and a hurried escape from the media waiting at the dock, Pepe and Tico were back at the hotel. After a brief meal and a shower, they both slept a deep, grateful sleep in the overly cool hotel room, bundled up in blankets and thankfulness. Pepe had wanted to order a computer keyboard as soon as he returned but was too exhausted from their ordeal. He vowed to do it as soon as he awoke, after he called his wife. His dreams were at first nonexistent yet one had found its way into the center of his rest. It was a dream of a time when he was just a boy of about seven. His best friend had lost his grandmother. They shared a new emotion in their friendship, one of grief. They were standing in the street, talking about her, his friend trying not to cry. Pepe had not yet been to a funeral and had not seen a dead person except in the movies. At the age of seven, death was an insult to their freedom.

The dream continued as an alternative ending to what happened that day. He walked to the church where his friend's family was gathered inside, paying their last respects. He stood outside the church, afraid to go in and more afraid of what to say when they came out. Suddenly, the double doors of the crowd opened, and the grandmother stood in the center of the crowd of her family. They happily escorted her down the stairs. It was a miracle!

Pepe awoke slowly, wondering what would have happened if he had gone to the church to be with his friend but was faced with a curious sight to think about instead. A flashing police light was seen through the center of the partially drawn drapes. It was just dawn. More trouble he did not want any part of this new day. He wanted to go home to his wife.

He slid out of bed, surprising himself with his own agility, and opened the curtain to reveal four policia cars and ambulance parked in the street. His first instinct brought his around the bed to his phone. He found the marine store's phone number and called immediately, giving the part number for the computer keyboard for his boat to the customer service attendant, along with the address for the hotel. He hovered his card when prompted and asked for rush delivery. She said it would be there in three days. He thanked the girl and hung up with purpose, giving a reassuring nod to Tico, who had just rolled out his slumber with a far-reaching stretch and yawn.

Before going outside to see what the matter was, he called Paloma to tell her what happened the previous day, at least most of it for now.

Chief Arajo stood at the side of the pool, teasing the edge with his belly. Other police and staff were in the pool, surrounding the body of the maintenance man's carcass mostly covered in the stiffening white muck that partially cemented him to the bottom of the pool. A variety of insects had stuck to the goo. An effective trap for bugs, he thought, and a very embarrassing way to die. While taking a sip of his iced coffee while snapshots were being taken, a variety of hotel guests, staff, and bystanders looked on. An uncomfortably warm breeze blew through the trees near the pool. Several four-foot insets clung to the swaying trees, blending well in the foliage. Arajo's wrist phone rang. Stooping to place his coffee on the cement poolside tried the strength of his waistband.

"Sergeant Arajo," he said with authority.

"Sergeant, we have a report of another attack," an officer said evenly. "The carniceria on Eighth Street called at nine forty-five this morning. He went to dispose of his morning trash in the compactor, and a large insect sprang out. He threw the trash and ran back inside. He is okay. We have a car there now."

The sergeant paused to think and then responded. "I will stop by later this morning. Keep a man there until I arrive."

The sergeant closed the phone and reclaimed his coffee. After taking a good drink, an officer approached with an electronic pad. "Chief, the man died of excessive blood loss. His jugular vein was pierced in four places." He offered a picture on the screen for the boss's approval.

His response was put on hold when a familiar voice called his name from beyond the yellow police tape. Looking over, he saw Professors Sanchez and Alba behind the line, wanting to talk to him. Aroja waved to the attending officer, and they ducked under the tape, marching to the scene poolside.

"It looks like your little bugs are not so little anymore," Aroja said, pointing into the pool. "What information can you give me about these things? I need to know."

"Sergeant, we are just now beginning our tests. It will be some time before we have a full report. We do know that they feed on blood from hosts either dead or alive. They exude a white liquid. It seems to be some kind of immobilizing web with a tendency to harden in sunlight," Alba added with earnest.

"I can see what it did to that man in the pool. Is there anything else I should know? The sergeant looked intently at the pair. Sanchez met his accusative gaze with a firm reaction.

"You know all that we know, Sergeant. We had planned to take the specimens back to Merida to do our tests. I think now that would be a mistake. We should do the testing here. Can you provide us with a facility?"

"I can get you a room at the city morgue. Get your things together. I will have a car in the front of the hotel to take you there in half an hour. Anything you need, the coroner will get for you," the corpulent cop added with an atypical tone of concern.

"I will be in touch. We hope dissection will give us more clues to any weaknesses they might have that we can exploit. We have to prepare. I will call you later. Thank you." Sanchez shook his hand. The academics marched off to their rooms, pleased with the new arrangements.

The alien's insects in the trees considered the convening cluster of people. Keeping still and away from sight appeared to them as the best course of inaction.

*****

Nick and Charley sped back to the barn in twenty minutes. Taking the long driveway slowly, nothing out of the ordinary struck either of them for the length of the trail. Charley parked in front of the lab and was out of the car and into the box of guns when Nick stopped him, seeing a police car enter the drive.

"Hold it. The cops are here. Put them in the trunk."

With the guns hidden under an old blanket in the trunk, the two doctors waited for the police to roll into the lighted yard.

Two young officers approached. Nick explained the situation and, after a twenty-minute search of the grounds, admitted that no one was on the premises. During their infrared scan search, Nick was more concerned about the illegal guns than someone snooping around his land. Maybe it was a kid or a hunter. The cops, eager to be elsewhere, handed a small disc with a record of their scans and apologized for not finding anything. They prompted Nick to be careful and to call them if there was detection. They returned to their car and bounded along the road out of the highway.

"Nothing else we can do about this. Get the guns and let's start some tests," said Nick, apparently not ready to rest from the day's trials. Charley agreed silently and brought the gun cases into the pole barn, setting it on one of the table on the right.

"If we do a fifteen-minute survey of each of the eras, we will have a general idea of what we are going to be up against and the best time slot to try your pressure experiment. I will familiarize you with the systems. Then after a few, if you would like to try, I think it will add to your understanding of holography."

Charley knew it was pointless to disagree with the doctor at this juncture. He joined him at the control computer and reviewed the locator arm function and the power inline. Charley felt as though he knew how to operate the machine after a brief lesson. Nick called the satellite station and asked Burt to grant his access through the night. Soon, the relay dish was accepting microwaved solar energy, charging the system with a familiar power hum.

Nick reset the locator to the second position that according to the reading jumped back to five million years BC. Charley committed the controls to memory and took some time to become familiar with the various screens and moderating systems, while Nick dressed in the wet suit and geared up his cameras. He added a few smoke bombs, a flashlight, and a considerably larger hunting knife to his bag. After a review of the gun operation, he tucked one of each, sort it on his belt, giving his assistant a "thumbs-up."

Charley initiated the heliolocator. Blue light crept through the box. Nick waited at the view door for the image to coalesce. As the blue light became trees and rocks, Nick viewed the soundless location with controlled wonder.

"It is a forested area with a rocky soil. Maybe there is a mountain nearby. I'll check it out."

He took the short stairs and then opened the lid now swathed in the light. One step and then another as if standing in a bathtub of light.

"I'll be back with some tape in fifteen minutes. This time please do not shut me down. I think you should watch me from the peek door," Nick said from a sitting position, eager to enter the past. Charley closed the lid and then followed the stairs down. Once he opened the peek door, Nick was standing in another time.

Pine needles covered the rocky forest floor. Beyond the landscape of less than fifty feet, the land sloped rather steeply into an open vale covered in scrub and grass. Turning around, a hill was revealed that sat in front of a majestic purple mountain green with trees against a partly cloudy sky. The scent of pine invaded his lungs, making them work harder to take in more of the uncommonly fresh air. Nick sniffed, detecting water, perhaps from a stream or river that must have been nearby. After a few minutes of appreciation, he went to work, filming the scene, narrating as he panned his head in a 360-degree pattern. Other than some less than noisy birds, there wasn't any sign of animal life, something he had hoped to see. Fifteen minutes passed quickly in the idyllic spot, Nick, satisfied with his pictures, assumed the supine position and rolled back into the blue zone. Nick lay on the ground, and then within seconds, Nick was back, feeling refreshed, stepping out of the PFC.

"See how easy it is! I have it all here on tape! It was a small forest at the foot of a mountain, nothing short of breathtaking."

Nick reset the machine to the next entry, ready to continue cataloging.

"The next trip I will make is to a time that was created from a fossil that originated fifteen million years ago."

Charley looked on approvingly, starting to get anxious to try it himself like a young boy looking on before his first roller coaster ride.

Nick reentered the box, finding himself in a wet bog. Mist filled the spaced between the wide branches of a variety of willow trees and other wetland flora. While still on the ground, feeling the spray of a light rain on his face, he noticed a cricket in the hollow of a tree, exposing the majority of its roots.

Standing quickly to expedite filming, he faced the sullen reminder that he had unexaggerated fear of water and the creatures that lived beneath its surface. He stood on the bank of a dank-smelling marsh. Something was rotting nearby. He made a spread of the area, describing many felled and falling trees amid several small islands. Frogs squeaked and leaped away from the cinematographer from the future. Suddenly, a swell twenty yards ahead sent ripples in his direction. Taking a couple of automatic steps back toward the box while filming, the firmer ground reminded him that escape was near.

The mist covered the sun, not giving him an easy guess at the time of day; it probably was late afternoon. This film wouldn't yield pretty pictures like the other times, yet he had some good shots of frogs. While giving one last slow pan, something hit his shin. He looked down, bending the camera's eyepiece away, to see the largest frog he had ever seen; it was the size of a German shepherd. Its tongue held his leg. Its open mouth filled with an eerie row of small sharp teeth pulled and jerked, actually bringing Nick a step closer to the water's edge. The frog gave a guttural croak that was loud enough to scare him. He drew the stun gun from his belt and fired off one shot to its black-green topside. The frog tipped on its side, twitching spasmodically, its tongue still affixed to his leg. Nick put the gun in his belt and then took the plastic bag from his belt, searching for the knife. His hand searched while scanning ore of the peculiar ripples in the water. During the time it took to find the knife and unsheathe it, five or six huge, hungry frogs had flopped to the shore, apparently having eaten their fill of smaller frogs, and ready to take on something bigger, him. Without thinking, he cut away the stuck tongue. It fell away with ease. Nick stepped back, followed by the hungry amphibians already flipping the sticky tongues at him. Barely evading being snatched like a buzzing insect, he dropped to the muddy bank and rolled haphazardly into the light.

Once confirming that he was completely in the box, he pushed the lid open and stood, half expecting to be pulled back by several hungry frogs.

Charley stood next to PFC box. He came to his friend's side, helping him down the stairs.

"That was incredible. Those things were as big as truck tires. Are you okay?" Charley stopped, looking at Nick's wet suit that should have been covered with mud. It was clean.

"There is no residue. It must stay inside the hologram. This is the most amazing thing I have ever seen. Nick, you've got to let me try this. You look like you need a break anyway."

Nick assessed his state of mind, finding not being chased or eaten for a bit might do him some good. Charley had better instincts when it came totaling with physical situations. He tried to not think of how he would feel if he lost his friend to a freak of light, dirt, and computer gymnastics. Though somehow it would be an end, Charley wouldn't mind as much as the authorities would.

Knowing that Charley would persist anyway, he conceded. Nick insisted that the wet suit would not fit him, but Charley said it was rubber and it would stretch to fit his mildly ample belly. Soon, Charley was dressed more than snugly in Nick's wet suit and equipped with the cameras, guns, and plastic bag.

Nick moved the indicator up another globe, bringing light to the next phase in geological time to the Miocene era somewhere around twenty-three million years in the past. This particular sample was the first sample retrieved from the continental United States, somewhere in Montana.

"Okay, Charley, you know how to use the camera, and I hope you can use the gun. Get in the box and roll past the light. You will be able to push through the light with some force. Get fifteen minutes of footage. Don't bother with the audio. I will fill it in later. If it gets dangerous, leave. I don't want your death on my conscience. Understand?"

Nick finished his preaching, taking the stairs to enable the holo-imager, chuckling inwardly at Charley in the ill-fitting wet suit.

Charley took the steps like a kid finally getting his turn for the largest roller coaster, ever. He lifted the lid and began to step in. Nick called to him from the console.

"Wait. Let's take a look and see what you are stepping into."

Nick came around opening the peek door. A rushing stream cascaded down from a rocky incline. It was nearly dark. Nick had a moment of trepidation sending Charley into the oncoming night. Rather than stop the experiment, he sent him in anyway after a check for any hostile beasts.

"Okay, it looks like a stream near a rock formation of some kind. Take fifteen minutes of film then roll back through the perimeter," Nick said, keeping watch at the door.

Charley stepped in and was on his back, waiting for Nick to close the lid. Charley looked up with a stretch of his neck to see the silent water rushing along a loose copse of woods. With a bit more strength than needed, he rolled into the blue barrier. He was on his stomach for a few seconds, orienting himself to the damp ground under his nose.

"This is unbelievable," he said, spinning around to a sitting position. "The air is alive with light mist, and the sun had already reached below the ten-story rock formation about fifty yards ahead behind the water that seemed more like a river than a stream." He stood with a smile, wiping dirt from his face, documenting his findings.

He activated the camera and pulled the snake eyepiece in position. His pictures were not even as Nick's. (They would find out later.) He had made a full circle, including the ravine that ran away opposite the stream into a valley fed by rushing water. He thought there must be a waterfall along the course of the river downstream. He took a few steps to the shore, minor insects bouncing away from his footfalls.

Once he reached the shore, movement on the rocks across the river stopped his amateur panning. A very large animal appeared to be sort of a bear. Its light brown fur drenched with water made it blend in with the rocks. Its head and snout was elongated and was larger than any bear he had ever seen. He tapped the telephoto to see more. It was enjoying a great bizarre-looking fish, pawing it apart with claws that had to be at least ten inches long.

It had not seen him. He thought it would be a good idea to step back from the shore for safety. As he was moving back, a sudden snarl came from above. He looked up to see several mean-looking spotted cats that threatened the bear. They bared their teeth and, roaring, bounded down along the rocks with incredible agility for their size. Charley hoped they were growling at the bear and not him. All at once, the docile-looking bear saw its nemesis careening down the rocks at him. There were at least six of them closing fast. The bear took three graceless steps away from the rocks and though the water in Charley's direction. It would not be long before he was nose to nose with the frightened bear.

He turned and ran, heaving his less than fit body to the safety of the blue light. After a few moments, he was sitting on the ground next to the perimeter. He looked over to see that the bear had crossed the river and was lumbering its wet mass directly at Charley. The cats were on the other bank in pursuit. Charley thought if these cats were afraid of water like the ones he knew, they might not follow, but he did not plan to stay long enough to find out. Hefting himself in retreat, he felt the heat of the animal coming sickeningly near.

Diving prematurely to roll into the light, he couldn't get through. He was still on the ground with the mad bear less than ten yards away. He rolled himself harder against the light, and he found his way through with the proper amount of exerted force. Nick opened the box, helping his friend out. Charley was gasping, still with a smile on his face from the encounter.

After a few deep breaths, he was able to say only a few words.

"THAT WAS AWESOME!"

CHAPTER 35

$\mathbf{D}$r. Alba was proud of her vast experience in biological dissection, yet it had been a few months since she had cut into a dead body and several years since she had done an insect. They had comparably simple yet curious anatomies than those of reptiles and mammals. This specimen, she hoped, would be a mutated deep-sea species and not an extraterrestrial. If it were, she would undoubtedly come up against some political mayhem, which she would rather avoid, thinking the opportunity to catalogue a species with off earth origins would certainly put her in the history books. She did not like publicity.

With the advancements of space rock mining and deep space travel as of the year 2168, no life signs of any sort had been found in space. Scientists were still disappointed that no trace of life had been found on Mars after several missions to the desiccated riverbeds and polar caps. Life was yet to come.

She and Sanchez were escorted past the security desk through the hallways of Progreso's city morgue. It was really an unimpressive place, but then who did a morgue need to impress? It served a twenty-five-mile radius, mostly dealing with elderly customers. As the average life expectancy of humans peaked one hundred years with the help of chromosomal preservation drugs, it is quieter than usual. More people seemed to die of accidents and occasional homicide than old age.

The coroner seemed too young to hold such an important position, but he seemed to be comfortable with his surroundings, at least by his casual shorts, sport shirt, and gym shoes. He brought the doctors to a medical examination room equipped with a full supply of dissection tools. Alba had seen more sophisticated analysis instruments; nevertheless, she was capable with the old-fashioned laser scalpels and clip clamps.

The canvass bag was ready on the examination table. Its smell filled the room. The coroner walked to the exhaust fan and turned it on with a scowl of disgust. "If it is all the same to you, I'd like to stay and watch. It's not every day we dissect giant sea spiders."

"It isn't a spider," said Sanchez, putting on the rubber gloves from a table of instruments.

"You are a coroner, and we want to treat this dissection as identification. It will be in professional confidence.

He helped himself to a pair of gloves as Sophia abruptly unzipped the bag. The translucent exoskeleton was covered in the dried goo. Alba took a paddle-like instrument from the table and moved the skins aside. To their amazement, the creature was gone. All that remained were the tangled skins and more bad smell. Upon inspection, the bag had been torn open from the bottom, perhaps with the help of the acidic nature of the spetum.

"It's not here," said Sanchez.

He looked around the room.

"The officers brought the bag from your truck last night, and this room has been locked since then," the young man explained.

"It had all night to escape. They could be anywhere. Could you please phone the sergeant, tell him the specimen is alive and have escaped? Dr. Alba and I will be here for an hour or so, making some observations," Sanchez directed the young man to action.

He responded like a good student, leaving them to their work. At first sight, the skins seemed larger than the ones originally found in Benito's goody bag. They carefully transferred the skins to the examination table. The skins were splayed out on the stainless steel table, one on its back and the other on its underside. Six small openings under the legs were tipped with dark curved claws, looking very much like a crab, something Alba would have not tasted for anytime soon. Alba recorded data into her electronic book, while Sanchez took the measurements.

"Rene, bring up the DNA report from the lab. I want to compare data with that of the tardigrade."

Sanchez had the information in a couple of minutes and then reading aloud.

"These creatures, sometimes called water bears, retract their legs, forming a thick double cuticle around itself for protection. The life process in this state is barely detectable. They can last for decades in this position. In this position, they have been called Tuns. The Tuns can survive in liquid helium and exposure to ionizing radiation. Toxic chemicals and temperatures up to 272 degree Celsius have no ill effect upon the Tuns. The clinical term for this ability to survive environmental extremes is anabiosis . . .

"It seems that our guests at least exhibit some features of the tardigrade, and perhaps they entered the Tun state after being attacked as a defense mechanism," Sanchez added, looking to his partner for an opinion.

"Rene, it said something about Tuns theoretically being able to survive space flight. You remember how you started this expedition looking for the meteors that landed off the peninsula. What if these things came from the asteroid belt or anywhere else in the universe for that matter? We have found either a new species or an alien exhibiting survival aspects of the Tardigrade.

"Subatomic analyses can be done or, more specifically, elemental componenting, but that may take time. For now, these things are eating Progreso for lunch."

Sanchez recalled the events of the past week in the quiet of his mind while taking another long look at the crab-like spider skin, hoping a plan would coalesce. Then looking at Alba, he said plainly, "Sophia, I think we will not find what we are looking for at the subatomic level. We should be examining the rocks we found at the impact site. Remember, there were two distinct versions. What is their relationship?

*****

Charley stood reorienting himself to normal surroundings, searching for works to describe his experience. Nick smiled knowingly for a time and then reset the machine, allowing Charley to compose himself.

"I've been thinking of a name for this. We can't call it virtual reality of holography. It's way beyond that. I've been toying with the idea of temporal reality. Let me know if you have any ideas. Are you ready to go back?" Nick indicated to the box.

"Yeah, man, I am so ready to go back. How far this time?"

"Twenty-seven million years to the Miocene Epoch."

"So it is still too late for the dinosaurs? I am not going to run into any giant lizards?" Charley asked, seriously looking like a strangely dressed kid waiting for another ride on a new roller coaster.

"No, for the most part, all life at this period is relatively dinosaur free. Theoretically, thanks to our friends Louie and Walter Alvarez's research, a mile or larger-sized asteroid sixty-five million years ago destroyed them. We are not there yet. Okay, let's take a look at what is going on then," Nick said, enabling the system. Blue lights refilled the PFC, and once the humming reached its pinnacle, Charley opened the peak door.

Rock and scrub on a small scale peppered the flat rocky terrain. Charley's first impression was that it looked like Nevada, remembering the view from the plane from his trip to Las Vegas three years ago.

Without as much ceremony as the last trip, Charley found himself standing in a hot rock desert. Before filming, he checked the ground for scorpions and the air for vultures, animals he imagined would be in this terrain. He saw nothing like that here.

Filming was uneventfully ordinary. He hoped another time would offer something more exciting. Naturally, Charley toyed with the idea of capitalizing on temporal reality, offering temporal tours for a juicy 1,000 WD card. He knew better than to bastardize Nick's vision but would certainly help develop a business model if he ever came to his senses.

After an uneventful fifteen minutes, he assumed the position and rolled back into the box.

"Not much there to look at. It was very hot. There were plenty of rocks, hardy little plants, but no monsters."

"This next epoch is known as the Oligocene still in the Tertiary period. I know from the limited data here that it is forty-seven million years in the past. The sample was gathered from Oregon. We have many Oregon samples. In fact, the next five epochs are from the same location at John Day Fossil Beds National Monument. This place is incredible. The crickets seemed to do well there for a long time. I have a theory that the consistency of their concentrations at this locale has significantly influenced the success of this system." Nick gave an empty look at Charley and then with slight begrudgement, popped his bubble. "I would like to see this one myself."

Charley couldn't argue. It was Nick's project. He took off the suit and gear.

Nick visited John Day National Park in Oregon three years ago not only because it was famous for its abundance of fossils but also that it represented five subsequent epochs of samples. He collected them himself with some acquaintances he had met from the local university. Now was his chance to see if it was as beautiful a terrain almost fifty million years in the past.

Charley reviewed the troubleshooting screen monitoring power fluctuations and any red lights that might pop up. The system seemed rather stable, which was a credit to Nick's thoroughness, something Charley envied about his lifelong friend.

Nick entered the box, taking some time to observe the blue redwoods for danger. Noting nothing ready to eat or stab him, he rolled into the lush-living early Oregon. He stood for a long time before activating his camera in awe of the grove of fantastic trees. Immense redwoods independently owned the forest like great fathers rooted in the spacious forest floor. They stood with a victorious majesty, proudly claiming their right to bask in the sun and drink from the earth. These were the kings of the world.

He stood in the shadow of the noble tree, craning his neck to see as high as he could before stepping back to widen his view. A crackling of twigs from one step followed by another turned his attention from the tree to the forest floor. He wasn't stepping on twigs at all; it was a swarm of insects. His foot sank with a live crunch into a nest of very large black crickets as big as his thumb. He hopscotched around uneasily at first, sinking where he thought to find solid ground, finding the ground completely subjected by the bugs.

After a few less than graceful leaps, he found solid ground, the crickets dispersing in confusion. He hadn't seen a nest of them before like this. Without delay, he began filming the strange colony living beneath the leafy carpet. There were millions of them crawling over one another but not like a stampede or confusion but rather naturally as if the hive belonged closely connected. Nick took some shots of the trees, still keeping a wary eye on the living carpet of leaves. The sun was nearly masked entirely by the wide canopy of limbs and leaves that offered a kind of haven to the crickets below. Satisfied with his footage and not wanting to sabotage their ecosystem any more than he had already, Nick sat at the blue boundary of the PFC for a minute or so. He thought of Ada and tried to imagine what she would say about this moment. After a feckless moment, he rolled back with a full body surge, placing himself once again into the confines of the PFC.

He looked to the left, startled to see Charley's smiling face in the peek door. It closed abruptly. The lid of the coffin opened. Nick stood, removed himself from the box, and came down the stairs.

"I think I killed some crickets. I stepped on them" was the only thing Charley could say.

"It's only a few bugs. History will never miss them. Don't freak out on the timeline thing. A handful of smashed crickets are not going to alter our reality. A prehistoric moose must have killed thousands walking around in a day," Charley said, steadying a shaking Nick.

"We can't just go into the past and start destroying things. Most theorist discuss macroscopic time travel. What happened in there was on the microscopic level, man. It freaks me out! Think of the theories cramming thousands of textbooks. You are right to be careful of what you do back then, but you are missing the best part. This is your chance to study the truth of what actually happens. We can start flushing dozens of theories right now based on what we've seen. We are dealing with sub, sub atomic matter. I bet that we will not affect the future events by our actions in the past. What has past has past. If we go back and shoot a moose, that would have caused a tree to fall later that day while scratching its ass against it. What if that tree would have hit Og the caveman on the head, causing him to go crazy with pain and beat his family to death? So he doesn't kill his family and one of his boys grows up to live and die like millions of other people over time, so what?"

"Nature will make the adjustments. It has the power to do that. Og will have a happy life and maybe some more grandkids than if we didn't shoot the moose. Do you understand? This is prehistory. We are not plotting to kill Hitler here. In the great scheme of life, it's just one being over millions of years. I hate to sound so anti-individual right now, but think about it. Nature will compensate, so calm down." Charley finished catching Nick's gaze, knowing he was making sense.

Nick nodded silently, knowing that from this point on, the phrase "theoretically speaking" was not going to get much play. They could test actual causal stimuli. This wasn't what he wanted to think about at this time. He wanted to get as many of the samples tested as he could tonight. He engaged the next time globe, finding strength in silence. He went to the box. Before climbing the stairs, he turned to his friend and said frankly, "I think to an extent we are intruding in the past. My goal at this point is to observe and document without having any impact upon the environment. It is more like a polite visit than a safari hunt. I'm going in carefully fifty-two million in the past. This may be a good spot to try your lens compression system theory. Care to watch?"

Charley opened the box, indicating with his hand in a mock gentle manner. Nick shook his head and climbed in to the Oregon forest five million years later. It was amazing to him how similar the area was five million years later. This was stable environment, apparently unaffected by floods, volcanoes, or forest fires. If such natural events did occur, time seemed to restore order. Nick recorded the area, keeping close to the box. He was standing a section of the redwood forest, but there were several varieties of fir trees in the distance. He was about to finish his filming when he noticed a cricket on a protruding root sitting in the sunlight, apparently basking in its warmth. Nick telephotoed the camera and took a tight shot of the happy creature soaking up the sun-thesis cover.

The relationship between the cricket and the sun had lasted for millions of years. This constant exposure perhaps had programmed the sun's recorded cycles in its DNA. Its simplicity was almost embarrassing, that sunbathing crickets would carry the sun code recorded across millions of generations in was very constitution. Light holds the secret to life and now to time. He filmed the dreaming cricket for a minute, thanking it for showing him the way through time.

The remainder of the Oregon samples offered wonderful footage, yet nothing was around to attack Nick. This period was markedly abundant with insects of all sorts. At one visit, Nick noted the trunk of a large fir completely covered with honeybees the size of strawberries relocating their nest.

Dragonflies hung from the low-hanging boughs of another fir, adorning them like Christmas ornaments. It was an amazing sight that he recorded with appreciation. However, the most memorable sight from the John Day Park samples was the cicada-like swarms of the infested area of fifty-two million years back.

Everything was covered with the seemingly robotically moving insects. Their skins were everywhere. The air was thick with the flying buzzers whose song resounded in the forest at a near-deafening volume. He spent the least time at this period because they seemed to be not beyond swarming on him in search of food. Nick climbed back into the PFC and then rolled back to 2168.

At the end of the Oregon epochs, it was well past one o'clock Friday morning. They were tired despite the excitement. Nick stopped the tests, agreeing with a sluggish Charley Porter that they should wrap it up for the night. They shut down the system for the night.

"Charley, we should go over the shutdown sequence again, just in case. You might as well sleep here tonight, though I didn't change the sheets on the bed, but you won't mind," said Nick though a yawn.

"No, I won't mind," Charley said under his breath, taking the computers offline at Nick's instruction. As the screens came down, Charley remembered the intruder situation, hoping that someone wasn't aware of this technology.

Moving back from the chair, he recalled the tire tracks and the spicy perfume in the night air. He wasn't sure why he thought of it now. It might be the computer. The new ones do tend to give off a bit of an odor after they have warmed up.

*****

At La Fuentes, Pepe and Tico spent their time early that Friday morning watching television and relaxing in the hotel. Soon, the novelty of luxury made the two fishermen anxious to at least go back to the boat and clean it while they waited for the computer board to be shipped. The police activity at the hotel stepped up their pace. They went to the lobby, where several patrons were asking questions about their safety. A policeman was explaining that a maintenance worker had fallen into the empty pool. An electric bulletin board announced that the pool was closed and that patrons were asked to pardon the inconvenience while exterminators were at work. Pepe stopped listening to the recording of the young lady on the screen and read the text below to verify what she said.

"I don't think they want to alarm the people. Tico, something tells me that man did not die by falling in the pool," he told his dog, noting the dead fish smell from the passing covered gurney. People were asked to step behind barriers as the paramedics brisked the body into the truck.

"Someday they will take Pepe away in one of those wagons, but it sure as hell will not be because of one of those bugs got me. Not on your life. As soon as we get the boat running, we are going back home to Mommy."

They grabbed a donut from the lobby and took a walk to the marina to see his friend Jose and get some better coffee. Pepe watched the people on the street. At first, he did not notice the elevated agitation of the people amid his thoughts of getting the boat back home. It seemed that the people were more than usually cautious walking and driving along Progresso's streets that had become even more of a haven for *La Touristas* since he had been here on business last two years ago.

Tico trotted along, respectfully acknowledging trash cans, mailboxes, and other people with whom another dog might have a rude sniff fit. They soon found the familiar white plastic timbers of the dock, following the path to the marina. Workers were cleaning ships. The smell of insect spit and ammonia battled in the air for the right to make him sick. Tico gave a sudden sneeze as they entered the machine-cooled marina.

Several American tourists and a few fishermen were shopping or having breakfast when they walked in, and none of them were happy.

"I haven't smelled anything this bad since I spent what I thought was the worst vacation in Key West. The shore was covered with these fecal grease balls or at least that's what they called them. They looked like some freaking fruitcake pirates had a shit war on the beach. I won't go back there," said the American, wearing a Hawaiian shirt and a baseball cap.

"I know. This infestation is bad. They figure these things are some deep-sea crabs that were swept into the gulf after hurricane Frederica. The lack of pollution has allowed some species to go crazy. In my grandfather's day, we had animals under control. Now that we stopped poisoning the water and air, they're taking over," the other American said, taking a savored sip of his oversized Bloody Mary.

Pepe listened while Jose waited on a customer. Tico stamped around politely, knowing he was in the place that usually rendered some good beef jerky.

"Senor Pepe, we haven't ever had you stay this long in Progreso. Who would think that some big crabs would keep you here so long?" he said, pouring a cup of coffee.

"I thought I would be away for a couple of days, but now my keyboard is fried. I ordered a new one. So I will be around until it comes. Did you hear about the guy that died at the hotel? They say he fell into the pool. But I think one of those bastard bugs got him." He looked his friend in the eye with new seriousness.

"Don't think those things are getting in here." He reached under the counter and sneaked his shotgun for Pepe to see. Pepe nodded, lifting his shirt to reveal his stun pistol tucked in his belt.

"We have to be ready. These bitches are fast, Jose. Keep your garbage sealed. They like that too. They are blood-sucking scavengers. I will be right back. We need to get some things from the boat." They turned their heels for the door.

There was a commotion on the dock. Men were running and looking into the water. No sound could be heard, yet the scene indicated that someone had fallen into the water. Pepe livened his step to see what was going on.

Several ship hands were yelling as splashing and horrible screaming came from dockside thirty paces from the shore.

"Get a rope and throw it to him! Somebody get a rope!" an onlooker said frantically.

Pepe sprinted to see what was becoming a familiar sight. An insect had ensnarled one of the workers in his fangs and legs. It rolled and pierced his chest, making the blue water dark with blood. The man's screaming was heard sporadically when he was able to fight his way to the surface for air. The monster pulled him beneath the water with ferocious might. The small man was not able to break free. He waved pleadingly to the people on the deck with one hand while trying to alternately stay afloat and wrest the mandible from his chest with the other. His face was stricken with fear and desperation, a sight ordinarily unseen on peaceful fishermen.

Pepe drew his gun, hoping to stun it. Once his big fingers released the safety, it was too late. It had overpowered the man, pulled him below the surface, and was scuttling away along the bottom, leaving the water to calm with only his straw sun hat floating in the bright sun-rippled wake.

CHAPTER 36

Gerhard Steele sat in his cool basement office for a worldwide videoconference with his board of directors and investors. Steele preferred the chill quiet of the dim lair. It allowed him to focus closely on the faces of each of the participants. He could better understand the effect of multiple screens, directing questions to those expressions indicated they might not completely concur. Steele did not like dissention. Yet his mind occupied other thoughts. Steele, with his best capacity for organizations and innovation, whirled uncomfortably with the new information given to him by Leslie Davis. He had the schematics for the defense of *MoonCorp*, yet the further invention of Dr. Nicholas intrigued him much more deeply.

For centuries, science has spun wild philosophical on the subject of time travel, and now here it was. Of all the deals, associations, and contracts he had made, this was by far the most lucrative. Obtaining time would be the greatest acquisition not only of his lifetime but also of all time. He had difficulty putting it out of his mind as the idea and its haunting possibilities occupied the front of his brain.

Steele reminded himself he needed to focus upon this conference. The defense system would have to wait to be announced in a later meeting pending the adaptation engineering. They would be satisfied with Skylar's improvements. Modification for the use with the expensive nuclear reactors was a vital hurdle. It would save millions; moreover, he felt if the new local defense could take the flag, the game would be his.

He had recruited some of the finest engineers money could buy. In many cases, he created them. Fees paid to universities and companies for talent would now pay off. It was a foregone conclusion that in light of the accident on the moon, the board would surely not approve Stan Duncan's fee. A grim stiffness tightened his neck at the possibility that more investors would pull out if he asked for more money. All faith would be lost. No. He chose not to bear the thought of losing support this late in the project. He would tell them all they needed to know, which meant what they wanted to hear.

The large center screen offered a collage of the group at a virtual table simulating a traditional meeting. Steele observed the members in their seat each, having substantial capital as they logged in to the conference. There were fourteen in all, each having substantial capitol committed to *TerraLuna*. 9:00 p.m. approached. He had several topics to cover regarding the state of the repairs, insurance, and defense issues. He would close the meeting with a garish graphic of menu options, giving them a vote on the meals served during the grand opening. With two more members yet to log in, he readied a recording of his image listening intently. This was to be used to allow him to use the camera to get close up shots of the other board members. When it was time to speak he would change camera angles as part of an expensive production package.

The final two members appeared on the screen just before nine. A prompt on his conference coordinator program signaled that all were present.

"Good Morning, *TerraLuna!*"

The group adjusted themselves in their seats, at attention now that the boss was on line.

"Thank you for being here on time. I have several topics to cover, all of which are positive. I am proud to announce that *TerraLuna* is back on schedule, and our next conference will be in a grand ballroom on the moon."

A murmur passed through the crowd. Steele adjusted the volume down, continuing. "We have a fantastic crew on-site that brought us back on schedule. I would like to congratulate Dave and his people for their extra efforts after our little setback. I would like to extend condolences to the families of those lost last month. The company has provided for those losing loved ones as well as extending them a free week at *TerraLuna*. A committee will form at our next meeting to erect a memorial to our fallen employees, which brings me to the issues of future security. I have spent several hours with Ben Skylar. We sifted through quite a bit of information concerning the bogey that found us last month. It appears that the region of space from which our visitor arrived has never yielded a threat in the history of recorded observation of space. It is a virtual dead zone. However, it is not apparent that the threat from that sector is real. Ben has upgraded his satellite defense system to include not only this region but several others as a precautionary measure."

Edna Cosgrove, the young daughter of investor Bruce Cosgrove of London, sat listening patiently and then interjected at Steele's pause. She was nearly thirty, nearly attractive, and primarily concerned with her father's investment.

"Mr. Steele, I cannot speak for anyone here other than myself and my father. He had a concern that we feel deserves some attention. We understand that the *MoonCorp* organization has a rather innovative local defense system currently that deflects all micrometeorite material from damaging the edifice. Studies have shown that hundreds of millions of tiny rocks have indeed eroded the surface of the moon over the eons. How do you propose to protect *TerraLuna* from such impacts?"

Steele kept his tone even. He was prepared for this question. He singled her image, enlarged it, and replied, beginning with a bit of a laugh.

"Ms. Cosgrove, I am glad you have brought that up. I was actually saving that part for later. We have good news in the local defense area. Currently, I have several of our staff engineers working on a simple modification of the artificial gravity structure that will have a similar effect in protecting us from all sizes of meteoric encounters. In addition, our chemists are working on a sort of protective paint that will re-strengthen the outer walls from minute erosions. Safety is tantamount only to our guests' satisfaction. Further, these projects are being conducted using current staff and within normal budgetary parameters."

He searched Cosgrove's face for traces of doubt. His response seemed to satisfy her and the group. Steele hoping the issue would close, switched on the live camera.

"I am happy to inform you all that the insurance payment has been received to cover the rebuild. We are again on track to meet our goals. We must persist in a positive light in our reservation drive. This mishap is behind us. The only thing that will keep us from our aim is if we lose faith in our reservation drive. The mishap is behind us. The only thing that will keep us from our aim is if we lose faith in the dream. It begins with you.

"You are by far some of the most prominent figures on Earth in business and society. Your opinion matters. The one element that can hinder our success is doubt. I want to ask all of you to keep positive. We must 'calm down' the rumors and allegations. If we are to make this work, we must remain positive to sustain customer interest.

"Granted, we have lost 17 percent of our reservations since the accident. I charge all of you to spread the good word that *TerraLuna* is not only safe but also in the universe. I want you to know that it is safe for your family and friends. My vision is for all to share. After our stay at *TerraLuna*, you will want to come again and share the experience with your loved ones. Grandmother and grandfather will be receiving trips to the moon for anniversary gifts. Graduates will come. Birthday boys and girls, retirees, singles, second time arounders and of course, newlyweds *will come*. I have some pictures I will send to your screens now of our bridal suite. We have spared no expense in making this the most elegant, if not opulent, place to spend your honeymoon. In fact, I am considering getting married again someday simply to honeymoon at *TerraLuna*. As you can see, we have beefed up defense, and now we must beef up our marketing attitude. To demonstrate how confident I am in this matter, I will not be taking a young female guest to the opening ceremonies. Yes, I realize many hearts will be broken, but I will make my point in our success. At the New Year's Eve celebration welcoming in 2169 at *TerraLuna*, I will be escorting my own mother."

Steele paused, having cranked them up high enough that they needed a break from his tirade. He adeptly scanned the faces close up with the spin of a dial, looking for someone who was not crying or at least not smiling. They were persuaded, if not motivated, as evidenced by the round of extended applause echoing through his speakers. With a self-congratulatory twist, he turned the speaker volume up, revealing in what sounded like pleased audience, while analyzing each face for signs of dissent. From what he could discern, all were happy, even Edna Cosgrove, whom Steele would make a point of introducing to his mother.

The call lasted another forty minutes, comprised of general hype, menu selections, color and design schemes, and promises, most of which were perfectly legitimate. After ending the call, leaving the board still clapping, Steele recalled everything he said to protect himself. It was all true, except for the part about the defense system, which was almost true. It was a system being modified. He omitted the part about it being stolen from *MoonCorp*. Nodding with action to the onset of ridiculous guilt and, more importantly, patent infringement, Steele arranged a meeting with his engineers for next week to modify the power fed for the defense technology to adapt to the reactors. Even with his less than limited scientific prowess, he felt that it should be feasible. After all, power is power.

Still on an up from the conference call, he phoned Leslie in hopes of setting some additional business in motion before lunch. He rang her pocket phone, which she answered after two rings.

"Hello?" she said, waiting for the next pallet of supplied for unloading.

"Leslie, this is Gerry. How are you, darling?" he said, his voice more than enchanting.

"I am waiting for another pallet of slave labor work if you really want to know."

"I called to thank you for a job well done, Leslie. Have you mailed the package?"

"Yes, I mailed it early this morning."

"Excellent, my dear. You have helped do a great thing for the corporation. I know you are tired of playing the game down there, but I recommend that you continue the charade and fulfill Dana Kim's course requirement. Soon, we will be together, enjoying some vacation time. Now since you are going to be there for the balance of the summer term, I want you to do me another tiny favor."

Leslie held the phone at a subjective distance, waiting for him to drop the next bomb that she would have to catch.

"What would that be?" she said, staving off sarcasm.

"Well, think about what you told me last night. Think about what you have stumbled across while listening in to your physicist friends. It seems to me that a scientist of your degree would appreciate their findings more than most. Take a guess, my little plum. I would like more information about this temporal box experiment you have described. If you can get a copy of it, that would be outstanding." He paused to get a sense of her reaction.

"Listen, I did what you asked me to do. I do not want to take another chance at blowing my cover. Can't you let him have his glory? It is his work. Why must you have it too?" she said, keeping her conversation as private as she could.

"Leslie, my dear, I do not want to steal it. I merely want you to get to know the general principles. I am interested in what may be the greatest discovery of mankind for humanitarian purposes. Perhaps later, I can offer some kind of financial support for his project. From what I can tell, he seems to be working on it at home, which excludes any claim of *MoonCorp*. Nicholas may benefit from some mentoring in such a delicate arena. Do I make myself clear?"

"Yes," she replied with some effort.

"Wonderful. Collect what you can, and I will calculate your bonus based on what you find. They like you. Ask them if you can come over for a barbecue. Tell them you have a recipe that you are itching to try out. You are a resourceful woman, Leslie. Use your talents, or they will waste away. Think of this as a research project, or think about visiting the past. It is a breakthrough. It fascinates me to say it. Ultimately, you will be doing them a favor by enlisting your expertise to the cause. Do this thing for me, and I will secure your future in ways you haven't started to think about, Leslie."

"Okay, I'll do it, not for science or profit. I am doing it for you," she said closing the phone.

*****

Work on the remaining sections of time had to be put on hold for at least a couple of days. Nick and Charley woke early, scarfed a quick breakfast, and then prepared to drive to separate locations. They agreed to meet later that night to continue observing and recording the past. Before eight, they were on their separate ways, Nick to *MoonCorp* headquarters, where the virtual bot station was waiting for him to supervise work on the defense tubes, and Charley to the desert to work on the transport endeavor. After a couple of miles, Charley unhappily remembered that he promised to take Dana out tonight. It was Friday after all, and he turned her down yesterday. He was anxious to do something as well. This always happened to him. Some important research conflicted with his social life with strange regularity. He scrolled his mind wearily through the list of past relationships gone sour for the sake of science.

He would like to take her along to Nick's lab, but Charley knew the he would never allow it. Nick would have to show his findings to someone sometime. Dana would be as good a witness as any. He had time to think of a way out of trouble with her. Postponement was the only answer he had. He continued to drive the sunny trip, soon forgetting about Dana, his thoughts gathering at the temporal experiment and what he would encounter tonight.

Nick entered through the main gate of *MoonCorp* with his yellow Buick, waving to some of the morning joggers. These middle managers found either peace or political safety in jogging around the complex before work time or at their lunch break. He did like the "cool suits" they wore to prevent exhaustion by cooling the air in the suit using the heat energy conversion idea *Thermalsol* found in space suit technology. Nick shouldered the usual guilt for not working out more regularly to tone up and maintain good cardiovascular as he continued to his parking spot.

He was scheduled to meet his VB people at 9:30 a.m., offering him some time to get a coffee and check with Eleanor to get up to speed after his "working" vacation. After some briefing with the secretary, he sat at his computer, reviewing items of interest that had accumulated over the past week. There were routine e-mails, a brief note from Zonic, as well as announcements from a variety of associations that sent him regular newsletters. He subscribed to *Archeological Daily*.

It offered information concerning modern digs and discoveries all over the world. He did this to further the span of his cricket collection. Since he had some time before the bot session, he read an article on the team that went to the bottom of the Gulf of Mexico to retrieve asteroid pieces from an impact earlier this summer. The article mentioned some unusual samples that were reported to be atypical of asteroids found to date. The article further told of strange infestations of sea insets in the area. Naturally, the combination of old rocks and insects caught his attention. He made a tab on the article, telling the computer to route all information concerning the Progreso, Mexico, incident to his terminal.

Nick remembered that Zonic had a sample of the same asteroid he had taken from the lab. Nick sent a quick electronic message to Kerry Mumphrey, a student he met while getting his doctorate. *TerraLuna* employed Kerry. He would be going to the moon soon on transport detail. He was to be the pick-up man for Zonic. Nick knew that Kerry idolized him and would have no problem with this favor.

Kerry,

I have a favor to ask. My friend Ed Zonic is one of the chief engineers at TerraLuna. *He has a package for me. It is something I want you to pick up from him for me. Try to keep it under wraps. He'll be expecting you to contact him. Call me when you get back to Earth.*

Your friend,
Nick Nicholas

Nick sent the message and closed the computer. He had enough time to get some coffee and head over to the bot staging room.

"Well, it is nice to have you back, Nick. I was lent out to some visiting consultants, not one of which had any interest in taking me out to lunch," said Eleanor, giving him her familiar genuine smile, feigning disappointment, which genuinely did something to Nick.

"I have so much to do here, but there is no way that I could do it without a few freedom lunches with my favorite office girl," Nick said, going out the door, still nervous with his advances, if he could call them that. Eleanor respected him. He respected that. Again, he sighed to himself, bemoaning the lost perfection he revisited in his dear dead Ada. A voice in his mind calling from some recess told him it was time to move on. She was such a great girl. Habit had taken the majority of his sensibilities. She was a great, true habit and a hard one to break.

The bot room was at the lower level beyond with limited access. Recognition identification cameras monitored the entrance closely. Anyone not assigned to be there would be sequestered immediately. Facial recognition system was more than a precaution. It was standard operating procedure. It hadn't detected someone trying to enter the lower level unauthorized the entire time installed. Nick passed his ID badge through the reader, opening the elevator door. He placed his briefcase on the floor to check the time, regarding the nearly empty cup of coffee in his other hand. The caffeine had certainly taken effect as he found himself comfortably on edge, waiting for the car to stop. He was excited about working with the bot. It was such a fantastic technology yet still very secret. In the wrong hands, it would be disastrous. The car stopped his thoughts as it smoothed to a halt and opened the door. Taking the empty modestly lit tan-colored corridor to the staging area with lively steps, Nick felt good about himself. It seemed like a long time since he had such a deep feeling of well-being. This could be the payoff for years of waiting. Still unwilling to accept victory over defeat and depression an aegis that had ruled his life for so long, he turned the corner and through the double steel doors with a reserved smile for Stan Duncan, Robert Franz and the support crew for the bot procedure. Stan, attempting to be comfortable in his plum sport shirt and casual slacks, greeted him with a handshake.

"Good morning, Dr. Nicholas. Welcome back! Are you rested, Nick? I trust you didn't work too hard at home again. I need you to be fresh for our bot today." They walked together past several double door areas to a set of doors that had a sign that read "VB STATION." They pushed through the doors.

"Herr Franz, I was curious. The last time I saw a sample of the bot in action, there were some glitches. You've worked those completely out, haven't you?" said Nick.

Franz felt an itch on his scalp. When he was asked to defend his position even on the simplest of issues, the skin on his head moved.

This movement perhaps expressed this desire to give a correct and precise answer yet most certainly disengaged more than a few hairs.

"Nick, you know I couldn't allow an in situ exercise to take place without proper testing," Franz said through an instinctive forced smile. He spoke with a German accent yet tried to acclimate his speech to Standard English.

Nick looked at the persisting queerish smile with pause.

"Of course, you have the kill button this time. It is within reach if a malfunction does occur. It has been placed within reach, on the new control box in the V chamber. We use a larger red button, so you miss it."

"Thanks, Franz."

They entered the area where a large video screen placed seventeen *MoonCorp*'s builders ready for their briefing on the delicate procedure of connecting and servicing Nick's defense system. Stan took the small clip-on microphone from its holder and addressed the group. Politically, the bot system's use on the moon would be used to promote distribution.

"Yuri and everybody, this is San Duncan. We have come a long way in a short time. We are very proud and excited and hope to maintain our dedication to precision in every aspect of *MoonCorp*. By this time, you are all aware of Dr. Nicholas's defense matrix that will be installed in three tiers around the building and then across the top. The pipes that you will be installing need to be perfectly sealed to ensure proper operation of the system. Dr. Nicholas is here with us this mornings, and with the help of Robin and the virtual bot suit and his instruction, you will learn the properties of the system and its maintenance."

"I want to stress to you the terms of your nondisclosure contracts you signed with *MoonCorp* that forbid sharing any of this information. It is not only grounds for dismissal but will incur legal action. So please bear this in mind, and now I give you Dr. Nicholas."

During his talk, Franz helped Nick into a light gray bodysuit with wires interwoven very tightly throughout. Franz, buzzing around Nick like a tailor, connected an attached hood and form-fitting wired gloves.

"Thanks, Franz. Robin, can you hear me?"

A silver space-suited head turned to the camera with a modest nod.

"Yes."

A young American female voice returned.

"I know you have heard of the virtual bot. I realize you drew the short straw or something like that to have this honor."

The group gave a chuckle heard through the wall speaker in the fluorescent room.

"I want you to remember to relax. There is no danger in this procedure. The suit you are wearing is linked with mine. The small neural tap at the base of your neck will allow me to control your bodily movements. We will not take over your thoughts or normal body functions, those over which you have complete control. If you do move, the link will be delayed. Therefore, if you must scratch, let us know, and we will have someone do it for you. We are going to start with a basic connection between the delivery pipe and one of many generation boxes that work together to create the A-antigravity field. The "A" stands for anti. Some have suggested I simply call it A2, but it is a bit more complicated than that. I won't go into specifics. The main thing to remember is that it allows the expertise of system designers to work with the stamina of the young crew. It is very efficient. So, Robin, if you will move to the box, we can get started."

A voice entered the room from the speaker.

"Dr. Nicholas, is it true someone died in the VB experiment?"

Nick held still for a moment the VB system vibrating, slightly warming his muscles, not really wanting to go into detail now, yet despite a false oversight and a discouraging expression from Stan, these people deserved a dismissal of the rumor with a quick story.

"Yes. Early in the testing stage, an aging and still almost famous entertainer of the Broadway stage was asked to participate in a trial. They placed her onstage wearing the VB suit under her old costume she wore for early thirty years for yet another reprisal of her very physical dance number. A young dancer would dance the same steps backstage, and theoretically, the venerable old dancer would have the feeling of moving the way she used to, and it had all sorts of positive psychologically healing effects and so forth. We instructed the old girl to keep perfectly still like we are now, Robin, and waited for the music to start. Well, the young dancer backstage had quite a bit of pizzazz or whatever they call it in show business. She went out there and danced furiously. Sally moved like she did thirty years back, whipping, flipping, and kicking it up all over the stage. It was really an amazing use of the VB. Two minutes into her routine, the stress on her body caused a massive heart attack. Testing on the VB was halted after an investigation. Its use was classified to professionals like ourselves. A side note about Abbie: they said she died with a strange smile of satisfaction on her face. I suppose she died doing what she enjoyed. In some odd way, it isn't so bad when that happens." Nick ended the story to the quiet of an apparently affected audience in the room and on the moon.

A set of tools identical to those ready for use moon side sat on a table alongside a generator box and pipe sections. Nick nodded to Franz who had taken his place at a computer to monitor the interface. Franz typed a few strokes. The suit conformed slowly to Nick's body like a vacuum seal. The wires bulged over the suit like the veins of some skinless monster.

"Okay, let's start with the first phase of connection. The pipe you have there has a thick screw slot. If some of you can lift that pipe and bring it to Robin. Robin, I want you to take the thread fusing tool there and be ready."

Two workers took a twenty-foot section of pipe, holding the end to the generator box. It floated up rather easily in the gravity free environment. As usual, the workers were amused with gravity-free fun. They laughed a bit as they floated the pipe up to waist level.

"The rest of you, be prepared to install the mounting brackets. After I show Robin how to perm thread the connection, I will show her how to fuse the outer connection ring. When this is complete, we will reverse the process using the separation system. Eventually, you will be able to repeat these processes on your own, but it is important that you have some *hands-on* experience."

Franz handed Nick the tool and moved closer to the box. Robin's body responded as each step he took was mimicked through her body.

"I feel like a zombie or something, Dr. Nick. This is weird," said Robin, trying to relax and allow Nick to work through her body.

Nick raised his other arm, waving in the air.

"Hi, Mom!" he said. Robin's arm repeated the motion simultaneously, and they all laughed at the sight. After a dry look from Stan, he continued to instruct the crew on every aspect of set up and break down. He reminded them that at a later date he would be operating through twenty suits simultaneously, an idea they seemed to like.

Robin became accustomed to the puppet-like sensations. Soon, she settled her muscles, letting Nick take over, and concentrated on learning the procedures that turned out to be more delicate than she had anticipated. All totaled the experience had a more profound effect than an instructional video. Thankfully, his movements were slow and deliberate. Robin didn't feel as happy as Abbie but close enough.

CHAPTER 37

Friday felt like Friday as Charley entered the hanger. Shipments of supplies were always on schedule. Once a week, the JC would haul tons of essentials to the rapidly growing *MoonCorp* surface. His regular duties had become monotonous. He enjoyed coming to work to see Dana, and the paycheck was nice, not that he was desperate for money. Charley went about the routine of work as his thoughts churned exclusively on time travel. Working with holograms all these years, he had adopted sort of a self-imposed expertise on the subject. What Nick had done was to take it to the next level, a level that no one imagined could exist.

He sat in his chair at the entrance, nodding hello to the workers as they filed in for another day. After things got under way, he would go into the cafeteria for some coffee; he did not need any right now. His musings on the possibilities of actually being in the past satisfied his need for caffeine fix, for now. He also wanted to wait to avoid the chance of seeing Dana, still not ready to tell her that he was going to stand her up tonight.

He did not need another failed relationship because of what one of his former girlfriends called outside circumstances. He never thought it would overwhelm him to the point where he had to choose between a woman and his work. Women eventually demand "the choice," which leads him to formulate "the exit strategy" from the relationship.

Tired of thinking of it, he focused on the sound of a truck making its way along the road from the front gate. A voice crackled on the radio. "Porter, here comes another shipment. Happy unloading."

"Thanks a lot," he said back to the radio with an unusually low level of sarcasm. Charley stood and tapped a couple of keys on the computer. A pleasant recorded female voice began to sound throughout the complex.

"Unloading detail at hangar door 2. Unloading detail at hangar door 2. All personnel, please report immediately."

The truck would delay having to talk to Dana until later. Charley checked the truck into the side entrance where some of the workers were already gathered, ready to work. The truck backed in, and within a few minutes, a line of hands unloaded a variety of boxes onto low handcarts, which were meticulously packed in the canister. Charley checked for Dana. She was nowhere to be seen. He took this opportunity to get some coffee.

He walked across the expanse of the hangar with an important stride, leaving the thought of unloading the truck far behind. It was an unspoken practice for everyone to pitch in to unload trucks. Stan and some of the visiting investors would lend a hand when they were there. The others expected him to help as well, but Charley tried to find something else to do. He walked into the cafeteria to find Dana walking out, tossing her cup into the trash.

"Good morning," she said, stopping in the doorway.

"Hi, Dana," he said, nothing else to say, and then continued. "I was just coming to get a cup of coffee. Would you like to have lunch together today? I have to work tonight, so it will be our only time to talk."

She looked at him, trying to hide her disappointment, leaning in the doorway, expecting more of his attention.

"You said we would go out *tonight*, Dr. Porter. If you weren't a dedicated scientist, I would be a jealous girl. I should respect the kind of work reappropriating a Friday night date with me! It must be important. Being in college, I suppose I'm still a kid in some ways, you know, party, party. Hey, you know what would be great? If I were to come along and take notes, I could write an article on whatever it is you are doing. It may help me in my thesis. Extra credit?" She ended almost pleading, only to find him staring at her with empty eyes.

"Dana, you must realize this is Nick's life work. We've known each other since we were kids. I have to respect his request for privacy. It's not only a professional thing. It's personal too. It involves some close observations. Nick is nervous. I am helping him, and I am sure when the time is right, if he needs help, he will ask for it, OK? So I do not know if he will need me tomorrow, but if he does, I will be there. It shouldn't take very much longer. Believe me. If he asks for additional opinions, I will mention you," he said, attempting some finality and needing some coffee.

Dana looked back at Charley, forcing a wry smile. "I understand completely." She stopped leaning against the door, it feeling unprofessional to her.

"See you around, Dr. Porter," she said, walking away, leaving him with the sort of mixed feelings that might win her a last-minute change of heart.

Charley looked on as she filed into the work force they say getting under way around him.

"What about lunch?" he called ineffectually after her. He paused for a dull moment, filled with confused emotions. His off-base question stopped logical thought and replaced his brain with a wet, twisted towel: quite useless. Turning into the cafeteria for some coffee and sweet donuts would help him sort these emotions. He was sure of that.

*****

Pepe and Tico did not stay for the police to arrive at the marina. They took the stairs built into a hill to the street as people were coming down to see the creatures that were attacking the town. After hearing of attacks of people dragged off into the trees or the water, Pepe thought waiting at the safety of the hotel for his keyboard was a good idea, and the next thing on his mind was getting back home.

An American lady with her young daughter, each wearing large sunhats, were half-running, perhaps to the hotel as well. Pepe and Tico reached the halfway point to the hotel from the marina, when he spotted some commotion in the street up ahead. Several youths walked slowly, talking and jeering as they made their way toward Pepe's direction. As they approached, Pepe saw the children dragging something behind them on a tarp. It was a large skin unmistakably shed by one of the creatures, only it was three times as large. It had to have been the size of a small horse. As they passed, the American lady called to them in textbook Spanish.

"Where are you taking it?"

One of the children yelled back with glee, "To the police station! Maybe we get a reward!"

Pepe thought for a frightening instant how easy it would be for an insect of that size to take a person down.

"If they grow any larger, they won't think about eating you little Tico. You would be too small for their appetite," he said as they turned into the hotel. Pepe went to the desk and inquired about the mail.

The slim clerk responded, "No, Senor Fernandez, nothing has come for you, maybe tomorrow."

Pepe and Tico took seat on the couch by the window overlooking the street, enjoying the cool lobby for a few minutes. He noticed that several patrons were in line, apparently checking out of the hotel, bringing their vacation to a close a bit sooner than expected. Taxis lined up outside on the street managed by the doorman in his rather warm-looking gold-trimmed white suit and hat.

"I could call Mother to come and get us, but I am afraid she would be too worried during the drive. We wait another day for our keyboard, and then we will take the boat home."

Pepe looked at his little friend. He seemed to be upset, looking out into the street. Pepe turned to the large window when all at once, a man flew against the glass, shaking it hard. Pepe flinched, afraid the glass would break. An insect larger than any he had ever seen, the size of a cow, was pinning the man against the glass, forcing its four long sucking teeth into his back. The man's face splayed hard into the glass by the larger legs of the creature while the smaller legs were poking and pinching him along the sides. Soon, the man stopped struggling, and a wave of goo ejected around the body, swirled with the red blood from its helpless victim. Pepe stood and ran to the front door his dog, following him closely. He picked the dog and handed him to the doorman.

"Senor, please hold my dog for a minute." Pepe drew the stun gun from his belt and went out into the scorching air, people running in all directions, screaming, dropping what they were carrying and ran, some putting children over their shoulders, others looking on incredulously.

The insect had the man still firmly against the glass. Pepe held his position under the canopy leading to the street. Taxi sped off without their fares. It held Pepe's gaze for a few moments. He took in the awful sight with a bit more horror than before. The creature did not stop at simply sucking the blood of the victim. It was chewing at the man's back, eating the flesh after the small mouth ripped pieces away with small ferocious bites. Pepe's anger took control. He activated the gun to the maximum stun and aimed it at the creature's long multi-segmented back. He fired four shots at the monster and was ready for more.

The chitinous body lurched at the impact of the six-inch red bolts, its legs squirming uncontrollably from the impact. It stopped its eating and took the man with the small legs, holding him to its underside, and came down slowly from the window to face Pepe. It looked at him as a serious contender but was acutely aware of its reduced mobility. It reeled around and began to scurry down the opposite direction. Pepe took two large steps and fired four more shots at the monster. The numbing effect of the blasts finally took effect. The nervous system of the bug completely useless, its palsied legs twitched and fell over onto the sidewalk, blood and white goo staining the sun-bleached walk a sick pink.

Some men looking on approached with some caution to try to help the man. Pepe called to them with a warning.

"Be careful! It is only stunned! Try and get him out quickly!"

The men ran to the body nearly twice as long as the person was high. They pulled the man free. Little legs gave way freely from the bloodied body. People stood around in a circle, amazed at the sight of the enormous insect.

A voice called from the crowd, "Get back! It will come back alive!" The crowd parted a bit to allow three young men, shirts covered in blood, carrying axes and bats. They began beating and chopping violently at the creature. It convulsed slightly, perhaps not feeling much other than the dull pressure of the axes that separated its body into several parts.

*****

Gerhard Steele found each day leading up to his trip to the moon to be busier than the last. Virtual press conferences, television interviews, and phone calls with presidents and dignitaries thrilled him with tech efficiency. Steele rehearsed his speech to himself for the National Conference of Hotel Proprietors in the wings of the Dallas convention center of which he owned 82 percent. The crowd assembled, representing the largest group of hotel owners in the world, and sat in the gold-draped auditorium, waiting to hear Gerhard Steele give a talk about his crowning achievement, *TerraLuna*.

He paced in the wings, conjuring his posture to make him seem more erect, more complete, and in control of his body and voice. Blotting out all outside influences, he took his speech, which was memorized and reviewed it again simply as a nervous gesture. He knew every word. A stagehand with a small headset kept him ready or his cue. He looked to her and said a single word, "Mirror?"

The girl, now used to his vain requests, offered him a hand mirror that Steele used to double-check his flawless hair. He adjusted his wire-framed glasses and popped another piece of pungent mint gum to the waning piece already in his mouth. He handed her the mirror and checked his manicured nails and gold ring, coming closer to the feeling perfection he was looking for, when his picket phone rang an executive tone. He quickly put the phone to his ear.

"Gerhard Steele," he said with silent approval at the relaxed yet firmly secure sound of his own voice and accepted the light stroke of his ego taking a call at this high-test time.

"Mr. Steele, this is Pat Beck. I wanted to tell you about the findings on that piece of asteroid that hit us. We have been running some tests, and we have some information I think you should know." Beck paused for approval from his boss.

"Pat, it is a bad time. I am ready to give a speech. Give me the basics quickly," he said, switching the minty gum to the other side of his toned cheeks.

"Well, sir, our tests show that is more than simply an asteroid. It is comprised of some biological properties, which is rather unusual for space-faring rock."

"What sort of biological properties, Pat?" Steele inquired, a bit interested.

"It is comprised of reproductive material specifically make reproductive material. I have confirmed this with our experts. We have some theories that we would like to run by you, but as you said, now is not the time. If you can call me back when you have some time, I will go into detail."

"This is something I would like not to be a problem, Beck. Have some digital sent to me by 8:00 a.m. Monday. I have to go. Have a nice weekend."

He turned the phone off, pocketed it, and began pacing again to find his rhythm. The lights dimmed in the house, cueing the crowd to settle. The stagehand held up a single finger to Steele and said, "One minute."

Upbeat music began to fill the room. Steele took some deep breaths, hoping to properly file the new information he received from Pat Beck. The active part of his mind wanted to find some explanation for the attack on *TerraLuna* that could be blamed on Duncan. Not making any sense to him at this time, he focused on his speech as the stagehand pointed a single finger, prompting him to step onto the stage.

The crowd erupted as he approached the podium center stage. Steele adored the cascade of applause. After thirty seconds, he waved the crowd down with a couple of "thank yous" and addressed the convention with his unique confidence.

"I am very grateful for your warm reception today, ladies and gentlemen. It is in the designers, investors, builders, and dreamers I represent here today. All of us at *TerraLuna* are excited about our grand opening in less than two weeks of the first hotel and convention center off the planet Earth."

He paused eloquently to solicit a response, and it came with cheers, whistles, and applause.

"Thank you, thank you all. *TerraLuna* began almost four years ago as a brainstorm. We are indebted to the Independents Space Commission for carving the mold for any kind of off-world endeavor. They took an independent space program inundated with governmental procrastinating and unrealistic budgeting and turned it into the one of the largest grossing businesses in the world today. With costs so low and competition too high, we are able to explore space and capitalize on its resources for the sake of the people of America and the world. Independent space programs have created seventy-five thousand jobs, and those numbers will increase with more construction on the moon and beyond. Other projects such as space mining, solar power research, and space-plane vacations are projected to increase 8 to 10 percent in the next year alone. It is plain to see that we are on the doorstep of the universe, the future of Earth."

Steele paused, taking a sip of water from the glass on the table next to the podium as the crowd offered some approval. Looking around the room below the dimly lit chandeliers, he estimated about four thousand people listened, representing all the hotel conglomerates and many independent owners. He cleared his throat briefly and continued.

"Your presence here had done so much for our little enterprise that I would like to offer some discount coupons in your *TerraLuna* packets, which will be distributed after today's sessions. I hope to see all of you try our low-gee handball, golf, and aerobics, swimming pool with Earth glow dome and dance floor just some of the recreational wonders available at *TerraLuna*. The brochure is included in the packet. Yes, the moon offers us great pleasure in its perspective to the Earth, sun, and planets in our observatory lab. It also offers some recently encountered dangers.

"Pieces of interplanetary material are constantly bombarding Earth, the moon, and each other. We have a staff of some of the finest science engineers the universities can offer. They have developed a new field barrier to further protect our guests beyond our current defense strategies conducted by cutting edge indepenent space industries. With this new technology, we will be 100 percent safe on the moon and beyond. I must remember I am speaking to hotel owners who are regarded as the finest in their field in the world. I will let you in on a secret. Within the next three years, plans will be brought to my boardroom for the first hotel complex . . . on the planet Mars, making you hotel owners who are regarded as the finest in the universe! How do you like that?"

The room thundered with the approval of so many motivated, wealthy, and important people. This truly was a different sound from any concert or presidential rally Steele had ever heard. These people were excited, and he was certain that they would be a fine pool from which to draw some investment capital.

The audience took their time with the revelry, giving Steele a few moments to think. With these advocates, he would be able to do ten times the business as *MoonCorp* or any other comers. He thought of Duncan and how he would be affected by this win. One thing was certain. He had limited need for Stan Duncan. Old balding Stan could be up here now receiving the same laud, Steele thought, if he had shared the local defense technology. He reveled in the sensation of knowing it was all his. An insuppressible suspicion still existed that Duncan tried to sabotage *TerraLuna*, and Steele might manufacture a way to have Duncan's corner of this market as payback. It was a magnificent plan to him. His cheeks glowed with appreciation from the audience, and a smile rose to his face, and it stayed there. He couldn't remember a time when he held a smile for such a long time.

CHAPTER 38

After a full six-hour shift, Nick's presence at the virtual bot station was certainly not needed. The high-capacity workers of *MoonCorp* were able to apply the assembly technique quickly, soon performing the tasks with varying degrees of accuracy. This activity secured their coveted jobs they worked hard to attain. Nick was pleased with their performance but would certainly check in on their progress from time to time. With the defense system under way in good well-trained hands Nick's concern drifted to tonight's continuing experiment. He called Charley, telling him to meet him at the lab at seven o'clock. Charley was more eager to continue adventuring temporal fantasies than being with the young doctoral student.

After a brief meeting mostly of a congratulatory nature with Stan Duncan, Nick took to the road, meeting the continuing heat of summer without complaint. What would be the practical application of his breakthrough? It was going to be a difficult and slow process arranging a format for what could very easily be dangerously exploited. He curbed waxing thoughts of a private time museum until testing was complete. It had to be safe and free from any sort of interference, he thought finally, agreeing with himself to chill the automatically developing idea.

Nick slowed the Buick to his mailbox and retrieved his mail that included another package that undoubtedly held a fossil sample from a dig in Italy. This site was relatively young as were several others that had been collecting dust in the cabinet not suitable for the experiment. The fossil samples under ten thousand years were not initially part of the experiment. In light of recent developments, these newer samples may prove useful.

He pulled the Buick into the garage, checking his security screen, the light coming on automatically in the darkness of the garage. He went to the washroom, washed his face and hands hoping Charley would come early to get something to eat before they started.

Almost on cue, he heard a car crunch along the gravel. He scanned the selections available for dinner and opted for the beef stew. The doorbell rang before he was able to get himself a drink. He activated his phone to call Charley and to unlock the front door from his phone. Soon, they were enjoying a hot meal and a cool drink.

Nick ate half of his meal, his interest moving from the stew to the experiment. Charley ate ravenously as usual, pausing begrudgingly to get up and refill his large glass of soda.

"You are aware that tonight we will be going back to a time where there were dinosaurs? I understand if you want to stay back and work the board. I won't think you are a coward," Nick said, looking at Charley.

"Seventy million years ago sounds about right. You might encounter some extinct creatures. I will be sure to get some footage. People love dinosaurs," Charley said with half a mouthful of food.

"People are not going to see this stuff tomorrow, maybe not ever. You persist to visualize this project from behind a cash register. I will not until it is entirely safe. How else do you want me to explain it to you? It will be *In Secretum*." Nick's appetite waned.

He activated the computer screen built into the kitchen table to check his messages, while Charley silently fought the urge to ask for another plate of food.

Nick accessed his interest files and several entries, some of which were calls of assistance to the scientific community by Dr. Rene Sanchez. *The situation in Progreso has worsened.* Nick read the articles intently. Photos accompanied the text showing huge insects resembling a cross between a lobster and a centipede. Nick's attention drew closer to a group of pictures of the mysterious rocks that were collected from the seafloor. Sanchez held that these are the eggs from which these creatures hatched. Nick stared for a few moments at the texture of the shell of the "eggs," The shell was covered with a fossilized coating. Nick took a sudden interest in these observations. He pulled the keyboard out from under the table and typed a note to Sanchez:

Dr. Sanchez,

I am Dr. Nick Nicholas from San Bernardino, California. I have been working on several fossil experiments over the years, and your insect samples interest me. I am concerned about the age of the eggs you have found. They look rather fossilized on the outside, suggesting considerable age. Have you run tests to determine how old these things might be? I would be interested in sharing that data for my own research. This might also help you in learning about the species. It seems unusual that a new species would have fossilized eggshells. They have been deep-sea dwellers for a very long time. You may have evidence of an entirely unknown form of life. Perhaps the age of the sample will help in your work. I am happy to help in any way I can if you need temporal analysis facilities I have ready access to the equipment.

Sincerely,
Dr. Nick Nicholas
San Bernardino, CA

Nick sent the letter with a tap of a key. Looking up, he saw Charley munching a cookie.

"When you are finished, I would like to get started."

"I'm ready now," he said, taking the last bite of cookie.

*****

Getting out of the sleepy little town of Progreso would never again be so difficult. The busses were filled with standing passengers, and the highway out was packed and moving at an excruciatingly slow pace. All boat traffic was banned in and out of the harbor. Taxis and private car services were working overtime.

When Pepe heard the tv news, he and Tico walked to the city morgue to find Dr. Sanchez. The streets were rather vacant. They walked fast along the abandoned road usually packed with shoppers and electric cars with the stun gun pistol in the "on" position. They arrived at the morgue without incident. No one was in the lobby. He followed the signs to the morgue where the front desk said he was working.

Tico tapped his little feet along the way behind his master aware that something was wrong and hoping they would be back home soon. He opened the door marked "Morgue." "I am looking for Dr. Sanchez."

The coroner looked up from a desk.

"Three doors down on the left, lab 22," the young coroner said. Under the circumstances, he assumed Pepe was on some delivery and did not question his presence.

Pepe and Tico thanked the young man, turned on his heel, and went to the workroom, where he found Sanchez and Alba working at a portable computer. A small television was on the table with hit volume low as well as some books and a telephone.

"Dr. Sanchez, Dr. Alba, it's good to see you." He went to shake their hands. Tico received, copious pettings and was glad to see his new friends now some days after their adventure.

"Senor Fernandez, it is good to see you. How is the ship coming along? Are you here to say goodbye?" Sanchez smiled, offering some sort of worried smile.

"No. I am afraid they have cancelled all incoming and outgoing boat travel from the docks. It seems I will be here for some time yet. There is no telling when my keyboard will get here. I do not expect it to be soon. Tico and I thought that while we are here we could be of some help to you, if you will have us."

Sanchez consulted Alba with a quick nodding glance and turned a serious eye to Tico.

"You know, I do believe we have use for a good watchdog and someone handy with a stun pistol. Yes, amigo, we would be glad if you would keep us company," said the professor.

Pepe shook his hand again, pumping it with natural vigor. "Thank you."

"We will help any way we can. Did you know that the police asked people to leave town if they have somewhere to go? The highway is filled with cars and busses. Others are arming themselves, going on hunting parties to defend their homes. There is a meeting tonight at the high school gymnasium. It is like a war out there. The people are complaining that they need help from the military. Sergeant Aroja said they should be here soon. My Paloma is beside herself to have her boys home. I told her that I would be home soon. How long do you think it will take to get rid of theses damned things?"

Sanchez shook his head, pointing to the computer.

"We have been sending out messages, including their DNA code, to scientists worldwide to help us identify these insects and offer some effective answer to their find their weakness. The sergeant has given us some bad news. He says that their shells are getting so tough as they grow that old ballistic bullets have no effect. It took ten shots with a stun pistol to bring one down outside the library this morning. Some people rushed it then hacked it apart with axes and chainsaws."

Pepe listened with attempted composure and then returned a bit uneasily.

"Have you found some way to kill them?"

"The military will undoubtedly have laser rifles bombs of some sort. This will be terrible for the town. Dr. Alba suggested that if we were to have some way of luring them away from the city and centralize them, we could use localized explosives or poison. The only thing we can think of is bloody flesh like we used to catch the one on the boat. It is like catching fish on land, eh, Pepe?"

Pepe looked to the dog, considering the idea with sober silence.

The television on Pepe's phone suddenly came on, drawing their attention. A news flash reported something about a bus under attack. Dahlia Morales was on location at the side of a road, leading out of town.

Behind her was a charter bus lying on its side with various emergency vehicles parked and personnel milling about. She spoke into a handheld microphone.

"I am here just one mile outside of Progreso where a chartered bus heading to Merida was attacked by seven of the marauding insects that have been terrorizing our usually quiet town. The creatures rammed the bus until it fell onto its side. They mutilated them quickly, killing twenty-five people. Ten passengers managed to survive. We are extending a warning now to stay in your home, preferably in your basement. Emergency vehicles will patrol the streets, offering food, water, and any medical assistance. If the infestation persists, all residents will be informed as to evacuation procedures. Please stay calm and stay tuned for the latest on Progresso's greatest challenge. I am Dahlia Morales."

They watched the newscast with more disgust than fear. Words came to none of the three as they watched footage of the bus with it windows smashed and blood running down its sides. A beep interrupted their thoughts. An incoming message appeared on the computer. Sanchez took the call, reading it to himself with concern. Alba came over to see what was happening.

"What is it, Rene?"

"It is a response to our science call. It is from a Dr. Nick Nicholas in California."

Sanchez read the letter with gratitude at the offering of input. Dr. Nicholas's suggestion confirmed the evolving theory that the phenomenon maybe of an extraterrestrial nature. Sanchez sent a response.

Dr. Nicholas,

Thank you for your suggestion. In fact, we have dated the material and the fossilized egg material has registered 65,056,345.987 years. I find it amazing and frightening that such an old sample could be fertile after such a long period. Progreso is a war zone. These creatures are growing quickly and feasting on people. Any help you can offer us will be appreciated. As of now, Dr. Alba and I are the frontline science team. Military support is on the way. I am sure they will ask our opinion. We would greatly appreciate any support. My question for you is one concerning their geological origin. Why did they hatch now? Perhaps if we knew that it would help us to destroy them. I will send you the photographic and genomic data I have compiled to thus far. I would appreciate any suggestions based on our findings."

Again, thanks for the input.
Dr. Rene Sanchez, University of Merida

Nick read the portentous pleas from his new acquaintance on the beach city in Mexico. He had to send him a quick note back, feeling the gravity of their situation.

Dr. Sanchez,

Your findings certainly point to some fantastic conclusions. They are the best ones in science as far as I am concerned. I think your situation is in need of some information about what to expect from the imago or adult form of the creatures. That information is expectedly unavailable. What is their next stage of their rapid development? If it is extraterrestrial, your research would also benefit from sub molecular testing to detect any weaknesses they may have. I have done extensive work with sub molecular samples. I am very interested in running some tests. Keep me posted on your data. I will offer any assistance possible.

Yours truly,
Nick Nicholas, *MoonCorp*

Charley looked over his shoulder, showing a growing interest in Nick's letter as he finished it, and sent it off. "Now you want to go to Mexico. You have many irons in the fire, Doctor," said Charley.

"Yes, I do. It seems that Dr. Sanchez has a fossil insect sample from sixty-five million years ago. I happen to be missing that particular time in my collection, which, if you recall, is a very important time in Earth's history. Can you dig it? If it's Okay with you, let's get to work," Nick said with finality.

Within twenty minutes, they had the computers up and running. Nick spent half an hour time running a diagnostic on the globe selector. Finding time slipping away, he called over to Charley, reviewing footage from the caveman epoch on the big screen.

"Call Bert and tell him to give us some power. We can begin as soon as he boots us in."

"Sure thing, boss," said Charley, activating his wrist phone.

"Say, Bert, how is it with you? Charley Porter here."

"Well, if it isn't Mr. Hologram. How the heck are you? It's been a long time since you have come over. The kids are asking about you less and less now. You had better make an appearance, or they will forget they even have an Uncle Charley. I do not want you to be a vague memory for these kids," Bert said, closing his statement with a friendly chuckle.

"I know, Bert. I have been busy with my new job with *MoonCorp*. I will have you know I am coordinating assistant now. So have a little respect. I am a key man," Charley said, enjoying talking to his old friend. "I am here with our colleague Dr. Nicholas. He has a special request for some love from above. Do you think you can plug us in for this evening's experiment?"

"Well, you know I am the dude with the juice. Who else are you going to call? This time it will cost you a visit, both of you. I want to invite you to the birthday event of the year. It is next month, and I want to give you ample advance notice. I will mail you an invitation anyway. Please do not let these kids down. I don't know why they love you so much. Apparently, they have their reasons. They will be disappointed if Uncle Charley isn't there. So with your acceptance, I will turn on the power," Bert said, plainly finalizing the deal.

"I have no choice other than to accept unconditionally. Thanks for the juice, Bert. We'll see you soon."

He closed the phone and set the computer to display the satellites power link.

Nick ran another twenty minutes of tests, satisfied that the system was still at peak operation. He began to climb into the wet suit, aware that the slight shake in his hand must be because of the excitement of being the first to see a world that countless others have depicted from bones and dust. He felt some pride in the notion that he had actually recreated past time from same dust and bones, sunshine, and good record keeping. Once he was dressed and equipped, he made his way to the box, addressing Charley as he went.

"Charley, I want you to be ready for anything. If I come back wounded, call Dr. Tecani and no one else. If I die, carry on the research. It is willed to you with the provision that you cannot sell it. So whatever happens, I trust you will carry out my wishes for nonbastardization. I will haunt you if you screw it up. I'll bring Ada with me. I am sure you do not want to be haunted by her. Let's do this thing activate globe ten."

Charley, finding silence to be his best way to respond to Nick's overdramatic last request, set the blue lights free to dance through the machines and globes with the tap of a computer key. Nick opened the peek door and looked in to see the pastoral scene image itself in a blue and white. The box was located on the edge of a great wooded valley. Lushly leaved trees and shrubs cascaded along the green slopes with a clear sky beyond the opposite rise spanning nearly three hundred yards. Secure that there wasn't an immediate danger, he stepped into the box, assumed the supine position, and closed the lid. With a trained thrust, he rolled into at time nearly seventy million years in the past. The sun seemed different from the other visits. It could have been because this sample is taken from Gubbio, Italy, or perhaps because it was so very early in the morning from the position of the sun from across the valley. Each epoch had a different feel like when one traveled among the states. California has a distinct flavor compared with Florida, and they are both different compared with Wisconsin. There was a mineral scent in the piney air, and it was not as humid as some of the other visits.

He stood nearly thirty feet from the rather steep slope down into the valley. Looking around, he saw a loose grove of trees behind him. He inspected them for dangers using the camera as efficiently as his time. Satisfied that a hungry beast hadn't already sized him up for dinner, he walked slowly to the magnificence of the sprawling valley.

Checking to see that he hadn't come too close to the edge, he then continued searching for some sort of movement among the strange trees below. A sudden wind blew past him, affecting the trees in the distance. It sounded very peaceful. Welcoming the private peace calmed him for a moment until a winged shadow entered the top of his viewfinder. He looked up quickly to see a huge winged pterosaur fly overhead with intents of covering the distance of the valley, perhaps looking for some prey. The trees behind him must have been forty feet long. Instinctively, he crouched inward, stepping back for cover, but the creature was certainly not looking for the likes of him.

Nick took a few steps to the left to get a different view. He pushed the snake viewfinder away for a moment to get a full view as something caught his attention in the trees below. It was dark and long like a rock outcropping, but it had moved. As he inched faster along the edge, it came into view. It was the tail of massive creature nearly sixty feet in length. He immediately identified it as an ankylosaur. Its armored body came into view. Stiff plates of bony protection protruded from the center of its back. Its legs festooned with spiked horns, obviously for defense. The creature grazed casually on some tall grasses. Nick found himself rapt with the creature for an undetermined time and then started filming. He spoke a single word, "remarkable," the beast came into view. Glad that he was far enough to not be slurped up like a giant cricket lunch, he focused the camera for a clean shot.

A sudden booming crack lifted his head. He found himself farther away from the blue light. It hit again. The ground shook, and trees fell in the distant expanse of the valley. He sidled at a near run to get a glimpse of what might be making the noise. He counted thirty paces from the box, searching for the sources of the commotion, his heart beating markedly faster.

Having traveled quite a way along the ridge, he saw an incredible sight. It was some sort of prosauropod. An enormous plant eater with elephantine legs and a long neck reached up into the trees to feed. It tore branches away from a tree and munched peacefully. Nick noted how unusually accurate the artists of his and earlier times had predicted how these creatures would look. The creature was nearly ninety feet long. The two beasts were unaware of each other, concerned entirely with their grazing. Nick bent to one knee and filmed the creature with the telephoto feature. It was fantastic.

After nearly ten minutes, he felt it was time to head back. He wanted to pan the creature again to give a depiction of its size. A rustling was heard when the trees below once again brought his eye away from the viewfinder. A smallish creature standing on hind legs sporting a mouthful of teeth sprinted a path toward the ankylosaur. It let out a screech that echoed throughout the valley. It was either a small Megalosaurus or some sort of raptor, obviously a carnivore. It ran across the bottom of the valley enraged, perhaps by hunger, and snapped at the larger beast. The ankylosaur swung its tail covered with spikes in defense. The many toothed demon ran again at the upper end of the tail jaws first, hoping to get a damaging bite. It missed and then scrambled back, barely missed by the huge flailing tail. The little monster was determined to attack the prey despite the fact that it was much larger. Tail and jaws played a game for another few minutes until it ended abruptly when the tail struck the little Megal squarely on its side. It flew into the nearby trees and, after a bit of shaking, was motionless, probably dead by what he could see at max telephoto.

That's a hard lesson to learn, Nick thought. He was satisfied with the film much like the beasts seemed satisfied munching in their own private spheres. He trotted briskly back to the friendly blue light that would take him back.

*****

Gerhard Steele sat in his comfortable stateroom aboard the space plane, reviewing the latest financial reports for the grand opening of *TerraLuna*. Scanning with a steady eye for the likes of excessive spending or ambiguous expenditures was not a task for him but rather an executive passion. His room offered a view of space through a twelve-inch window, which he ignored as he reclined in a leather chair amid darkened tranquility. His pocket phone chimed three times before he answered not wanting to break his concentration.

"Mr. Steele, this is Dave. How is the trip?" said Dave from his office in the control center on *TerraLuna*.

"Fine, David. It is more pleasant than travel in Earth's atmosphere once you break from the gravity. This new plane is going to be as amazing as *TerraLuna* herself. What is on your mind? I am busy," said Steele, dropping niceties.

"*The Motivator* is going to rendezvous with B2 ahead of schedule according to our latest telemetry. I thought you would like to know that we will be in position thirty minutes after you arrive." David paused professionally, a bit put out by Steele's shortness with him.

"Very good. I want to be there. I am sure my presence will encourage Mr. Zonic to not screw up. Make sure he knows I will be there so he can mentally prepare for a flawless execution. I want that thing nudged or obliterated and out of the equation quickly without any more bad press. See you soon, David." Steele closed the phone and resumed his reclining review of the space planes systems.

The space plane accommodated one hundred, including crew. Guests had their own cabins as well as a takeoff and landing area, much like an ordinary airplane. During space flight, artificial gravity allowed passengers to enjoy a ride much like an ocean liner with a minimum of discomfort even for those prone to space sickness. Sensitive riders can opt to undergo a sleep takeoff, making the trip available for the old, young, and those with health risks. The new space plane replaced the previous plane with these and many improvements. Now it was safe for anyone to travel to the moon without the risks of conventional space flight of the past, though the costs remained out of most people's budget.

Steele's landing was routine having flown space plane trips quite frequently during the past several years. The plane made a horizontal landing on the moon strip and taxied to the air lock on the western side of *TerraLuna*. Once the plane had stopped and the air lock secured, he briskly undid his seat belt and made his way to meet Dave. Other passengers included mostly relief workers and some media people. They made their way through the spaceport, very eager to experience the actualized *TerraLuna*. Welcoming staff guided passengers to their destinations. Dave caught sight of Steele and waved a raised hand. They met and shook hands as they walked directly to Motivators control center.

Kerry Mumphrey saw Steele meet Dave and followed them to the control room, hoping to connect with Ed Zonic soon before the plane took off later that day. He had to take packages back to Earth and deliver it to Dr. Nick. It was important to keep it in secrecy. Kerry had been a favorite student of Nick Nicholas and did not mind doing him a favor.

Ed Zonic sat in the high-back mission chair in the darkened sim cockpit, ready for the moment he had waited more than a week to arrive. Simey reset the timer four times, adding time to the countdown for manual control. The automated systems jockeyed *The Motivator* into position in front of the speeding megalith. It was his job to land the ship once Simey matched speed and position. A brief moment passed with a message to Ed from Simey that Steele was on *TerraLuna* and would be watching the maneuver. Steele annoyed Ed, and Ed knew his boss tried to unnerve him simply because it was part of the arrogant bastard's nature. Zonic's self-control was legendary. Nothing the German egomaniac sent his way ever made it past Ed's icy cool demeanor.

Ed waited for Simey's cue to surge ahead of B2. He was flying adjacent to it at a safe distance from thereto, flying off the sides and rear.

"How are we doing, Simey?" he said into his headset.

"Trajectory is stable by seven tests. Take her twenty miles closer and resumed current speed," Simey said from his station behind the curtain.

Ed shifted the control, taking *The Motivator* into his command, bringing her into position a mere three miles from the speeding rock nearly the size of a mall parking lot.

"Everything looks good from here," said Simey as professionally as he could. Gerhard Steele was now standing over his shoulder, literally breathing down his neck.

Ed referred to his gauges one last time and then urged the craft forward passing it and then twisting the ship around matching its speed. With all the skill he had and some luck, he positioned to land in front of the rock.

"Heat readings are at 45 percent …tolerable. Landing gear enabled."

Ed flipped a switch, keeping an eye on the computer readout that soon gave the green light for landing. Ed took her down consulting both visual screens and computer read out for the best place to land.

"I detect optimal landing sight. Matching speed is holding. She is all yours, Captain," Simey said evenly.

Ed held his gaze on the screen while fingering the control carefully as *The Motivator* eased onto the rocks surface.

"Landing sequence is complete. Engaging leg lock," Ed said, unworried.

Two of the six legs drilled their hold on the semi smooth surface. Movement ceased both on the ship and in the virtual chair. Ed took a small breath and consulted a new screen to enable the reverse thrust. The view window didn't give much of a panorama of the surface of the rock as the ship was not designed for tourism. He activated the auto photographic program that would take pictures from a variety of angles.

The craft revolved on two massive legs, offering an antimatter engine ready to push against the oncoming strength of the monolith. Once the ship was revolved, the other four legs were disengaged from their holding positions and anchored the ship onto the speeding rock.

"Antimatter thrust reversed. Bracing legs drilling for stability. Initiating fuel diagnostic. We will be ready to redirect in five minutes," said Ed, now a bit surer of himself.

Steele stood with his arms folded, looking around the control center, exerting his CEO status upon the busy staff with executive glances and nods. Dave stood next to Steele, observing his boss's king-like demeanor but was mostly concerned with Simey's screen.

Ed sat in his chair, hoping to get this job done, and let a rookie fly *Motivator* back in the pilot seat. For all he cared, Steele could take the thing home and land it next to his pool. Zone eased away from reality for a moment, working out the math for such a project until he was interrupted by a green light flashing again, signaling the end of the diagnostic.

"Simey, I am going to initiate a three-quarters full blast and hold for two minutes based in the date here. Do you think that will be enough?"

Simey made some quick calculations and concurred with his colleague.

"That sounds right. If it is going to veer from its course, that should do it."

"Beginning firing package," said Ed, flipping switches and tapping keys deliberately.

The Motivator lit up against the underside of the rocky surface of the speeding meteor, attempting to push it upward against its natural course. Extreme force assaulted the rock with severe intensity for five minutes. All eyes were watching the engines assail themselves against the alien rock. Simey and Ed monitored the gauges with waning hope; *The Motivator* not seeming to make a difference.

"We need at least four degrees changes to make a viable trajectory shift from our safe zone, Ed. We have barely taken her away one-tenth of a degree. She will regain that in momentum after five hundred thousand miles in rotation. Shut her down.

"Ed, we'll have to take her to plan B," Steele said, surprising them all with a nimbly acute ascertainment of the situation.

IMAGO

CHAPTER 39

Sanchez stood near the stage set into the wall of the Progreso Public High School gymnasium. The coffee he had been sampling from his large plastic urn was uncharacteristically bad for a Mexican coffee. Perhaps it had been stored a long while in the cafeteria. High school students today probably didn't drink as much coffee as he did when he was thirteen.

Chairs were set up to accommodate two hundred Mexican army troops and nearly as many concerned citizens ready to confront the blight that had descended on their peaceful town. It was not quite five-thirty on a Saturday morning. Outside, assault vehicles were stationed in a numbered grid pattern in the fading darkness of late July. Most of the military were from the national reserves; only twenty-five percent are from the regular army. Normally, the guardsmen, men and women, were very positive at the prospect of seeing some action. There hadn't been a war in Mexico in more than two hundred years. The reserves had been on call for natural disasters the country has never seen. The national volcano showing signs of possible activation and several minor earthquakes were the closest thing.

Pepe stood holding his dog next to Dr. Alba as the crowd began to find their chairs at a silent hand wave command of Gen. Jaime Gonzales, who was called in from Mexico City to handle the plague of Progreso. He was a short, thick man, standing his ground firmly and always seeming to have a grin on his face, the rest of which held an incongruously stoic demeanor. He was dressed in military fatigues and sported a red beret bedecked with pins of achievement. As the men took their seats, he tested the microphone and gave another silent hand wave for the academics to join him on the stage. Sanchez topped off his coffee and made his way to one of the six chairs waiting behind the podium.

"Please take your seats." said Gonzales, his voice strangely thin for a general as his voice was patched through the gymnasiums public address.

The crowd included assortment of civilian businessmen and civic leaders flanked by employees, sons, and nephews ready to defend their interests. They looked on edge, having spent the day reviewing tactics and laser weapons use; all were anxious to start hunting.

The general began with reserved authority. "Ladies and gentlemen, we are faced with one of the worst situations in military conflict, the unknown foe. We *do not know* more than we know about these creatures. Let's review what we do know. The creatures originated from the sea, they feed on blood. They attack much like a spider springing on its prey. We know they are growing. Their skins are shed as they increase in size. Our intelligence has shown that they are now impervious to normal ballistic bullets and stun pistols have been marginally effective. We do not know how they grow so large and so quickly or the extent of their presence. We have with us from the University of Merida Dr. Rene Sanchez and Dr. Sophia Alba. They have been researching the physiognomy of these beings for some time and will be assisting me in the coordination of our attack. We will conduct attacks on the creatures in squads directed by our satellite location system programmed with the DNA signature of the creatures. We will systematically attack and eliminate these creatures in the surrounding areas furthest away from the civilian buildings with infrared locating technology, first using aerial bomb and laser attacks. For local defense, handheld RPGs, bazookas, and grenades are to be used with care to preserve as much of the town as possible. Your job as attack squad within the city limits will be to use high-impact rifles to eliminate the threat, locating vital concentrations of the insects within highly populated area points through your satellite locators. Stun rifles are on hand to initially weaken the creatures' defense. Report to command central all assaults as they occur. Keep your communication headsets on and be ready for extraction and remobilization."

The general surveyed the crowd that appeared questionless. He continued within increased confidence as his control status was confirmed.

"At this time, we have one hundred and seventy-two insect locations. This number is growing by the minute. Our goal is to eliminate all within eighteen hours. Report to your squad positions and await deployment."

"Dismissed."

The general briskly walked to his captain, already wearing a headset equipped with a pull around video screen offering satellite feed. As planned, they began to coordinate the assault before the sun rose as the troops filed out into the parking lot.

Pepe stayed behind with the doctors who were now at a table next to the communications specialist's station, observing the various radar dots on an enlarged map of the area. The creatures were very mobile. Gonzales looked worried for a moment at the sight, yet they began the attack with his usual calm.

"Okay, strike force one, begin perimeter attack on target number one."

The two-man attack jet had been circling the area with their targets on the green screen for nearly half an hour, waiting the go-signal to attack. The vid-screen displayed an area a mile from the northwest corner of the town. A group of insects was traced in a field moving away to the countryside.

After thirty seconds since the signal to attack, the pilot came in low and slow, riding with the rocket-firing safety off, very sure of the location of their target.

"Target one located. Missile guides locked, firing for effect," the young pilot said, evenly sending four rockets at the pinpointed yellow blip. A detailed view appeared on their console screens from the mini-onboard rocket cameras as the rockets approached.

The creatures materialized in the screen frame. The sight of their numerous appendages and hulking torso widened the eyes of the pilots momentarily. All four missiles slammed into the bugs as they convened against a small tree, blasting it and the tree apart, setting the area afire, and bringing an early light to the dark, cool Mexican countryside. The other pilot spoke into the microphone, controlling his young exuberance.

"Command central, target group one- direct hit. Confirm takedown, ready for next target."

The general consulted the information offered by the soldier at the screen with a nod and then switched his headset to public address.

"Target one eliminated."

"Good job, strike team one! Proceed to target two. Let's clean them out ahead of schedule." The general spoke with sure approval for his men.

The jet altered course nearly half a mile to the south where the satellite screen showed two bugs near a barn with a farmhouse, not twenty yards away glowing red on the dark screen.

"Hold fire on target two and three. We need to confirm the area is clean of civilians."

The general motioned to the satellite scanner, checking the area for signs of life with a human DNA pulse scan. He responded, "All clear."

"Let's come back to this one strike. We want minimal structural damage. Proceed to target number four."

The satellite scanner ran his area scan, allowing a few minutes to collate the new locations. A slow shade of pale grew upon his face as a large concentration of red, orange, and yellow infrared depictions of insects nearly engulfed the entire screen.

"General Gonzales, we have eyes on multiple targets within the school perimeter on the roof of the gymnasium! They are here."

The general moved quickly behind the radar man and said, "How many of these things can the satellite see at one time?"

The young radar man looked blankly at the screen, referring to the overlapping, swarming concentration of aliens on the screen.

"Depending on the size of the quadrant, hundreds, maybe more. I will place peripherals in position. The wider the area, the fewer locations it can detect accurately. I will focus on a one-hundred-yard radius of our position."

The screen responded with a satellite picture of the school that detected at least fifty targets within the field. The general looked sharply to his waiting captain.

"Transmit these coordinates to the parking lot. Engage mobile units one through eleven and secure the area all personal inside, on windows and doors, now!"

The captain carried out the command. Screens lit up in the assault vehicles as lounging soldiers spread to attention receiving orders to prepare to attack. A searchlight, mounted on the roof of a truck, clicked into action, bathing the school building with light trying to locate insects. Several vehicles, having honed in on their targets, rolled away checking their weapons and computers. A special tactics team pulled quickly to the wall of the school, and soon, three ropes brought armed men up the side of the school gym where the spotlight stayed fixed on the edge of the roof. The team took the roof within a few minutes and readied the stun rifles fixed with flashlights.

The locater screen picked up the DNA signature of a bug near an air-conditioning unit. It huddled ominously, possibly thinking itself hidden. A muffled hiss, sounding like a hungry whisper, came from it. The creature was motionless in the lights for a while. The men raised their guns thinking it was injured or frightened, but before they could fire, the beast the size of an adult cow lunged forward, scraping its rear legs along the pea-graveled rooftop, sending a spray of rocks pelting the rooftop.

The soldiers spread apart in reaction, letting several shots off at the airborne monster. It was a young adult with untried wings. The red bolts hit its somewhat unprotected underside below the chutneys shell, affecting its landing and nearly hitting one of the soldiers with a flailing claw as it landed.

The gunmen spread out and opened fire at the slowing creature now straining to move at its assailants, with its hissing changing from hunger to anguish.

Red flashes popped in the dark morning like silent firecrackers, casting quick flashes upon the roof and the soldiers. After more than two dozen shots, it lay beaten and comatose. They stared at it for a silent minute, then jarred by a chillingly unfamiliar guttural call resounding from below. From their vantage, they saw an explosion like red firecrackers in the darkness, as another attack occurred beyond the parking lot on the tennis court.

A soldier activated his communication node in his helmet. "Roof subject is down by laser fire, please advise."

General Gonzales looked to the professors who looked back blankly. The general spoke into the headset. "Make sure it's dead."

*****

Nick removed his video headset as he was climbing down from the box, eager to replay the fantastic footage of living prehistoric beings in their natural habitat. He placed the node into the computer, and his friend Charley, full of questions, followed behind.

"What the hell was there? You were gone almost half an hour."

"The most fantastic thing ever filmed. Forget frogs and bears, let's see some dinosaurs."

They watched the video straight through without talking much at all, as the pictures said that which speech could only fail at representing.

"The earlier tests are going to have to wait. The system has tested true for thirteen epochs. It knows the effect of the sun's exposure to the cricket genealogy."

Charley looked at him, still piecing together Nick's thought process, and he felt good that he understood where he was coming from.

Nick stood with a start, walking briskly up the metal stairs to shut the system down. When the lights and power feed were completely off, he went to the cabinet across from his workbench and stared for a time at the dozen or so small mailing packages on the top shelf. He gathered them with Charley's help and brought them to the table to review the labels of fossilized crickets dated at various times throughout the last ten thousand years. He sorted them to find the five latest samples.

They sat on the tall stools and turned on the magnifying circular lights to illuminate the table copiously with white light. Nick stared at the samples dated within the past ten thousand years. He felt an ominous sensation of power as he considered the samples. The thought that he may be able to enter the past of the modern world at the same time entranced him and filled him with a terrible feeling of foreboding.

He slowly took a package bearing the date of 2080. It was recently found in Hawaii. The eruption of Mount Kilauea during the 2080 Olympic Games was big news at the time. The opening ceremonies shocked the world when Kilauea erupted in the background.

He put the box aside, his attention focusing on another box dated with the words "Southern California forest fire." A large portion of forest had allegedly burned away from the fire started by an arsonist. Many homes were lost, and more than twenty people died. It was a time of political unrest for the state and was a vehicle for the reconstruction of the state. The president had visited the San Bernardino to offer support. It was documented as some of the worst natural disasters in California's history.

Nick opened the box and emptied the contents onto an observation tray. It looked darker than most of the other samples since the fire and ash were responsible for the fossilization. He took a scraping tool and began to collect the fine dust containing the vital yet desiccated material of a cricket unfortunate enough to have been caught under the pressure of tons of burned timber from the forest fires of the mid-twenty-first century.

Satisfied with the dark powder, he put it aside, covering the glass tray with a form-fitting sterile glass cover. He took the flask of clear suspension fluid from the shelf and placed it on the Bunsen burner. He went to the cabinet to retrieve the gloves, sterile globes, wire, and glass solder to prepare the most exciting chapter in this experiment. He looked at Charley, who watched him with nothing to say. He was happy that Nick had drifted back into the more daring part of experimentation, not caring to talk idly.

Nick worked carefully preparing the globe too focused to make small talk about Charley's new girlfriend. He made several trips to the computer documenting his progress.

"You have a message here from Dr. Rene Sanchez. Would you like me to read it?"

Nick raised his head slightly, handling the globe in the special soft glove.

"Sure. What does he say?"

"We are under attack in the school gymnasium. The creatures have grown and are aggressively searching for food. The government quarantined the town. People here are very concerned. Any ideas you have on how to stop them would be appreciated."

Charley brought the portable computer and showed the photos of the insects that were infesting the coastal city of Progreso.

"They look like giant crickets," Dr. Porter said flatly.

Nick paused for a moment, looking deeply at the images of the insects. Turning the globe over in his hand, he considered if the sample he held would be able to be interpolated in his system and if it could bring him to a near enough time that might allow a visitor from the past to actually affect future modernity. The thought held him for a moment. Equations found their way into his silence like a lost child to his worried parent. *What would happen if extraterrestrial elements were introduced to the cricket genealogy?* Star shine affects the universe from incredible distances. What would the blue light offer him then?

The chance of finding empirical data by examining the sub-atomic dimensional strata from an alien world was now the next level in the experiment. The prospect of seeing the sixty-five-million-year marker was tantalizing indeed, yet this new concept raised the bar for Nick beyond previous expectations. He needed to get some of Sanchez's sample and was ready to go to Mexico to get it. The potential idea of saving some lives offered an antidote to the gnawing guilt of not being able to save Ada from an early death. Rationalizing his latest theory rather quickly, Nick adjusted his plan. The 2003 test must be postponed. He preferred the new sample to rest for a couple of days. He resumed his work, now setting the copper wire into the globe. He called to Charley, "Send him a reply. Tell him this: *Dr. Sanchez, I may be able to provide some solutions to help you deal with the insect plague at Progreso. I understand travel in and out is restricted. Ask the military commander if a plane can pick me up and bring me to your location. I can stay only a day, but if I have DNA samples I can send you improvements for the locating program, but I will need to run some special tests on your samples. Let me know as soon as possible. I hope I can help. Sincerely, Dr. Nick Nicholas,* MoonCorp "Did you get all that?" he asked, still balancing the globe in steady hands.

Charley typed the message as he heard, it wondering what made his friend so concerned. "Yes, I have it. Is there anything else?"

"That should do it. I am almost finished here. Come and see this."

Charley sent the message to Sanchez, then walked to the table to find Nick setting the fluid-filled globe on the tall metal stand and began soldering it closed with the hot, clear glass from a gun-like dispenser.

"The globe needs to be soldered, then it must rest. I am going to try to be back by Monday. We will run the experiment then. According to the resolution diagnostics I ran earlier, we get a more refined picture after the sample has settled in the globe for twelve hours. I had no idea it would refine as well as it did. We must let the globe settle in the little toaster for twenty-four hours. I expected Dr. Sanchez will send a plane for me. I need you to stay here, lower the temperature to 107 degrees after twelve hours, then remove the globe using this glove, and place it in the holder in the cabinet at eight sixteen tomorrow night. Under no circumstances should you touch the globe with your bare hands. Any questions?"

"No, Nick."

Dr. Nick completed soldering, then he gingerly took the globe across the room, followed by his dedicated observer, and placed it in the little oven. He closed the door and set a timer to eight sixteen Saturday.

"There it is. Perhaps the second greatest experiment I have ever conducted is officially in the oven."

"What's the first?"

Nick looked up sprightly. "I haven't made it yet." Nick said hearing the beep of an incoming message on his computer.

"We will perform that experiment when I return from Mexico. That beep will be Dr. Sanchez, I presume," said Nick.

"*Sí*. I presume," said Charley.

*****

Zonic sat in the simulator, not feeling much like taking a break in effect, milling around at the coffee urn choosing donuts. This was mostly because Gerhard Steele was present. Talking to him usually involved frequent considerations of telling him to go to hell and then quitting. As he sat with eyes closed in the now inactive comforts of the command chair, very focused on the success of the *Motivator*, he heard the curtain get pulled aside and, still at ease, caught a whiff of Dave's cologne.

"We want to take a break here, Ed. Why don't you go get a coffee or something?"

"I'll break right here. Liquids make me nervous."

"Ed, Gerhard Steele is here. He wants to talk to you."

"Send him in."

Ed exhaled, finding the little composure he needed to handle Steele. He resolved not to overexert himself to challenge a man who he knew held himself at dangerously fluctuating levels of self-esteem.

Steele walked with an erect saunter through the curtains held open by Dave, attempting to take command of the room, yet he looked a bit stiff in the small sim-cockpit. Ed opened his eyes and spun the chair with exaggerated executive flair to face Steele, whose extended hand accompanied a charming smile.

"Ed. How are you doing, man? That rock out there is a bit large to motivate. You know this is the first time we are attempting alternating nukes to pull her apart. Do you feel up to the job?" Steele said with what may have been mock concern.

"I can handle it," Ed replied.

"I know that you can. You are the best, buddy. The one thing we are concerned about is the location of the bogey. It may precipitate into Earth's safety zone, adversely affecting *TerraLuna*. We cannot have that after our run in with B1, that's bogey one. We should begin the sequence in about five minutes to stop B2. Are you in top form? You're not overstressed? Depressed, or in any way incapable of executing the maneuvering task?" said the executive with a piercing glance.

Ed slightly ground his teeth, holding back a snappish reply. Yet the tone of his answer was not without corruption.

"No, not at all. I am fine and ready to do this. I could do it in my sleep, I often do. That's why I am sitting in this chair right now. I am the best. I know you trust me, so let us get on with it without the bullshit pep talk." Ed held Steele's gaze for a bit longer than necessary, fortifying his point.

Steele took his hand off the back of the chair, leaving Zonic to his space, inviolate. Zonic hated to be prodded almost as much as he hated being patronized. Steele always took time to push Ed Zonic's button.

"We should look at the placement patterns Mr. Simon has prepared. Do you have access?" Steele sidled up to the console, sending the hairs on his neck bristling upward.

"Yes, I have them here. We have the chevron, or baseball stitch pattern, the zigzag, and the circle blowout available. I favor the circle blow out in this instance. Many times in simulation it breaks the bogey in two pieces, easy, you go your way I'll go mine."

Ed's screens displayed the three simulation blast patterns.

"The circle blowout does tend to offer a better result for nudging off course than the others, but I am concerned that it may be too large and not as effective as the zigzag. If it does not break apart, we have a meteor with a hole still barreling toward *TerraLuna*. I do not want to endure my hotel to another trauma."

"Earth may be in danger as well from a meteor shower. Zig zag is sloppy. Why is the Earth second on our priority screen? Last time I checked, it had much more gravity and a few more people than the moon."

"The ninety-seven billion world dollars of my investors is at the top of my screen, Mr. Zonic. Occupation of the moon is a necessary function of man's colonization of the universe. How can we control it if we cannot first control its basic safety?"

"The seven billion people on Earth are more concerned with there being a sunrise tomorrow than spending a million world dollars on a trip to *TerraLuna*, or should I say, your moon. Do you own the moon? Is it your property? How long will it take you to divide and conquer it? Will you not be satisfied until you are renting space to the insensitive rich, young moon-lifestyle addicts who must have a condo on the moon to impress some girl's family? I know your target customer, Gerry. Where will it end? Can you tell me that?"

Steele could rarely be pressed or chided by anyone. Blankly staring ahead in a stance usually held by Ed Zonic, he did not face the *Motivator's* pilot.

"Aside from your tenable employment by *TerraLuna*, you hate your job. What other reason do you have to threaten the safety of this operation? If you want to work for Stan Duncan, frankly, I will gladly let him have you. It comes full circle back to the reason we do anything, Mister Zonic, and that is for the money! You challenge me like some sort of grassroots rebel. I know the risks to the Earth, and for your information., *I am* concerned. If I wasn't, I would not be here right now protecting the frigging human race! This may come as a bit of a surprise to you, but I have family there, too. So if you would like to take a handsome severance package, I will arrange a seat for you on FIDO and drive you across the yard to *MoonCorp* myself!"

Silence was Ed's answer. In a way, Steele was right. Memories of being poor flashed across his memory like a shock of pain. Ed's only identifiable response was a quick adjustment of the computer's monitor. Dave emerged through the curtain, interrupting the silence. Ed hoped he hadn't been there the entire time.

"We would like to not miss our window here, gentlemen. We should begin."

Dave and Steele left Zonic to the quiet of the cockpit.

Ed sat for a moment, fathoming his reasons for not taking Steele up on his offer. *Why do I put up with the guy?* He almost thought aloud, his mind cascading away into a pensive stare, which was startled back by the unfamiliar voice of Kerry Mumphrey.

"Hi. Ed? I am Kerry Mumphrey. Dr. Nicholas wanted me to pick something up for him?" He said halfway into the room, obviously nervous.

"You have some timing, kid." Ed said as he produced the silver cylinder from his jumpsuit pocket, handing it to Mumphrey.

"Be careful with that. Get it to Dr. Nicholas as soon as you can. Do not open it. Thanks. Now, get out of here." Ed turned in his chair at the sound of Simey's prompting.

"Simey, I like the zigzag pattern a tad more than the circle because it is a deep rock. Circle pattern will be like making a hole to plant a big tree. We can crack it with wavelength at one hundred and fifty. We should unload all the nukes simultaneously for maximum effect rather than in cascading series. Starting where we are now, I (the computer) suggest this pattern." His fingers poised for Simey's agreement.

As he spoke, a screen offered a computerized image of the meteor. Zigzag lines appeared, indicating the drop point for the explosives at generally equal intervals like a patternless zipper across the circumference of the meteor.

"Run the density algorithm pattern from the most recent scans."

"They just came in. Twice as many nukes across sectors six, seven, and eight will get the job done. The computer detects the regions here to be the weakest points. This should crack her apart. I can add them into the drop plan if you would like to concentrate on navigation."

"That's fine with me, Simey. There seems to be quite an obstacle course out here. I want to be ready to deal with any guidance problems. How much time do you need?"

"We are ready now," Simey cued with surety.

Ed adjusted in the tall black chair, snapping his seat belt onto place, and commanded the motivator to spin back to normal position. The main cabin spun slowly on its axis and was soon sitting squarely on the speeding meteor, which didn't seem to be moving as fast as it actually was thanks to speed compensating. Ed disengaged the fastening legs that retracted along the sides of the craft. The lower section reformed to reveal the large double tread gear to roll along the uneven surface. In four minutes, it looked quite like a different vehicle. Ed brought the tread controls online, and he slowly urged *Motivator* along using the red indicator dot on the screen as a guide to steer along the computer-generated zigzag pattern. The drop points were indicated by green triangles at the apexes of the zigzag.

"Approaching first drop point fifty yards from current position," he said, rumbling in his seat as the ship moved along the surface.

Ed surveyed the rocky surface displayed on the screen to the left of the navigation pattern. The plotted course kept him on an even track. Along the way, Ed noted steep drops and sharp outcroppings of iron and rock, avoided by a carefully planned course along the severely potholed surface.

"Okay, Ed, the first drop is coming up. Take her twenty-seven feet and put her in neutral."

"Roger that," Ed said, consulting the distance meter at the corner of the screen. He pulled the ship to a halt and engaged the brake.

From the control panel, Simey opened the specialized bomb bay, releasing a nuclear device the size of a small keg. The device was carried out on a small conveyor. The plank-like device folded back, leaving the barrel on the surface. Ballast controls initiated. The outer metal surface melted after three flashes of a red signal light at the top of the apparatus, surrounding the bomb sending liquid tendrils onto the meteor and immediately fusing it firmly in place on the surface of the hurtling rock.

"*Point One* in place. Proceed to *Point Two*," said Simey, with usual surety in his voice.

Ed followed the zigzag pattern, leaving a red line dotted with the green triangles. After the better part of an hour, seventeen kegs were deployed along the half-mile wide bogey. Simey rechecked the bombs that were actually small yields as far as nukes go. He engaged a computer simulation to predict the outcome of the explosions.

Ed was almost expecting Steele to come back and continue their discussion. He had some choice words in the periphery of his mind in the event that he appeared through the curtain. Zonic stared at the screen without really looking at it until Simey's outcome simulation calculations for of the blast materialized on his screen, charting out the outcome in tactical graphics. It played again and again to many screens across *TerraLuna*.

"Ed, 87 percent is not bad. Ready to activate to M1 return status. Unless you have anything else?" Simey offered.

"I hope seventeen is your lucky number. Let's get ready to take her home," Ed said coldly.

Ed automatically flipped the switches and tapped the computer to retract the treads and re-establish *Motivator's* landing legs. The multipurpose ship was soon ready to blast off the meteor. Skylar was in progress of refurbishing *Motivator* for other specialized functions as needs presented themselves moving forward into space. From serving as a freshwater manufacturing plant to serving as a mobile artificial gravity generator, its mutability was nearly as impressive as its ability to stop a meteor millions of miles away from Earth. As Ed waited for the ship to re-modify, he couldn't help thinking of the money spent on these operations. Skylar might very well be the richest man on Earth. He provided equipment and crew for these operations, and he was an emperor among businessmen, rivaled only by the JC of Yokomoto/Chen. He was satisfied with the idea that Steele had to pay for this. It was the only sincere way to affect the man—through his wallet.

Ed changed the screen to monitor the ship's ascent. The chair rumbled, and within minutes, he was slicing through space back to *TerraLuna*. Simey changed Ed's screen to that of the meteor now laden with nuclear charges. The tension of the crew could be felt from behind the black curtain as Ed sat comfortably, waiting to be out of range of the blast, as a counter displayed the number of miles to go before detonation. As it clipped down to the last ten thousand miles, he called to Simey.

"You have determined that I will be safely away from danger, Mr. Simey. I would hate to think that you would use this opportunity to destroy the only person on *TerraLuna* capable of beating you at Ping-Pong," he said accusingly with a trace of humor.

"We'll find out in less than a minute, won't we?"

Ed put his protective sunglasses out of habit waiting for the explosion. It came in time. The blasts were timed simultaneously in order to provide maximum effect. The countdown ticked down with very few of Earth's inhabitants even aware this was taking place. Why scare six billion people for the sake of media panic that would amount to global hysteria?

All the elite screens became entirely illuminated. The screen in Ed Zonic's was dramatic, totally filling Ed's silent cabin with light. He stared at it in wonder. It seemed to have meaning. Ed was observing with cavernous reflection, contemplating mostly unspoken things, yet this happening offered advanced answers to the blackness of his mind. It grew and glowed, changing colors of white, red, and yellow, dazzling the eye, yet Zonic saw definite hints of blue and orange. He heard the excitement of the crowd in the control room at the destruction of B2.

Something remained from the blast, even from the sight of Ed Zonic. Something at the core shot through the conflagration. It was black, roughly oval, nearly thirteen hundred yards diameter with a smoother surface than the meteor. It was not made of rock, and it was still on course for Earth.

Chapter 40

Nick walked into the airport, carrying only a large green rucksack he had used while at school. The coolness of the lobby accosted him with somewhat less of the generic unfriendliness of strangers about their travel plans. Perhaps it was the time of night he was traveling. Usually, he was sound asleep after 2:00 a.m. He hoisted his pack and walked to the information desk to find the military concourse where the Mexican plane was waiting to take him along the coast of Progreso. After a brisk walk, he found the military check-in station, where a wide-eyed woman of about twenty-four welcomed him with a large smile in a formal Mexican military uniform.

"I am Dr. Nicholas. I think you are expecting me."

"Yes, of course, Dr. Nicholas. Welcome. I am Major Reales. We are waiting for you. May I please check your back and see your identification, please?"

After the usual formalities, Nick and the young major were aboard the idling plane. They were the only passengers. One steward served them a rather luxurious Mexican dinner. The flight lasted more than four hours. The major seemed to make herself unavailable for questioning by busying herself with her military communication device for the better part of the trip. The modern midsized jet offered a gentle ride and quite comfortable accommodations, undoubtedly reserved for officials. The captain announced their landing, leaving Nick wanting to deplane as soon as possible. After a less than polite landing, the major escorted Nick through a manned underground corridor leading to a private parking lot where a tan sedan bearing military license plates waited for them.

"It is a twenty-minute drive to command central. General Gonzales and the science team are set up in the high school gymnasium. I should inform you that the city is under attack, and it is dangerous. I am armed."

Nick looked at her with the usual glance she received from men that are unaccustomed to dealing with a woman in a military situation.

"Have you seen these things up close?"

She wanted to look at him while speaking, seemingly her habit, but shared her attention with the dusty road leaving the airport parking lot.

"I have been briefed and read some holodiagrams, but I have not been in direct contact. You must be very important to Dr. Sanchez. You are the only one to come here from the scientific community. Do you know how to stop these things, Dr. Nicholas?"

She said, finally turning to offer him a warm look.

"I have some tests I must run which will tell me if I can do anything about it. I hope to be of some help."

"I hope you can. It is a mess down there."

The remainder of the trip included innocent small talk. Nick was able to avoid talking about his work as they pulled up to the military outpost that passed them in without more than a wave of recognition. The dusty road led through the outskirts of Progreso, which seemed rather unimpressive to Nick, being used to the larger vacation cities of Mexico he had visited some years ago.

An occasional military vehicle rode past them without incident, and Nick noticed that, in the early light of dawn, as farms and homes began to appear, not a single civilian was to be seen. All evacuated, he assumed. Major Reales made several communications relaying their location, each familiar with her friendly female coterie.

The city began to accumulate around the car. Nick looked behind to see two military vehicles behind them, possibly as an escort. The deserted town looked unnatural and gave Nick a chill along his back. The stores, restaurants, and homes, motionless and without life, greeted them with unconscious cheer.

"This looks like a nice place to visit. I'll have to come back when all this is over."

The major smiled and spoke into her small handheld radio. "We are five minutes away."

"Come in, Major, we are waiting for you," the voice responded through the little speaker in her hand. Reales brought the car down a wider street, revealing the high school. Military jeeps and trucks replaced the usual faculty and student vehicles turned the school into command central.

The guards at a makeshift checkpoint waved them in. A small jeep took its place in front of the large glass doors beyond where teens normally gathered for basketball games and pep rallies; Nick thought briefly of his own high school days and wondered how long this would last. *These people's lives should not suffer.*

They exited the car, and the major took him into the gym to find large cables across the floor, connecting various tables covered with computers, radios, lights, and other equipment. A man not in military uniform, with a bristling dark mustache, wielding a cup of coffee looking to be the most academic person in attendance, and seeming oddly in place among the local militia, raised his hand upon Nick's entrance into the gymnasium. Nick walked toward him with his free hand outstretched.

"Dr. Nicholas! I am Rene Sanchez. This is Dr. Alba and our ship's captain, Pepe Fernandez. We are so glad you are here. Come. We have much to do."

A table was set up at one end of the gym. Several sample boxes, papers, and computers scattered its top. Nick noticed a man in a red beret talking on a telephone. *Obviously, the man in charge,* he thought.

"I want you to see the latest footage of these creatures. They really are quite fantastic."

The three doctors pulled up chairs and huddled around the army's latest footage of an insect under attack by gunfire. Seemingly unaffected by the barrage protected by their hard outer shells, they fought fiercely, now having claimed two troops in the battle.

"Look here how the jaw has four protuberances. We can ascertain, the upper pair is for piercing and the lower two are specialized, smaller for cutting and this series of elongated organs for sucking bodily fluids. Have you seen anything like this, Dr. Nicholas?"

"It bears resemblances to several species. The body strikes me as that of a common cricket, while the numerous legs are like those of a centipede. That does not include many other features akin to a variety of creatures. I would say it is a new species or some kind of mutation. I am not a biologist. I can be of assistance to you by doing a sub-molecular analysis. I am sure the army has satellite DNA scanning in place. I can break into atomic system to view how it works and then perhaps I can tell you how to undo these things if possible. Do you have a sample of the fossilized eggshell?"

"Yes of course." Dr. Sanchez dug into his locking metal box and produced a chunk of the egg, and a plastic bag of insect skin.

Nick took it into his hands studied it, gingerly rolling it over in his long fingers.

"I hope you can spare this piece. You will get it back, of course. I think the tests I will run will provide some missing information. This material may tell me where these things came from and hopefully how we can neutralize them more efficiently. May I take it?"

He said with a true interest, nudging his glasses back into place.

"Naturally. I would suggest you put it into your sack before the general comes over to meet you. Not that he would have any objections, it's only that you never know when the military may decide to be restrictive in dire situations. Take this sample of its molted skin," said Dr. Alba, handing him a plastic bag with a skin sample sealed within.

"I agree, Dr. Alba," said Nick, slipping the samples into his rucksack and zipping it closed.

As if on cue, the general, now concluding some official strategy, began to walk over to greet his visitor.

"Dr. Nicholas, I trust our accommodations were satisfactory? We reserve the jet for high propriety individuals, mostly the president and foreign dignitaries. We are happy to have you here to help us."

"Thank you, General. I will do all I can to help, but I am afraid I will have to return to my lab to conduct the vital research necessary that may help you stop these things," said Nick, now becoming uncomfortable with the military setting as he considered the startling sound of rapid gunfire in the distance.

"We have neutralized twenty-two percent of the known infestation. The others will be harder to attack given their current location. Another problem has arisen. It seems that more of this pestilence is emerging from the sea. We could use some help the attack. Inform me personally." He gave an involuntary smile and turned back to the center of the gym.

The remainder of the morning was spent reviewing not only the target intel data collected but also the assault plans designed by the general. Nick observed the attack matrix proposed by Dr. Sanchez and Pepe. Many of the insects are hiding in areas where collateral damage is an issue. The team has devised a land bait strategy that Nick thought to be rather inhumane considering the livestock, yet it had real potential for luring the bugs out of hiding. Several cows, sheep, and pigs were placed in a simple corral near the location of some imbedded insects. Once the bugs came in the open for some fresh blood, the troops would quite simply open fire.

Nick was more eager to return with the sample and run tests on the fossilized egg, yet the live battle coordinated from the gym seemed exciting. Not being war-like by nature, the concept of coordinating a war from a school kept him more interested in the offensive than he typically would be. The day wore on, and before they had a chance to invite him to stay, Nick Nicholas's mind was eager to return to his pole barn laboratory.

"I have what I need. I really should get back to my lab, the sooner the better. My plan is to try to isolate the chemical assets of their DNA and try to counter it with a designer poison if you will, one that is specialized to kill only the particular gene format."

"The Mexican government is very much against the use of poisons in the environment. It was altogether abandoned as a method of combat. I suppose if it works, they may allow its use. Do you have to go today?" said Dr. Alba with disappointment.

"I can be more help to you running tests on these samples. I belong in the lab. I will excuse myself from lunch and catch the next plane home."

"There is something else. We have consulted with a xenobiologist from New York City, Fr. Vincenzo Sardi. He has helped us project into what the creatures may evolve with his artistic depiction of where they are going as they mature. He suggests that the excessive rapidity of their growth is in relation to their very long state of dormancy."

"May I have copies of your files concerning the Imago?"

"Yes, of course. Dr. Nicholas, you refer to them as Imago, which is the adult form of the insect, those ready to mate. How do we know they have reached maturity?" Sanchez asked.

"I fear that their rate of growth will summit at the point of sexual maturity leading to the next generation, which may happen sooner than we think." He stopped himself short, not wanting to hypothesize prematurely, then added, "How much bigger will they grow?"

Sanchez and Alba stopped, looked at each other blankly and offered no response.

*****

When Nick left for Progreso Airport at 1:00 p.m, Charley took a nap in the back room, sure that the sample in the oven will have cooled in the oven later that night.

Nick preset the timer before he left. When Charley woke in the warming morning sun, he enjoyed the early country sounds for a few minutes before being encouraged to rise by the alarm clock and thoughts of some breakfast.

After a large batch of pancakes and coffee, he went out to the barn to remove the globe as per Nick's instructions which he found written out for him, taped to the front of the super fridge. He reviewed the globes in the holder set carefully in the cabinet while still wiping the sleep from his eyes. Dredging the thought of having to go to the base from his mind, he closed the barn and went in for a shower. He redressed in the same clothes from the previous day and took the drive in to *MoonCorp*'s staging facility.

The fact that it was Saturday was not apparent in the mood of the workers. It was another day of work. *MoonCorp* was moving ahead tirelessly. Stan Duncan kept a fierce pace with Gerhard Steele who had been taking reservations for New Year's Eve for six months.

The *Junk Colossus* was returning today with some extra cargo, trash, and a group of workers changing shifts. *MoonCorp* was thirty percent complete, and from the real time images on the great screens hanging above the hangar floor, Charley noted that it was beginning to take an impressive form.

A tap on the shoulder surprised him, and for a moment dreading the sight of Stan Duncan with a pink slip, he turned to see Dana Kim smiling cheerfully.

"Dinner tonight?"

"Hey, that sounds like a good idea. I am sort of house sitting for Nick tonight. Why don't we have dinner there? We can order a pizza."

Dana thought for half a second and then returned, "That sounds great. I'll follow you there after work."

The rest of the day, the crews were detailing and checking the engines of the JC, preparing it for flight late Monday. Three o'clock came quickly. Charley found Dana waiting for him at the door after a quick trip to the cafeteria.

"Nick lives about twenty miles down that road. Can you keep up with me?"

"I'll give it a try."

The cars rolled past the gates and down the road toward Nick's house. At the halfway mark, Charley called to order the pizza with precise timing for it to arrive a minute after they got there. Charley was sure to outline his pizza timing process to Dana over the phone as she followed him closely, taking a moment to check her eye pull. It looked like it was holding. She tensed a bit now in preparation to take advantage of this experiment she had heard them talk about earlier that week. It would not be much longer that she would have to play this game. She hoped it would end soon. Charley had become much more than a friend to her. She had to stay close to him to do her job, but that closeness was more real than she admitted to herself. Charley's appeal to her was different from her affection for Steele. Not wanting to deal with a comparison headache, she turned the car into the driveway behind Charley, bringing it onto the gravel parking area in front of the pole barn, this time as an invited guest.

"Nice place Nick has here," Dana said walking in the coolness of the dark living room.

"Well, Nick has done rather well for himself. Stan has had him on the payroll for close to ten years now. I worked for him four years before I was let go for reasons I do not care to talk about much now; patent pending."

Charley gave a brief yet distracted tour, which was interrupted by the pizza delivery kid.

Dana unwrapped the food while Charley prepared some large icy soft drinks. They dug into the pizza, enjoying each other's quiet company. Charley broke the not uncomfortable silence. "I think I would like to get a house in the country. Those pole barns make great laboratories, which reminds me, I have to check on an experiment." He stood up, followed closely by Dana.

"I don't know if I should take you into the lab. This experiment is really top secret. Nick does not want anyone to know . . . " His voice trailed off, meeting her undeniable glance.

"Charley, I like to think of myself as more of a scientist and less of a student. When I am around you, I feel like a kid. You can show me the lab, I am an intern! I am taking this degree to be on the cutting edge of technology, not safety strapped in the back seat. *It is a PhD, remember?* I promise I will not tell anyone what I see, especially Dr. Nicholas. You have kept this secret, and you can't keep secrets from me. It's not right." She touched his chest delving deeper into his eyes.

"Dana, this is a big breakthrough. If I show you what is in there, I want your sacred oath that you will not tell anyone."

She looked at him for a moment of what seemed to Charley like intense appreciation, and silently, she kissed him. She pulled away, taking her purse from the chair and leading him by the hand to the front door. Charley followed along, checking his watch to see he had fifteen minutes to remove the sample from the oven. He grabbed their drinks (and a piece of pizza) and half ran across the gravel lot.

Charley entered the code in the door lock, and Dana found herself drinking in the sights of the lab as if for the first time.

He turned the lights and the computer on and moved quickly to the oven.

"It still had eight minutes to cool."

"What is it?" she demanded.

"In a nutshell, Nick has been doing holographic experiments with fossilized insect material in hopes of recreating an enhanced image. He succeeded by even more than he had originally expected. Rather than recreating an image, he has somehow opened a portal into the past where when in this box, one can actually be transported into the time when the fossil originated. It is the most remarkable thing I have ever seen."

Dana was without words. She moved to the projector, inspecting further the line of gloves and then the black box, lightly touching the components, then finally brought herself to ask, "How is it possible?"

"It's complicated. He has used a record of the cycles of the sun. He traced the sun's pattern thousands of years old. Somehow is allows entry into specific dimensions of time. Where genetically traceable life once existed now there is a multiplicity of times that we can actually experience. It's a mind-blower."

The bell rang on the oven. Charley ran over and, taking the glove, removed the globe from the oven and placed it in the holder.

"Impossible," she said, hoping for more.

"I'll show you, but you will need to swear that you will not tell anyone," he said searching her eyes for any shred of doubt. He found none.

Charley made a quick call to Bert and started up the system allowing concentrated radio solar power to be sent to his breakthrough solar panels. Charley felt a rush of excitement considering the newness of the last sample still warm from the oven. It will depict the latest sample recorded to date. He went to the holder, brought the globe into the empty slot, and connected the wires to the frame.

"When entering the box, we wear that rubber suit. You have to push your way through the light barrier. We are not going to do that now, but Nick has installed a peek window to see what is beyond. Let's take a look."

Charley said, moving the indicator to the last globe representing a period in the middle years of California in the twenty-first century. Soon, blue light entered the projector and moved into the final globe and onto the black box. The hum of power introduced through the jostling cables sent a chill along Dana's arms.

"Do you know when Nick is coming back?"

"He did not say. I expect a call anytime from him. When I get the call, you had better leave. I would rather not explain your presence here. It's too important to him to have any exposure. Come on, look at this."

They went to the peek door and opened it to reveal the world just over one hundred and fifty years ago. It was a typical Californian forested area with ravines seemingly recently ravaged by fire.

"I was inside and interacting with the past. We are obviously extremely careful about the applications this discovery presents. It is really exciting. I need a drink."

"I need one too. I'll get them." Dana went to the computer where the drinks were. After a quick look back, she fished out the knockout drug in a paper pouch and emptied it into his drink. She brought the drinks back, handing him his and taking a sip of her own.

She looked for a minute more, then timing the reaction the drug needed to take into effect so she can get him into a chair before he passed out. Dana knew that the antidotes would work quickly; he would be of the mind that he simply dozed off for a minute.

"This is remarkable," she said, walking toward the desk, looking around, and then taking a chair, hoping he would follow her, and he did.

"I have been suggesting to Nick some positive applications, but he is really concerned that it will be bastardized. We need to do more tests to determine the effect of our presence in the past. It could have horrible ramifications if misused." He took another deep swig of the drink.

Dana took a cue and stood, then moved behind him to offer a back massage.

"It seems to me that you are working very hard on this as well. All this and your regular job at the hangar must make you so tired. Now, I understand what has been wearing you down. It is a fantastic experiment."

"Yes, it is. Wow, that really feels good."

He said, flexing his neck in tandem with her touch. In a minute, he lay comatose in the wheeled chair. Dana looked around to see his head tilt forward to sleep.

She wasted no time walking fast to the computer and producing a blank data node and inserting it into Nick's computer. As the files were copying, she eyed the coffin-like box. She had to test this thing herself. With nervous hands, she removed the node and shoved it into her purse. She donned the rubber suit that was a few sizes too big. She rolled the sleeves and adjusted as well as she could. She put on the rubber cowl and gloves took a deep breath and took the steps to the inner glow of the black box.

Lifting the lid, she instinctually sniffed, noting the power burn but dismissing it as incidental, not dangerous. She stepped in, discovering the rules of the box. After some exploring, she found herself in the supine position, and she remembered what Charley said about pushing against the light barrier. She rolled with some force then found herself passing through what could only be described as a dream.

After a few moments of clenched eyes, Dana Kim was behind a rocky cliff overlooking a valley covered with trees. Before she had time to react to the natural wonder of this new dimension, she was fixed with an image that occupied her thoughts immediately.

A man was lying prone on the ground at the edge of the cliff. He was holding a rifle trained at something in the valley. All at once, she was aware of the sound of a large group of people in the valley. She wanted to look but stood frozen in her place. Then, a voice with some authority, obviously aided by a microphone, was addressing the crowd. She could make out most of the speech.

"In light of this disaster, we are comforted not only by our brave firefighters and abatement forces, but by the faith of the people of California."

The crowd erupted with cheers and applause.

It was apparent to her that this was someone important; it might even be the president. She thought back to her recollection of California history and remembered a terrible forest fire sometime in 2063. Presidents were known to travel to comfort the victims of such disasters. The gunman was very still, his head leaning hard against the stock of the gun.

She abandoned fear of drugging Charley and stealing into the box and replaced it with one narrowing thought. *She had to stop the gunman.* Moving as silently as she could, she started a quick jog at the gunman, and then jumped, aiming her feet at the neck and forcing all her weight hoping to disable him with one pounce. She landed right on the mark. She heard the subtle crack of his neck. His body went limp.

Now in a position to see further into the valley, she saw a large group of people, several thousand rallying around a podium bearing the American presidential seal. Taking in the sight for as long as she could before regaining her balance, she stepped back from the cliff, leaving the gunman limp and most certainly dead. *Karate finally came in handy*, she said to herself. Starting to reel a bit from what she had done, she moved back to the bar of blue light. Taking one final look around feeling rather important, after all having had prevented an assassination. She rolled along the rocky ground and found herself back in the box.

Back on the cliff, the gunman was still, now getting stiff but not from the crushing blow to the neck, but rather from the snakebite that had finally taken effect, perhaps while he was waiting for the president to come into place. The gunman would never have been a threat. He was dead before she hit him.

Dana composed herself in the box for a moment, then rose, instantly taking off the suit and placing it back in the place she found it. A glance over to be sure Charley was still sleeping eased her heavy breathing. She ran up the steps and closed the box then went down. She walked to her purse and found the special smelling salts containing an antidote that would revive Charley instantly. She took her place behind him when she was giving him a backrub and snapped open the smelling salts then waved them under his nose. After a few seconds, Charley revived to the soft touch of his girlfriend still rubbing his neck.

"Wow, that was some back rub. I think I fell asleep,"

Charley said, finding his voice behind a yawn.

"Did you hear what I have been saying? Charley Porter, I hope the next time I decide to pour my heart out to you, I suppose I am going to make sure you are awake," she said ending with a convincing pouty tick of her tongue.

"I am sorry. I must have been exhausted. Your touch was so soothing. What did you say?" Charley said, sounding close to worry.

"Oh, never mind. The moment is gone. I might remember later." She took the glasses and walked to the door. "I am going to get some refills. You had better shut that thing down before your boss comes back. I'll be inside."

Charley stood begrudgingly. Removing the last globe from the machine, he then placed it in the holder. He shut the system down, and crunched his way back to the house.

CHAPTER 41

The plane trip back afforded Nick some time to take nap, the setting sun prompting him pointedly to catch up on several lost hours of sleep. Before he ceded to rest, he gave a call to Charley. It was nearly nine o'clock when Charley answered his phone.

"Nick. How's Mexico?" Charley said, rather than a hello.

"It was a bit buggy from what I saw of it. They have an off-the-charts situation down there. I am on the plane back. I should be there around ten thirty. Did you remove the sample from the oven?"

"Of course, I did. It is in the holder cooling down now."

"I will be doing more sampling when I get back. It you want to stay and help, that would be great. I think you might want to see what comes next."

"I'll be there. See you at ten thirty."

Charley closed the phone and looked over to his girlfriend sitting beside him on Nick's couch where they had spent the last two hours by candlelight and whose mood he had been trying to decipher for the last half an hour. Either he was a bad judge of the female temperament (only of late), or she was good at hiding her feelings. She looked at him expectantly, moreover with a bracing mien, preparing for some bad news.

"That was Nick. He will be here at ten thirty."

"I am not angry with you. I find this experiment utterly fascinating. I think I should stay and document the experiment. Nick will understand."

"You are out of your mind. Absolutely not," Charley said, his tone frenzied.

"Well, here, it is a Saturday night, and I have to drive back to my little apartment and go to bed. Maybe I will stop at a bar and see if I can get lucky."

"Dana, please. I showed you this lab, something I wasn't supposed to do, and now you are making me feel guilty. Cut it out. You see how important this is. Understand I have a responsibility to someone, something. You have to know what that is like. You are a responsible person. Can you accept that I am respecting his work? How can this not mean anything to you?"

"Yes, Charley. I know what it means to be responsible. What I don't know is what *I* mean to you. Okay, I will leave. Call me tomorrow?" she said, with a surge of bogus jealousy laced with her natural feminine ease.

"Thanks for understanding. We'll find time to do something fun next week, I promise. I keep my promises, you know."

"Yes, Charley, I know."

She reached up on her toes and gave him a nice kiss on the lips, took her purse and walked out of the lab, with Charley looking after her like a puppy left home alone. After a few minutes alone in the chair, a pang hit Charley in what he would term as his true spot. He reckoned with this spot less and less lately, but no matter how he avoided it, he was there. *What did he really feel for Dana?* He certainly had addressed this issue on the surface but after weeks of the problem sitting center deep in his mind, it traveled into his gut. He loved her. She had everything he had dreamed of in a woman, and yet he was managing to turn her away time and time again.

He rubbed his head, hoping to reach some resolve. It became clear. He had to tell her. He had to do it, or she will disappear. Sitting on the couch, he wrestled with what might be the inevitability of a lifetime.

Dana Kim could be the answer to his life, yet he wanted to be certain. Not knowing how to find evidence of this made the feeling seem less and less like an experiment and more like an emotion impossible to properly express. *Maybe love is not science,* he thought, making his way back to the chair to think some more on the subject. Scientific method was probably the wrong approach when in love.

His phone interrupted his thoughts. "Charley Porter."

"Charley. It's Nick. I am about ten minutes away. Is everything all right there?"

"Couldn't be better. I'll be in the lab."

"Be there in nine-point-five," Nick said, closing the phone.

After the last turn onto the main road, Nick pulled up to the mailbox and, to his surprise, found a package from Kerry Mumphrey, the intern from *TerraLuna*. There wasn't a postmark on it. He must have dropped it off by hand. He gathered the mail and drove along the gravel path and into the garage. Parking the car and leaving the other mail in the passenger seat, he walked to the lab.

Charley gave a last-minute check of the lab to ensure that Nick would not suspect he had been using the holoimager. Things seemed normal. He sat in the chair and flipped through a science magazine until Nick came in carrying his rucksack and a small box.

Nick came into the lab in a hurry and quickly opened his tabletop computer and began accessing his e-mail.

"Yo, Doc," Charley said casually.

He found a note from Ed Zonic:

Nick,

Kerry Mumphrey has the sample and will drop it off personally. He was afraid to send it in the US mail. I do not blame him. The latest scanning technology may have flagged it. The rumor mill around TerraLuna is going to be a shocker. Are you ready for this? The meteor sample is comprised of some sort of cryobiotic organic compound. They say it contained alien reproductive material! What? Let me know what you make of it-Ha. —Zone.

"Here is a fragment from the meteor that hit the moon." He placed the box on the computer desk. He opened his rucksack and produced the piece of shell found at the bottom of the Gulf of Mexico.

"Here is the fossilized shell that has been dated sixty-five million years ago."

Charley looked at his friend still half following his girlfriend's train of thought.

"I have both of the pieces of the puzzle, boy and girl. Only two pieces, so the answer is easy," Nick said, his mind stretching into the potential of the new information.

"They seem to be using Earth as a sort of a Petri dish. Okay, now what are we going to do with them?"

"Experiment, of course. I'll bet you want to know what I am thinking? Yes. Yes, you are Charley Porter. We are going to make a globe out of each of these two beauties and place them in the system. What I hope to see is if my system can be used as a reference to show us the origin of these samples. We have the egg that is dated sixty-five million years. It has been on Earth that long and therefore subject to all those years of Earthly influence. The other sample's the male aspect of this species that seems to have arrived earlier this month in 2168. My system may be able to do it. Each sample is a reference point for the others. I think that's how it works—solar cycles being the constant. Do you see? Point 'A' and point 'B' can be connected. Come on, you need to help me. Tomorrow, if this works out, we will be able to see not merely into the past but into an alien past. Hopefully, we can find a way to stop them. Well, Charley, is this progressive enough for you?"

Charley made his way without speaking, forcing his mind further away from those of Dana. They gathered the samples and began to work.

*****

Tico and Pepe sat on the long cement flowerbed that spanned the side of the school soon after dawn of the next day. An average day would have them already at sea, fishing. Military vehicles came and went as they waited the assaults to end. Thoughts of home and fresh fish dinners in the comfort of their kitchen waded in and out of their minds as a truck they hadn't seen before pulled into the parking lot. Pepe recognized it as a livestock truck, bearing a load of cows doomed to be land bait on which the pestilence will feast. It would be their last meal.

The trap was to be set up in a park on the edge of town. The cattle would be tethered to a communication pole, and when gathered, the military would blast them. Pepe had overheard the general saying that they would kill one of them to propagate the smell of blood. hoping to draw them more quickly. A terrible waste, but ultimately, he thought, it would be worth it to eliminate the damned things.

Military personnel came to be parked truck and inspected the beasts. Within fifteen minutes, the truck pulled away with an escort of personnel, supply, and assault trucks.

A large half-track truck pulled up, carrying Sanchez and Alba. The window came down. Sanchez called out to Pepe.

"Senor, would you like to come along and see the trap being set? You two look like you could use something to do today."

"There is not much else to do. I would not mind seeing more of these devils destroyed. Come on, Tico, let's go for a ride."

They climbed in the truck, carrying two other armed men and rode off to join the convoy. After a fifteen-minute ride, the public park could be seen in the distance. Pepe looked out with Tico on his lap taking in the scenery and enjoying the air-conditioned ride in the clean truck which was obviously not used very much and was probably kept in the garage for some time—it was, after all, the Mexican national guard. A voice over the military radio cracked on with a message.

"We have a major group gathering at coordinates North 78 and West 27. Unit 55, please investigate and report," the voice instructed.

The driver looked back to his passengers.

"It is only five minutes from here. The general wants us to check it out."

The half-track pulled ahead of the convoy and turned off a side ride to investigate the call. Dr. Alba felt a warm sensation in her stomach at the sudden change of plans and braced herself silently for whatever might happen. Soon, their objective became apparent.

"It's a radio tower. It is covered with them. There must be over one hundred of them all the way up the tower."

The driver informed the voice on the other end of the radio.

"Proceed to a safe range. Send us some pictures from the telephoto mobile video. Satellite feeds are interrupted by some sort of interference. The general wants to study this activity before taking action," the voice replied.

The driver activated a video camera with a link to the command center located in the front grill of the truck. A screen in windshield flipped from navigation to telephoto footage of the insects climbing over each other to find position. The academics watched soundlessly, forming hypotheses as the image telephotoed to a proper view, with the truck inching closer to the tower and rifles held firmly in the hands of the soldiers.

As they approached, a sound joined the pictures. At first, it was faint, then it grew louder as they closed in, sounding more like a buzzing vibration than anything else. The soldier in the passenger seat took the window down slowly to get a clearer idea of the noise. One of the guardsmen opened his window to half, letting the hot air into the truck along with a seething chorus of throbbing emanations. Dr. Alba opened her window and listened.

"It sounds much like the cicada in late fall. I thought they were loud. This is almost hurtful."

She closed the window, thinking for a moment she saw the glass vibrate from the insects' relentless song. The camera continued to relay the footage to the command center.

General Gonzales looked intently at the screen, then to his captain.

"What are they doing, Captain?"

"I do not know, sir. I can remember that other insects used a call like this to attract a mate. That is their way of letting the members of the opposite sex know where they are."

"Are you saying that is a mating call, Captain?"

"I cannot say, sir."

The soldiers parked at a safe distance from the radio tower. The swarm of increasing size climbed over many others to reach nearly its full length. Then, a somehow audible pop was heard in the sky. A flash of light drew the attention of the passengers of the parked military vehicle in silence. A red flaming ball was seen cascading its way Earthward with a white plume of smoke in its wake. As the bogey entered the atmosphere, it began to change. Its outer shell flaked away as it went, and soon, something living emerged during the flight to Earth. Still curled up and safe from its cryptobiotic journey, the object hurtled closer to the radio tower. Its descent was interrupted by a natural separation. It split into two pieces. Friction-warmed air treated the bodies of two insects, adults in search of their brood, called by their progeny from their new world. The Imagoes came.

*****

After preparing two globes containing the alien components for life, Nick found his way to his bed for some well-deserved sleep while it cooked in his specialized oven. Charley, not prepared to sleep without some food, stood at the super fridge to pick out a late-night snack. After some more meatloaf and mashed potatoes covered in fantastic gravy, he went to the back bedroom and slept.

Nick woke after ten. His first thought was of the two hours and forty minutes remaining before the latest samples would be ready for testing.

His second thought was of some breakfast. He found his way into the kitchen. Charley's snoring resounded down the hall.

He took a long shower, recapping the numerous events of the last twenty-four hours. Relishing the chaotic flurry of events as he toweled dry and dressed averted his usual morning bout with the blues.

Leaving the bedroom, he heard the telltale sound of the food machine dispensing another meal for Charley. Nick walked into the kitchen, meeting his friend's gaze who was holding two plates of food.

"You are unbelievable," he said, going for a coffee mug.

"I need the basic nutrients for survival."

"You eat as if you are an endangered species."

"I may be the last one of my kind. I must feed."

"I want to run some quick tests before we start. There will be time. The samples need another couple of hours to cook."

Charley scooped his scrambled eggs onto a large biscuit, unsuccessfully attempting to make a sandwich.

"Nick, I have a question. To whom should we bring this experiment? Should we get some technical advice first, or take it directly to Stan? You know he will want the action on this. Remember, he does technically own the rights to your experiments."

"This work was started before I worked for *MoonCorp*. I have documentation of that fact. Not that I have discluded Stan as a backer—it is simply not in his area of concern. There are some scientists I have considered sharing with, no one conclusively."

"I think bringing a fresh mind in may help you clean the system up a bit. Someone who will ask basic questions may balance out the highly technical mode of thinking you have been in, resulting in new insights," he said, giving Nick a pointed glance then taking a large bite of his tenuous egg sandwich.

"I assume you have someone in mind?"

"Well, as a matter of fact I do. I think my friend, the PhD candidate Dana Kim would offer an objective point of view. She has a brilliant scientific mind and . . ."

"And you like her," Nick finished he sentence.

"That is well, beside the point. It's true, yet beside the point."

"I'll think about it. Finish your breakfast. I am going to get the lab started up." Nick topped off his coffee and left the kitchen.

Twenty minutes later, Nick found himself staring at some probability problems posed by the infusion of the alien substances. A long sip of coffee offered little help. Many variables wrestled with this attention. One item did ring as a necessity, that being the irradiance modulator from sample one to sample thirty-six. Luckily, the data Ed Zonic sent him on the original meteor included the sector of space from which it originated. Adjusting the contact sensitivity from the sun to that sector in space to detect the constant, though faint exposure would need to be tested until the system, linked the two samples by their association to photonic exposure strong and consistently enough to turn the system over. He rearranged the globes with the highest slot for the sixty-five-million-year sample available for the globe with the new sample containing a suspension from the eggshell found on the sea floor at Yucatan. He positioned latest sample of the male alien sample into the last slot now totaling thirty-six globes.

"The sensors in the PFC will test the atmosphere mixture, temperature, and other qualities of the alien world. I imagine it should be similar to Earth since the creatures have little problem surviving in Mexico. Hand me sensor from the bottom drawer of the desk"

Charley opened the drawer without a word and brought the sensor to Nick. He plugged it in to the computer, programmed it and then inserted it into the jack on the side of the PFC.

He went to the computer, activated the indicator to the alien fossil year globe and engaged the system. It would not activate. Nick stared at the system, then after a few minutes of readjusting the globes to properly align in the rack. He tried again—still no activation.

"I need to calibrate the sensitivity. I am not sure of which sample is not aligned. I am going to leave it on and adjust the levels from either sample." Dr. Nick said over his shoulder to his assistant. "Let me know if there is any change!"

After fifteen minutes of leveling the sensitivity factors, the system came alive with a lurch of refined solar electricity bringing the familiar blue light into being.

"It's there!" Charley shouted.

Nick spun out of his seat and stood in awe at the PFC bathing in the esoteric blue light.

"The imager has tapped into the alien world!" Nick scanned the readings from the sensor hanging in the box with quick glances, eyes widening as he read the results.

"Sensor readings are available. Temperature 83 degrees Fahrenheit, atmosphere mix contains ample oxygen, radiation levels within safe parameters. This is amazing. Its atmosphere is like Earth—a bit hotter, but I will not burn up."

"You are going in now?" Charley said.

"I will wear this compact Aqua-Lung and mask for protection."

After being sure he was not exposing any bare skin, he said to Charley. "I am going in, why not?" Nick dressed in the wet suit. Nick moved with a quicker step than Charley had seen in some time. Taking the bag of standard supplies, including the new personal motion detector belt, he eagerly climbed the stairs to the black box. He paused to pull the guns from his rucksack and place them in the bag. He checked the sensor wire from the box and climbed in looking over his shoulder to Charley, "Keep an eye on me buddy. I installed a live feed on the computer. Just open the 'Live Feed' icon."

"That's what worries me," Charley countered.

"What?"

"That you will end up *live feed* . . . for the aliens!"

Nick assumed the supine position, with his eyes scanning the blued surroundings beyond the temporal haze. It seemed darker than the other epochs he had visited. Before rolling in he retrieved his flashlight from the bag, tucked it under his arm, and rolled in, holding his breath as a precaution.

Nick found himself in a place immediately warmer than his laboratory. It was dark. He assured himself that the ultra-blue light limned his escape from behind. As his eyes adjusted, glints of red light focused his eye to the distance. After a moment, he connected the heat with the faint red light. He was apparently within proximity to some sort of volcanic activity.

The atmospheric readings from the remote sensor still registered a breathable atmosphere. He removed the Aqua-Lung and slowly attempted to breathe. The air was acrid and warm yet not unfriendly to his lungs. After a few drafts of air punctuated by some coughing, he stabilized himself, finding a need to see where he was. He took the binoculars from the bag. He set the switch to night vision mode and keyed in on the distance between himself and the cracking, rocky ground. The area was crawling with hundreds of very large insects centralized in the middle of a large rocky plain that seemed roughly circular. A forest of dark, thick-branched trees bearing leathery leaves encircled the raised mound, with most of its vegetation burned off by the heat emanations from below. Nick was located rather far from the edge of the volcanic area, two hundred yards ahead, with the forest forty paces behind him. Amidst the hot, sulfur-laced air, he still felt a large looming chill run up behind him.

After a sharp look behind him, he took the motion detector belt from the bag and clipped it snugly in place above his headband camera on his head (which he had been able to do with greater and greater ease from repetition), and he began taking footage. He snapped on the motion detector which would send an indication of any movement within seventy-five yards of his position. Nick adjusted the telephoto as he walked with deliberate steps toward the activity around the center of the hot hill ahead.

The insects had an odor that stood thick in the air around him. The entomological musk impeded his senses. They owned the planet. He adapted by breathing with shallow breaths. As Nick took the rise in the landscape, his legs absorbed the strain, and after traveling just twenty paces from the box, he noted he was sweating. Moving forward, wanting a clear picture, he stopped and looked around, adjusted the camera and observed the scene ahead.

The insects seemed to move faster than the ones he saw at Progreso. He touched the control on the camera to focus on what they were doing around a raised hill at the very center of the forest-lined area. With random bursts of energy, an individual insect would run up the hill (perhaps due to the heat) and shake its rear section for a minute or so, leaving something behind. Without hesitation, it scurried down the hill and into the swarm below. Nick pulled the camera to the side and used his binoculars to get a closer look at the top of the hill. After a bit of focusing, he saw what the insects were doing. The top of the hill was strewn with what were unmistakably eggs. An insect ran into his view and laid an egg that seemed translucent at first, covered with an ample amount of whitish goo that quickly dried, perhaps as a protective coating to preserve the eggs from the heat. After ten minutes of egg laying, a pod of at least five hundred coalesced eggs was alone on the hill.

Armed with what he thought would be indistinguishable from professional footage, Nick lowered the camera and filmed the swarm of insects alive with communal buzzing at the bottom of the hill.

The choral, rhythmic sounds reminded him of a swarm of feral ants or bees if the sound were amplified—dangerous in their heighted state of frenzy. It brought him back to a feeling he remembered as a child. The cicada-like song faded in and then out, heralding a variety of ends of summer days. Trees covered them from sight, offering a clever angle to their domination as of the voice of nature.

Without warning, the ground lurched below him, nearly knocking him to the ground. A resounding crack from the beneath the center of the hill shook the ground and exploded, small fissures all around him spewing steam and rocks into the air. After regaining his balance, he turned to the hill. It had risen at least fifty feet higher than before; the cache of eggs still glued to the top, supported by a column of rock.

Scree rolled down the hill from the ensuing tremors. Insects scrambled away to the burned forest, to escape what looked like an impending explosion. Nick backed up, sidestepping toward the PFC, hoping not to be caught in a stampede of insects that may come his way. The camera had fooled his eye. The swarm was actually further away, and it seemed he would be able to make it back. With newly bought time, he adjusted the camera and started filming, now carefully stepping backwards and taking in the frantic retreat of the crazed female insects ahead.

The ground was swelling. The hill had raised more than one hundred feet. Red-hot glowing lava began to light the dark terrain and dripping down the hill. Minor explosions beset the flat around the hill sending lava streaming in the air falling upon the fleeing swarm. He spun the camera to capture the effect of the lava on the creatures and squinted for want of comprehension at what he was seeing.

As the lava sprayed over the insects, rather than seeing them melt away from the excruciating heat, they remained intact in the molten rock. The insects turned in upon themselves, bringing the head forward to its rear, their legs clenching the underside of the body. A surge of white goo could quickly be seen about them, and then much like when laying the eggs, the insects hardened, forming a protective coating about them and initiating a completed physical change.

An array of dark balls sat in pools of lava. How long could they be protected from the lava with this defense? Heat certainly was not a problem for these creatures, he noted as something to remark to Dr. Alba when he returned. They were like the tardigrade from Earth in their ability to secure themselves from severe elements.

Still stepping back, keeping the lava and insects safely at a distance, he looked again at the hill that seemed to rise higher yet into the night sky. Constriction in the ground, now feeling hotter beneath his feet, indicated increased turmoil in the bowels below.

Looking back, the box light appeared just beyond his reach. Nick regripped the camera, balancing it skillfully before his eyeglass lens. He wanted to stay as long as it was safe to see what would happen. Safety was kicked from his senses with an explosion that rocked the area, sending him flying in the air with his arms and legs reeling for control. He hit the ground flat on his back, hoping he could raise his head to see. Luckily, his neck worked.

He saw what must have been the entirety of the lava lit hill, along with much of the surrounding terrain, nearly a mile across, blast off into space propelled by a fiery column of flame, rock, and lava. The heat against the air could nearly be seen rushing at him at an unimaginable speed. The hill itself that was now rocketing skyward was now an entity in and of itself—with a purpose, like a spacecraft. Soaring upward from the power of the blast, it turned and rolled into the thinning atmosphere beyond. *Incredible!* Nick thought.

He ran as fast as he could to the blue light looking ironically like a coffin. He spastically rolled to the light first missing, and then another roll brought his body partly into the box. Somehow his foot was lodged beyond the light. It was caught on a rock. He pulled it. Standing with his arm upstretched like the Statue of the Liberty to open the lid of the box and then jumping onto the stairs with a bounce, he was out of the box, with his shoe smoking as the rubber coating burned off.

Charley looked at Nick, his hair tangled about his head, glasses askew, and breathing heavily. He stood and nearly doubled over taking a quick assessment of his body.

"Nick, are you hurt?"

"No. I am fine. I'm out of breath."

He took the headband off and handed it to Charley who was ready to help.

He took slow steps to the computer station, easing his way up the stairs. He switched off the helioladder of globes, then re-aligned the indicator to the second alien sample.

"Download this onto a node. I need to see what happened at the second alien sample."

Charley transferred the video onto a blank node and then brought the camera back to Nick, who was adjusting the imager. The lab was cool to Nick in contrast to the volcanic world and with his heart not beating as fast this time.

"What happened in there?" Charley said, searching Nick for information.

"It was more incredible than the dinosaurs. I was on another planet. The insects had eggs on a volcanic surface that exploded into space. Apparently, these creatures have unusual intricate propagation habits. I am going back to the . . . meteor event. We will review the video after I film this next period."

He said as he commanded the machine's sliding reader methodically along the line of globes to the very last one in the thirty-sixth position.

Nick turned and climbed into the box.

Charley looked after him, trying to remember the last time he saw Nick this excited about anything. He followed him the box, helping him close the lid. Charley then opened the peek door and watched as Nick disappeared into the ambiguous blue.

He prepared himself for the change in the atmosphere, holding his breath and taking short gasps of alien air until his lungs become accustomed to the slight yet present difference.

He sat up to get his bearings. Looking around, he found that it was daylight. The alien sun was at least three times larger in the sky than Earth's sun. He kept his eyes nearly shut while adjusting to the brightness; the goggles helped very little. From what he could see, the scenario was similar to the previous period. He stood near the edge of a large circular plain surrounded by thick trees. They seemed to have more leaves than before; obviously, it was a different season—an alien spring. Insects gathered near the center of the plain where a large hill protruded, cracked with fissures and steam.

He started the camera still at maximum telephoto, giving him very impressive pictures despite his distance from the center. Insects systematically crawled up the hill to do what he perceived as a similar communal duty. Once at the top, the creatures shook their abdomens, excreting white patches on an outcropping that had been added to for what must have been some time, for it was large as a school bus. Afterward, a copious amount of the protective secretion was added to protect the specimen.

Nick left the camera running, moving the arm over and using his binoculars to get a better view. Swarms of nearly a thousand males coagulated at the ridge below the hill, writhing in an exciting frenzy. He noted that they were moving faster that their female counterparts. They were spinning on a firm axis perhaps with one of their claws, anchoring them in the rocky ground. After several spasmodic spins, the males excreted a large glob of thick, whitish semen, planting their seeds on the burgeoning hill in the preparation or the impending catapulting into the heavens. It was a most amazing system to send the sperm to meet with the eggs back on Earth across the galaxy. It was the slowest metabolic act of reproduction he had ever seen. He couldn't help thinking if other planets were infested by this method or if perhaps Earth was the only one. Maybe they did not know themselves. Was it a joint instinctual effort of trial and error, or was there some gravitic navigational function in place?

The ground shook, sending a spasm of insects scurrying back into the ridge, foretelling repetition of the activity from the ancient egg exodus. A section of the hill near the center exploded, realigning the shape of the hill and sending tremors back at Nick who had replaced the camera lens to his eye to get some quality photographs.

A rivulet of magma oozed from the side of the hill, slowly nearing the sperm sacks. A low rumble had ensued after the explosion and continued to herald what Nick thought could only be a repetition of the last event that sent the egg clutch into space and perhaps consciously toward Earth.

He noted (and filmed) that as before, insects that had come in contact with the lava rolled themselves into impenetrable balls protecting them from incineration.

Still filming Nick, felt a vibration at the small of his back. Immediately, he knew it was the motion detector alerting him of movement behind him. He turned to see several insects coming from the trees, slowly at first, then all at once, they rushed to him with fangs first. Too far to dive into the box light, he fumbled with the plastic bag and grabbed one of the guns. Luckily it was the laser weapon. He flipped off the safety and began rapid blasts at the creatures while edging his way to the light. Two immediately were stopped as if hit by a brick wall, the others unaware of an assault continued at him. He fired multiple shots until all the insects were left screaming and twitching their bodies ripped apart by the virulent concentrated beams of light. The grounds rumbling from behind him indicated that the hilltop was going to explode sending, the seminal compliment toward Earth that would lead to the infestation of 2168.

He sidled up to the box light, hoping to get pictures of the actual eruption, while watching the forest edge for any signs of further attack. None came. He remained for another fifteen minutes until the climactic explosion finally came, sending what seemed to be a somewhat smaller section of the hill cascading into the white sky and turning it black and red by sending a shower of rocks and smoke into the air in its wake. He stayed for as long as he could. A running fissure quickly breaking its way in his direction prompted him to escape back into the light. Soon, he was back in the confines of the box still holding his gun, with Charley's wide face staring through the peek hole. He was surprised by the sight yet, after the alien ordeal, it was certainly welcome.

"Shut it down!" Nick yelled to his assistant looking to him with urgency. Charley moved to the shutdown sequence. The blue light slowly faded as Dr. Nicholas sat up in Photonic Focusing Cabinet.

CHAPTER 42

Leslie did not go to a bar. Driving back to her apartment, she tuned in to a classical music station, regretting that she never studied music as it offered her great comfort. The slow melodic strings played very personally to her heart as the dark highway unfolded. She knew what was happening as she brushed a dark tear from her eye. It was Charley. She could not think of anything else. Perhaps it was his gullibility or it was his honesty that she all at once defined as a great resource, something missing in her life lately.

The music swelled. It brought upon a slow exhale with a soft, intent piano movement. She felt a twinge in her lower abdomen, and there was Charley. He was so loyal. He loved his work, was true to his friends and had a genuine passion for science. Her criteria for a mate had always included someone with financial potency. Of course, Charley was not poor by any means, yet he certainly did not have the resources of Gerhard Steele. Carefully, she began to rethink her motives for admiring the man that had put her up to this ridiculous scam.

The subject of Steele planted itself in her mind as she pulled up to her apartment complex. Honesty was a trait that could not be used to apply to the man, and for the first time this, angered Leslie. Why should the basic human precept of honesty be something to shove aside for decadence and glory? What was more important?

She took the car into the garage under the building, thinking again of the scope of the defense system and the time experiments, fathoming the purity of its scientific integrity, and tears welling up in her eyes. Putting the car in park and taking a tissue from her purse, she toweled her eyes. When she finished and used her cleared sight, there was an image of Charley again. Consulting her adult sense of emotion perhaps more seriously than usual, she admitted to herself that she loved him. There was no way she could betray the concept of truth she had built her life around for the sake of Steele's shallow manipulation. Moving out of the car with purpose, she admitted silently that the information she possessed could ruin Charley's resource of honesty that she so suddenly, terribly wanted to keep intact.

She tumbled the lock of her temporary home's door, welcoming the peaceful quiet. Leaving the lights off, she showered and dressed immediately into warm flannel pajamas, ready to review thoughts anew with the random consideration of dreams. A red indicator light pulsed from her phone. The phone had been off for some time. She pushed the power button and accessed the video e-mail. It was Steele.

"Leslie. I need to talk to you. Tomorrow is Sunday. Call me from a holophone at eleven o'clock. I am at *TerraLuna*."

Steele's visage disappeared from the screen.

Leslie set the phone on the table resisting, the temptation to slam it down. Still in darkness, she turned the radio on and tuned it from the popular music station to the classical station, wanting to continue the way she felt earlier. Once in the bedroom she crawled into bed, soothed by melodic swells, and was soon asleep.

She woke to the continued strains of horns and strings gently overlapping and after a sound sleep, her purpose encountered the need for change. She had to confront Steele. She dressed quietly then made a cup of tea and toasted half of a bagel. The apartment seemed rather tamed by the nightlong exposure to the music. She sat in safe silence for a few moments, wrapped in the warm atmosphere created by the music.

Soon she was on the highway again to meet with Steele at the holophone center and was rehearsing what she would say. They had a history of arguments that always seemed to end with her being seduced by some power offer. Remembering the foolish things she had done made her feel alone. The need to purge this weak idiocy from her memory grew as she approached the holophone center in San Bernardino.

The center was rather new. A bright, sun-lit circular lobby included a ring of comfortable chairs. The length of the facility was lined with individual doors leading to private calling rooms where a three-dimensional image of the person to whom you wished to speak appeared complete with surround sound. She walked in and was pleased to see that it was not very busy. The receptionist greeted her with a warm smile.

"Good morning, Ma'am. Will you be making a holo call today?" The young girl asked with sincere innocence.

"Yes. I need to place a holo call to the new station at the *TerraLuna* resort. You know the one on the moon? You can connect me, can't you?"

"Wow, the hotel on the moon. Have you been there?"

"No. Not yet."

"Do you have a code card for the *TerraLuna* holostation?"

Leslie opened her purse and produced the card Steele had given her. She handed it to the girl, who inspected the raised numbers set upon a smiling picture of Gerhard Steele and the *TerraLuna* logo.

"This will work just fine. You have used our station before?" The girl asked politely.

"Yes, I have. I know how to use it. Which room may I use?"

"Room number four is ready for you. Enjoy your call."

Leslie took the card and walked into the wide hallway to the room with a holographic "Number 4" hovering above the doorframe.

The room consisted of a control panel with touch-tone numbers and a card reader. The lighting system was rather dim, but she could see the dozens of imaging projectors placed on the walls and ceiling used to create the three-dimensional image of the other party. Leslie was on time. It was just eleven o'clock. She placed the card in the reader and entered Steele's personal number. The small computer screen in the console read: *Thank You. We are processing your request.*

After a few seconds, the lights dimmed even further, and the holo projectors came to life, creating a life-sized three-dimensional image of Gerhard Steele. He was smiling an innocent smile, very much unlike that of the receptionist at the front of the store.

"I see my little geisha girl is looking rather fine this morning. I can only imagine the effect you have on those boys at *MoonCorp*," Steele said, flashing a white smile, surprisingly dressed in his blue business-as-usual suit on a Sunday morning.

"Thanks, Gerry. You look good too. How is the weather up there, and why didn't you tell me you were going to the moon? Wasn't I supposed to go with you? That is what you told me, isn't it?" she said, unconsciously pouting.

"Actually, there isn't any weather up here. There isn't an atmosphere. You know that. I had to come up yesterday, quite unexpectedly. We have had some developments that needed my personal attention."

The lights flickered, distorting his image. It was not a fully detailed holograph, like the ones she saw in Charley's apartment, one that gave a less-than-perfect image of actual presence.

"I need personal attention too, Gerry. I really do not think even you have enough to spend on me," she said, resetting the tone of the conversation.

"You are mad because of the speech I made about taking my mother to the grand opening of *TerraLuna*. She will be there, but she won't be staying in my suite, you will," Steele said, hoping to mollify her.

"What? Are you sure about that, Mr. Steele? What makes you certain that I do not have other plans?" she blurted, striking a firm while still slightly unreal holographic pose.

"Other plans for the grand opening? You are angry about something. Stop your general bitching and get to the point. Tell me what they are, these other plans?" he replied, standing in his blue suit at the *TerraLuna* holostation.

"Now, I have you listening. This could be a first. Maybe it's time for you to hear some specific bitching. When I first met you, I was infatuated by you, Gerry. You took me out to exquisite restaurants on a whim, tossed me fur coats and whisked me away to other countries, barely able to take my lab coat off. You have been making steady purchases of my time, in exchange for what I thought was affection. I see now I was nothing more than a stupid lure to catch a stupid fish. Has it occurred to you how insulting that is to me? I have been doing these errands for you for two years, and it has transformed into criminal activity." She began to pace, limited more by the parameters of the phone room than by her anger.

"You are upset about something. What could I have done to irk you? I promised a great job and something much more valuable—my devotion. I want to be with you. This current sortie of ours is really not as important as us. *TerraLuna* is opening soon, and I realize I haven't had much time for you. Is that it? You must tell me what has turned you suddenly so sour. I deserve an answer," Steele said, studying her image, appearing upset as his holophone clearly indicated.

Leslie raised her arms and flapped them uselessly to her sides.

"It's wrong, Gerry. What you made me do was wrong. These people are genuine scientists, and they deserve recognition and respect for what they are doing. I will not be party to your exploitation of their sincerity."

Steele watched her image that, despite the fair reception, expressed her dismay very well. He had calmed her before when she was upset, but this time, he was unable to touch her. Their holograms were still for a few seemingly unnatural moments.

"Leslie, think about how I can help them . . ."

"You are only concerned about helping yourself, and I refuse to participate anymore. I will complete my fake stint at *MoonCorp*, and after that I want nothing to do with you or *TerraLuna*. I hope a meteor smashes the damned place." Leslie fought tears yet lost, sending holographic moisture down her cheeks.

"Leslie . . ."

"I am not finished. If you install that defense system, I will publicly confess as Dana Kim that I stole the plans as a direct agent for you, for money. It's true. Then freaking Dana Kim will disappear forever, and I can have my blonde hair back."

"What has come over you?"

Steele said, extending a holographic hand to try to wipe away her tears.

Leslie recoiled, slapping through his hand made of light.

"Also, I will expose you if you utter a syllable about Dr. Nicholas's other experiment. Yes, I spied for you, and I am in the wrong too. Dana will take the fall, but you are the puppeteer behind the screen. Once all media outlets are fully notified, Leslie Davis will disappear as well. This is what will happen, Gerhard Steele, and there is nothing you can do about it," she concluded, now closely facing his stunned image squarely as it searched for words. Steele looked at her quizzically, trying to evoke some angle with which to sway her. He was not certain that any temptation would change her mind. Then, a creeping suspicion finally found its way into the rapid workings of Steele's mind.

"You slept with him. You have gone and fallen in love with either Nicholas or Porter or both of them, and now you champion their cause. How romantic. Let me tell you this, Miss Davis. I have offered you all that is mine. If you had completed this task and not had this flight of righteousness, it would be all yours. Have it your way. Make the sacrifice, it becomes you. You should think again, very carefully about what you are throwing away!" he said smugly and tapped the console. His image disappeared. Leslie pulled the card from the reader and fell back into the chair with closed, weeping eyes and failing to compose her emotions yet relieved that she had done the right thing.

*****

All screens from the generals down to the cooks in the cafeteria at the high school were now trained on the fantastic pictures of two insects the size of dump trucks soaring the skies above the communication tower. Luckily, the mission had excluded the media, or at least for the time being, according to information last given to the general. It would not be long before Ms. Morales would be linking video for a story to send to the world from the Media Center. As the general weighed the decision to go to the field, he witnessed the unfurling of the insects' massive wings. Large wafting stretches of wing looking leather-like and seeming like sails on an ancient ship expanded and found the wind.

The general maintained his strategy to observe the pattern of the creatures now obviously enervated on the tower, making short, erratic movements along its length and increasing the cadence of their rhythmic song. The larger insects did not look exactly alike. One was nearly a fifth smaller and had a slightly different shape to the abdominal area. They flew in nearness, indicating that they were going to the same place, and that place was the tower. After fifteen minutes of what appeared to be acrobatic flying for the sake of drying their giant wings, the huge bugs focused their flight and began descent.

Jaime Gonzales opened the radio channel, speaking clearly and pointedly in the fashion to which his troops had become accustomed.

"Air command, ground crews, and all other on- and off-site tactical teams, our primary function at this time will be reconnaissance. If these insects have a purpose, we must learn what that is, as these creatures are growing more and more resistant to our weapons. We do not know what they will do next. Stand by."

Flying at what Dr. Alba thought to be a very steep angle, the large insects came into view, nearing the tower, turning, and hovering to manage a landing while taking wide spans of space with their rapidly beating wings. She recalled how flies move and now was experiencing the same effect, only millions of times larger. She sat in the vehicle, as did the other passengers holding their hands to their ears for nearly fifteen minutes until a supply truck arrived with protective ear wear.

They finally reached the ground, their many legs tamping and flopping, testing its viability. They seemed to have fewer legs than the smaller variety; perhaps they lost them over time. Dr. Alba wondered how old these creatures might be. Despite their age, the legs were many times longer than baseball bats and their fangs were like large machetes. The centipede-like head turned and stretched for some reason, perhaps testing the breathable surface air. The creatures seemed to be anxious and skittish, ready to fly off at a moment's notice. Making revolutions in one place looked like they were surveying the area, yet after more observations, Dr. Alba detected that it was some sort of dance, an assortment of movements conveying communication.

The dancing had torn the grass very badly. Clumps of sod flew into the air, punctuating the message that must be of some importance to the towering audience still chirping what sounded like a chorus of approval. After more odd gyrations, the insects began pounding their bodies onto the ground, moving up and down rather regularly to create a cadence.

All at once, the smaller insects on the tower filed down along themselves and scampered to rally about the elder bugs. For nearly a minute, they crawled all over them as if to offer affection. Then without much to do, majority of the insects clung tightly to the larger undersides of the adults. Fewer took fastening positions in various crèches beneath the wings, under the throat and along the top. They adjusted the wings to allow the maximum amount of passenger room. Ultimately, there was not enough room for all of them. The several dozen remaining continued to jump up to gain some hold on the impending departure.

Without warning, they sprung to the air with tremendous force propelled by their thick wings. Several insects lost their grasp and fell to the ground into the crowd below, undoubtedly disappointed at the loss of transport. The passengers clung together, tightly fusing themselves flat to help with aerodynamics.

They veered in a southerly direction with purpose. The extra weight did not hinder the flight by much. It appeared to increase their momentum as they were soaring into the midday sun. The insects on the ground began a unified exodus in the direction of their fortunate flying brothers and sisters. They ran in stampede fashion along the rocky scrub, totaling four or five dozen at first glance.

"Follow them and keep at least a half of a mile distance. Be ready to attack, especially if they head for population. Ground crews in the area, continue to maintain reconnaissance. I want those stragglers hot on radar. Let's see where they are going," the general said with a shade of coyness in his voice.

The planes that had been hovering beyond took a course and pursued the envoy of insects flying in the direction of Campeche and keeping to the coast. The truck with the academics started. The navigation screen changed, offering a local road map. The soldier wheeled to the main road, following the planes ahead.

"They must know where they want to go, Rene, but I haven't any suggestions of where or why, do you?" Alba asked sincerely.

"Sophia, they are remarkably intelligent and have a sense of organization. Therefore, they must have a purpose. This we will know soon enough. I must confess that the general is doing the right thing by not destroying them, a surprising move even for the Mexican military. Those larger versions are strong. We do not know what they are capable of. Above everything else, this scares me the most," Dr. Sanchez said, and then resorting to professional silence, he took a sip of coffee.

The wind displaced beneath the insects' wings would surely at least tear shingles off roofs. Large masses of air moved under the bugs as they made their way across the Mexican terrain. As flight speed increased, the smaller bugs clung more intently to their parents.

A convoy of ten vehicles had joined the parade along the thin highway that led through the country, including jet tanks, rocket launchers, troop transport, medical vehicles, and supply truck. Others periodically joined the general in monitoring the insects from the planes on a long-range video array. The captain surveyed the terrain map, and noting the limits of the country's land mass here, he called the general over to the screen.

"General, it looks like they are flying along the ocean side. They seem to be keeping on the coast. Their altitude is only 1,500 feet." Gonzales eyed the map.

"Why the hell would they stay on the coast? They had a very small distance to travel to get to the sea here in Progreso. They must not want to get back to the ocean. We need more intelligence."

The general took the communicator, opened a channel to the vehicle with the doctors aboard, and addressed them directly. "Drs. Sanchez and Alba, could you possibly give me some insight as to the behavior of these creatures? Where are they going?"

The passenger soldier took the wireless microphone and handed it back to Sanchez who responded, "We were just now weighing some options. It must know where it is going. The complex communicative skills they are demonstrating tell us that wherever it is, it is a specific place, probably a place of safety. We will contact you if we have any suggestions. Over and out."

He handed the microphone over to the soldier who was grinning at Sanchez's attempt at military radio jargon.

*****

"It's an interplanetary alien life cycle. If they leave any of us behind after they have had their fill, we can hope it's us and the Nobel Prize people. If they do, I'm sure they will have some final words for you. Nick, this is the ultimate science fair project. Big blue ribbon all the way, man!" Dr. Nicholas said, viewing the insect videos.

"How they navigate themselves beyond the light atmosphere of the planet is the most intricate example of parent or offspring homing instinct that I have ever witnessed. I have to tell Dr. Sanchez that they resort to a cataleptic or hibernating state—I'm not sure which—when exposed to extreme heat. They roll in on themselves for protection like an armadillo, but it's more than that," Dr. Nicholas said.

"Their legs almost fuse in creating sort of a chrysalis, obviously able to withstand great temperatures as we see them floating in molten lava, not to mention space flight," he paused, catching himself repeating something he had touched upon earlier and reminded of the need to record this information. The clock said 7:07 a.m. Charley was propping his sleeping head on his fist.

"I need a more captive audience. It's not too early to call Dr. Sanchez."

He opened his wrist phone, then spoke Sanchez's name. The voice recognition system placed the call to the professor in the convoy.

"Rene Sanchez here," said the professor a bit sleepily.

"Professor, this is Nick Nicholas. Good morning. I have been working on those samples for you. I may have some information that can help. How is the situation there?"

"The situation has grown graver. Two Imago insects much larger and able to fly have joined the smaller ones. We do not know where they came from. The general wants us to follow them. Dr. Alba and I are in a military vehicle heading after them. This is most fantastic. What information did you find from the samples?"

Nick paused shortly, not wanting to tell him how he came to his conclusion, and then he began to explain.

"By analyzing the components of the DNA and subjecting it to tests, I have found that the creatures have an ability to create some kind of shield around them when exposed to very high temperatures. You must tell the general to use flamethrowers or some kind of heat-based weapon. I am quite sure it is the only way to have any real effect. They will resort to a protective posture. It is their natural response to heat that may give you the edge," Nick said with effective urgency.

"I will find out if they have anything like that. I will call you back."

He tapped the soldier on the shoulder, attempting to speak in a non-condescending way.

"Excuse me, I need to know if the military had flamethrowers in their arsenal. Would you know if they do?"

The soldier looked back sporting a knowing grin. "We can get anything, senor. I have never seen anyone have a need of a flamethrower, but the general can get any weapon."

"Call the general. I have some information for him."

The soldier activated the communication port immediately.

Sanchez nodded, then turned to Dr. Alba.

"Dr. Nicholas may be onto something. One thing we do know is that these creatures have evolved to travel."

The military jets kept their half-mile distance consistently for most of the afternoon. After heading along the coastline, the Imago took an abrupt turn at Veracruz Llave, now heading into the western sun placed brilliantly before them. The sudden shift in direction brought the command center to its feet. General Gonzales watched the captain plot the potential course and felt a change of heart as the Imago closed in on Mexico City, the capital of Mexico.

"General, radar readings put the insects 198 miles due east of Mexico City."

The captain reported, hoping for some new orders.

"Would they drop their passengers off in a populated area like Mexico City for a reason you can think of, Captain?" the general said, baiting his second in command.

"I can only think of one thing that they would want there, sir. More food."

"This is my thinking as well. Bring the fighters within one half mile; keep them on alert."

The giant adult insects sped onward with increased intensity, chasing the sinking sun burning richly in the five-o'clock sky and aware of the new closeness of the jets.

"They are approaching the city of Tlaxcala, a city of more than eighty-five thousand. Approximate time of arrival is fourteen minutes. The flight team is awaiting orders, Sir," the captain said, watching another mile tick off the indicator to Tlaxcala.

Gonzales narrowed his eyes, watching the altimeter and monitoring the height of the bugs, waiting for it to drop before attacking. Sweat appeared on the general's forehead. During the next ten minutes, the altimeter remained a +- of one hundred feet. Weights of iron seemed to rest on his shoulders as he kept thinking and rethinking the possibilities of chastisement for allowing these creatures to infest another city. He would surely be court-martialed, yet he would emerge a wise and victorious leader who had the foresight to refrain from attacking and using intelligence to combat the enemy. The captain broke his concentration with an update.

"Two miles and closing, still no change in altitude. They may fly over, Sir."

"Yes, I believe that is what they are going to do. I only hope they are not passing up a light snack for the feast that is Mexico City. Recalibrate your sensors for the capital."

CHAPTER 43

The convoy following the pair of insects and their passengers streamed into the afternoon sun, closing in on the capitol of Mexico. Sirens rang throughout the city, a fearsome sound heard only upon occasional testing. This time, it seemed louder. The public emergency system instructed people to stay in their homes, offering scant details via the public holomonitors that were normally alive with advertisements. The people on the streets rushed home for their Sunday meal, now not very hungry in the face of impending doom.

They took a stop at a local village for a washroom break and a candy bar. Pepe and Tico, more than any one on the convoy, were eager to the brink of anger to end the events of the past month, yet ironically, they found themselves resolved enjoying seeing much of Mexico that they had not seen before.

The general must have been busy since he hadn't called the professor. Sanchez asked the soldier to call twice more and still got no response, understandably due to the Imagoes abrupt change in course toward the capitol of Mexico itself. They waited for the call, listening to the radio reports while trucking across the countryside during most of the day not speaking much, each wrapped in thoughts of possible outcomes and what affect it could have on the world.

From a distance, the captain reported via video feed, to the general the diminishing expanse between the planes and the aliens.

"Range, four miles and closing. Altitude dropping to sixteen thousand feet, General."

Gonzales hated sweating and was now forced to towel his brow as he faced the most important decision of his career. He took the communicator with slow, quiet dignity and spoke to the pilots. "Air command, decrease distance to one-quarter mile and place all weapons on ready. Await my orders."

Immediately, the nimble fighter planes pushed forward to what seemed to them a threatening distance yet certainly dangerous to the Imagoes and their riders. Flying intently most of the day, the Imagoes illustrated their stamina to all watching their progress from intermittent satellite feeds. As they barreled toward their destination, a heightened sense of threat accosted their senses. Hearing and feeling the presence of the military planes shook them uneasy from their flight path. The flight pattern involved a coursing up and over agitatedly, much like a fly being chased by an insect-eating bird. This continued for a short time, as their patience with intimidation was brief. Some of the smaller insects facing the rear of the abdomen observed the impending planes and began to make buzzing sounds which vibrated through the body of the adults. They communicated what they saw, and what they saw was dangerous.

The larger of the two took a sudden turn to the left to see for itself what could be risking their evolutionarily perfect design. It was sizing up its attacker, and after flying off course for a quarter mile, it abruptly lurched sideways, aiming itself like a rocket with an incredible force at the nearest plane. Within several seconds, the plane was T-boned directly at its center, not before a feeble attempt at outmaneuvering the insectoid missile. The force kicked the plane sideways and over in a spiraling descent. The pilot fumbled with inactive controls, with the inertia bringing nausea to the point of unconsciousness. After repeated unresponsive attempts, he hit the eject button. The top of the plane flew open, sending a queasy pilot tethered to a blue parachute upwards and a doomed jet cascading down into the small town below.

The pilot held his parachute straps tightly, breathing rapidly into the mouthpiece attached to the emergency oxygen tank that was activated by the ejection. His breathing started to become more irregular. The pilot gasped hard from the air tank as he fathomed the insect that spun around and went speeding toward him. His eyes grew wider as he made out the horrible visage of the four machete fangs opening as it made its final approach. The pilot was snatched in the massive jowls of the enormous arthropod, swallowing him nearly whole like a mosquito plucked from the sky by a predatory bird. After a few shags of its head, the machete fangs scissor away the parachute strings, leaving the billowy satin tarp to float away into the wind, as though it was an instant and maudlin tribute to the pilot being chewed whole in mid-flight.

The plane fell randomly, spinning terminally at high speed. A public suburban park heretofore safe sat below. Most of the people saw it coming and were able to run out of the way. It hit a newly erected state-of-the-art playground; parents were running off and pulling their children away from the death blow of the descending plane. Swing sets, slides, and benches that were not annihilated from the impact flew off into the reaches of the park.

A slide hit a moving car, and chain swings wrapped themselves around light poles. The escaping crowd crouched for fear of being hit with ejecta from the rather large play area that was now a tangle of metal, flame, and smoke.

The other plane maintained its position several miles behind, while the second plane held its position, hoping to be called out of its newly unsafe position. The attacking bug rejoined its mate and progeny now flying faster to the outskirts of the city, sharing what could have been concurrent vibrations of family satisfaction.

Gonzales kept even eyes on the altimeter as most of the staff took data on the plane crash, with a video now coming in from a reconnaissance craft over the sight of impact.

"General, the creatures have come within two miles of the city," the captain said, adjusting his screen now ready with a topographical view of the capitol. Gonzales weighed his decision, and with a final fated sureness, he snapped on the communicator.

"Number 2, this is General Gonzales. I want you to fire a volley of laser fire within fifty feet of the creature. Do not hit it. See if you can't change their course," he said with overcompensated authority.

The pilot engaged his laser guns affixed to the underside of each of his wings. He urged the plane forward and disengaged the tracking device and then fired several blasts of laser power on the right side of the smaller one with hope of affecting its flight path.

The Imago was shocked with what looked like indignation by the attack, swerving away to the left and lowering its altitude. The pilot fired again, careful not to hit them, and carried out his orders, pushing them further to the south, hoping they would respond, and wanting to be called away after the warning shots.

The creatures shuddered all abuzz with what seemed like fear. The pilot watched carefully and held back his fire to see what they would do. All at once, a splat of white viscous fluid hit the windshield of the cockpit. It was followed by more, larger such gobs of material apparently coming from the chased bugs. All at once, a large spray hit the glass, completely covering it and removing his entire field of vision. The pilot cursed and took the plane to a slower speed, switching navigation to radar control. The white goo began to form hard crust overt the front of the plane. The pilot was totally blind. Remembering that he had questioned the autopilot feature, he now thankfully engaged the satellite navigation system to bring him back to the base. As he fell back and away, the Imagoes began to cross into Mexico City's airspace.

The commercial satellite operator unknowingly opened his mouth as the screen at long last fed pictures of the creatures being chased by the Mexican air force.

"We have pictures!" he said, to the approval of his colleagues.

Within minutes, they were ready to be broadcasted on the television and holo sources throughout the world. Dahlia Morales, always ready for a broadcast, was given her cue as the holoprompter displayed her scripts in heavy black writing in the air against a clear sky near the transmitter tower outside Progreso.

"We have shown you where the insects had gathered here outside of Progreso, and now, thanks to our satellite forces center, we have live pictures of the insects as they are carried by adult versions referred to as Imago insects, just outside Mexico City." Dahlia paused.

The word "pause" in parentheses moved slowly across the sky. Her holoprompter fuzzed in with impressive definition for a satellite feed. For nearly a minute, not a word was said, the camera releasing the shocking unimaginable images to the world. Across the globe, people viewed the communal insects with the same silence. Fears mounted and took real form as people came to the unspoken conclusion that these monsters from beyond the solar system had some purpose that were nothing less than dastardly.

The general, choking back orders, watched the tireless flotilla maintain altitude high over the city. A new wave of pilots kept a two-mile distance with weapons hot and hands easy on the controls now that their intention was actually not to descend on the capitol city.

Stronger wings beat the air with new authority flying them past the city and into the Michoacán region. The television screen in the windshield displaying the familiar face of Dahlia Morales had sharper images of the insects than the military cameras on the dash monitor. Military vehicles tuned in to her CNN report.

Dahlia's visage reentered the windshield with her latest account.

"It has just now been confirmed that the company of insects have cleared Mexico City airspace and are flying into the mountains of Michoacán. All citizens in the region are asked to stay inside. Wherever you are, go to the nearest building, store, school, or home and remain off the streets and open areas until the military offers further instructions. These creatures are dangerous and will probably cause you physical harm if contact is made."

"What could they want in this area?" Sanchez oddly said to himself in the rather cramped confines of the back seat of the vehicle.

"Let's see what they could be after," he said, zooming in on the region map, his computer board secured in the space provided in the back of the forward seat.

"There are mountains there. I know the town of Zamora is there. I have a cousin in Zamora. I hope they do not land there," said Pepe with emerging concern, trying to allay his fear by tersely inspecting other sites from the map. Sanchez studied the terrain with Pepe, Alba, and Tico looking on as they spanned the highway through Mexico City.

A function undetectable to humans or their technology began to increase in the sensory system of the insects as they flew into the mountain of southwest Mexico. Their brains pulsed sonar signals and then responded with slight adjustments to their course. After another forty miles of such changes, another sense came into effectiveness. All at once, the Imagoes stopped flapping their leathery wings and coasted, dropping several hundred feet. The wings closed over the body, and they plummeted with precision toward the mountain range ahead. As they dropped, an acute sensory detection skill overtook the primary sense of the adults as well as the young. Focusing entirely on the activity during coasting put them in what would seem up close as nearly a comatose state. Their hard outer skins opened slightly with many tiny spiracle holes allowing air to enter the sides of their bodies more than usual. The bodies throbbed as they took in what equaled large breaths of air, testing it systematically for the location of something vital to their existence.

*****

Gerhard Steele sat for few moments as he contemplated Leslie's assertion to expose him in the holophone booth on *TerraLuna*. She had struck a deep, rarely affected nerve he long protected with all his defensive faculties. Modification of Dr. Nicholas's defense system had proven so far to be nearly impossible. If they could manage to convert the nuclear power sources of *TerraLuna* to operate it, any inquiry investigation would reveal that the core generation system was the design of the young man.

Steele could be exposed, sued, and consequently heavily fined. The money would be replaced; it was the tarnishing of his reputation that would negatively affect his organization, leaving him in the public eye as a thief and a fool.

His teeth ground with bad intent as he reviewed the list of supporters he had worked so fervently to rally support for his dream. He could not let disgrace enter his world. That cost was too great. His alternative was to pay Stan Duncan's price. Cash flow was limited. His CP position already promised out hundreds of free trips, reducing liquid revenue. This option was one he dreaded. By paying Duncan's price, he would have to drop out of the Corporate Point system by lowering his principle under ten billion world dollars, excluding *TerraLuna* from global corporate trading privileges. This impossible no-win situation was a place he willfully veered from every day of his life. Time would bring things back to normal. Not wanting to figure how long it would take to financially recuperate, he sat in the holophone room, wondering if luck would find him a way out of this predicament. Looking to the holo apparatus above him, there was no luck to be found.

*****

Uninterested in the prospect of the population in Mexico City, the Imagoes continued their course over the Uruapan region and toward the mountains that rose respectfully, meeting the insects' senses with innate satisfaction. The planes kept a two-mile distance with their weapons locked on the target in readiness. The day drifted deeply in the west as it usually had done as they began their descent into the mountainous region of the Volcan Paricutin.

The public alert system quickly informed the residents with routine warning procedures that certainly upset the small town that already lived in fear of El Monstre, the newest volcano born in Mexico. It had recently reactivated in the past two years and often threatened the area with unnerving rumbles and ash clouds.

Finding power from somewhere within their hulking segmented bodies, the Imagoes coursed with renewed furor, taking a steep plunge in altitude toward the volcano. The spiracles on the sides of the big and small bugs opened and closed with increased rapidity, ingesting the scent of the volcanic fumes playing innocently to the sky from the seething magma below.

Pushing faster in the setting sunlight, they soon circled the top of the looming cone, flying through the whiffs of steam and smoke. After a second flyover, they landed on a ridge just below the base of the living mountain relieved the flight was over. The Imagoes walked along the ground, testing it much like it did when they first landed. They tamped the ground with a motion like clumsy jumping, sniffing the disturbed dust with gleeful approval.

The young clung to the elders during the test and then slowly dislodged themselves from the self-imposed glue. Falling off, they shook with spastic undulations to unstick the dried residue and then began the same testing tamping dance acclimating to the environment.

Sanchez and his backseat companions watched as the satellites feed came into focus after transmission adjustments. They were driving away from Mexico City into the mountains.

"They have landed at El Monstre," he said upon consulting his computer.

"It is a live volcano," added Pepe with a simple flair for the obvious.

"Excuse me, Officer, could you route the satellite feed into my computer in the back. It is hard to see from back here," said Sophia, furrowing a brow of concern.

The soldiers looked at each other, wanting to comply with the doctor's request. Acute images of the activity at the bottom of the volcano soon popped up in the rear of the moving vehicle. Sanchez immediately directed his computer to record the images. After several minutes of observation, he entered the live feed into an electronic envelope and sent it to Dr. Nicholas. The computer beeped when the link was established. Sanchez opened his phone and called his American colleague.

"Dr. Nicholas? This is Rene Sanchez. The insects have landed outside of the town of Uruapan at the foot of the Cordillera de Anahuac range. They are right below the volcano we call El Monstre. We are almost two hundred miles from the mountain. You said these creatures went dormant when exposed to heat. Yet here they are at the hottest point in Mexico. Why are they coming here?" he said.

Nick sat at his computer desk, already looking at the live link snuck in from the truck's computer feed. Charley sat deep in thought watching the screen with silent respect. Nick pushed his glasses up onto his nose with a slow movement, thinking the answer was simple: that they sought a region similar to the terrain of their home planet; yet, he stopped himself, not wanting to expose the sources of his information to the professor.

"Wherever they are from must have a higher average ambient temperature. It looks like they have been able to locate a comfortable spot to live. Any form of intense heat weapon will be most effective. We are sure that they are susceptible to extreme heat. It is like the way people are when we want to be around a campfire but not in it," Nick said, quite pleased with a rare well-quipped analogy.

"I understand. I will tell the general. It is amazing how you can deduce these things from sub-atomic analysis. I will call you back when we arrive at the Volcan Paricutin. Call me if you conceive some way to help our situation. Sanchez out," Rene said in military style.

A quick snorting giggle came from the young soldier in the front seat, covered quickly by a fake cough. "Excuse me," he said. The truck continued along the road to the volcano.

*****

Nick and Charley spent that day documenting the newly attained alien data. They were aware of the conclusion that the adult forms of the insects offered problems that could not be solved with a flamethrower. Nick was doubtful that a flamethrower would be effective in putting the creatures into a dormant state.

"If those little ones want to be as big as their older relatives, they will have to live a very long time and consume a great deal of food. I have to conclude that feeding is going to become a major concern eventually. Their plan is to find a home away from home. That volcano reminds them of their home world." Nick said compiling items on his tablet.

"What are you thinking Charley?" Nick added.

"We could blow up the volcano. The lava would pour over them, then we could pick them out and dispose of them somehow," Nick said off the cuff.

"Then we would destroy several Mexican towns and wreak environmental hazard for millions of people in the area. No, that is not going to be our professional suggestion, Dr. Nicholas," Charley said with some sarcasm.

"We know it is getting dark there and the military is two hours away. They could pick them off one by one by air with radar by night, but the terrain there is rough. They may disperse and hide in the mountains, near the volcano, of course. This doesn't give us enough time to save the day here."

Charley watched the movie again of the insects forming a rough ball shape after being immersed in the lava of their home planet. "When I designed the receptor technology for the radio power modules, others were working on various aspects of applications for high power output. Skylar kept us estranged from his uses, but it has access to radio solar power. I highly suspect defense technologies were created as well as environmental temperature control. It was designed to keep the polar ice caps cold and cool the deserts." He paused, then followed up with a pointed glance at Nick.

"Skylar may have developed a weapon. He may be convinced to let us use it considering the gravity of the situation unofficially if possible," he offered with some closure.

"You said 'gravity,' Charley. That is it! Skylar developed the gravitic engine. He consulted with me on some engineering problems. I was sworn to secrecy so you know nothing about it, but you probably do," Nick said with a rare flurry of excitement.

"A gravitic engine exists and it has solar radio satellite powered weapons?"

"You have heard of *The Starship*?"

"The *SummerStar*, as it is also referred to, is the gravity-powered ship shaped like a five-pointed star that hovers over cities and warms them over a cold weekend, changing a winter day into a balmy seventy-five-degree day. It will go public soon, Skylar is still testing. Not much use for it around here, but they love it on Chicago winter construction sites."

"If we can get Skylar to lend it to us for a day, we can create a heat wave for our guests."

He activated his wrist phone and said, "Ben Skylar."

*****

The cramped trip into the region of the Volcan Paricutin ended at the beginning of dusk. Since the base of operations needed to be near the volcano, the military mobile command unit and shelter buildings were quickly erected, an enormous plastic oval pumped with air from several high velocity fans. After setting up camp in the foothills by high-intensity lamps mounted on the trucks, most of the crew settled down for some sleep.

Hunt One was the name formally given to the squad to begin the search for the Imagoes and their young. They prepared weapons, gear, and communications for the early dawn excursion. Sanchez set his computer on his lap, sitting in the military cot, and then reviewed a list of available heat generating weapons. He had hoped for some word from the General.

A shadow appeared on the plastic screen separating his room in the vast tent; it was Dr. Alba who feigned a knock on the screen with a vocalized, "Knock, knock, Rene? I heard that Gonzales is on his way here. He should arrive sometime during the night."

Sanchez raised the small radio-powered lamp on a folding table next to the cot.

"That is good news. I have been looking at these weapons logs, and I am afraid so far, there isn't much that they can use against these things. Dr. Nicholas will call with some insight."

Sophia came to the cot and looked over to see the screen. She sat, and they scanned the variety of weapons in the international military weapons database. After half an hour, she was lying next to Sanchez, their bodies warm from casual contact. After an hour, they were both asleep with satisfaction from innocent intimacy.

The early morning crews of soldiers, armed with flamethrowers and high-energy laser rifles not a part of regular Mexican military weaponry, began their walk into the still cold hills. They appeared from an unmarked truck in the middle of the night. Briefing took half an hour. It was a simple weapon, yet much larger than ordinary laser rifles due to the larger power source housed in the butt. Night vision goggles were affixed to their helmets rigged in with satellite feeds and radar access. It was not much of a hunt. The DNA of the creatures stored in the computers locked them onto their targets positioned over a small ridge ahead.

The captain spoke clearly in an even, low tone into his microphone wire.

"Base, this is *Hunt One*. We are fifty yards from target and continuing approach."

General Gonzales sat in his chair, with his captain again monitoring the satellite feeds.

"Engage at will. Our goal here is to verify the weapons' effectiveness. Let's see what these imports can do."

The slow walk continued. A soldier not seeing a fallen branch stepped hard on it and cracking it with a loud snap. The team made ready the dim orange ready light of the large heat guns moving in synchronization with their reassessment of their advantage.

A moment of stillness punctuated by the sounds of the night held them in place. Continuing forward in the green filter of night vision, they took the ridge when all at once, seven or eight insects rushed to the team with jaws flailing from countless springing legs. Four of the men were instantly overcome. Several shots were fired, lighting the night with orange laser flame. One of the insects was hit. A soldier in the line of the rushing fangs attempted to activate the flamethrower. Much to his surprise the alien increased its ferocity in the presence of the flame. With the devilish velocity the monsters ripped open his chest. The onslaught was total. The entire fellowship of soldiers was struck at once. Within minutes, it was over. The aliens drank deeply before the new day came. They chirped a group song of contentment atop the soldiers' remains, observably pleased in their newfound home.

The night was filled with most of the usual summer activities, yet the end of summer was the time of the year for carnivals. In Mexico, the celebration before the Lenten season was a great celebration for people to get the crazies out before the sober sacrifices of the Catholic season. The summer carnivals had rides and attractions and came during the self-affirming heart of summer, punctuated with bright lights, music, and the smell of all sorts of food. It resembled the spring carnival. The region needed this expression to confirm life. A large bonfire was lit in the town square of a small town just north of Paricutin. People of all ages reveled regardless of the news of an alien threat. Yet, as so much preparation had gone into the event, the numbers in attendance were only slightly reduced.

The scene looked quite sumptuous to the Imagoes and their young who, while attracted to the bright lights and scents as a heat source, were rather there to satisfy their longing for fresh blood. A tent was arranged with tables where many diners sat, enjoying the treats offered in the seemingly friendly summer breeze. The swarm approached from the south, carefully walking and scuttling in between the cars and calmly waiting in the lot just beyond the tent. Its open sides allowed the swarm access and the numbers and sizes of people offered something for every sized insect.

The adults pounced in, taking quick, lethal bites from the larger patrons, while the smaller ones grabbed the slower and more accessible prey. Most of the children ran away, or they were simply not as appetizing to them. The slaughter did not last long. The Imagoes ate at least two persons to quench their thirst from the long flight to the capital. It was a horrible scene. Soon, the horde exited back to the parking lot engorged with blood, sniffing and taking the temperature of the air to find their way to El Monstre.

CHAPTER 44

Ben Skylar never had a negative thought walking through his arboretum. Oxygen engorged air from the many waterfalls, and aeration pools kept the atmosphere quite cool and crisp, leaving visitors far from mental or physical stagnation. Open ceiling discs allowed the fresh night air to linger onto the damp cement floor, offering a revitalizing mixture of air, water, and plant life. A phone call interrupted Ben between appreciative snoots of rare humors.

"Ben here," he said, still savoring the special conglomeration of fragrances.

"Ben, it's Nick Nicholas. How are you tonight?"

"I am fine, Nick. I was watering flowers. What can I do for you?"

"Well . . . we—that is, the Mexican army and I—are trying to work on a plan to eradicate these alien insects. I am sure you have heard about in the news?"

"Really, Nick, when did you get involved with alien zoology? Francine told me you had other interests. I suppose she was right as well. Let me guess. I have some technology that will destroy these supposed aliens, and you want to borrow it," Ben said, his enduring smile naturally spreading across his aging face.

"Sort of, Ben. I have an idea based on some sound evidence, and I am led to believe your *Starship* might be able to help. How hot can you make an area?"

"That is classified information, to use a term I learned from the government. I have become a great number of things to a great number of people, none of whom want to deal with liability or responsibility. You can come here or use your holophone feature in that computer I built for you to show me your thesis, all your research, and what you propose I can do for you," Ben said with a decreasing smile.

"That program is in the computer you built for me?" Nick said, surprised.

"It is filed under BS/HP\. Open it. Consider it a gift." Ben opened an eyeglass case-sized box and exposed three, inch-thick silver discs.

"Install it and download your data into the program as it prompts, and I will see the three-dimensional version right here in my garden. Make your case for my technology, and if it saves the day, your prize will be a new set of portable holo-imaging discs. You know I am big on motivational incentives."

"Yes, I know," said Nick, already activating the dormant program now sending images of the insects, documents of calculations, and other pertinent information.

Ben Skylar sat on the edge of one of his turtle pools, with the three holo-imaging discs spaced three feet apart. Upon activation using his handheld pilot, they cast images of Nick's information just three feet above the ground. Casting a phosphorescent glow on his well-tanned skin, the floating images of the insects morphing into rock like magic widened the sage eyes of the corporate genius.

"At some time in the future, I will tell you how I came across the footage. What is important to know is that if we can recreate temperatures as hot as that lava from the *Starship*, we can stop these things. How precisely can the ship focus the heat? Can we do this?"

Ben looked at the text accompanying the images, which were noting temperature of the air and magma. Other notes including atmospheric composition, air pressure, and radiation levels stiffened his eye with attention, yet, not wanting to press him for the origin of this information, he said nothing.

"Nick, I think we should get to work on this right away."

During the following two hours and a modicum of trial and error, the scientists worked hypothetical calculations to determine what it would take to actualize the ideas Nick had proposed. They raised and lowered the altitude of the *Starship*, increased and decreased the intensity of the heat waves that would normally be used to raise the ambient temperature of a small city, narrowing the waves to bake highly resistant aliens into submission. Skylar cut the air with his hand, holding a holographic stylus tucked into the pilot case.

Numbers appeared on Nick's screen. Ben's work was sent as an animation to a corner of his video screen. Ben, now convinced that the configurations they decided upon would work, encountered the thought of a break which includes some lotus tea in the warm, humid garden. He liked being a go-to guru.

Reviewing the suspended "pages" of holographic calculations again, a weathered smile returned to his face now adopting the familiar posture of bearing success, he said, "Dr. Nicholas, though the citizens of Varnamo in Jonkoping, Sweden might be disappointed that their visit by *SummerStar* will be delayed, I think she has somewhere more important to be tomorrow."

"I am expecting to leave for Mexico today. I will be in touch."

Ben closed the line. His mind was now accepting the onset of fatigue, so he pressed the off button deactivating his imager. Sitting for a moment in the humid dark, he found new peace in his latest achievement and went in for lotus tea.

"I want to go to Mexico and see this. Call Dr. Sanchez and tell him we want to be there to coordinate the plan," Charley said in a flurry of excitement.

"You know, I think we need to explain this to the general in person. He could use a few good thoughts. Ben and I have reworked the *Starship*; it should work. I will call Stan Duncan later and tell him you will not be at work for a few days. I am calling Sanchez now," said Nick, feeling focused.

The phone activated, waking Sanchez out of his early sleep. He was pleasantly surprised to see Sophia warmly cuddling on his chest. With a smooth adjustment, he rolled over with the phone and answered the call.

"Rene Sanchez . . . yes, Dr. Nicholas." He listened carefully to Nick and methodically reached for his notepad, which he used to take notes during the conversation.

"Essentially, the *SummerStar* will lower itself over the insects to about four hundred feet and focus an adjusted heat beam onto the insects. They will revert to a cataleptic state, and then we will have to find a way to dispose of them. It is better than most of the ideas we have heard of so far. The general should really hear this from you, Doctor."

"The insects have disseminated near El Monstre, and our camp is set up at the foot of the mountain. They attacked a carnival and many persons are dead. We need to put a stop to this immediately. I will tell them to send a military transport for you and Dr. Porter. Someone will call you back with the flight time. It should be sometime early tomorrow, so be ready. Sanchez out."

He closed the phone and went to find the general.

Charley, fathoming a free trip to Mexico and a chance to see aliens up close; it was finally beginning to be a good day.

"Sanchez says that we should get the call to leave at any time. I am going to start packing. You have enough to wear in that back closet, so don't think about going back to your place. We don't have time," said Nick transferring data to his portable computer with the plans he and Skylar had worked out earlier.

They shut down the lab in record time, and while returning to the house, Nick got the call from Gonzales' assistant that their flight would be at 9:45 a.m.

"We lift off at 9:40 a.m. We should get a few hours of sleep. Pack now, we'll load the car tonight," Nick said, reviewing his fluctuating list of things he needed.

Charley nodded from within his own imagination of the potential experience that would occur during the next seventy-two hours. He fished through his adopted spare closet in Nick's back bedroom, finding clothes he hadn't seen in some time and some he had forgotten he had. He found a duffle bag and began to casually fill it. A phone call interrupted his packing

"Charley? Hi, it's Dana."

Charley listened for more from her and feared having to tell her that he would be gone for a few days. The conversation was poked forward with habitual decorum.

"Hi, Dana. How are you? Hey, I have some news."

"I have some news too. I was hoping to see you later today."

"That might be a problem. You see, Nick and I are flying to Mexico tomorrow first thing to help with the alien problem. We have been working on a plan with the Mexican military and Ben Skylar. Our military flight is at nine forty. Yes, it is important."

"Well, I won't complain that what I have to tell you is more important than saving the world from alien invaders, but I still think that what I have to tell you might rank high in percentile," she said riding the emotional moment.

"It will have to wait until I get back. If you can't tell me over the phone, now I am worried that you want to dump me. Is that what this is about? Are you afraid to dump me unless you are standing in front of me?"

"No. I have to show you something."

She was upset. Her voice shook, her fingers fumbled with the phone, she hung up.

Charley continued his packing. After realizing the need for clean clothes, he spent most of the night doing laundry and eating, unable to sleep. By two o'clock he found his body giving in to its capacity to sleep. With a sudden radical disregard for the time of night, he thought about calling Dana but stopped himself, not knowing what he would say to her.

At seven o'clock they were in Nick's Buick sailing to the airport. The usual fleeting coolness of the morning welcomed them if only for a short time. They reached the airport, parked in the garage, and made their way through the busy airport. Sifting with purpose through the crowd, Nick and Charley walked briskly through the main concourse.

"You will like the Mexican army food. I can't explain it, Charley, other than it is simple and satisfying."

"It sounds good. Don't give me a hard time, Nick. I have a taste for a soft pretzel, and I see them just around the corner. Do you want one?" said Charley ever hungry.

"No. I am too nervous to eat, but you go ahead. The military boarding center is right ahead. I will meet you there, okay?"

"No sweat, Doc. I'll be there in a few minutes." Charley walked across the concourse into people traffic, excusing himself as he geared himself for his favorite snack. Soon after he happily settled into line, he felt a hand grab his arm. Turning, he found the searching gaze of Dana Kim fixed upon his face.

"Dana, what the hell are you doing here? My flight leaves in thirty minutes," Charley said, utterly surprised.

"I had to see you today. Today is the day Charley. We have to talk tight now. If I didn't come now, it wouldn't be right.

"What wouldn't be right? You are not making much sense, Dana. I have a plane to catch, and I'd like one of these pretzels."

"There isn't time for pretzels," she said with force, grabbing his hand and pulling out of line into the concourse.

"Do you have your world dollar card?"

Charley hesitantly produced the card that Dana quickly took. She grabbed his hand and they ran across the concourse to the in-airport motel rooms and scanned across the reader above the door handle. A green light came on opening the door charging the card the less-than-reasonable price of a twenty-four-hour hotel room.

They walked in briskly, with Charley feeling very much not in control as she double locked the door and then turned to face him, expelling a long breath. She fixed a deep fathoming gaze on his eyes and then ran to him, giving a long, deep kiss as though it would be her last. Charley responded by dropping his backpack, embracing her with his strong arms harder than he ever had. He pulled her away and said, looking deeply into her eyes, "What has gotten into you?"

"Charley, do you only love me physically? Do you love me mentally? Tell me how you love me," she said, melting herself into his chest.

"I love you in those ways. You know that. I want to learn to love you in more ways if you tell me what this is about!" he said with a furrowed brow.

"I know our love will change in a very short time." He attempted another Elysian kiss.

She pulled away, picking her purse from the floor and walked toward the washroom.

"I hope that you will feel the same way after what I have to tell you. I haven't been completely honest with you, and it is time to come clean. I have to wash my hair. Sit on the bed and listen."

She pushed him on the bed and proceeded to dig into her purse, retrieving a plastic bottle. She walked silently into the washroom and then turned on the water.

"You are going to wash your hair? Now?" Charley said, very confused.

"I am not a college student. I lied to get into the *MoonCorp* intern program. I already have my PhD." She turned bent over and began to wet her hair in the large sink and then squirted the bottle into her hair.

Charley sat, watching streams of dark liquid fall from her hair. Thinking it best to say nothing, he watched and waited. After another application from the bottle and more rinsing, her ebony hair returned to its original blonde color.

Charley pretended not to be surprised, then said, "You may have to rinse a few more times. There is still a little left."

She looked at him plaintively for a moment, then said, "I have been hired to spy on *MoonCorp*, particularly on Nick. I used you to get to him. For the record, this ridiculous disguise was not my idea."

She marched to her purse and took the skin puller out. She placed herself squarely in front of him, activated it, and began to pull her slanted eyes back to their original shape. She stood before him with black hair dye running down her neck and waited for a response.

"Are you telling me that the time we have spent together was fake? All of this was so you could steal trade secrets?" he said, his eyes trying to firm a grip on her new face.

She looked back with what might have been a penitent expression, muddled with the truth that he was looking at someone he didn't know. Her appeal for forgiveness must have seemed to him like a cry for pity, she thought.

"Charley, I did what I did for the wrong reasons. I know this now. You have shown me something I have known all along. I needed such an enormous amount of proof. My hypothesis is so outrageously obvious that it must be fact. It is easier for me to believe and accept. Overkill, right? I am a scientist first. I am a lot of things to a lot of people—a spy much further down the list," she said, feeling warmth from her heart faintly rising and glowing into her words. After searching his visage for some sign of anger, he gave a response she had not expected.

"What do you expect me to say? Here you are, someone I do not know, admitting guilt. I mean, I know you, Dana. I know you very well. At least, I thought I did. Now, I think I deserve more information, I need more proof. Don't you see I fell in love with *you* way beyond all of this?" Charley said, his voice rising in the beginnings of desperation.

"Who are you working for?"

"It shouldn't be hard to guess, Charley. It's Steele. He wanted the defense system for *TerraLuna*. He has it now, but I told him if he used it, I would expose him. The lawsuit brought on by Duncan would set him back farther than he wants to be. He will not use it. I know him," she said, searching his face for clues of forgiveness.

Charley shifted his stance, absorbing information. He sent a sigh upwards, rolling his eyes, and then turned back to her.

"So all along, you are this blonde spy running me for a nice commission. How much did he pay you? What was the price for breaking my heart? I loved you. Now, I want to hate you. How can this possibly balance out into world dollars for you, Dana?" he said, balancing anger and pain.

"It doesn't matter. I haven't taken any money. He is an arrogant user, and I am his victim. It's my sad truth. Now, he will probably have to buy the system from Duncan and that should hit him where it really hurts—right in the world dollars," she said, searching his face for understanding.

She felt oddly comfortable now that the truth was in the open. She took the towel from around her neck and continued to dry her hair. Charley sat on the bed looking at her deal with her hair, an activity that had always intrigued him about women. He thought of the numerous women he had been associated with, none of which had the personality and scientific acumen that Dana possessed, and he wanted all this to not be happening.

Leslie came to him and kneeled on the floor in front of him, putting her hands on his knees.

"You have more than enough reasons to hate me. This has been an attempt to make amends for my crime. I fell in love with you, Charley. I won't say it is the only reason I am stopping this, but it is a major one. I am not the kind of person that acts on emotions, but when I do, it is full tilt! I see it in your eyes, that you love me too. I want to know that you were in love with me all along, not this falsity. I doubted this job from the beginning, but it was you who made up my mind, not only that it was illegal and unethical but also that there is something more valuable here, and that is the truth. My name is Leslie Davis. I hold a PhD in Astrophysics and have been employed by Gerhard Steele for seven years, doing research and occasional political tasks for that son of a bitch. How do you do?" she paused, needing to regroup now that the truth was made clear, then extended her hand.

Charley studied her face, thinking about how she lied to his genuine affection. His heart was splitting with his mind, nothing came to either place for a few moments. Then he began slowly, "Dana, I mean Leslie, I have had relationships on and off for a long time. The reason I am not married is the fear of committing to someone and finding out they have a hidden motive and not truly sincere. This is *my* sad truth proving itself again. So I will lay it out for you. You have been the best thing that has happened to me. You have come closer to me than anyone has in a long time. You love science, you are beautiful and like me for who I am. Now, I know this isn't the case. I cannot go on seeing you after this. Yet how can I wake up next to you and remember that you nearly betrayed a lifetime of work simply for money. I realize you have tried to make reparation for what you did, and I will not say anything, but I won't ever feel comfortable doubting your agenda."

Leslie looked at him without tears, then wordlessly stood up and began walking to the washroom. She stopped and turned with last effort.

"I need you to know that I have had a change of heart after the deed was done. If you choose not to forgive me, this is something I need to learn to accept. I had planned us to reconcile here today, but I see that that isn't going to happen and the worst of it is that your response makes me want you even more," she said, unable to cry any tears further.

Charley looked at his watch. "I need to save the world from an alien invasion. I was hoping you would be around when I get back for some hero sex. Will you go to work next week?"

"Yes. I will continue until the middle of August. I do not want to draw any suspicion."

"You won't have any problem. I won't rat on you," he said plainly. "I have a plane to catch. I will be sorting this out—up in the air."

He gave her a quick disimpassioned look for a lack of something else to say, took his backpack, and left the room. Leslie Davis stood for a moment, staring at the closed door, and then went into the washroom to wash her hair again, slamming the door behind her.

CHAPTER 45

Sophia sat with her computer in the makeshift commissary. Smells of a promising lunch taunted her senses in the late morning of their first day at camp outside Paricutin. The mountain camouflage walls of the tent were tautly spread over a fiberglass frame. They were made of Polylon, a poplar material that was both strong and light, providing an impressive heating and cooling from its electric hvac mesh. Tempered sunlight illuminated the large room, with support poles and ceiling wires offering the lighting needed at this time of day. The hard Polylon derivative floor had been rolled out and seamed together with long fastening strips. It was surprisingly flat, thanks to a series of simple pressing machine applications that evened it.

Despite its size, the commissary was comfortably cool in the full Mexican midday sun. Soldiers had been setting economically-sized tables and chairs to accommodate the growing staff arriving in trucks and aerial craft. Sophia sat with her computer, filing through data beginning back when they first encountered the creatures aboard *La Fresca*.

She was intrigued by the rate growth exhibited by the alien metabolism. Now, with a large Imago as a model for their evolutionary path factored into the equation, Sophia worked her way back through a growth chart to determine how long it would take the new hatchlings to grow to adulthood. She scanned photos and noted that they were not growing at an even rate; some were certainly larger and healthier than the others were. She quickly concluded that some were better nourished than others, sadly by the ingestion of blood. She stopped to think of the wildlife and livestock living in and around the area that already must have suffered by the fledgling aliens. A tremor of fear passed across her eyes, thinking that humans would offer better nourishment than mountain cats and prairie dogs but not as fine a meal than a cow or a horse. The aliens would most probably continue their hunt for human blood. She concluded that their purpose must be to inhabit the planet because of its comfortable temperature firstly. Secondly, they are here for its abundant food source, and their growth could be determined by the amounts of food ingested.

Gunfire from outside the tent reissued a tremor of fear. This time, it pulled deep from her instinctive lower abdomen. Soldiers scrambled with communicators in hand for orders. Sophia was not sure if she was the first to see the shadow of an insect perched on top of the tent. Without time to think, she screamed—the fastest way to alert the milling soldiers to the chewing insectoid face emerging through the Polylon. Soldiers reached for their side arms and began firing. After a few moments of fearful staring at the creature, a soldier hauled her away and down an artificially-lit hallway away from the fracas.

"My computer!" she yelled, back pulling herself down from the burly soldier.

"I'll get it," he said pulling his weapon.

Sophia looked as the man collected her things. At this point, the creature's head had come past the thin membrane. Undaunted by the gunfire, it attempted to urge its way through the small opening with some difficulty. As he jogged away with her things, the ceiling ripped free, and the alien fell to the floor, adroitly landing on its many legs.

With pause and a defensive rearing of its head, it let out a screech, setting the troops back a step with fear. With a feral-pointed spring, it propelled its body at the nearest soldier, catching him squarely in the chest. The man fell limp in the creature's grasp, with his blood spewing in all directions. Sophia looked on, and with grasping hands for her computer, a splash of blood hit her in the face. They ran together down the hallway. After several large strides, Sophia looked back to witness her worst fear actualized. The insect was barreling down the hall, its fangs still dripping with blood. She staved off the desire to faint, pushing herself along the hallway. Ahead was a four-way corridor connecting three other tents. They burst into the center section suddenly flanked by soldiers with ready fire. The beast met a force of laser fire with a shock, slowing its advance. Alba and her protector ran off to the double doors leading outside. The creature's momentum hurled it into the men attempting to hold their ground. Ballistic guns blaring could be heard, as well as the unmistakable sounds of fangs hitting flesh, before it was finally blasted apart..

The area around the tent was busy with soldiers. She looked for Rene as they made their way beyond the line of gunmen scrambling to the tent, aiming for a parked Humvee. He put her in with a firm hand and said, "Stay here you will be safe."

Sophia sat in the truck, composing her mind after the rare, sudden vigorous activity. She was breathing heavily, fumbling with her computer and too disoriented to activate it. Rene sat in the truck, interrupting the filing of her thoughts. A smile came over her face, and she embraced him briefly.

"Are you all right?" she said with concern.

"Yes, I am fine. You?"

"I'm a little shook up. I am glad you are here." She gave him a fast kiss of assurance. Rene looked back, noting her sincerity. He put his hand on her shoulder and squeezed it, composing himself. She embraced him to stop the her shaking.

Streams of soldiers affronted the tent. Sanchez noticed the keys were in the ignition and took a sure bet that it might help to gain a view of the situation from a distance. He got out of the Humvee and entered at the driver's side. Starting the massive vehicle, he looked back to Sophia. "Do you want to stay in the back? Am I your chauffer?"

She moved to the front seat with an unnoticed glee, reminding her of the lost pleasure of carefree spontaneity. Rene turned the truck around while her counterpart activated her phone to call Nick Nicholas. "Hello, Nick? This is Dr. Alba. We are having some serious trouble here. The insects have attacked the command tent at the foot of El Monstre. We are outside now watching. How soon will you be here?"

Nick and Charley were at the military car pool waiting for their ride. He stood looking out at four cars parked at either end of the small lot. Nick started a fast walk to the soldiers and stood around waiting for what Nick did not know. They eyed his gait with something near suspicion.

"We are at the carpool in Mexico City. We will be leaving now?" he said explicitly nodding to the driver for understanding.

The young soldier, aware of Nick's urgency nodded and got into the car.

"It shouldn't be an hour's drive. We have been fine-tuning our plan. At least we have one that could work. We think it will work. I'll keep you up-to-date on our location." They sped out of the parking area and out onto the ramp to the highway toward Paricutin.

*****

Pepe and Tico sat in the assault utility vehicle for nearly half an hour while the battle for the tent raged on in surreal silence. They had been checking out the new extra duty hydrogen engine in the AUV. Pepe had not seen one in person until today. His next track would certainly have an engine with this magnitude of horsepower fueled by a hydrogen cell. He hoped that the check from the university would be supplemented by some funds from the military for his help or his inconvenience. He hadn't been of much assistance lately, so there he sat.

Tico sat on his lap and slept for lack of anything better to do. They had parked forty yards from the ramp with the main road in sight. Pepe kept his eye on the road for reinforcements that may be needed. According to regular radio report, three insects had entered, one was dead and the other two still inside. He wanted to be glad to know that Dr. Sanchez and Alba were okay; moreover, he wanted this ordeal to be over and be home again with Paloma. He drew a life-affirming breath, yet the smell of laser fire and blood of this odd summer day from the open window did not offer the usual warm feeling of the open sea.

A car coming up the road turned his attention abruptly away from thoughts of home. A cloud of dust followed it into the perimeter and into a cluster of defensively positioned vehicles. It backed into a re-made slot, creating a tighter circle of cars ready facing outward.

Two men and two soldiers got out and moved into the circle talking, while their attentions were fixed on the tent under siege in the not-too-far distance. Another car came from the opposite side, wobbling on the uneven ground. It was Drs. Sanchez and Alba coming to join the two scientists. Pepe had a feeling something was finally going to be accomplished. He opened the car door. Tico leapt out, followed by his master, as a soldier directed Sanchez to park in the circle. Pepe walked to Nick, his hand outstretched.

"Hello, I am Pepe Fernandez. This is Tico. You must be Dr. Porter and Dr. Nicholas."

"Good to meet you. I am the captain of the ship the doctors used when we first found these things. I have been here helping them ever since. If Tico and I can be of any help, please let us know."

"We will, Pepe, for sure," said Charley, who seemed to hit it off with him immediately.

Rene walked up to introduce himself, smiling easily. "Rene Sanchez. It's a pleasure to meet you both. We have had this latest trouble going on here for about an hour. We should leave it to them. It will give us time to coordinate our data."

"That tent would be more impressive if that large hole wasn't in the roof," Charley said to Pepe for approval. The big fisherman responded with an agreeing shake of his head.

Dr. Alba had set her computer on the hood of the car and was ready to get to work. She offered to one of the several soldiers standing nearby, "Maybe you should call the general and tell him they are here."

"The general knows you are here. He will be here soon. Our latest report indicated that there is only one bug left inside," said one of the soldiers to Dr. Nicholas.

"It would be nice to link the military programs with our system indoors, but we could run this from here if we had to," said Nick to Sanchez.

"I agree. The military satellite has the aliens' DNA programmed on the D-Sat, so locating them isn't a problem. Can you tell us something about what you propose to do? We have some dangerous choices that we would like to consult with you about," Sanchez said with expectation, affirmed by the others with silent accord.

"Essentially, these creatures are highly adaptive especially when exposed to extreme temperatures. We propose to expose them to high levels of heat in order to revert them to a state of anabiosis. At that point, we can deal with them without the chance of being attacked," Nick said.

"How are you going to generate this heat?" said Pepe, as he collected Tico who had been running around excitedly meeting new friends.

"We will be using some climate-adjusting technology modified for our purposes. In fact, I think it's time to bring her in," Nick said, turning to his wrist phone.

"Hello, Ben. We just arrived in Paricutin. The Imagoes have attacked the command center here. I am hoping to get under way here as soon as we coordinate the D-Sat with *SunStar*," Nick said.

Skylar's sat phone system picked up Nick's GPS signal and automatically referred it to the flight coordinator. The pilot entered the course. "Nick, I am amazed at how many names my climate craft has. I must say I have never heard that one. I thought of filing a sole proprietary on the name for patent purposes, but everybody seems to love her in their own way, so I keep calling my lawyer and adding, 'also known as.' The IFDA can call them anything they want. They have ordered several currently in production. The Independent Fire Department of America wants them to put out

Californian forest fires. Okay, right now she is coming over the ridge, over your right shoulder. It looks awfully warm down there."

Before Nick could turn, he felt an unusually cool breeze running across his back. The group turned their heads upwards to see a silver star-shaped craft, emanating a nearly invisible stream of light with beautiful coolness cascading gently from its points and center.

"Is it cool enough down there for you? I can take it down a few degrees," said Skylar over the radio, looking at the group around the circle of cars on his monitor aboard his *SummerStar*.

It hovered a few hundred feet above them, casting a well-placed glistening shadow and keeping them cool from the pulsing sun. During a timeless regard for the ship, the general pulled up in his covered jeep, breaking the spell. He stepped out, ready to meet the science team. With a diplomatic stride, he greeted Nick and Charley with impressive handshakes.

"Now that we are all here, I am afraid our meeting room is currently unavailable. There is still one insect, but it is severely wounded. It will not be very much longer for threat level. Dr. Nicholas, I see you have brought some backup. Let's see your proposal," the general said, ready to strike back.

Nick looked at his audience. With a prepared breath, he set his portable computer on the hood of the car and began to outline his plan of assault.

"Basically, the insects are highly adaptive to a certain level of heat. We think it is why they have coagulated here at the volcano. From my DNA testing, I have found that at extreme temperatures, they hibernate much like the microscopic tardigrade insect found in Earth's oceans. In this state called cryptobiosis, they should be able to be collected and disposed of," Nick offered carefully to his mixed audience.

The general stopped him. "How do you propose we do that?"

"Dr. Porter and I have fielded several options. One would be to transport them off world into orbit with the help of some heavy lift craft provided by Mr. Ben Skylar who has graced us with is assistance. He is up there in the *SummerStar*. Say hello, Ben."

"Hello, everyone. You have a beautiful country from up here. Francine and I will have to come back for a visit using more conventionally transportation, of course," said Ben from the speaker on Nick's computer.

"As you know the *SummerStar* has helped to deter some global warming. She is used to warm or cool a region, offering relief from extreme temperatures. What we propose to do is to subject them to highly concentrated sunlight and bring them to their comatose state. Our second option is to off load them to another planet, perhaps Venus, where the high temperatures will keep them dormant indefinitely." Nick looked at the group all silent, save for Sanchez who offered a question.

"How will we transport them once they have gone dormant?" asked Sanchez.

"I was hoping the general would help us with some bulldozers and hydraulic shovels. A heavy lift container is on the way. You might also want to alert the fire abatement crews to be on hand with plenty of heat-protective suits. There will be ground fire. It will be very hot out here. It is the only way to stop them from settling in the region, which I believe is their goal. They are planning on staying for some time," said Nick.

The general and his assistant began to coordinate the request for additional equipment while Sanchez and Alba reviewed the plan again, peering onto Nick's screen.

"The *SummerStar* should start linking with the D-Sat location system. It had been rather helpful so far. I think we should not waste time," said Sophia, eager to help.

"Naturally. All the military systems are available to Mr. Skylar," said the general's assistant who began to speak with Skylar to enable his ship with the necessary functions. They broke off into groups and started to work.

An hour's time passed. The last insect was destroyed, dragged out of the tent, and now burning in a controlled bonfire, their defense system notwithstanding after death. Pepe and Tico stood and watched the insects shrivel and crack in the blaze.

"To hell with you demons! I hope you all swell up today and leave us to our planet." Pepe kicked a rock that landed with a plop in the flames.

Sophia and Sanchez drove up to the fire and stood for a time with the fisherman and his dog. Sanchez wanted to express thanks for all Pepe had done yet found it difficult to begin.

"I want you to know that I spoke to the university, and they agreed to increase your fee for all the help you provided. It will not be enough to buy a new boat, but it will be enough for a nice down payment on one of those hydrogen engines I heard you admire so. Thanks, senor. We are grateful for your help," said Sanchez, offering a hand that turned into a bear hug from an exuberant Pepe.

"Thank you. It has been quite an adventure. You know after this is over, I want you and Dr. Alba to come over to my house. Paloma will cook us a big fish dinner, and we can tell her about our war with the aliens. What do you say, Dr. Alba?"

"We would love to come. I think before she plans the menu, we should pray that Dr. Nicholas and Mr. Skylar's plan works," said Alba, looking up to the sky.

"Yes, a prayer could not hurt," added Sanchez.

They stood for a time, silently watching the cracking carcass of the three invading insects and hoping that it would soon be the end of the Imago and the beginning of a return to their normal lives.

*****

SummerStar hovered noiselessly during the twenty minutes it took to coordinate computers. DNA locks had been logged for nearly forty targets. Ground forces had taken back the camp without a casualty. A perimeter around the tent had been set up, consisting of local police reinforcements trucked in from Mexico City. The assault was ready yet waiting for the arrival of the disposal vehicles, including a heavy lift tank. Ben Skylar sat in the command chair next to his pilot who was already into his second mango juice. He touched an electronic pad, opening his COM to General Gonzales.

"General, we have an estimated time of arrival on the heavy lift at ten minutes. I think now would be a good time to review our strategy." Gonzales sat in his newly reclaimed command room at the center of the makeshift complex.

"I will have the livestock placed in the cleared area. This will avoid excessive brush fires. Upon the request of Dr. Alba, we will hope to attack as they enter a fifty-yard radius of the bait. Actually, I consider preserving the bait a better idea than waiting until they gather to feed. I have never been accused of inhumane acts against animals. I'd like to keep it that way," Gonzales said into his headset.

Nick, Charley, and Pepe sat around a small table within view of the general's command table, discussing the Imago over packaged snacks and juice drinks. Tico slept under the table, somehow knowing that whatever was going to happen, he could do nothing to help.

"Their rate of growth indicates to me that something in our atmosphere is acting as a catalyst, perhaps something that is available in miniscule amounts on their home planet. It could be something we have an abundance of here, hydrogen, carbon, even oxygen. This, in combination with the lack of food during an undetermined amount of time spent dormant in space to find us, is causing these things to rapidly increase in size," Dr. Nick said.

"I wonder about those larger versions. Are they parents? I am not sure if they are the same species. What do you think, Doctor?" said Pepe.

"I cannot say. I am concerned that they will certainly be harder to destroy than the smaller ones. My hope is that the *SummerStar* will have an effect on them," said Charley.

The walls of the tent moving from some outside force ended their snack. They all turned, hearing the engines of what must be the heavy lift vehicles. They moved to the exit.

The heavy lift was very much like the *Junk Colossus* yet smaller. The canister sat below, with the ship resting upon it beyond the circle of vehicles. Several soldiers rode to greet her. The men stood to view the ship, none as enthralled as Pepe.

"It is magnificent," was all he could say.

The general's assistant came from behind Nick, tapping him on the shoulder.

"The general has asked for you to ride with him to the sight. He says we must leave immediately. The bait animals are in place."

The men were picked up in a large armored utility vehicle. The ARUV took them along a newly beaten road. Nick sat in the front seat his computer fixed in the holder provided. He was able to help coordinate the attack with Skylar, Gonzales, and Sanchez. Screens provided several aerial views and an abundance of distances, matrixes, and perspectives on the insects' locations in reference to the bait and the outlying region.

Soon they were in view of the two dozen cows tethered to a pole. Cars and trucks mounted with guns and earth-moving equipment were jockeying to form a defensive circle within not more than 150 yards distance.

Ben Skylar's disembodied voice filled the truck, quickly bringing all to attention. The driver shook a bit, obviously on edge. "I see they are edging their way nearer. Can you see that, General, Nick?"

The general responded, nearly stepping on Skylar's words. "Yes. Yes, I do. I see no reason to hesitate. Head to the nearest one, and let's see if this works."

Ben pointed to a red blip on the screen, and the pilot nodded and veered the *SummerStar* a few degrees, with the DNA satellite guiding the way. It descended to an ominous four hundred feet from the surface. The outline of the spokes of the *Starship* was covered with circular actuators. A large half circle actuator sat in the center. Looking like a giant starfish hunting above the terrain, it honed in on its first target, moving with stealthy precision.

"I have the first target, which is actually two moving together. Dr. Nicholas has configured that the cryptobiosis process occurs at 720 degrees Celsius. The only known creature on Earth with this ability is less than two hundredths of an inch. These targets are many thousands of times larger. I hope we can get her hot enough.

"Our thermal setting is for seven hundred degrees Celsius. We have power and a locked target, General. Should I pull the trigger?"

"You have a green light, Mr. Skylar. Fire when ready."

All watching the screen tensed. The ship began to glow. The pilot increased power to the insulator array, adjusting for the extreme temperature. Rays of light beams began to file down, instantly scorching the terrain. It was so hot that any small fires extinguished themselves and all oxygen burned away from the area. In a moment, two alarmed insects exposed to the heat hunkered down, curling themselves together. A dark cuticle began to emerge, trying to seal itself in response to the fire above.

After thirty seconds, they frantically scurried about, looking to escape the heat. The cuticle grew thick around them, seemingly in an involuntary manner as they walked in a peculiar semi-upright position, with their outer shell creating a natural curved shape in response. Skylar kept them in a twenty-yard circle of effect for just inside of a minute, and then hit the COM touch pad.

"It is working slowly. I will have to increase the intensity. I am taking it up to nine hundred degrees. We are able to attain this temperature but not for long periods." Skylar made the adjustment then consulted his screen.

The intensified heat sent ironic shivers through their recombining bodies. The pilot kept them with slight decreases of the circle's brightness and increases in intensity; the smaller the circle, the higher the temperature.

"Temperature increased to seventeen hundred degrees," said Skylar.

After being exposed to the incredible heat, which to them seemed like a welcome state, the aliens popped up a few feet from the seared ground as if like popcorn and landed in a nearly perfect sphere, steeping in the smoking charred ash of the burned soil. After some adjustments the sealing process entombed the creatures in a final defensive ball.

General Gonzales called into his headset. "Retrieval crews, move out. Let's pick up these things before they cool off." Firetrucks were on the move in the same minutes as the order was given. Steel link plates were affixed to the tires to protect them from heat contact."

"I have a group of eleven, coming within half a mile of the bait. They are closest. Shall we try this again, General?" said Skylar.

"No time like the present," said the general amid the elated soldiers in the command room.

SummerStar adjusted its efficient gravitic engine with minor effort, and within moments placed herself above a swarm moving tersely across the scrub.

"I will keep the setting at seventeen hundred degrees. Let's see if we can get them all," Skylar said, activating the heat.

The aliens began to pulse and bake, adjusting to the sudden heat seemingly confident in their ability to compensate yet still adjusted to their newly-found instinct. After another minute, they jumped and landed like steaming pool balls tossing and bouncing against each other until they stopped.

The AUV containing Nick and Charley was parked within sight of Dr. Sanchez and Dr. Alba who waved excitedly, offering a "thumbs up" sign for success.

The hydraulic shovel rolled over to an area beyond the first two balls black with soot and still smoldering. It crept closer and sunk into the surface nearly two feet of ash before finding solid ground. It flew into reverse. The driver's radio came alive with the voice of Jaime Gonzales.

"Hold off with that shovel. The firetruck will foam a path to let it cool."

The truck pulled up within minutes, and three firefighters in fire protective suits unrolled hoses and began spraying thick foam liberally at the burned ground. It sizzled and melted in the ash. After few minutes, the shovel received the order to move in. It sank slowly in the somewhat hardened ashen sludge as it carefully rolled in to reach the spheres with the shovel aided by firemen with hooked poles.

Nick's radio clicked on with Ben Skylar's voice. "I have taken a ground temperature reading, and those fire trucks are going to melt their tires off! Let me cool a path from up here. Stand by." The *SummerStar* actuated a cooling beam, making a path for the trucks to reach the arrested aliens.

The trucks moved in slowly and finding terra firma began to collect them. In two tries, it scooped them with reasonable amounts of mud and backed out, making its way to the heavy lift canisters. The cameras mounted on the surveillance hover pods recorded the retrieval sending pictures to a rapt audience.

Another crew of shovels and firetrucks were on the way to the second site, encouraged hearing that the first two were safe in the canister. Yet, not far beyond the new human optimism, perched at the lip of the volcano, the Imagoes sat in stillness, watching the scene from a safe distance contemplating how to take control back from the humans.

The *SummerStar* continued, scorching groups of aliens with relative ease throughout the afternoon. The general's crews worked efficiently with Skylar; by three o'clock they had collected well over one hundred balls and deposited them into the large dark canister. Ben Skylar tapped a switch to check the weather report. He called on the radio channel secured for the general.

"General, we may have a problem. The weather might not be very cooperative later this afternoon. A storm system is moving in. We are closing in on some of the more deeply set bugs in the forested areas. These will be harder to retrieve."

"Keep on schedule," replied the general.

"We are approaching what we think is the last group D-Sat has detected. They are imbedded in the forest, which will not be there for very long," said the soldier.

The ship lit the heat wave, evaporating the forest below. After a minute of intense heat, the thinned, charred tree trunks cracked and fell apart. The seven remaining bugs fell, metamorphosed among piles of smoking twigs that were once great trees.

With the help of several bulldozers clearing the way the decimated topsoil, and Ben Skylar cooling the way, the hydraulic shovels were able to make their way to the last of the downed aliens. The trip to the canister was a bit longer, the terrain rough, yet all were happy to know that they had retrieved all 143 detected.

Nick and Charley had moved from their original position and drove to the canister just west of the tent. Dr. Sanchez and Alba were there as well, standing with Pepe and Tico who were looking on as the last spheres were polled into the can. "It is amazing that we have captured them all in one day," Pepe observed.

"This has been one of the most efficient operations I have ever seen. We have you to thank. Without your expertise, these monsters would be feasting on the town council of Paricutin," Sanchez said, patting Nick on the back with gusto.

"I am glad to help. Yet we are not out of the woods yet. I am concerned about the other two Imagoes. The general said they have been located on the volcano itself. I do not know if the *SummerStar* can generate enough heat to transform them. Since they are airborne, it will be easy for them to escape the heat rays," Nick said, feeling the need to strategize with the general.

Nick's sentence was mostly unheard as the heavy lift ship descended upon the canister after reaching two hundred feet and four thick cables were dropped swinging above the can. Two ready technicians sprinted up the built-in ladders to fasten the cables to the tank. Within the span of five minutes, the tanker was lifting slowly into the air, all heads lifted with relief, and the blight was now on its way to Venus to be incinerated. The option of placing the can in an outer orbit would leave remote chances that they might find their way back to Earth. Thus, the decision for Venus was decided upon without much dialogue.

Almost unheard over the radio was the observation coordinator's voice.

"The Imagoes have left El Monstre. We are tracking them heading to the camp."

Sirens immediately followed, sending people for cover and soldiers to their weapons. Several combat trucks mounted with laser ballista rolled into action. They were the best offense available against the large aliens used regularly to raze buildings easier than the old bulldozers used in the twenty-first century.

The ship had lifted the tank nearly one hundred feet when the giant insects flying at very high speed in a state of agitation zeroed in on the suspended tank. They collided with the tank wrapping themselves around the girth and width and with ferocious bites attempted to chew the cables. The laser ballista, still milling for position, was not be able to fire a shot.

The creature sliced one of the cables, dropping the can suspended by the remaining three. It was only a matter of moments until the can came crashing down to the ground, sending the tank several feet into the earth and spouting ejecta about the area.

The tank seemed intact, as were the cooling insects within. The first bug shimmied across the breadth of the canister and with the alacrity of insects they maneuvered themselves about the task of releasing the young from impending danger.

CHAPTER 46

Mayhem and confusion of a surprise attack engaged the few remaining soldiers who were now blasting the air wantonly at the giant insect's manic intent on opening the canister filled with their dear young. Moving incredibly fast for their size, they were able to dodge the majority of the energy bolts. Those that hit them did not seem to be causing any damage. The larger of the two flew away from the site as if in retreat and then turned around flying full force at one of the vehicles. With consciously lethal momentum, a supply truck was struck from behind, sending it rolling into another truck and both into a ball of flame.

Soldiers and fleeing onlookers alike were amazed at the insect's ability to act with such precision. The second bug performed a similar maneuver, aiming itself at the heavy lift canister. It barreled into it, nearly turning it on its side. With devilish quickness, it scuttled along the side of the can to the side hatch using its front legs attempting to wrest it open.

Poorly aimed laser fire followed. Several blasts actually hit the insect. It recoiled with annoyance at first, then after continued strikes, it flew up and away and out of range. Deep gouges maligned the canister's side door. Charley looked on with binoculars bringing it to the others' attention.

"I wonder how long those things need to snap out of their heat sleep." Nick thought aloud.

"If the canister is damaged, there is no way it can take flight to Venus. We may be faced with having to find another way to dispose of these things and fast." Sanchez pulled his communicator on and addressed the *SummerStar*, "Mr. Skylar, this is Dr. Rene Sanchez. Can you tell if the canister has been damaged from your vantage point?"

Skylar, hovering beyond the scene, scanned the canister with a simple touch pad move, then replied, "It doesn't look good. The small claws must have been able to work at the seam. The lock is not broken but it has been damaged. I doubt heavy lift will want to take the chance of interplanetary space. I will link the video now. Be careful. Those things are stronger than we thought they were."

The next voice was that of General Gonzales.

"Science team, I am looking for some fast answers on how to deal with these new developments. Take cover in the tent. Meet me in the command room now."

The team assembled themselves to the tent. As they went, laser fire volleys notwithstanding one of the beasts careened into an assault vehicle, sending it into the brush like a discarded soda can. This time, the creature came closer than it had ever been to the four doctors, Pepe and Tico. Hidden fears reaffirmed in their quickened steps, and they made their way safely to the tent. The battle raged on once they were in the command room. Gonzales stood watching the battle rather calmly, Nick thought as he approached him.

"General, I am concerned with the insects inside the canister. Being exposed to heat for enough time to achieve cryptobiosis tells us little about how long before they will stay that way," Nick said.

"Do you have any answers, Dr. Nicholas? We could use a good one."

"The answer has been in front of us all along."

The others all turned to Nick, waiting to know his idea. He continued.

"The volcano, El Monstre, has a constant heat factor that that should be hot enough to keep them dormant. Since my research is still incomplete, I do not know how long they will remain incapacitated. We should act fast. I hope the heavy lift has another cable it can drop. We attach it to the canister and drop it into the volcano."

The general's assistant radioed the heavy lift without being asked, reporting that it is equipped with an auxiliary eyehook in the tip of the can. "Also, a thick gauge cable is available aboard the craft."

Dr. Alba looked on with quiet concern during common approval of the idea, and then said, "I'd like to point out that aside from the likelihood that El Monstre will be able to keep them, we should think to the future. In the event that the volcano erupts, we would have the same problem, reconstituted aliens cast about the country. We may be merely postponing a disaster."

The general fielded her point without hesitation. "Dr. Alba, my job is to ensure the safety of this area, today I cannot put the country in danger based on the chance of something like that happening many years in the future. You must understand that."

Charley, who had been unusually quiet still digesting the icy reality of Dana Kim's betrayal of his trust, was freshly engaged with engineering adders to the latest plot and felt the need to interject. "General, I think Dr. Nicholas has a great idea. Yet someone is going to have to ride out there and manually attach the cable to the can. Those adult bugs may not be happy about someone attempting that activity."

Gonzales regarded Charley differently, noting the energy pistols purposefully strapped to his belt. "Am I to guess, Senor Doctor, that you would like to help? I have noticed this guns you carry here are not legal in this country, and to my knowledge, not so in any country. Don't worry, I won't tell.," he said, covering a smile.

"Well, I feel like I need to contribute, if not scientifically, then strategically. I could provide cover. These guns are really effective. Furthermore, since I am not a legal citizen of Mexico, I wouldn't be breaking any local rules," Charley said impressively.

He looked at Charley again, then activated his radio, "Heavy lift one, prepare a grapple to lift the tank. Personnel will be on hand to attach. You will proceed to El Monstre and await further action."

He addressed his captain. "Have an AUV sent to the western door now. Okay, you may ride along, but please exercise caution, Dr. Porter, and allow our personnel to do their duty. Meet the truck at the side door. Fall out," he said with official resolve.

Sanchez opened the tent door to find an assault vehicle waiting for him with the door open. Another soldier, standing ready at the back, operated a large laser anti-aircraft gun mounted on the roof. The driver waved him in the back seat with a smile.

"Dr. Porter?" he said.

"I am Leo. This is Armando, our gunner. We are ready to go. I see you have some heavy handguns. Those are very illegal, senor."

"I know. So what? What's the plan?"

"We ride out there. I climb the ladder to attach the hook, then we ride back. You provide cover. We will need it. Those are the orders."

The thin young soldier said, simulating playing the drums on the steering wheel seeming to always be fidgeting with something yet not in a nervous way. Charley nodded without much else to say, hoping that some action would take his mind off the reappearing despair he felt at occasional thoughts of Dana. How could he be so gullible? He tried so hard, but he was a better romantic than a detective. Who would have thought this cute, bright sex bomb would be working for Gerhard Steele?

The insects were still engaged with the soldiers in the distance. From the vantage point of the AUV, Charley saw a hover recon rammed airborne by the force of the Imago. It fell onto some parked cars. Gunfire seemed to have minor effects on the aliens, yet he thought they must feel the blasts. They had an annoying habit of coming out of nowhere and fast. He checked the guns' power level and sat ready as the truck idled.

His attention was drawn to the east. Four dark images flying toward them gradually made themselves out to be some sort of jet plane.

"Those look different. Where are they?" he said to the driver. Leo responded, craning his neck to see the jets.

"Those are the new M-2 fighters, very slick with lots of extras. They will be our real cover."

The gunner laughed aloud. This was the first noise Charley had heard from the young man standing behind a large laser cannon, not unlike the ones he had seen demolition crews use to raze a building but much more efficient than the bulldozers of the twenty-first century.

Above, the heavy lift ship had come into place, hovering over the damaged canister. A cable began to descend, swaying in the wind as it fell. The radio came alive with orders. The truck sped out to the tanker, nearly three-fourths of a mile ahead to the west of camp. El Monstre loomed in the background. As they approached, Charley could now see thin wisps of steam or smoke rise from the cone. With the windows down, Charley checked the sky for bugs. It was clear that perhaps the frequency of the blare from the heavy lift was keeping them away, Charley considered.

Leo pulled up to the side of the tank without incident. He regripped his gun with disappointment at the size of the ladder.

"Okay, let's do this. Cover me!" he shouted over the noise.

Jumping from the truck, Leo took the built-in ladder, holding onto the railing. Looking up, the cable swung beyond his reach by nearly fifteen feet. He waved a down signal to the pilot. The cable began to lower. As he raised his arms to retrieve the locking hook fingertips beyond his reach, an Imago appeared from over a nearby hill. Armando spun the laser cannon and tried to opened fire during the short time it took the creature to reach the tank. Charley held his gun outside the window trying to manage a clear shot. With a singular movement, it snatched Leo from the top of the tank. Gnawing at his chest as it flew away followed by laser fire, it escaped back into the hills, with Leo's blood dripping unseen onto the brush below.

Charley sputtered a curse and got out of the backseat, holstering his gun and knowing what he had to do. "I've got this one, Armando. You only live once. I have done that. Just remember this: when you fall in love, make sure you have someplace to land," he said, reassuring the young driver.

Giving a fast look at the unfamiliar tank ladder, he took the railing in hand and, with a spring, climbed up to complete Leo's mission. He cleared the stairs trying to keep an eye on the sky. Crouching on the smooth surface of the tank, he looked around, ready to draw his pistol. *It looked easy enough*, he thought, as small quick steps took him to the center.

He took the hook and cable swaying above. His hands were wet with sweat. The hook mechanism was large and clumsy to operate. Charley shook his head to remove the sweat stinging his eyes, not wanting to release the hook. He tried to attach the hook again, his big, slimy hands untried on the foreign mechanism wanted to learn faster.

A sight forced his body to a lower crouch. From the hills dead on, he faced an Imago, its white fangs seemed to be aiming at his chest even from half of a mile away as his fingers fumbled uselessly with the hook. Another check upwards showed the monster had spanned more than half the distance from the hills beyond. Back to work, Charley doubled his efforts, and after another try, he finally hooked the cable and scuttled back away to the ladder. As the Imago neared with deadly precision, he lowered himself onto the stairs using the tank itself as cover. The alien swooped over and away, creating its own gust of wind. Armando shot the cannon, hitting the creature only a couple of times yet providing enough cover for Charley to find his way down and into the driver's seat of the truck to make a speedy escape back to the tent base.

The M-2s broke formation to create a circle around the tank. One the protective pattern was established; the heavy lift pulled upwards, taking its embedded load off slowly from the earth. The jets came into position, yet as they were unable to get a clear shot, their task was defensive. The canister must reach the volcano.

After rising one hundred feet, its course changed for the volcano nearly two miles away. The planes tightened their circle ready for another attack on the regrouping monster, with the tank swinging along below.

Alerted by the activity, the second Imago brought itself in position, flying out from recovery from minor laser burns. Sensing what the humans had in mind, it spanned the distance with great speed to the tank, swinging from the cable.

One fourth of a mile from the edge of the volcano, the ship's captain was given the order to drop the tank once it was over the center of the opening. The space insect came around again undaunted by the fighters. It flew what seemed like an evasive pattern as it rapidly closed the distance. Its previous contact with aircraft fueled its approach.

The planes finally opened rocket fire on the Imago as it focused its body to hit the tank. Several shots streamed past it as it landed on its top with a monumental grasping effort. The creature scrambled to hold fast to the smooth surface and soon was about the task of chewing through the cable.

The increasingly accurate laser blasts then began to hit more often as the tank breached the opening to El Monstre, yet the alien's tough exoskeleton provided sufficient armor avoiding major damage.

Wisps of smoke and steam from the molten lava below cascading around the tank seemed to be enjoyable to the insect, its flavor reminding it of its home planet. Its mandibles chewed at cutting away at the cable, and its smaller appendages neatly tossed away the cable until it finally began to show weakness. The creature's body tensed, its legs grasping the metal surface with stretching clutches. Before the cable gave way, the beast began to flap the gigantic wings in a monumental attempt to fly away to safety with the canister and its young inside. The massive wings pushed against the sky while working the cable.

The command center screens all displayed the scene from the ship's video feed as well as from the Humvee. Nick, Sanchez, Alba, Pepe, and Tico were fixed closely on the actions taking place. The general kept his hard eyes on the distance over the center of the volcano. He gave the order. "Release the cable!"

Now, directly over the center, the pilot touched a control, and the cable was released from the underside of the ship. The tank and the Imago began to fall. Sensing victory, it renewed its effort, and chewed the final strands and cut away the cable. It took every ounce of strength of the hundreds of legs and beating wings to keep the tank aloft. It held the tank with ferocity. For a few moments, it floated, battling for equilibrium. As the Imago established command of the tank, its progeny took its bearings and began to veer off perhaps to the safety of the ocean in the western distance. However, before it covered any latitude, the half-mile of industrial cable crashed down on top of the alien and the tank, collecting itself in a weighty piling heap. With its wings made helpless, the Imago failed to fly off and was now entangled in the cable plummeting in the smoky expanse below.

The tank splashed deep into the chasm, hitting an expanse of lava and sending molten spray all about. The Imago hit the lava; its legs and wings helpless to save itself, it sank below the surface with a burning hiss that muffled its alien screams. Instantly, the great insect father morphed in the heat, rolling ultimately into is protective sphere.

The pilot of the heavy lift spacecraft had looked forward to the trip to Venus. He figured as he brought the ship around for a view of the gaping expanse of the volcano filming the metamorphosis. The heat of the second planet would of course be greater than that of Mexico's El Monstre. If this heat source was not enough to destroy the insect aliens that had come to be known as the Imago, how long would they remain in anabiosis?

With her particular point of view of coordinating all the camera views available at the command station, a young female soldier had filmed some very dramatic events, yet none had remained in the minds of humans as that of the second Imago that was now climbing, jumping, and flying its way to the top of the volcano. Picking a feed from the military satellite, the frame focused in on the mother Imago that had flown to the volcano instinctively to the aid of her children. It bounded and scurried with a sense that bordered between fear and hope that it would find its lost family. Periodically, it would "stand," if that expression could be used for an insect, as it was one that had exhibited fantastic skills originating on a far-away planet in a hidden solar system. It sniffed the air with assurance that it was on the right path, until she breached the edge of the pit of hot lava.

Carefully, it sent feelers across the lip of the steaming mountain. It knew her family had gone into the furnace below. To the creature, the fire was rather hope than death. The very nature of molten rock held the alien promise of a new life. With less trepidation than drama, it hurled itself over the edge, tucking itself together with a kind of poise into the fire.

The noise it made, if it could have been heard, might have sounded like pain; it certainly looked painful to the camera, yet was rather a sweet relief. The Imago soon turned into a sphere of exoskeleton and floated peacefully away into the bowels of El Monstre to join her family, protected by the ironically redeeming high temperatures that would certainly be a burning hell to any Earth creature. There, they would remain preserved by the fiery rock until time and temperature would allow them to change.

Printed in the United States
By Bookmasters